STORIES *to* READ AGAIN *and* AGAIN

STORIES *to* READ AGAIN *and* AGAIN

A SELECTION OF THE FAMOUS AND FAMILIAR

Edited with an introduction by
SARAH ANNE STUART

BRISTOL PARK BOOKS

The acknowledgements on pages 369 to 370 constitute an extension of the copyright page

First Bristol Park Books edition published in 2015

Bristol Park Books
252 W. 38th Street
NYC, NY 10018

Library of Congress Control Number: 2015944165

ISBN: 978-0-88486-590-2

Text and cover designed by LaBreacht Design
Cover illustration: *The Window Seat* by Jacquelyn Bischak

Printed in the United States of America

Contents

Introduction

Storytelling is an art as ancient as cave drawings and as contemporary as yesterday's headlines. The short story encapsulates that art into a popular literary form. Here, character meets action; there is a climax followed by a resolution and often a "take-away"—a truth for the reader to discover and ponder for days thereafter. Some of the greatest writers in the English language have used this form to tell their most compelling stories.

The stories selected for this volume represent those writers in the English language, from the mid-eighteenth century to the twenty-first century, whose works gained recognition and a lasting reputation for quality and originality. Some titles will be immediately recognized. Others are written by writers of famous works in longer form—novels, memoirs, biographies, and histories—and their storytelling skill shines through in these chosen short story formats.

Here you will find authors like Ernest Hemingway, F. Scott Fitzgerald, Alice Munro, and John Cheever; and stories like *Rip Van Winkle, The Gift of the Magi, Wee Willie Winkie,* and *The Diamond as Big as the Ritz.* The writers have received numerous awards: Pulitzer Prizes, Nobel Prizes, and many national honors from their country of birth. All were selected because of their enduring fame and familiarity—writers of stories that you will want to read and re-read, again and again.

It is my hope that as you enjoy this book you may discover new works by your favorite writers and be introduced to writers who might have been unfamiliar to you but have earned your respect and praise through their wonderful art of storytelling. May they all be famous and familiar to you.

Sarah Anne Stuart

STORIES *to* READ AGAIN *and* AGAIN

About Washington Irving

He was born in New York City on April 3, 1783, and named after America's hero, George Washington. After studying law he abandoned it to write, finding inspiration in the lives of Dutch settlers of New York and along the Hudson River. Biographer, diplomat, and storyteller, he advocated for the recognition of writing as a legitimate profession with copyright protection. In 1859, completing his biography of George Washington, Irving died at his home, Sunnyside, in Tarrytown, New York.

Rip Van Winkle

A POSTHUMOUS WRITING OF DIEDRICH KNICKERBOCKER

Whoever has made a voyage up the Hudson must remember the Kaatskill mountains. They are a dismembered branch of the great Appalachian family, and are seen away to the west of the river, swelling up to a noble height, and lording it over the surrounding country. Every change of season, every change of weather, indeed, every hour of the day, produces some change in the magical hues and shapes of these mountains, and they are regarded by all the good wives, far and near, as perfect barometers. When the weather is fair and settled, they are clothed in blue and purple, and print their bold outlines on the clear evening sky; but, sometimes, when the rest of the landscape is cloudless, they will gather a hood of gray vapors about their summits, which, in the last rays of the setting sun, will glow and light up like a crown of glory.

At the foot of these fairy mountains, the voyager may have descried the light smoke curling up from a village, whose shingle-roofs gleam among the trees, just where the blue tints of the upland melt away into the fresh green of the nearer landscape. It is a little village of great antiquity, having been founded by some of the Dutch colonists, in the early times of the province, just about the beginning of the government of the good Peter Stuyvesant, (may he rest in peace!) and there were some of the houses of the original settlers standing within a few years, built of small yellow bricks brought from Holland, having latticed windows and gable fronts, surmounted with weather-cocks.

In that same village, and in one of these very houses (which, to tell the precise truth, was sadly time-worn and weather-beaten), there lived many years since, while the country was yet a province of Great Britain, a simple good-natured fellow of the name of Rip Van Winkle. He was a descendant of the Van Winkles who figured so gallantly in the chivalrous days of Peter Stuyvesant, and accompanied him to the siege of Fort Christina. He inherited, however, but little of the martial character of his ancestors. I have observed that he was a simple, good-natured man; he was, moreover, a kind neighbor, and an obedient, hen-pecked husband. Indeed, to the latter circumstance might be owing that meekness of spirit which gained him such universal popularity; for those men are most apt to be obsequious and conciliating abroad, who are under the discipline of shrews at home. Their tempers, doubtless, are rendered pliant and malleable in the fiery furnace of domestic tribulation; and a curtain lecture is worth all the sermons in the world for teaching the virtues of patience and long-suffering. A termagant wife may, therefore, in some respects, be considered a tolerable blessing; and if so, Rip Van Winkle was thrice blessed.

Certain it is, that he was a great favorite of all the good wives of the village, who, as usual, with the amiable sex, took his part in all family squabbles;

and never failed, whenever they talked those matters over in their evening gossipings, to lay all the blame on Dame Van Winkle. The children of the village, too, would shout with joy whenever he approached. He assisted at their sports, made their playthings, taught them to fly kites and shoot marbles, and told them long stories of ghosts, witches, and Indians. Whenever he went dodging about the village, he was surrounded by a troop of them, hanging on his skirts, clambering on his back, and playing a thousand tricks on him with impunity; and not a dog would bark at him throughout the neighborhood.

The great error in Rip's composition was an insuperable aversion to all kinds of profitable labor. It could not be from the want of assiduity or perseverance; for he would sit on a wet rock, with a rod as long and heavy as a Tartar's lance, and fish all day without a murmur, even though he should not be encouraged by a single nibble. He would carry a fowling-piece on his shoulder for hours together, trudging through woods and swamps, and up hill and down dale, to shoot a few squirrels or wild pigeons. He would never refuse to assist a neighbor even in the roughest toil, and was a foremost man at all country frolics for husking Indian corn, or building stone fences; the women of the village, too, use to employ him to run their errands, and to do such little odd jobs as their less obliging husbands would not do for them. In a word Rip was ready to attend to anybody's business but his own; but as to doing family duty, and keeping his farm in order, he found it impossible.

In fact, he declared it was of no use to work on his farm; it was the most pestilent little piece of ground in the whole country; everything about it went wrong, and would go wrong, in spite of him. His fences were continually falling to pieces; his cow would either go astray, or get among the cabbages; weeds were sure to grow quicker in his fields than anywhere else; the rain always made a point of setting in just as he had some out-door work to do; so that though his patrimonial estate had dwindled away under his management, acre by acre, until there was little more left than a mere patch of Indian corn and potatoes, yet it was the worst conditioned farm in the neighborhood.

His children, too, were as ragged and wild as if they belonged to nobody. His son Rip, an urchin begotten in his own likeness, promised to inherit the habits, with the old clothes of his father. He was generally seen trooping like a colt at his mother's heels, equipped in a pair of his father's cast-off galligaskins, which he had much ado to hold up with one hand, as a fine lady does her train in bad weather.

Rip Van Winkle, however, was one of those happy mortals, of foolish, well-oiled dispositions, who take the world easy, eat white bread or brown, whichever can be got with least thought or trouble, and would rather starve on a penny than work for a pound. If left to himself, he would have whistled life away in perfect contentment; but his wife kept continually dinning in his ears about his idleness, his carelessness, and the ruin he was bringing on his family. Morning, noon, and night, her tongue was incessantly going, and everything he said or did was sure to produce a torrent of household eloquence. Rip had but one way of replying to all lectures of the kind, and that, by frequent use, had grown into a habit. He shrugged his shoulders, shook his head, cast up his eyes, but said nothing. This, however, always provoked a fresh volley from his wife; so that he was fain to draw off his forces, and take to the outside of the house—the only side which, in truth, belongs to a hen-pecked husband.

Rip's sole domestic adherent was his dog Wolf, who was as much hen-pecked as his master; for Dame Van Winkle regarded them as companions in idleness, and even looked upon Wolf with an evil eye, as the cause of his master's going so often astray. True it is, in all points of spirit befitting an honorable dog, he was as courageous an animal as ever scoured the woods—but what courage can withstand the ever-during and all-be-setting terrors of a woman's tongue? The moment Wolf entered the house his crest fell, his tail drooped to the ground, or curled between his legs, he sneaked about with a gallows air, casting many a sidelong glance at Dame Van Winkle, and at the least flourish of a broomstick or ladle, he would fly to the door with yelping precipitation.

Times grew worse and worse with Rip Van Winkle as years of matrimony rolled on; a tart temper never mellows with age, and a sharp tongue is the only edged tool that grows keener with constant use. For a long while he used to console himself, when driven from home, by frequenting a kind of perpetual club of sages, philosophers, and other idle personages of the village; which held its sessions on a bench before a small inn, designated by a rubicund portrait of His Majesty George the Third. Here they used to sit in the shade through a long lazy summer's day, talking listlessly over village gossip, or telling endless sleepy stories about nothing. But it would have been worth any statesman's money to have heard the profound discussions that sometimes took place, when by chance an old newspaper fell into their hands from some passing traveller. How solemnly they would listen to the contents, as drawled out by Derrick Van Bummel, the schoolmaster, a dapper learned little man, who was not to be daunted by the most gigantic word in the dictionary; and how sagely they would deliberate upon the public events some months after they had taken place.

The opinions of this junto were completely controlled by Nicholas Vedder, a patriarch of the village, and landlord of the inn, at the door of which he took his seat from morning till night, just moving sufficiently to avoid the sun and keep in the shade of a large tree; so that the neighbors could tell the hour by his movements as accurately as by a sun-dial. It is true he was rarely heard to speak, but smoked his pipe incessantly. His adherents, however (for every great man has his adherents), perfectly understood him, and knew how to gather his opinions. When anything that was read or related displeased him, he was observed to smoke his pipe vehemently, and to send forth short, frequent and angry puffs; but when pleased, he would inhale the smoke slowly and tranquilly, and emit it in light and placid clouds; and sometimes, taking the pipe from his mouth, and letting the fragrant vapor curl about his nose, would gravely nod his head in token of perfect approbation.

From even this stronghold the unlucky Rip was at length routed by his termagant wife, who would suddenly break in upon the tranquillity of the assemblage and call the members all to naught; nor was that august personage, Nicholas Vedder himself, scared from the daring tongue of this terrible virago, who charged him outright with encouraging her husband in habits of idleness.

Poor Rip was at last reduced almost to despair; and his only alternative, to escape from the labor of the farm and clamor of his wife, was to take gun in hand and stroll away into the woods. Here he would sometimes seat himself at the foot of a tree, and share the contents of his wallet with Wolf, with whom he sympathized as a fellow-sufferer in persecution. "Poor Wolf," he would say, "thy mistress leads thee a dogs life of it; but never mind, my lad, whilst I live thou shalt never want a friend to stand by thee!" Wolf would wag his tail, look wistfully in his master's face, and if dogs can feel pity I verily believe he reciprocated the sentiment with all his heart.

In a long ramble of the kind on a fine autumnal day, Rip had unconsciously scrambled to one of the highest parts of the Kaatskill mountains. He was after his favorite sport of squirrel shooting, and the still solitudes had echoed and re-echoed with the reports of his gun. Panting and fatigued, he threw himself, late in the afternoon, on a green knoll, covered with mountain herbage, that crowned the brow of a precipice. From an opening between the trees he could overlook all the lower country for many a mile of rich woodland. He saw at a distance the lordly Hudson, far, far below him, moving on its silent but majestic course, with the reflection of a purple cloud, or the sail of a lagging bark, here and there sleeping on its glassy bosom, and at last losing itself in the blue highlands.

On the other side he looked down into a deep mountain glen, wild, lonely, and shagged, the bottom filled with fragments from the impending cliffs, and scarcely lighted by the reflected rays of the setting sun. For some time Rip lay musing on this scene; evening was gradually advancing; the mountains began to throw their long blue shadows over the valleys; he saw that it would be dark long before he could reach the village, and he heaved a heavy sigh when he thought of encountering the terrors of Dame Van Winkle.

As he was about to descend, he heard a voice from a distance, hallooing, "Rip Van Winkle! Rip Van Winkle!" He looked round, but could see nothing but a crow winging its solitary flight across the mountain. He thought his fancy must have deceived him, and turned again to descend, when he heard the same cry ring through the still evening air: "Rip Van Winkle! Rip Van Winkle!"—at the same time Wolf bristled up his back, and giving a low growl, skulked to his master's side, looking fearfully down into the glen. Rip now felt a vague apprehension stealing over him; he looked anxiously in the same direction, and perceived a strange figure slowly toiling up the rocks, and bending under the weight of something he carried on his back. He was surprised to see any human being in this lonely and unfrequented place, but supposing it to be some one of the neighborhood in need of his assistance, he hastened down to yield it.

On nearer approach he was still more surprised at the singularity of the stranger's appearance. He was a short square-built old fellow, with thick bushy hair, and a grizzled beard. His dress was of the antique Dutch fashion—a cloth jerkin strapped round the waist—several pair of breeches, the outer one of ample volume, decorated with rows of buttons down the sides, and bunches at the knees. He bore on his shoulder a stout keg, that seemed full of liquor, and made signs for Rip to approach and assist him with the load. Though rather shy and distrustful of this new acquaintance, Rip complied with his usual alacrity; and mutually relieving one another, they clambered up a narrow gully, apparently the dry bed of a mountain torrent. As they ascended, Rip every now and then heard long rolling peals, like distant thunder, that seemed to issue out of a deep ravine, or rather cleft, between lofty rocks, toward which their rugged path conducted. He paused for an instant, but supposing it to be the muttering of one of those transient thundershowers which often take place in mountain heights, he proceeded. Passing through the ravine, they came to a hollow, like a small amphitheatre, surrounded by perpendicular precipices, over the brinks of which impending trees shot their branches, so that you only caught glimpses of the azure sky and the bright evening cloud. During the whole time Rip and his companion had labored on in silence; for though the former marvelled greatly what could be the object of carrying a keg of liquor up this wild mountain, yet there was something strange and incomprehensible about the unknown, that inspired awe and checked familiarity.

On entering the amphitheatre, new objects of wonder presented themselves. On a level spot in the centre was a company of odd-looking personages playing at ninepins. They were dressed in a quaint outlandish fashion; some wore short doublets, others jerkins, with long knives in their belts, and most of them had enormous breeches, of similar style with that of the guide's.

Their visages, too, were peculiar: one had a large beard, broad face, and small piggish eyes; the face of another seemed to consist entirely of nose, and was surmounted by a white sugar-loaf hat set off with a little red cock's tail. They all had beards, of various shapes and colors. There was one who seemed to be the commander. He was a stout old gentleman, with a weather-beaten countenance; he wore a laced doublet, broad belt and hanger, high-crowned hat and feather, red stockings, and high-heeled shoes, with roses in them. The whole group reminded Rip of the figures in an old Flemish painting, in the parlor of Dominie Van Shaick, the village parson, and which had been brought over from Holland at the time of the settlement.

What seemed particularly odd to Rip was, that though these folks were evidently amusing themselves, yet they maintained the gravest faces, the most mysterious silence, and were, withal, the most melancholy party of pleasure he had ever witnessed. Nothing interrupted the stillness of the scene but the noise of the balls, which, whenever they were rolled, echoed along the mountains like rumbling peals of thunder.

As Rip and his companion approached them, they suddenly desisted from their play, and stared at him with such fixed statue-like gaze, and such strange, uncouth, lack-lustre countenances, that his heart turned within him, and his knees smote together. His companion now emptied the contents of the keg into large flagons, and made signs to him to wait upon the company. He obeyed with fear and trembling; they quaffed the liquor in profound silence, and then returned to their game.

By degrees Rip's awe and apprehension subsided. He even ventured, when no eye was fixed upon him, to taste the beverage, which he found had much of the flavor of excellent Hollands. He was naturally a thirsty soul, and was soon tempted to repeat the draught. One taste provoked another; and he reiterated his visits to the flagon so often that at length his senses were overpowered, his eyes swam in his head, his head gradually declined, and he fell into a deep sleep.

On waking, he found himself on the green knoll whence he had first seen the old man of the glen. He rubbed his eyes—it was a bright sunny morning. The birds were hopping and twittering among the bushes, and the eagle was wheeling aloft, and breasting the pure mountain breeze. "Surely," thought Rip, "I have not slept here all night." He recalled the occurrences before he fell asleep. The strange man with a keg of liquor—the mountain ravine—the wild retreat among the rocks—the woe-begone party at ninepins—the flagon—"Oh! that flagon! that wicked flagon!" thought Rip—"what excuse shall I make to Dame Van Winkle!"

He looked round for his gun, but in place of the clean well-oiled fowling-piece, he found an old firelock lying by him, the barrel incrusted with rust, the lock falling off, and the stock worm-eaten. He now suspected that the grave roysters of the mountain had put a trick upon him, and, having dosed him with liquor, had robbed him of his gun. Wolf, too, had disappeared, but he might have strayed away after a squirrel or partridge. He whistled after him and shouted his name, but all in vain; the echoes repeated his whistle and shout, but no dog was to be seen.

He determined to revisit the scene of the last evening's gambol, and if he met with any of the party, to demand his dog and gun. As he rose to walk, he found himself stiff in the joints, and wanting in his usual activity. "These mountain beds do not agree with me," thought Rip, "and if this frolic should lay me up with a fit of the rheumatism, I shall have a blessed time with Dame Van Winkle." With some difficulty he got down into the glen: he found the gully up which he and his companion had ascended the preceding evening;

but to his astonishment a mountain stream was now foaming down it, leaping from rock to rock, and filling the glen with babbling murmurs. He, however, made shift to scramble up its sides, working his toilsome way through thickets of birch, sassafras, and witch-hazel, and sometimes tripped up or entangled by the wild grapevines that twisted their coils or tendrils from tree to tree, and spread a kind of network in his path.

At length he reached to where the ravine had opened through the cliffs to the amphitheatre; but no traces of such opening remained. The rocks presented a high impenetrable wall, over which the torrent came tumbling in a sheet of feathery foam, and fell into a broad deep basin, black from the shadows of the surrounding forest. Here, then, poor Rip was brought to a stand. He again called and whistled after his dog; he was only answered by the cawing of a flock of idle crows, sporting high in air about a dry tree that overhung a sunny precipice; and who, secure in their elevation, seemed to look down and scoff at the poor man's perplexities. What was to be done? The morning was passing away, and Rip felt famished for want of his breakfast. He grieved to give up his dog and gun; he dreaded to meet his wife; but it would not do to starve among the mountains. He shook his head, shouldered the rusty firelock, and, with a heart full of trouble and anxiety, turned his steps homeward.

As he approached the village he met a number of people, but none whom he knew, which somewhat surprised him, for he had thought himself acquainted with everyone in the country round. Their dress, too, was of a different fashion from that to which he was accustomed. They all stared at him with equal marks of surprise, and whenever they cast their eyes upon him, invariably stroked their chins. The constant recurrence of this gesture induced Rip, involuntarily, to do the same, when, to his astonishment, he found his beard had grown a foot long!

He had now entered the skirts of the village. A troop of strange children ran at his heels, hooting after him, and pointing at his gray beard. The dogs, too, not one of which he recognized for an old acquaintance, barked at him as he passed. The very village was altered; it was larger and more populous. There were rows of houses which he had never seen before, and those which had been his familiar haunts had disappeared. Strange names were over the doors—strange faces at the windows—everything was strange. His mind now misgave him; he began to doubt whether both he and the world around him were not bewitched. Surely this was his native village, which he had left but the day before. There stood the Kaatskill mountains—there ran the silver Hudson at a distance—there was every hill and dale precisely as it had always been. Rip was sorely perplexed—"That flagon last night," thought he, "has addled my poor head sadly!"

It was with some difficulty that he found the way to his own house, which he approached with silent awe, expecting every moment to hear the shrill voice of Dame Van Winkle. He found the house gone to decay—the roof fallen in, the windows shattered, and the doors off the hinges. A half-starved dog that looked like Wolf was skulking about it. Rip called him by name, but the cur snarled, showed his teeth, and passed on. This was an unkind cut indeed—"My very dog," sighed poor Rip, "has forgotten me!"

He entered the house, which, to tell the truth, Dame Van Winkle had always kept in neat order. It was empty, forlorn, and apparently abandoned. This desolateness overcame all his connubial fears—he called loudly for his wife and children—the lonely chambers rang for a moment with his voice, and then all again was silence.

He now hurried forth, and hastened to his old resort, the village inn—but it too was gone. A large rickety wooden building stood in its place, with great gaping windows, some of them broken and mended with old hats and petticoats, and over the door was painted, "the Union Hotel, by Jonathan Doolittle." Instead of the great tree that used to shelter the quiet little Dutch inn of yore, there now was reared a tall naked pole, with something on the top that looked like a red night-cap, and from it was fluttering a flag, on which was a singular assemblage of stars and stripes—all this was strange and incomprehensible. He recognized on the sign, however, the ruby face of King George, under which he had smoked so many a peaceful pipe; but even this was singularly metamorphosed. The red coat was changed for one of blue and buff, a sword was held in the hand instead of a sceptre, the head was decorated with a cocked hat, and underneath, was painted in large characters, GENERAL WASHINGTON.

There was, as usual, a crowd of folk about the door, but none that Rip recollected. The very character of the people seemed changed. There was a busy, bustling, disputatious tone about it, instead of the accustomed phlegm and drowsy tranquillity. He looked in vain for the sage Nicholas Vedder, with his broad face, double chin, and fair long pipe, uttering clouds of tobacco-smoke instead of idle speeches; or Van Bummel, the schoolmaster, doling forth the contents of an ancient newspaper. In place of these, a lean, bilious-looking fellow, with his pockets full of handbills, was haranguing vehemently about rights of citizens—elections—members of Congress—liberty—Bunker's Hill—heroes of seventy-six—and other words, which were a perfect Babylonish jargon to the bewildered Van Winkle.

The appearance of Rip, with his long grizzled beard, his rusty fowling-piece, his uncouth dress, and an army of women and children at his heels, soon attracted the attention of the tavern politicians. They crowded round him, eying him from head to foot with great curiosity. The orator bustled up to him, and, drawing him partly aside, inquired "On which side he voted?" Rip stared in vacant stupidity. Another short but busy little fellow pulled him by the arm, and, rising on tiptoe, inquired in his ear, "Whether he was Federal or Democrat?" Rip was equally at a loss to comprehend the question; when a knowing, self-important old gentleman, in a sharp cocked hat, made his way through the crowd, putting them to the right and left with his elbows as he passed, and planting himself before Van Winkle, with one arm akimbo, the other resting on his cane, his keen eyes and sharp hat penetrating, as it were, into his very soul, demanded in an austere tone, "What brought him to the election with a gun on his shoulder, and a mob at his heels, and whether he meant to breed a riot in the village?"—"Alas! gentlemen," cried Rip, somewhat dismayed, "I am a poor quiet man, a native of the place, and a loyal subject of the king, God bless him!"

Here a general shout burst from the bystanders—"A tory! a tory! a spy! a refugee! hustle him! away with him!" It was with great difficulty that the self-important man in the cocked hat restored order; and, having assumed a tenfold austerity of brow, demanded again of the unknown culprit, what he came there for, and whom he was seeking? The poor man humbly assured him that he meant no harm, but merely came there in search of some of his neighbors, who used to keep about the tavern.

"Well—who are they?—name them."

Rip bethought himself a moment, and inquired. "Where's Nicholas Vedder?"

There was a silence for a little while, when an old man replied in a thin piping voice, "Nicholas Vedder! why, he is dead and gone these eighteen years! There was a wooden tombstone in the churchyard that used to tell all about him, but that's rotten and gone too."

"Where's Brom Dutcher?"

"Oh, he went off to the army in the beginning of the war; some say he was killed at the storming of Stony Point—others say he was drowned in a squall at the foot of Antony's Nose. I don't know—he never came back again."

"Where's Van Bummel, the schoolmaster?"

"He went off to the wars too, was a great militia general, and is now in Congress."

Rip's heart died away at hearing of these sad changes in his home and friends, and finding himself thus alone in the world. Every answer puzzled him too, by treating of such enormous lapses of time, and of matters which he could not understand: war—congress—Stony Point;—he had no courage to ask after any more friends, but cried out in despair, "Does nobody here know Rip Van Winkle?"

"Oh, Rip Van Winkie!" exclaimed two or three, "Oh, to be sure! that's Rip Van Winkle yonder, leaning against the tree."

Rip looked, and beheld a precise counterpart of himself, as he went up the mountain: apparently as lazy, and certainly as ragged. The poor fellow was now completely confounded. He doubted his own identity, and whether he was himself or another man. In the midst of his bewilderment, the man in the cocked hat demanded who he was, and what was his name?

"God knows," exclaimed he, at his wit's end; "I'm not myself—I'm somebody else—that's me yonder—no—that's somebody else got into my shoes—I was myself last night, but I fell asleep on the mountain, and they've changed my gun, and every thing's changed—and I'm changed, and I can't tell my name, or who I am!"

The bystanders began now to look at each other, nod, wink significantly, and tap their fingers against their foreheads. There was a whisper, also, about securing the gun, and keeping the old fellow from doing mischief, at the very suggestion of which the self-important man in the cocked hat retired with some precipitation. At this critical moment a fresh, comely woman pressed through the throng to get a peep at the gray-bearded man. She had a chubby child in her arms, which, frightened at his looks, began to cry. "Hush, Rip," cried she, "hush, you little fool; the old man won't hurt you." The name of the child, the air of the mother, the tone of her voice, all awakened a train of recollections in this mind. "What is your name, my good woman?" asked he.

"Judith Gardenier."

"And your father's name?"

"Ah, poor man, Rip Van Winkle was his name, but it's twenty years since he went away from home with his gun, and never has been heard of since—his dog came home without him; but whether he shot himself, or was carried away by the Indians, nobody can tell. I was then but a little girl."

Rip had but one question more to ask; but he put it with a faltering voice:

"Where's your mother?"

"Oh, she too had died but a short time since; she broke a bloodvessel in a fit of passion at a New England peddler."

There was a drop of comfort, at least, in his intelligence. The honest man could contain himself no longer. He caught his daughter and her child in his arms. "I am your father!" cried he—"Young Rip Van Winkle once—old Rip Van Winkle now!—Does nobody know poor Rip Van Winkle?"

All stood amazed, until an old woman, tottering out from among the crowd, put her hand to her brow, and peering under it in his face for a moment, exclaimed, "Sure enough! it is Rip Van Winkle—it is himself! Welcome home again, old neighbor—Why, where have you been these twenty long years?"

Rip's story was soon told, for the whole twenty years had been to him but as one night. The neighbors stared when they heard it; some were seen to wink at each other, and put their tongues in their cheeks; and the self-important man in the cocked hat, who, when the alarm was over, had returned to the field, screwed down the corners of his mouth, and shook his head—upon which there was a general shaking of the head throughout the assemblage.

It was determined, however, to take the opinion of old Peter Vanderdonk, who was seen slowly advancing up the road. He was a descendant of the historian of that name, who wrote one of the earliest accounts of the province. Peter was the most ancient inhabitant of the village, and well versed in all the wonderful events and traditions of the neighborhood. He recollected Rip at once, and corroborated his story in the most satisfactory manner. He assured the company that it was a fact, handed down from his ancestor the historian, that the Kaatskill mountains had always been haunted by strange beings. That it was affirmed that the great Hendrick Hudson, the first discoverer of the river and country, kept a kind of vigil there every twenty years, with his crew of the *Half-Moon*; being permitted in this way to revisit the scenes of his enterprise, and keep a guardian eye upon the river, and the great city called by his name. That his father had once seen them in their old Dutch dresses playing at ninepins in a hollow of the mountain; and that he himself had heard one summer afternoon, the sound of their balls, like distant peals of thunders.

To make a long story short, the company broke up, and returned to the more important concerns of the election. Rip's daughter took him home to live with her; she had a snug, well-furnished house, and a stout cheery farmer for a husband, whom Rip recollected for one of the urchins that used to climb upon his back. As to Rip's son and heir, who was the ditto of himself, seen leaning against the tree, he was employed to work on the farm; but evinced an hereditary disposition to attend to anything else but his business.

Rip now resumed his old walks and habits; he soon found many of his former cronies, though all rather the worse for the wear and tear of time, and preferred making friends among the rising generation, with whom he soon grew into great favor.

Having nothing to do at home, and being arrived at that happy age when a man can be idle with impunity, he took his place once more on the bench at the inn door, and was reverenced as one of the patriarchs of the village, and a chronicle of the old times "before the war." It was some time before he could get into the regular track of gossip, or could be made to comprehend the strange events that had taken place during his torpor. How that there had been a revolutionary war—that the country had thrown off the yoke of old England—and that, instead of being a subject of his Majesty George the Third, he was now a free citizen of the United States. Rip, in fact, was no politician; the changes in states and empires made but little impression on him; but there was one species of despotism under which he had long groaned, and that was—petticoat government. Happily that was at an end; he had got his neck out of the yoke of matrimony, and could go in and out whenever he pleased, without dreading the tyranny of Dame Van Winkle. Whenever her name was mentioned, however, he shook his head, shrugged his shoulders, and cast up his eyes; which might pass either for an expression of resignation to his fate, or joy at his deliverance.

He used to tell his story to every stranger that arrived at Mr. Doolittle's hotel. He was observed, at first, to vary on some points every time he told it, which was, doubtless, owing to his having so recently awaked. It at last settled down precisely to the tale I have related, and not a man, woman, or child in the neighborhood, but knew it by heart. Some always pretended to doubt the reality of it, and insisted that Rip had been out of his head, and that this was one point on which he always remained flighty. The old Dutch inhabitants, however, almost universally gave it full credit. Even to this day they never hear a thunderstorm of a summer afternoon about the Kaatskill, but they say Hendrick Hudson and his crew are at their game of ninepins; and it is a common wish of all hen-pecked husbands in the neighborhood, when life hangs heavy on their hands, that they might have a quieting draught out of Rip Van Winkle's flagon.

About Edgar Allan Poe

Born in Boston in 1809, Poe was orphaned at age 2 and adopted by the Allan family of Virginia. When he failed at the University of Virginia and then West Point, his adoptive family rejected him and he relied on his writing for sole financial support. He was a prolific writer of short stories and poems, many of which are renowned today. Yet he died in poverty in 1849, at age 40 in Baltimore, Maryland. His death has been attributed to alcoholism, brain congestion, and heart disease.

The Fall of the House of Usher

During the whole of a dull, dark, and soundless day in the autumn of the year, when the clouds hung oppressively low in the heavens, I had been passing alone, on horseback, through a singularly dreary tract of country, and at length found myself, as the shades of the evening drew on, within view of the melancholy House of Usher. I know not how it was—but, with the first glimpse of the building, a sense of insufferable gloom pervaded my spirit. I say insufferable; for the feeling was unrelieved by any of that half-pleasurable, because poetic, sentiment with which the mind usually receives even the sternest natural images of the desolate or terrible. I looked upon the scene before me—upon the mere house, and the simple landscape features of the domain—upon the bleak walls—upon the vacant eye-like windows—upon a few rank sedges—and upon a few white trunks of decayed trees—with an utter depression of soul which I can compare to no earthly sensation more properly than to the after-dream of the reveller upon opium—the bitter lapse into every-day life—the hideous dropping off of the veil. There was an iciness, a sinking, a sickening of the heart—an unredeemed dreariness of thought which no goading of the imagination could torture into aught of the sublime. What was it—I paused to think—what was it that so unnerved me in the contemplation of the House of Usher? It was a mystery all insoluble; nor could I grappled with the shadowy fancies that crowded upon me as I pondered. I was forced to fall back upon the unsatisfactory conclusion, that while, beyond doubt, there *are* combinations of very simple natural objects which have the power of thus affecting us, still the analysis of this power lies among considerations beyond our depth. It was possible, I reflected, that a mere different arrangement of the particulars of the scene, of the details of the picture, would be sufficient to modify, or perhaps to annihilate its capacity for sorrowful impression; and, acting upon this idea, I reined my horse to the precipitous brink of a black and lurid tarn that lay in unruffled lustre by the dwelling, and gazed down—but with a shudder even more thrilling than before—upon the remodelled and inverted images of the gray sedge, and the ghastly tree-stems, and the vacant and eye-like windows.

Nevertheless, in this mansion of gloom I now proposed to myself a sojourn of some weeks. Its proprietor, Roderick Usher, had been one of my boon companions in boyhood; but many years had elapsed since our last meeting. A letter, however, had lately reached me in a distant part of the country—a letter from him—which, in its wildly importunate nature, had admitted of no other than a personal reply. The MS. gave evidence of nervous agitation. The writer spoke of acute bodily illness—of a mental disorder which oppressed him—and of an earnest desire to see me, as his best and indeed his only personal friend, with a view of attempting, by the cheerfulness of my society, some alleviation of his malady. It was the manner in which all this, and much more, was said—it was the apparent *heart* that went with his request—which allowed me no room for hesitation; and I accordingly obeyed forthwith what I still considered a very singular summons.

Although, as boys, we had been even intimate associates, yet I really knew little of my friend. His reserve had been always excessive and habitual. I was aware, however, that his very ancient family had been noted, time out of mind, for a peculiar sensibility of temperament, displaying itself, through long ages, in many works of exalted art, and manifested, of late, in repeated deeds of munificent yet unobtrusive charity, as well as in a passionate devotion to the intricacies, perhaps even more than to the orthodox and easily recognizable beauties, of musical science. I had learned, too, the very remarkable fact, that the stem of the Usher race, all time-honored as it was, had put forth, at no period, any enduring branch; in other words, that the entire family lay in the direct line of descent, and had always, with very trifling and very temporary variation, so lain. It was this deficiency, I considered, while running over in thought the perfect keeping of the character of the premises with the accredited character of the people, and while speculating upon the possible influence which the one, in the long lapse of centuries, might have exercised upon the other—it was this deficiency, perhaps, of collateral issue, and the consequent undeviating transmission, from sire to son, of the patrimony with the name, which had, at length, so identified the two as to merge the original title of the estate in the quaint and equivocal appellation of the 'House of Usher'—an appellation which seemed to include, in the minds of the peasantry who used it, both the family and the family mansion.

I have said that the sole effect of my somewhat childish experiment—that of looking down within the tarn—had been to deepen the first singular impression. I here can be no doubt that the consciousness of the rapid increase of my superstition—for why should I not so term it?—served mainly to accelerate the increase itself. Such, I have long known, is the paradoxical law of all sentiments having terror as a basis. And it might have been for this reason only, that, when I again uplifted my eyes to the house itself, from its image in the pool, there grew in my mind a strange fancy—a fancy so ridiculous, indeed, that I but mention it to show the vivid force of the sensations which oppressed me. I had so worked upon my imagination as really to believe that about the whole mansion and domain there hung an atmosphere peculiar to themselves and their immediate vicinity—an atmosphere which had no affinity with the air of heaven, but which had reeked up from the decayed trees, and the gray wall, and the silent tarn—a pestilent and mystic vapor, dull, sluggish, faintly discernible, and leaden-hued.

Shaking off from my spirit what *must* have been a dream, I scanned more narrowly the real aspect of the building. Its principal feature seemed to be that of an excessive antiquity. The discoloration of ages had been great. Minute fungi overspread the whole exterior, hanging in a fine tangled web-work from the eaves. Yet all this was apart from any extraordinary dilapidation. No position of the masonry had fallen; and there appeared to be a wild inconsistency between its still perfect adaptation of parts, and the crumbling condition of the individual stones. In this there was much that reminded me of the specious totality of old wood-work which has rotted for long years in some neglected vault, with no disturbance from the breath of the external air. Beyond this indication of extensive decay, however, the fabric gave little token of instability. Perhaps the eye of a scrutinizing observer might have discovered a barely perceptible fissure, which, extending from the roof of the building in front, made its way down the wall in a zigzag direction, until it became lost in the sullen waters of the tarn.

Noticing these things, I rode over a short causeway to the house. A servant in waiting took my horse, and I entered the Gothic archway of the hall. A valet, of stealthy step, thence conducted me, in silence, through many dark and intricate passages in my progress to the *studio* of his master. Much that I encountered on the way contributed, I know not how, to heighten the vague sentiments of which I have already spoken. While the objects around me—while the carvings of the ceilings, the sombre tapestries of the walls, the ebon blackness of the floors, and the phantasmagoric armorial trophies which rattled as I strode, were but matters to which, or to such as which, I had been accustomed from my infancy—while I hesitated not to acknowledge how familiar was all this—I still wondered to find how unfamiliar were the fancies which ordinary images were stirring up. On one of the staircases, I met the physician of the family. His countenance, I thought, wore a mingled expression of low cunning and perplexity. He accosted me with trepidation and passed on. The valet now threw open a door and ushered me into the presence of his master.

The room in which I found myself was very large and lofty. The windows were long, narrow, and pointed, and at so vast a distance from the black oaken floor as to be altogether inaccessible from within. Feeble gleams of encrimsoned light made their way through the trellissed panes, and served to render sufficiently distinct the more prominent objects around; the eye, however, struggled in vain to reach the remoter angles of the chamber, or the recesses of the vaulted and fretted ceiling. Dark draperies hung upon the walls. The general furniture was profuse, comfortless, antique, and tattered. Many books and musical instruments lay scattered about, but failed to give any vitality to the scene. I felt that I breathed an atmosphere of sorrow. An air of stern, deep, and irredeemable gloom hung over and pervaded all.

Upon my entrance, Usher arose from a sofa on which he had been lying at full length, and greeted me with a vivacious warmth which had much in it, I at first thought, of an overdone cordiality—of the constrained effort of the *ennuyé* man of the world. A glance, however, at his countenance convinced me of his perfect sincerity. We sat down; and for some moments, while he spoke not, I gazed upon him with a feeling half of pity, half of awe. Surely, man had never before so terribly altered, in so brief a period, as had Roderick Usher! It was with difficulty that I could bring myself to admit the identity of the wan being before me with the companion of my early boyhood. Yet the character of his face had been at all times remarkable. A cadaverousness of complexion; an eye large, liquid, and luminous beyond comparison; lips somewhat thin and very pallid but of a surpassingly beautiful curve; a nose of a delicate Hebrew model, but with a breadth of nostril unusual in similar formations; a finely moulded chin, speaking, in its want of prominence, of a want of moral energy; hair of a more than web-like softness and tenuity; — these features, with an inordinate expansion above the regions of the temple, made up altogether a countenance not easily to be forgotten. And now in the mere exaggeration of the prevailing character of these features, and of the expression they were wont to convey, lay so much of change that I doubted to whom I spoke. The now ghastly pallor of the skin, and the now miraculous lustre of the eye, above all things startled and even awed me. The silken hair, too, had been suffered to grow all unheeded, and as, in its wild gossamer texture, it floated rather than fell about the face, I could not, even with effort, connects it Arabesque expression with any idea of simple humanity.

In the manner of my friend I was at once struck with an incoherence—and inconsistency; and I soon found this to arise from a series of feeble and futile struggles to overcome an habitual trepidancy—an excessive nervous agitation.

For something of this nature I had indeed been prepared, no less by his letter, than by reminiscences of certain boyish traits, and by conclusions deduced from his peculiar physical confirmation and temperament. His action was alternately vivacious and sullen. His voice varied rapidly from a tremulous indecision (when the animal spirits seemed utterly in abeyance) to that species of energetic concision—that abrupt, weighty, unhurried, and hollow-sounding enunciation—that leaden, self-balanced, and perfectly modulated guttural utterance, which may be observed in the lost drunkard, or the irreclaimable eater of opium, during the periods of his most intense excitement.

It was thus that he spoke of the object of my visit, of his earnest desire to see me, and of the solace he expected me to afford him. He entered, at some length, into what he conceived to be the nature of his malady. It was, he said, a constitutional and a family evil, and one for which he despaired to find a remedy—a mere nervous affection, he immediately added, which would undoubtedly soon pass off. It displayed itself in a host of unnatural sensations. Some of these, as he detailed them, interested and bewildered me; although, perhaps, the terms and the general manner of their narration had their weight. He suffered much from a morbid acuteness of the senses; the most insipid food alone was endurable; he could wear only garments of a certain texture; the odors of all flowers were oppressive; his eyes were tortured by even a faint light; and there were but peculiar sounds, and these from stringed instruments, which did not inspire him with horror.

To an anomalous species of terror I found him a bounden slave. 'I shall perish,' said he, 'I *must* perish in this deplorable folly. Thus, thus, and not otherwise, shall I be lost. I dread the events of the future, not in themselves, but in their results. I shudder at the thought of any, even the most trivial, incident, which may operate upon this intolerable agitation of soul. I have, indeed, no abhorrence of danger, except in its absolute effect—in terror. In this unnerved, in this pitiable, condition I feel that the period will sooner or later arrive which I must abandon life and reason together, in some struggle with the grim phantasm, FEAR.'

I learned, moreover, at intervals, and through broken and equivocal hints, another singular feature of his mental condition. He was enchained by certain superstitious impressions in regard to the dwelling which he tenanted, and whence, for many years, he had never ventured forth—in regard to an influence whose supposititious force was conveyed in terms too shadowy here to be re-stated—an influence which some peculiarities in the mere form and substance of his family mansion had, by dint of long sufferance, he said, obtained over his spirit—an effect which the *physique* of the gray walls and turrets, and of the dim tarn into which they all looked down, had, at length, brought about upon the *morale* of his existence.

He admitted, however, although with hesitation, that much of the peculiar gloom which thus afflicted him could be traced to a more natural and far more palpable origin—to the severe and long-continued illness—indeed to the evidently approaching dissolution—of a tenderly beloved sister, his sole companion for long years, his last and only relative on earth. 'Her decease,' he said, with a bitterness which I can never forget, 'would leave him (him, the hopeless and the frail) the last of the ancient race of the Ushers.' While he spoke, the lady Madeline (for so was she called) passed through a remote portion of the apartment, and, without having noticed my presence, disappeared. I regarded her with an utter astonishment not unmingled with dread; and yet I found it impossible to account for such feelings. A sensation of stupor oppressed me as my eyes followed her retreating steps. When a door, at length, closed upon her, my glance sought instinctively and eagerly the countenance of the brother; but he had buried his face in his hands, and I could only perceive that a far more than ordinary wanness had overspread the emaciated fingers through which trickled many passionate tears.

The disease of the lady Madeline had long baffled the skill of her physicians. A settled apathy, a gradual wasting away of the person, and frequent although transient affections of a partially cataleptical character were the unusual diagnosis. Hitherto she had steadily borne up against the pressure of her malady, and had not betaken herself finally to bed; but on the closing in of the evening of my arrival at the house, she succumbed (as her brother told me at night with inexpressible agitation) to the prostrating power of the destroyer; and I learned that the glimpse I had obtained of her person would thus probably be the last I should obtain—that the lady, at least while living, would be seen by me no more.

For several days ensuing, her name was unmentioned by either Usher or myself; and during this period I was busied in earnest endeavors to alleviate the melancholy of my friend. We painted and read together, or I listened, as if in a dream, to the wild improvisations of his speaking guitar. And thus, as a closer and still closer intimacy admitted me more unreservedly into the recesses of his spirit, the more bitterly did I perceive the futility of all attempt at cheering a mind from which darkness, as if an inherent positive quality, poured forth all objects of the moral and physical universe in one unceasing radiation of gloom.

I shall ever bear about me a memory of the many solemn hours I thus spent alone with the master of the House of Usher. Yet I should fail in any attempt to convey an idea of the exact character of the studies, or of the occupations, in which he involved me, or led me the way. An excited and highly distempered ideality threw a sulphureous lustre over all. His long improvised dirges will ring forever in my ears. Among other things, I hold painfully in mind a certain singular perversion and amplification of the wild air of the last waltz of Von Weber. From the paintings over which his elaborate fancy brooded, and which grew, touch by touch, into vaguenesses at which I shuddered the more thrillingly, because I shuddered knowing not why—from these paintings (vivid as their images now are before me) I would in vain endeavor to educe more than a small portion which should lie within the compass of merely written words. By the utter simplicity, by the nakedness of his designs, he arrested and overawed attention. If ever mortal painted an idea, tht mortal was Roderick Usher. For me at least, in the circumstances then surrounding me, there arose out of the pure abstractions which the hypochondriac contrived to throw upon his canvas, an intensity of intolerable awe, no shadow of which felt I ever yet in the contemplation of the certainly glowing yet too concrete reveries of Fuseli.

One of the phantasmagoric conceptions of my friend, partaking not so rigidly of the spirit of abstraction, may be shadowed forth, although feebly, in words. A small picture presented the interior of an immensely long and rectangular vault or tunnel, with low walls, smooth, white, and without interruption or device. Certain accessory points of the design served well to convey the idea that this excavation lay at an exceeding depth below the surface of the earth. No outlet was observed in any portion of its vast extent, and no torch or other artificial source of light was discernible; yet a flood of intense rays rolled throughout, and bathed the whole in a ghastly and inappropriate splendor.

I have just spoken of that morbid condition of the auditory nerve which rendered all music intolerable to the sufferer, with the exception of certain effects of stringed instruments. It was, perhaps, the narrow limits to which he thus confined himself upon the guitar which gave birth, in great measure, to the fantastic character of his performances. But the fervid *facility* of his *impromptus* could not be so accounted for. They must have been, and were, in the notes, as well as in the words of his wild fantasias (for he not unfrequently accompanied himself with rhymed verbal improvisations), the result of that intense mental collectedness and concentration to which I have previously alluded as observable only in particular moments of the highest artificial excitement. The words of one of these rhapsodies I have easily remembered. I was, perhaps, the more forcibly impressed with it as he gave it, because in the under or mystic current of its meaning, I fancied that I perceived and for the first time, a full consciousness on the part of Usher of the tottering of his lofty reason upon her throne. The verses, which were entitled 'The Haunted Palace,' ran very nearly, if not accurately, thus:—

I

In the greenest of our valleys,
By good angels tenanted,
Once a fair and stately palace—
Radiant palace—reared its head.
In the monarch Thought's dominion!
It stood there!
Never seraph spread a pinion
Over fabric half so fair.

II

Banners yellow, glorious, golden,
On its roof did float and flow

(This—all this—was in the olden
Time long ago);
And every gentle air that dallied,
In that sweet day,
Along the ramparts plumed and pallid,
A winged odor went away.

III

Wanderers in that happy valley
Through two luminous windows saw
Spirits moving musically
to a lute's well-tuned law;
Round about a throne, where sitting
(Porphyrogene!)
In state his glory well befitting,
The ruler of the realm was seen.

IV

And all with pearl and ruby glowing
Was the fair palace door,
Through which came flowing, flowing, flowing
And sparkling evermore,
A troop of Echoes whose sweet duty
Was but to sing,
In voices of surpassing beauty,
The wit and wisdom of their king.

V

But evil things, in robes of sorrow,
Assailed the monarch's high estate;
(Ah, let us mourn, for never morrow
Shall dawn upon him, desolate!)
And, round about his home, the glory
That blushed and bloomed
Is but a dim-remembered story
Of the old time entombed.

VI

And travellers now within that valley,
Through the red-litten windows see
Vast forms that move fantastically
To a discordant melody;
While, like a rapid ghastly river,
Through the pale door;
A hideous throng rush out forever,
And laugh—but smile no more.

I well remember that suggestions arising from this ballad led us into a train of thought wherein there became manifest an opinion of Usher's which I mention not so much on account of its novelty (for other men have thought thus), as on account of the pertinacity with which he maintained it. This opinion in its general form, was that of the sentience of all vegetable things.

But, in his disordered fancy, the idea had assumed a more daring character, and trespassed, under certain conditions, upon the kingdom of inorganization. I lack words to express the full extent, or the earnest *abandon* of his persuasion. The belief, however, was connected (as I have previously hinted) with the gray stones of the home of his forefathers. The conditions of the sentence had been here, he imagined, fulfilled in the method of collocation of these stones—in the order of their arrangement, as well as in that of the many *fungi* which overspread them, and of the decayed trees which stood around—above all, in the long undisturbed endurance of this arrangement, and in its reduplication in the still waters of the tarn. Its evidence—the evidence of the sentience—was to be seen, he said (and I here started as he spoke), in the gradual yet certain condensation of an atmosphere of their own about the waters and the walls. The result was discoverable, he added, in that silent yet importunate and terrible influence which for centuries had moulded the destinies of his family, and which made *him* what I now saw him—what he was. Such opinions need no comment, and I will make none.

Our books—the books which, for years, had formed no small portion of the mental existence of the invalid—were, as might be supposed, in strict keeping with this character of phantasm. We pored together over such works as the 'Ververt et Chartreuse' of Gresset; the 'Belphegor' of Machiavelli; the 'Heaven and Hell' of Swedenborg; the 'Subterranean Voyage of Nicholas Klimm' of Holberg; the 'Chiromancy' of Robert Flud, of Jean D'Indaginé, and of Dela Chambre; the 'Journey into the Blue Distance of Tieck'; and the 'City of the Sun of Campanella.' One favorite volume was a small octavo edition of the 'Directorium Inquisitorium,' by the Dominican Eymeric de Gironne; and there were passages in Pomponius Mela, about the old African Satyrs and Egipans, over which Usher would sit dreaming for hours. His chief delight, however, was found in the perusal of an exceedingly rare and curious book in quarto Gothic—the manual of a forgotten church—the *Vigilioe Mortuorum secundum Chorum Ecclesioe Maguntinoe.*

I could not help thinking of the wild ritual of this work, and of its probable influence upon the hypochondriac, when, one evening, having informed me abruptly that the lady Madeline was no more, he stated his intention of preserving her corpse for a fortnight (previously to its final interment), in one of the numerous vaults within the main walls of the building. The worldly reason, however, assigned for this singular proceeding, was one which I did not feel at liberty to dispute. The brother had been led to his resolution (so he told me) by consideration of the unusual character of the malady of the deceased, of certain obtrusive and eager inquiries on the part of her medical men, and of the remote and exposed situation of the burial-ground of the family. I will not deny that when I called to mind the sinister countenance of the person whom I met upon the staircase, on the day of my arrival at the house, I had no desire to oppose what I regarded as at best but a harmless, and by no means an unnatural, precaution.

At the request of Usher, I personally aided him in the arrangements for the temporary entombment. The body having been encoffined, we two alone bore it to its rest. The vault in which we placed it (and which had been so long unopened that our torches, half smothered in its oppressive atmosphere, gave us little opportunity for investigation) was small, damp, and entirely without means of admission for light: lying, at great depth, immediately beneath that portion of the building in which was my own sleeping apartment. It had been used, apparently, in remote feudal times, for the worst purposes of a donjon-keep, and, in later days, as a place of deposit for powder, or some other highly combustible substance, as a portion of its floor, and the whole interior of a long archway through which we reached it, were carefully sheathed with copper. The door, of massive iron, had been, also, similarly protected. Its immense weight caused an unusually sharp, grating sound, as it moved upon its hinges.

Having deposited our mournful burden upon tressels within this region of horror, we partially turned aside the yet unscrewed lid of the coffin, and looked upon the face of the tenant. A striking similitude between the brother and sister now first arrested my attention; and Usher, divining, perhaps, my thoughts, murmured out some few words from which I learned that the deceased and himself had been twins, and that sympathies of a scarcely intelligible nature had always existed between them. Our glances, however, rested not long upon the dead—for we could not regard her unawed. The disease which had thus entombed the lady in the maturity of youth, had left, as usual in all maladies of a strictly cataleptical character, the mockery of a faint blush upon the bosom and the face, and that suspiciously lingering smile upon the lip which is so terrible in death. We replaced and screwed down the lid, and, having secured the door of iron, made our way, with toil, into the scarcely less gloomy apartments of the upper portion of the house.

And now, some days of bitter grief having elapsed, an observable change came over the features of the mental disorder of my friend. His ordinary manner had vanished. His ordinary occupations were neglected or forgotten. He roamed from chamber to chamber with hurried, unequal, and objectless step. The pallor of his countenance had assumed, if possible, a more ghastly hue—but the luminousness of his eye had utterly gone out. The once occasional huskiness of his tone was heard no more; and a tremulous quaver, as if of extreme terror, habitually characterized his utterance. There were times, indeed, when I thought his unceasingly agitated mind was laboring with some oppressive secret, to divulge which he struggled for the necessary courage. At times, again, I was obliged to resolve all into the mere inexplicable vagaries of madness, for I beheld him gazing upon vacancy for long hours, in an attitude of the profoundest attention, as if listening to some imaginary sound. It was no wonder that his condition terrified—that it infected me. I felt creeping upon me, by slow yet certain degrees, the wild influences of his own fantastic yet impressive superstitions.

It was, especially, upon retiring to bed late in the night of the seventh or eighth day after the placing of the lady Madeline within the donjon, that I experienced the full power of such feelings. Sleep came not near my couch—while the hours waned and waned away. I struggled to reason off the nervousness which had dominion over me, I endeavored to believe that much, if not all of what I felt, was due to the bewildering influence of the gloomy furniture of the room—of the dark and tattered draperies, which, tortured into motion by the breath of a rising tempest, swayed fitfully to and fro upon the walls, and rustled uneasily about the decorations of the bed. But my efforts were fruitless. A irrepressible tremor gradually pervaded my frame; and, at length, there sat upon my very heart an incubus of utterly causeless alarm. Shaking this off with a gasp and a struggle, I uplifted myself upon the pillows, and, peering earnestly within the intense darkness of the chamber, hearkened—I know not why, except that an instinctive spirit prompted me—to certain low and indefinite sounds which came, through the pauses of the storm, at long intervals, I knew not whence. Overpowered by an intense sentiment of horror, unaccountable yet unendurable, I threw on my clothes with haste (for I felt that I should sleep no more during the night), and endeavored to arouse myself from the pitiable condition into which I had fallen, by pacing rapidly to and fro through the apartment.

I had taken but few turns in this manner, when a light step on an adjoining staircase arrested my attention. I presently recognized it as that of Usher. In an instant afterward he rapped, with a gentle touch, at my door, and entered, bearing a lamp. His countenance was, as usual, cadaverously wan—but, moreover, there was a species of mad hilarity in his eyes—an evidently restrained *hysteria* in his whole demeanor. His air appalled me— but any thing was preferable to the solitude which I had so long endured, and I even welcomed his presence as a relief.

'And you have not seen it?' he said abruptly, after having stared about him for some moments in silence—'you have not then seen it?—but, stay! you shall.' Thus speaking, and having carefully shaded his lamp, he hurried to one of the casements, and threw it freely open to the storm.

The impetuous fury of the entering gust nearly lifted us from our feet. It was, indeed, a tempestuous yet sternly beautiful night, and one wildly singular in its terror and its beauty. A whirlwind had apparently collected its force in our vicinity; for there were frequent and violent alterations in the direction of the wind; and the exceeding density of the clouds (which hung so low as to press upon the turrets of the house) did not prevent our perceiving the life-like velocity with which they flew careering from all points against each other, without passing away into the distance. I say that even their exceeding density did not prevent our perceiving this—yet we had no glimpse of the moon or stars, nor was there any flashing forth of the lightning. But the under surfaces of the huge masses of agitated vapor, as well as all terrestrial objects immediately around us, were glowing in the unnatural light of a faintly luminous and distinctly visible gaseous exhalation which hung about and enshrouded the mansion.

'You must not—you shall not behold this!' said I, shuddering, to Usher, as I led him, with a gentle violence, from the window to a seat. These appearances, which bewilder you, are merely electrical phenomena not uncommon—or it may be that they have their ghastly origin in the rank miasma of the tarn. Let us close this casement;—the air is chilling and dangerous to your frame. Here is one of your favorite romances. I will read, and you shall listen:—and so we will pass away this terrible night together.

The antique volume which I had taken up was the 'Mad Trist' of Sir Launcelot Canning; but I had called it a favorite of Usher's more in sad jest than in earnest; for, in truth, there is little in its uncouth and unimaginative prolixity which could have had interest for the lofty and spiritual ideality of my friend. It was, however, the only book immediately at hand; and I indulged a vague hope that the excitement which now agitated the hypochondriac, might find relief (for the history of mental disorder is full of similar anomalies) even in the extremeness of the folly which I should read. Could I have judged, indeed, by the wild overstrained air of vivacity with which he hearkened, or apparently hearkened, to the words of the tale, I might well have congratulated myself upon the success of my design.

I had arrived at that well-known portion of the story where Ethelred, the hero of the Trist, having sought in vain for peaceable admission into the dwelling of the hermit, proceeds to make good an entrance by force. Here, it will be remembered, the words of the narrative run thus:

'And Ethelred, who was by nature of a doughty heart, and who was now mighty withal, on account of the powerful of the wine which he had drunken, waited no longer to hold parley with the hermit, who, in sooth, was of an obstinate and maliceful turn, but, feeling the rain upon his shoulders, and fearing the rising of the tempest, uplifted his mace outright, and, with blows, made quickly room in the plankings of the door for his gauntleted hand; and now pulling therewith sturdily, he so cracked, and ripped, and tore all asunder, that the noise of the dry and hollow-sounding wood alarumed and reverberated throughout the forest.'

At the termination of this sentence I started and, for a moment, paused; for it appeared to me (although I at once concluded that my excited fancy had deceived me)—it appeared to me that, from some very remote portion of the mansion, there came, indistinctly to my ears, what might have been, in its exact similarity of character, the echo (but a stifled and dull one certainly) of the very cracking and ripping sound which Sir Launcelot had so particularly described. It was, beyond doubt, the coincidence alone which had arrested my attention; for, amid the rattling of the sashes of the casements, and the ordinary commingled noises of the still increasing storm, the sound, in itself, had nothing, surely, which should have interested or disturbed me. I continued the story:

'But the good champion Ethelred, now entering within the door, was sore enraged and amazed to perceive no signal of the maliceful hermit; but, in the stead thereof, a dragon of a scaly and prodigious demeanor, and of a fiery tongue, which sate in guard before a palace of gold, with a floor of silver; and upon the wall there hung a shield of shining brass with this legend enwritten—

Who entereth herein, a conqueror hath bin;
Who slayeth the dragon, the shield he shall win.

And Ethelred uplifted his mace, and struck upon the head of the dragon, which fell before him, and gave up his pesty breath, with a shriek so horrid and harsh, and withal so piercing, that Ethelred had fain to close his ears with his hands against the dreadful noise of it, the like whereof was never before heard.'

Here again I paused abruptly, and now with a feeling of wild amazement—for there could be no doubt whatever that, in this instance, I did actually hear (although from what direction it proceeded I found it impossible to say) a low and apparently distant, but harsh, protracted, and most unusual screaming or grating sound—the exact counterpart of what my fancy had already conjured up for the dragon's unnatural shriek as described by the romancer.

Oppressed, as I certainly was, upon the occurrence of this second and most extraordinary coincidence, by a thousand conflicting sensations, in which wonder and extreme terror were predominant, I still retained sufficient presence of mind to avoid exciting, by any observation, the sensitive nervousness of my companion. I was by no means certain that he had noticed the sounds in question; although, assuredly, a strange alteration had, during the last few minutes, taken place in his demeanor. From a position fronting my own, he had gradually brought round his chair, so as to sit with his face to the door of the chamber; and thus I could but partially perceive his features, although I saw that his lips trembled as if he were murmuring inaudibly. His head had dropped upon his breast—yet I knew that he was not asleep, from the wide and rigid opening of the eye as I caught a glance of it in profile. The motion of his body, too, was at variance with this idea—for he rocked from side to side with a gentle yet constant and uniform sway. Having rapidly taken notice of all this, I resumed the narrative of Sir Launcelot, which thus proceeded:

'And now, the champion, having escaped from the terrible fury of the dragon, bethinking himself of the brazen shield, and of the breaking up of the enchantment which was upon it, removed the carcass from out of the way before him, and approached valorously over the silver pavement of the castle to where the shield was upon the wall; which in sooth tarried not for his full coming, but fell down at his feet upon the silver floor, with a mighty great and terrible ringing sound.'

No sooner had these syllables passed my lips, than—as if a shield of brass had indeed, at that moment, fallen heavily upon a floor of silver—I became aware of a distinct, hollow, metallic, and clangorous, yet apparently muffled, reverberation. Completely unnerved, I leaped to my feet; but the measured rocking movement of Usher was undisturbed. I rushed to the chair in which he sat. His eyes were bent fixedly before him, and throughout his whole countenance there reigned a stony rigidity. But, as I placed my hand upon his shoulder, there came a strong shudder over his whole person; a sickly smile quivered about his lips; and I saw that he spoke in a low, hurried, and gibbering murmur, as if unconscious of my presence. Bending closely over him, I at length drank in the hideous import of his words.

'Now hear it?—yes, I hear it, and *have* heard it. Long—long—long—many minutes, many hours, many days, have I heard it—yet I dared not—oh, pity me, miserable wretch that I am!—I dared not—I *dared* not speak! *We have put her living in the tomb!* Said I not that my senses were acute? I *now* tell you that I heard her first feeble movements in the coffin. I heard them—many, many days ago—yet I dared not—*I dared not speak!* And now—to-night—Ethelred—ha! ha!—the breaking of the hermit's door, and the death-cry of the dragon, and the clangor of the shield—say, rather, the rending of her coffin, and the grating of the iron hinges of her prison, and her struggles within the coppered archway of the vault! Oh! whither shall I fly? Will she not be here anon? Is she not hurrying to upbraid me for my haste? Have I not heard her footstep on the stair? Do I not distinguish that heavy and horrible beating of her heart? Madman!'—here he sprang furiously to his feet, and shrieked out his syllables, as if in the effort he were giving up his soul—*'Madman! I tell you that she now stands without the door!'*

As if in the superhuman energy of his utterance there had been found the potency of a spell, the huge antique panels to which the speaker pointed threw slowly back, upon the instant, their ponderous and ebony jaws. It was the work of the rushing gust—but then without those doors there *did* stand the lofty and enshrouded figure of the lady Madeline of Usher. There was blood upon her white robes, and the evidence of some bitter struggle upon every portion of her emaciated frame. For a moment she remained trembling and reeling to and fro upon the threshold—then, with a low moaning cry, fell heavily inward upon the person of her brother, and in her violent and now final death-agonies, bore him to the floor a corpse, and a victim to the terrors he had anticipated.

From that chamber, and from that mansion, I fled aghast. The storm was still abroad in all its wrath as I found myself crossing the old causeway. Suddenly there shot along the path a wild light, and I turned to see whence a gleam so unusual could have issued; for the vast house and its shadows were alone behind me. The radiance was that of the full, setting, and blood-red moon, which now shone vividly through that once barely discernible fissure, of which I have before spoken as extending from the roof of the building, in a zigzag direction, to the base. While I gazed, this entire orb of the satellite burst at once upon my sight—my brain reeled as I saw the mighty walls rushing asunder—there was a long tumultuous shouting sound like the voice of a thousand waters—and the deep and dank tarn at my feet closed sullenly and silently over the fragments of the *'House of Usher.'*

About Mark Twain

Named Samuel Clemens when he was born in 1835 in Missouri, he became a licensed riverboat pilot on the Mississippi River. For his pen name he chose Mark Twain, sailor-slang for marking twelve feet. At the outbreak of the Civil War he went West to write stories of the gold miners in California. His writings brought him fame and national acclaim and he returned East to write and lecture. Memories of life on the river inspired his great works, *Tom Sawyer* and *Huckleberry Finn.* He died of a heart attack in 1910 in Redding, Connecticut, and is buried in his family's plot in Elmira, New York.

The Celebrated Jumping Frog of Calaveras County

In compliance with the request of a friend of mine, who wrote me from the East, I called on good-natured, garrulous old Simon Wheeler, and inquired after my friend's friend, *Leonidas W.* Smiley, as requested to do, and I hereunto append the result. I have a lurking suspicion that *Leonidas W.* Smiley is a myth; that my friend never knew such a personage; and that he only conjectured that, if I asked old Wheeler about him, it would remind him of his infamous Jim Smiley, and he would go to work and bore me nearly to death with some infernal reminiscence of him as long and tedious as it should be useless to me. If that was the design, it certainly succeeded.

I found Simon Wheeler dozing comfortably by the bar-room stove of the old, dilapidated tavern in the ancient mining camp of Angel's, and I noticed that he was fat and bald-headed, and had an expression of winning gentleness and simplicity upon his tranquil countenance. He roused up and gave me good-day. I told him a friend of mine had commissioned me to make some inquiries about a cherished companion of his boyhood named *Leonidas W.* Smiley—*Rev. Leonidas W.* Smiley—a young minister of the Gospel, who he had heard was at one time a resident of Angel's Camp. I added, that, if Mr. Wheeler could tell me anything about the Rev. Leonidas W. Smiley, I would feel under many obligations to him.

Simon Wheeler backed me into a corner and blockaded me there with his chair, and then sat me down and reeled off the monotonous narrative which follows this paragraph. He never smiled, he never frowned, he never changed his voice from the gentle-flowing key to which he tuned the initial sentence, he never betrayed the slightest suspicion of enthusiasm; but all through the interminable narrative there ran a vein of impressive earnestness and sincerity, which showed me plainly that, so far from his imagining that there was anything ridiculous or funny about his story, he regarded it as a really important matter, and admitted its two heroes as men of transcendent genius in *finesse.* To me, the spectacle of a man drifting serenely along through such a queer yarn without ever smiling, was exquisitely absurd. As I said before, I asked him to tell me what he knew of Rev. Leonidas W. Smiley, and he replied as follows. I let him go on in his own way, and never interrupted him once:

There was a feller here once by the name of *Jim* Smiley, in the winter of '49—maybe it was the spring of '50—I don't recollect exactly, somehow, though what makes me think it was one or the other is because I remember the big flume wasn't finished when he first came to the camp; but anyway, he was the curiousest man about always betting on anything that turned up you ever see, if he could get anybody to bet on the other side; and if he couldn't, he'd change sides. Any way that suited the other man would suit him—any way just so's he got a bet, *he* was satisfied. But still he was lucky, uncommon lucky—he most always come out winner. He was always ready and laying for a chance; there couldn't be no solit'ry thing mentioned but that feller'd offer to bet on it, and take any side you please, as I was just telling you. If there was a horse-race, you'd find him flush, or you'd find him busted at the end of it; if there was a dog-fight, he'd bet on it; if there was a cat-fight, he'd bet on it; if there was a chicken-fight, he'd bet on it; why, if there was two birds setting on a fence, he would bet you which one would fly first; or if there was a camp meeting, he would be there reg'lar, to bet on Parson Walker, which he judged to be the best exhorter about here, and so he was, too, and a good man. If he even seen a straddle-bug start to go anywheres, he would bet you how long it would take him to get wherever he was going to, and if you took him up, he would foller that straddle-bug to Mexico but what he would find out where he was bound for and how long he was on the road. Lots of the boys here has seen that Smiley, and can tell you about him. Why, it never made no difference to *him*—he would bet on *any*thing—the dangdest feller. Parson Walker's wife laid very sick once, for a good while, and it seemed as if they warn't going to save her; but one morning he came in, and Smiley asked how she was, and he said she was considerable better—thank the Lord for his inf'nit mercy—and coming on so smart that, with the blessing of Prov'dence, she'd get well yet; and Smiley, before he thought, says, "Well, I'll risk two-and-a-half that she don't, anyway."

Thish-yer Smiley had a mare—the boys called her the fifteen-minute nag, but that was only in fun, you know, because, of course, she was faster than that—and he used to win money on that horse, for all she was so slow and always had the asthma, or the distemper, or the consumption, or something of that kind. They used to give her two or three hundred yards start, and then pass her under way; but always at the fag-end of the race she'd get excited and desperate-like, and come cavorting and straddling up, and scattering her legs around limber, sometimes in the air, and sometimes out to one side amongst the fences, and kicking up m-o-r-e dust, and raising m-o-r-e racket with her coughing and sneezing and blowing her nose—and always fetch up at the stand just about a neck ahead, as near as you could cipher it down.

And he had a little small bull pup, that to look at him you'd think he wan't worth a cent but to set around and look ornery and lay for a chance to steal something. But as soon as money was up on him, he was a different dog; his under-jaw'd begin to stick out like the fo'castle of a steamboat, and his teeth would uncover, and shine savage like the furnaces. And a dog might tackle him, and bully-rag him, and bite him, and throw him over his shoulder two or three times, and Andrew Jackson—which was the name of the pup—Andrew Jackson would never let on but what *he* was satisfied, and hadn't expected nothing else—and the bets being doubled and doubled on the other side all the time, till the money was all up; and then all of a sudden he would grab that other dog jest by the j'int of his hind leg and freeze to it—not claw, you understand, but only jest grip and hang on till they throwed up the sponge, if it was a year. Smiley always come out winner on that pup, till he harnessed a dog once that didn't have no hind legs, because they'd been sawed off by a circular saw, and when the thing had gone along far enough, and the money was all up, and he come to make a snatch for his pet holt, he saw in a minute how he'd been imposed on, and how the other dog had him in the door, so to speak, and he 'peared surprised, and then he looked sorter discouraged-like, and didn't try no more to win the fight, and so he got shucked out bad. He gave Smiley a look, as much to say his heart was broke and it was *his* fault for putting up a dog that hadn't no hind legs for him to take holt of, which was his main dependence in a fight, and then he limped off a piece and laid down and died. It was a good pup, was that Andrew Jackson, and would have made a name for hisself if he'd lived, for the stuff was in him, and he had genius—I know it, because he hadn't no opportunities to speak of, and it don't stand to reason that a dog could make such a fight as he could under them circumstances, if he hadn't no talent. It always makes me feel sorry when I think of that last fight of his'n, and the way it turned out.

Well, thish-yer Smiley had rat-tarriers, and chicken-cocks, and tomcats, and all them kind of things, till you couldn't rest, and you couldn't fetch nothing for him to bet on but he'd match you. He ketched a frog one day, and took him home, and said he cal'klated to edercate him; and so he never done nothing for these three months but set in his back yard and learn that frog to jump. And you bet you he *did* learn him, too. He'd give him a little punch behind, and the next minute you'd see that frog whirling in the air like a doughnut—see him turn one summerset, or maybe a couple, if he got a good start, and come down flat-footed and all right, like a cat. He got him up so in the matter of catching flies, and kept him in practice so constant, that he'd nail a fly every time as far as he could see him. Smiley said all a frog wanted was education, and he could do most anything—and I believe him. Why, I've seen him set Dan'l Webster down here on this floor—Dan'l Webster was the name of the frog—and sing out, "Flies, Dan'l, flies!" and quicker'n you could wink, he'd spring straight up, and snake a fly off'n the counter there, and flop down on the floor again as solid as a gob of mud, and fall to scratching the side of his head with his hind foot as indifferent as if he hadn't no idea he's been doin' any more'n any frog might do. You never see a frog so modest and straight-for'ard as he was, for all he was so gifted. And when it come to fair and square jumping on the dead level, he could get over more ground at one straddle than any animal of his breed you ever see. Jumping on a dead level was his strong suit, you understand; and when it come to that, Smiley would ante up money on him as long as he had a red. Smiley was monstrous proud of his frog, and well he might be, for fellers that had traveled and been everywhere all said he laid over any frog that ever *they* see.

Well, Smiley kept the beast in a little lattice box, and he used to fetch him downtown sometimes and lay for a bet. One day a feller—a stranger in the camp, he was—come across him with his box, and says:

"What might it be that you've got in the box?"

And Smiley says, sorter indifferent like, "It might be a parrot, or it might be a canary, maybe, but it ain't—it's only just a frog."

An' the feller took it, and looked at it careful, and turned it round this way and that, and says, "H'm—so 'tis. Well, what's *he* good for?"

"Well," Smiley says, easy and careless, "He's good enough for *one* thing, I should judge—he can outjump any frog in Calaveras county."

The feller took the box again, and took another long, particular look, and give it back to Smiley, and says, very deliberate, "Well, I don't see no p'ints about that frog that's any better'n any other frog."

"Maybe you don't," Smiley says. "Maybe you understand frogs, and maybe you don't understand 'em; maybe you've had experience, and maybe you ain't only a amature, as it were. Anyways, I've got *my* opinion, and I'll risk forty dollars that he can outjump any frog in Calaveras county."

And the feller studied a minute, and then says, kinder sad like, "Well, I'm only a stranger here, and I ain't got no frog; but if I had a frog, I'd bet you."

And then Smiley says, "That's all right—that's all right—if you'll hold my box a minute, I'll go and get you a frog." And so the feller took the box, and put up his forty dollars along with Smiley's, and set down to wait.

So he set there a good while thinking and thinking to hisself, and then he got the frog out and prized his mouth open and took a teaspoon and filled him full of quail shot—filled him pretty near up to his chin—and set him on the floor. Smiley he went to the swamp and slopped around in the mud for a long time, and finally he ketched a frog, and fetched him in, and give him to this feller, and says:

"Now, if you're ready, set him alongside of Dan'l, with his forepaws just even with Dan'l, and I'll give the word." Then he says, "One—two—three—jump!" and him and the feller touched up the frogs from behind, and the new frog hopped off, but Dan'l give a heave, and hysted up his shoulders—so—like a Frenchman, but it wasn't no use—he couldn't budge; he was planted as solid as an anvil, and he couldn't no more stir than if he was anchored out. Smiley was a good deal surprised, and he was disgusted too, but he didn't have no idea what the matter was, of course.

The feller took the money and started away; and when he was going out at the door, he sorter jerked his thumb over his shoulder—this way—at Dan'l, and says again, very deliberate, "Well, *I* don't see no p'ints about that frog that's any better'n any other frog."

Smiley he stood scratching his head and looking down at Dan'l a long time, and at last he says, "I do wonder what in the nation that frog throw'd off for—I wonder if there ain't something the matter with him—he 'pears to look mighty baggy, somehow." And he ketched Dan'l by the nap of the neck, and lifted him up and says, "Why, blame my cats, if he don't weigh five pounds!" and turned him upside down, and he belched out a double handful of shot.

And then he see how it was, and he was the maddest man—he set the frog down and took out after that feller, but he never ketched him. And—

(Here Simon Wheeler heard his name called from the front yard, and got up to see what was wanted.) And turning to me as he moved away, he said: "Just set where you are, stranger, and rest easy—I ain't going to be gone a second."

But, by your leave, I did not think that a continuation of the history of the enterprising vagabond *Jim* Smiley would be likely to afford me much information concerning the Rev. *Leonidas W.* Smiley, and so I started away.

At the door I met the sociable Wheeler returning, and he buttonholed me and recommenced:

"Well, thish-yer Smiley had a yeller one-eyed cow that didn't have no tail, only jest a short stump like a bannanner, and—"

"Oh, hang Smiley and his afflicted cow!" I muttered, good-naturedly, and bidding the old gentleman good-day, I departed.

About Bret Harte

He was born in 1836 in Albany, New York. A journalist, essayist, and storyteller, he went to the Yukon and wrote about the lives of the miners and their independent spirits. Harte's stories were sent East and enthusiastically received. He returned East and toured the U.S. and Europe, lecturing on the Gold Rush. Eventually his popularity waned but he continued to write. He died of throat cancer in 1902 and is buried in Frimley, England.

The Outcasts of Poker Flat

As Mr. John Oakhurst, gambler, stepped into the main street of Poker Flat on the morning of the twenty-third of November, 1850, he was conscious of a change in its moral atmosphere since the preceding night. Two or three men, conversing earnestly together, ceased as he approached, and exchanged significant glances. There was a Sabbath lull in the air, which, in a settlement unused to Sabbath influences, looked ominous.

Mr. Oakhurst's calm, handsome face betrayed small concern of these indications. Whether he was conscious of any predisposing cause, was another question. "I reckon they're after somebody," he reflected; "likely it's me." He returned to his pocket the handkerchief with which he had been whipping away the red dust of Poker Flat from his neat boots, and quietly discharged his mind of any further conjecture.

In point of fact, Poker Flat was "after somebody." It had lately suffered the loss of several thousand dollars, two valuable horses, and a prominent citizen. It was experiencing a spasm of virtuous reaction, quite as lawless and ungovernable as any of the acts that had provoked it. A secret committee had determined to rid the town of all improper persons. This was done permanently in regard of two men who were then hanging from the boughs of a sycamore in the gulch, and temporarily in the banishment of certain other objectionable characters. I regret to say that some of these were ladies. It is but due to the sex, however, to state that their impropriety was professional, and it was only in such easily established standards of evil that Poker Flat ventured to sit in judgment.

Mr. Oakhurst was right in supposing that he was included in this category. A few of the committee had urged hanging him as a possible example, and a sure method of reimbursing themselves from his pockets of the sums he had won from them. "It's agin justice," said Jim Wheeler, "to let this yer young man from Roaring Camp—an entire stranger—carry away our money." But a crude sentiment of equity residing in the breasts of those who had been fortunate enough to win from Mr. Oakhurst overruled this narrower local prejudice.

Mr. Oakhurst received his sentence with philosophic calmness, none the less coolly that he was aware of the hesitation of his judges. He was too much of a gambler not to accept Fate. With him life was at best an uncertain game, and he recognized the usual percentage in favor of the dealer.

A body of armed men accompanied the deported wickedness of Poker Flat to the outskirts of the settlement. Besides Mr. Oakhurst, who was known to be a coolly desperate man, and for those intimidation the armed escort was intended, the expatriated party consisted of a young woman familiarly known as "The Duchess"; another, who had gained the infelicitous title of "Mother Shipton"; and "Uncle Billy," a suspected sluice-robber and confirmed drunkard. The cavalcade provoked no comments from the spectators, nor was any word uttered by the escort. Only, when the gulch which marked the uttermost limit of Poker Flat was reached, the leader spoke briefly and to the point. The exiles were forbidden to return at the peril of their lives.

As the escort disappeared, their pent-up feelings found vent in a few hysterical tears from the Duchess, some bad language from Mother Shipton, and a Parthian volley of expletives from Uncle Billy. The philosophic Oakhurst alone remained still. He listened calmly to Mother Shipton's desire to cut somebody's heart out, to the repeated statements of the Duchess that she would die on the road, and to the alarming oaths that seemed to be bumped out of Uncle Billy as he rode forward. With the easy good humor characteristic of his class, he insisted upon exchanging his own riding-horse, Five Spot, for the sorry mule which the Duchess rode. But even this act did not draw the party into any closer sympathy. The young woman readjusted her somewhat draggled plumes with a feeble, faded coquetry; Mother Shipton eyed the possessor of Five Spot with malevolence, and Uncle Billy included the whole party in one sweeping anathema.

The road to Sandy Bar—a camp that, not having as yet experienced the regenerating influences of Poker Flat, consequently seemed to offer some invitation to the emigrants—lay over a steep mountain range. It was distant a day's severe journey. In that advanced season, the party soon passed out of the moist, temperate regions of the foothills into the dry, cold, bracing air of the Sierras. The trail was narrow and difficult. At noon the Duchess, rolling out of her saddle upon the ground, declared her intention of going no farther, and the party halted.

The spot was singularly wild and impressive. A wooded amphitheater, surrounded on three sides by precipitous cliffs of naked granite, sloped gently toward the crest of another precipice that overlooked the valley. It was undoubtedly the most suitable spot for a camp, had camping been advisable. But Mr. Oakhurst knew that scarcely half the journey to Sandy Bar was accomplished, and the party were not equipped or provisioned for delay. This fact he pointed out to his companions curtly, with a philosophic commentary on the folly of "throwing up their hand before the game was played out." But they were furnished with liquor, which in this emergency stood them in place of food, fuel, rest, and prescience. In spite of his remonstrances, it was not long before they were more or less under its influence. Uncle Billy passed rapidly from a bellicose state into one of stupor, the Duchess became maudlin, and Mother Shipton snored. Mr. Oakhurst alone remained erect, leaning against a rock, calmly surveying them.

Mr. Oakhurst did not drink. It interfered with a profession which required coolness, impassiveness, and presence of mind, and, in his own language, he "couldn't afford it." As he gazed at his recumbent fellow-exiles, the loneliness begotten of his pariah-trade, his habits of life, his very vices, for the first time seriously oppressed him. He bestirred himself in dusting his black clothes, washing his hands and face, and other acts characteristic of his studiously neat habits, and for a moment forgot his annoyance. The thought of deserting his weaker and more pitiable companions never perhaps occurred to him. Yet he could not help feeling the want of that excitement which, singularly enough, was most conducive to that calm equanimity for which he was notorious. He looked at the gloomy walls that rose a thousand feet sheer above the circling pines around him; at the sky, ominously clouded; at the valley below, already deepening into shadow. And, doing so, suddenly he heard his own name called.

A horseman slowly ascended the trail. In the fresh, open face of the newcomer Mr. Oakhurst recognized Tom Simson, otherwise known as "The Innocent" of Sandy Bar. He had met him some months before over a "little game," and had, with perfect equanimity, won the entire fortune—amounting to some forty dollars—of that guileless youth. After the game was finished, Mr. Oakhurst drew the youthful speculator behind the door and thus addressed him: "Tommy, you're a good little man, but you can't gamble worth a cent. Don't try it over again." He then handed him his money back, pushed him gently from the room, and so made a devoted slave of Tom Simson.

There was a remembrance of this in his boyish and enthusiastic greeting of Mr. Oakhurst. He had started, he said, to go to Poker Flat to seek his fortune. "Alone?" No, not exactly alone; in fact—a giggle—he had run away with Piney Woods. Didn't Mr. Oakhurst remember Piney? She that used to wait on the table at the Temperance House? They had been engaged a long time, but old Jake Woods had objected, so they had run away, and were going to Poker Flat to be married, and here they were. And they were tired out, and how lucky it was they had found a place to camp and company. All this the Innocent delivered rapidly, while Piney—a stout, comely damsel of fifteen—emerged from behind the pine-tree, where she had been blushing unseen, and rode to the side of her lover.

Mr. Oakhurst seldom troubled himself with sentiment, still less with propriety; but he had a vague idea that the situation was not felicitous. He retained, however, his presence of mind sufficiently to kick Uncle Billy, who was about to say something, and Uncle Billy was sober enough to recognize in Mr. Oakhurst's kick a superior power that would not bear trifling. He then endeavored to dissuade Tom Simson from delaying further, but in vain. He even pointed out the fact that there was no provision, nor means of making a camp. But, unluckily, the Innocent met this objection by assuring the party that he was provided with an extra mule loaded with provision, and by the discovery of a rude attempt at a log-house near the trail. "Piney can stay with Mrs. Oakhurst," said the Innocent, pointing to the Duchess, "and I can shift for myself."

Nothing but Mr. Oakhurst's admonishing foot saved Uncle Billy from bursting into a roar of laughter. As it was, he felt compelled to retire up the canyon until he could recover his gravity. There he confided the joke to the tall pine trees, with many slaps of his leg, contortions of his face, and the usual profanity. But when he returned to the party, he found them seated by a fire—for the air had grown strangely chill and the sky overcast—in apparently amicable conversation. Piney was actually talking in an impulsive, girlish fashion to the Duchess, who was listening with an interest and animation she had not shown for many days. The Innocent was holding forth, apparently with equal effect, to Mr. Oakhurst and Mother Shipton, who was actually relaxing into amiability. "Is this yer a d—d picnic?" said Uncle Billy, with inward scorn, as he surveyed the sylvan group, the glancing fire-light, and the tethered animals in the foreground. Suddenly an idea mingled with the alcoholic fumes that disturbed his brain. It was apparently of a jocular nature, for he felt impelled to slap his leg again and cram his fist into his mouth.

As the shadows crept slowly up the mountain, a slight breeze rocked the tops of the pine-trees, and moaned through their long and gloomy aisles. The ruined cabin, patched and covered with pine boughs, was set apart for the ladies, As the lovers parted, they unaffectedly exchanged a kiss, so honest and sincere that it might have been heard above the swaying pines. The frail Duchess and the malevolent Mother Shipton were probably too stunned to remark upon this last evidence of simplicity, and so turned without a word to the hut. The fire was replenished, the men lay down before the door, and in a few minutes were asleep.

Mr. Oakhurst was a light sleeper. Toward morning he awoke benumbed and cold. As he stirred the dying fire, the wind, which was now blowing strongly, brought to his cheek that which caused the blood to leave it—snow!

He started to his feet with the intention of awakening the sleepers, for there was no time to lose. But turning to where Uncle Billy had been lying, he found him gone. A suspicion leaped to his brain and a curse to his lips. He ran to the spot where the mules had been tethered; they were no longer there. The tracks were already rapidly disappearing in the snow.

The momentary excitement brought Mr. Oakhurst back to the fire with his usual calm. He did not waken the sleepers. The Innocent slumbered peacefully, with a smile on his good humored, freckled face; the virgin Piney slept beside her frailer sisters as sweetly as though attended by celestial guardians, and Mr. Oakhurst, drawing his blanket over his shoulders, stroked his mustachios and waited for the dawn. It came slowly in the whirling mist of snowflakes, that dazzled and confused the eye. What could be seen of the landscape appeared magically changed. He looked over the valley, and summed up the present and future in two words—"Snowed in!"

A careful inventory of the provisions, which, fortunately for the party, had been stored within the hut, and so escaped the felonious fingers of Uncle Billy, disclosed the fact that with care and prudence they might last ten days longer. "That is," said Mr. Oakhurst, *sotto voce* to the Innocent, "if you're willing to board us. If you ain't—and perhaps you'd better not—you can wait till Uncle Billy gets back with provisions." For some occult reason, Mr. Oakhurst could not bring himself to disclose Uncle Billy's rascality, and so offered the hypothesis that he had wandered from the camp and had accidentally stampeded the animals. He dropped a warning to the Duchess and Mother Shipton, who of course knew the facts of their associate's defection. "They'll find out the truth about us *all*, when they find out anything," he added, significantly, "and there's no good frightening them now."

Tom Simson not only put all his worldly store at the disposal of Mr. Oakhurst, but seemed to enjoy the prospect of their enforced seclusion. We'll have a good camp for a week, and then the snow'll melt, and we'll all go back together." The cheerful gayety of the young man and Mr. Oakhurst's calm infected the others. The Innocent, with the aid of pine boughs, extemporized a thatch for the roofless cabin, and the Duchess directed Piney in the rearrangement of the interior with a taste and tact that opened the blue eyes of that provincial maiden to their fullest extent.

"I reckon now you're used to fine things at Poker Flat," said Piney. The Duchess turned away sharply to conceal something that reddened her cheek through its professional tint, and Mother Shipton requested Piney not to "chatter." But when Mr. Oakhurst returned from a weary search for the trail, he heard the sound of happy laughter echoed from the rocks. He stopped in some alarm, and his thoughts first naturally reverted to the whisky, which he had prudently *cached*. "And yet it don't somehow sound like whisky," said the gambler. It was not until he caught sight of the blazing fire through the still blinding storm, and the group around it, that he settled to the conviction that it was "square fun."

Whether Mr. Oakhurst had *cached* his cards with the whisky as something debarred the free access of the community, I cannot say. It was certain that, in Mother Shipton's words, he "didn't say cards once" during the evening. Haply the time was beguiled by an accordion, produced somewhat ostentatiously by Tom Simson, from his pack. Notwithstanding some difficulties attending the manipulation of this instrument, Piney Woods managed to pluck several reluctant melodies from its keys, to an accompaniment by the Innocent on a pair of bone castinets. But the crowning festivity of the evening was reached in a rude camp-meeting hymn, which the lovers, joining hands, sang with great earnestness and vociferation. I fear that a certain defiant tone and Covenanter's swing to its chorus, rather than any devotional quality, caused it speedily to infect the others, who at last joined in the refrain:

I'm proud to live in the service of the Lord,
And I'm bound to die in His army.

The pines rocked, the storm eddied and whirled above the miserable group, and the flames of their altar leaped heavenward, as if in token of the vow.

At midnight the storm abated, the rolling clouds parted, and the stars glittered keenly above the sleeping camp. Mr. Oakhurst, whose professional habits had enabled him to live on the smallest possible amount of sleep, in dividing the watch with Tom Simson, somehow managed to take upon himself the greater part of that duty. He excused himself to the Innocent, by saying that he had "often been a week without sleep." "Doing what?" asked Tom. "Poker!" replied Oakhurst, sententiously, "when a man gets a streak of luck—nigger-luck—he don't get tired. The luck gives in first. Luck," continued the gambler, reflectively, "is a mighty queer thing. All you know about it for certain is that it's bound to change. And it's finding out when it's going to change that makes you. We've had a streak of bad luck since we left Poker Flat—you come along, and slap you get into it, too. If you can hold your cards right along you're all right. For," added the gambler, with cheerful irrelevance,

"I'm proud to live in the service of the Lord,
And I'm bound to die in His army."

The third day came, and the sun, looking through the white-curtained valley, saw the outcasts divide their slowly decreasing store of provisions for the morning meal. It was one of the peculiarities of that mountain climate that its rays diffused a kindly warmth over the wintry landscape, as if in regretful commiseration of the past. But it revealed drift on drift of snow piled high around the hut; a hopeless, uncharted trackless sea of white lying below the rocky shores to which the castaways still clung. Through the marvelously clear air, the smoke of the pastoral village of Poker Flat rose miles away. Mother Shipton saw it, and from a remote pinnacle of her rocky fastness, hurled in that direction a final malediction. It was her last vituperative attempt, and perhaps for that reason was invested with a certain degree of sublimity. It did her good, she privately informed the Duchess. "Just to go out there and cuss, and see." She then set herself to the task of amusing "the child," as she and the Duchess were pleased to call Piney. Piney was no chicken, but it was a soothing and ingenious theory of the pair thus to account for the fact that she didn't swear and wasn't improper.

When night crept up again through the gorges, the reedy notes of the accordion rose and fell in fitful spasms and long-drawn gasps by the flickering camp-fire. But music failed to fill entirely the aching void left by insufficient food, and a new diversion was proposed by Piney—storytelling. Neither Mr. Oakhurst nor his female companions caring to relate their personal experiences, this plan would have failed, too, but for the Innocent. Some months before he had chanced upon a stray copy of Mr. Pope's ingenious translation of the Iliad. He now proposed to narrate the principal incidents of that poem—having thoroughly mastered the argument and fairly forgotten the words—in the current vernacular of Sandy Bar. And so for the rest of that night the Homeric demigods again walked the earth. Trojan bully and wily Greek wrestled in the winds, and the great pines in the canyon seemed to bow to the wrath of the son of Peleus. Mr. Oakhurst listened with quiet satisfaction. Most especially was he interested in the fate of "Ash-heels," as the Innocent persisted in denominating the "swift-footed Achilles."

So with small food and much of Homer and the accordion, a week passed over the heads of the outcasts. The sun again forsook them, and again from leaden skies the snowflakes were sifted over the land. Day by day closer around them drew the snowy circle, until at last they looked from their prison over drifted walls of dazzling white, that towered twenty feet above their heads. It became more and more difficult to replenish their fires, even from the fallen trees beside them, now half-hidden in the drifts. And yet no one complained. The lovers turned from the dreary prospect and looked into each other's eyes, and were happy. Mr. Oakhurst settled himself coolly to the losing game before him. The Duchess, more cheerful than she had been, assumed the care of Piney. Only Mother Shipton—once the strongest of the party—seemed to sicken and fade. At midnight on the tenth day she called Oakhurst to her side. "I'm going," she said, in a voice of querulous weakness, "but don't say anything about it. Don't waken the kids. Take the bundle from under my head and open it." Mr. Oakhurst did so. It contained Mother Shipton's rations for the last week, untouched. "Give 'em to the child," she said, pointing to the sleeping Piney. "You've starved yourself," said the gambler. "That's what they call it," said the woman, querulously, as she lay down again, and, turning her face to the wall, passed quietly away.

The accordion and the bones were put aside that day, and Homer was forgotten. When the body of Mother Shipton had been committed to the snow, Mr. Oakhurst took the Innocent aside, and showed him a pair of snowshoes, which he had fashioned from the old pack-saddle. "There's one chance in a hundred to save her yet," he said, pointing to Piney; "but it's there," he added, pointing toward Poker Flat. "If you can reach there in two days she's safe." "And you?" asked Tom Simson. "I'll stay here," was the curt reply.

The lovers parted with a long embrace. "You are not going, too?" said the Duchess, as she saw Mr. Oakhurst apparently waiting to accompany him. "As far as the canyon," he replied. He turned suddenly, and kissed the Duchess, leaving her pallid face aflame, and her trembling limbs rigid with amazement.

Night came, but not Mr. Oakhurst. It brought the storm again and the whirling snow. Then the Duchess, feeding the fire, found that some one had quietly piled beside the hut enough fuel to last a few days longer. The tears rose to her eyes, but she hid them from Piney.

The women slept but little. In the morning, looking into each other's faces, they read their fate. Neither spoke; but Piney, accepting the position of the stronger, drew near and placed her arm around the Duchess's waist. They kept this attitude for the rest of the day. That night the storm reached its greatest fury, and, rending asunder the protecting pines, invaded the very hut.

Toward morning they found themselves unable to feed the fire, which gradually died away. As the embers slowly blackened, the Duchess crept closer to Piney, and broke the silence of many hours: "Piney, can you pray?" "No, dear," said Piney simply. The Duchess without knowing exactly why, felt relieved, and, putting her head upon Piney's shoulder, spoke no more. And so reclining, the younger and purer pillowing the head of her soiled sister upon her virgin breast, they fell asleep.

The wind lulled as if it feared to waken them, Feathery drifts of snow, shaken from the ling pine boughs, flew like white-winged birds, and settled about them as they slept. The moon through the rifted clouds looked down upon what had been the camp. But all human stain, all trace of earthly travail, was hidden beneath the spotless mantle mercifully flung from above.

They slept all that day and the next, nor did they waken when voices and footsteps broke the silence of the camp. And when pitying fingers brushed the snow from their wan faces, you could scarcely have told from the equal peace that dwelt upon them, which was she that had sinned. Even the Law of Poker Flat recognized this, and turned away, leaving them still locked in each other's arms.

But at the head of the gulch, on one of the largest pine trees, they found the deuce of clubs pinned to the bark with a bowie knife. It bore the following, written in pencil, in a firm hand:

†

BENEATH THIS TREE

LIES THE BODY

OF

JOHN OAKHURST,

WHO STRUCK A STREAK OF BAD LUCK

ON THE 23D OF NOVEMBER, 1850,

AND

HANDED IN HIS CHECKS

ON THE 7TH OF DECEMBER, 1850.

†

And pulseless and cold, with a Derringer by his side and a bullet in his heart, though still calm as in life, beneath the snow lay he who was at once the strongest and yet the weakest of the outcasts of Poker Flat.

About O. Henry

William Sydney Porter was born in 1862 in Greensboro, North Carolina. At age 20 he went to Texas to write. He was a pharmacist, free-lancer, and bank teller. In 1892 he was convicted of embezzlement from the bank and sentenced to 4 years in prison. There he invented his pen name, O. Henry. When freed, he went to New York City to write. His stories are known for wordplay and surprise endings. A heavy drinker, O. Henry died in 1910 of cirrhosis of the liver. He was buried in North Carolina.

The Gift of the Magi

One dollar and eighty-seven cents. That was all. And sixty cents of it was in pennies. Pennies saved one and two at a time by bulldozing the grocer and the vegetable man and the butcher until one's cheeks burned with the silent imputation of parsimony that such close dealing implied. Three times Della counted it. One dollar and eighty-seven cents. And the next day would be Christmas.

There was clearly nothing to do but flop down on the shabby little couch and howl. So Della did it. Which instigates the moral reflection that life is made up of sobs, sniffles, and smiles, with sniffles predominating.

While the mistress of the home is gradually subsiding from the first stage to the second, take a look at the home. A furnished flat at $8 per week. It did not exactly beggar description, but it certainly had that word on the lookout for the mendicancy squad.

In the vestibule below was a letter-box into which no letter would go, and an electric button from which no mortal finger could coax a ring. Also appertaining thereunto was a card bearing the name 'Mr James Dillingham Young.'

The 'Dillingham' had been flung to the breeze during a former period of prosperity when its possessor was being paid $30 per week. Now, when the income was shrunk to $20, the letters of 'Dillingham' looked blurred, as though they were thinking seriously of contracting to a modest and unassuming D. But whenever Mr James Dillingham Young came home and reached his flat above he was called 'Jim' and greatly hugged by Mrs James Dillingham Young, already introduced to you as Della. Which is all very good.

Della finished her cry and attended to her cheeks with the powder rag. She stood by the window and looked out dully at a gray cat walking a gray fence in a gray backyard. Tomorrow would be Christmas Day, and she had only $1.87 with which to buy Jim a present. Her Jim. She had been saving every penny she could for months, with this result. Twenty dollars a week doesn't go far. Expenses had been greater than she had calculated. They always are. Only $1.87 to buy a present for Jim. Many a happy hour she had spent planning for something nice for him. Something fine and rare and sterling—something just a little bit near to being worthy of the honor of being owned by Jim.

There was a pier-glass between the windows of the room. Perhaps you have seen a pier-glass in an $8 flat. A very thin and very agile person may, by observing his reflection in a rapid sequence of longitudinal strips, obtain a fairly accurate conception of his looks. Della, being slender, had mastered the art.

Suddenly she whirled from the window and stood before the glass. Her eyes were shining brilliantly, but her face had lost its color within twenty seconds. Rapidly she pulled down her hair and let it fall to its full length.

Now, there were two possessions of the James Dillingham Youngs in which they both took a mighty pride. One was Jim's gold watch that had been his father's and his grandfather's. The other was Della's hair. Had the Queen of Sheba lived in the flat across the airshaft, Della would have let her hair hang out the window some day to dry just to depreciate Her Majesty's jewels and gifts. Had King Solomon been the janitor, with all his treasures piled up in the basement, Jim would have pulled out his watch every time he passed, just to see him pluck at his beard from envy.

So now Della's beautiful hair fell about her rippling and shining like a cascade of brown waves. It reached below her knee and made itself almost a garment for her. And then she did it up again nervously and quickly. Once she faltered for a minute and stood still while a tear or two splashed on the worn red carpet.

On went her old brown jacket; on went her old brown hat. With a whirl of skirts and with the brilliant sparkle still in her eyes, she fluttered out the door and down the stairs to the street.

Where she stopped the sign read: 'Mme. Sofronie. Hair Goods of All Kinds.' One flight up Della ran, and collected herself, panting. Madame, large, too white, chilly, hardly looked the 'Sofronie.'

'Will you buy my hair?' asked Della.

'I buy hair,' said Madame. 'Take yer hat off and let's have a sight at the looks of it.'

Down rippled the brown cascade.

'Twenty dollars,' said Madame, lifting the mass with a practised hand.

'Give it to me quick,' said Della.

Oh, and the next two hours tripped by on rosy wings. Forget the hashed metaphor. She was ransacking the stores for Jim's present.

She found it at last. It surely had been made for Jim and no one else. There was no other like it in any of the stores, and she had turned all of them inside out. It was a platinum fob chain simple and chaste in design, properly proclaiming its value by substance alone and not by meretricious ornamentation—as all good things should do. It was even worthy of The Watch. As soon as she saw it she knew that it must be Jim's. It was like him. Quietness and value—the description applied to both. Twenty-one dollars they took from her for it, and she hurried home with the 87 cents. With that chain on his watch Jim might be properly anxious about the time in any company. Grand as the watch was, he sometimes looked at it on the sly on account of the old leather strap that he used in place of a chain.

When Della reached home her intoxication gave way a little to prudence and reason. She got out her curling irons and lighted the gas and went to work repairing the ravages made by generosity added to love. Which is always a tremendous task, dear friends—a mammoth task.

Within forty minutes her head was covered with tiny, close-lying curls that made her look wonderfully like a truant schoolboy. She looked at her reflection in the mirror long, carefully, and critically.

'If Jim doesn't kill me,' she said to herself, 'before he takes a second look at me, he'll say I look like a Coney Island chorus girl. But what could I do—oh! what could I do with a dollar and eighty-seven cents?'

At 7 o'clock the coffee was made and the frying-pan was on the back of the stove hot and ready to cook the chops.

Jim was never late. Della doubled the fob chain in her hand and sat on the corner of the table near the door that he always entered. Then she heard his step on the stair away down on the first flight, and she turned white for just a moment. She had a habit of saying little silent prayers about the simplest everyday things, and now she whispered: 'Please God, make him think I am still pretty.'

The door opened and Jim stepped in and closed it. He looked thin and very serious. Poor fellow, he was only twenty-two—and to be burdened with a family! He needed a new overcoat and he was without gloves.

Jim stopped inside the door, as immovable as a setter at the scent of quail. His eyes were fixed upon Della, and there was an expression in them that she could not read, and it terrified her. It was not anger, nor surprise, nor disapproval, nor horror, nor any of the sentiments that she had been prepared for. He simply stared at her fixedly with that peculiar expression on his face.

Della wriggled off the table and went for him.

'Jim, darling,' she cried, 'don't look at me that way. I had my hair cut off and sold it because I couldn't have lived through Christmas without giving you a present. It'll grow out again—you won't mind, will you? I just had to do it. My hair grows awfully fast. "Merry Christmas!" Jim, and let's be happy. You don't know what a nice—what a beautiful, nice gift I've got for you.'

'You've cut off your hair?' asked Jim, laboriously, as if he had not arrived at that patent fact yet even after the hardest mental labor.

'Cut it off and sold it,' said Della. 'Don't you like me just as well, anyhow? I'm me without my hair, ain't I?'

Jim looked about the room curiously.

'You say your hair is gone?' he said, with an air almost of idiocy.

'You needn't look for it,' said Della. 'It's sold, I tell you—sold and gone, too. It's Christmas Eve, boy. Be good to me, for it went for you. Maybe the hairs on my head were numbered,' she went on with a sudden serious sweetness, 'but nobody could ever count my love for you. Shall I put the chops on, Jim?'

Out of his trance Jim seemed quickly to wake. He enfolded his Della. For ten seconds let us regard with discreet scrutiny some inconsequential object in the other direction. Eight dollars a week or a million a year—what is the difference? A mathematician or a wit would give you the wrong answer. The Magi brought valuable gifts, but that was not among them. This dark assertion will be illuminated later on.

Jim drew a package from his overcoat pocket and threw it upon the table. 'Don't make any mistake, Dell,' he said, 'about me. I don't think there's anything in the way of a haircut or a shave or a shampoo that could make me like my girl any less. But if you'll unwrap that package you may see why you had me going a while at first.'

White fingers and nimble tore at the string and paper. And then an ecstatic scream of joy; and then, alas! a quick feminine charge to hysterical tears and wails, necessitating the immediate employment of all the comforting powers of the lord of the flat.

For there lay The Combs—the set of combs, side and back, that Della had worshipped for long in a Broadway window. Beautiful combs, pure tortoise shell, with jewelled rims—just the shade to wear in the beautiful vanished hair. They were expensive combs, she knew, and her heart had simply craved and yearned over them without the least hope of possession. And now, they were hers, but the tresses that should have adorned the coveted adornments were gone.

But she hugged them to her bosom, and at length she was able to look up with dim eyes and smile and say: 'My hair grows so fast, Jim!'

And then Della leaped up like a little singed cat and cried, 'Oh, oh!'

Jim had not yet seen his beautiful present. She held it out to him eagerly upon her open palm. The dull precious metal seemed to flash with a reflection of her bright and ardent spirit.

'Isn't it a dandy, Jim? I hunted all over town to find it. You'll have to look at the time a hundred times a day now. Give me your watch. I want to see how it looks on it.'

Instead of obeying, Jim tumbled down on the couch and put his hands under the back of his head and smiled.

'Dell,' said he, 'let's put our Christmas presents away and keep 'em a while. They're too nice to use just at present. I sold the watch to get the money to buy your combs. And now suppose you put the chops on.'

The Magi, as you know, were wise men—wonderfully wise men—who brought gifts to the Babe in the manger. They invented the art of giving Christmas presents. Being wise, their gifts were no doubt wise ones, possibly bearing the privilege of exchange in case of duplication. And here I have lamely related to you the uneventful chronicle of two foolish children in a flat who most unwisely sacrificed for each other the greatest treasures of their house. But in a last word to the wise of these days let it be said that of all who give gifts these two were the wisest. Of all who give and receive gifts, such as they are wisest. Everywhere they are wisest. They are the Magi.

About Edith Wharton

Born Edith Newbold Jones in 1862 into "Old New York Society," Edith had all the privileges and constraints of the wealthy, gilded-age-world of her family. After her marriage to Edward (Teddy) Wharton in 1885 she wrote acclaimed novels and stories about their society. In 1902 she designed The Mount, in Lenox, Massachusetts, where she and Teddy lived until they divorced in 1913. Wharton won a Pulitzer Prize for *The Age of Innocence* in 1921. She died in France at the age of 75.

The Mission of Jane

I

Lethbury, surveying his wife across the dinner table, found his transient glance arrested by an indefinable change in her appearance.

"How smart you look! Is that a new gown?" he asked.

Her answering look seemed to deprecate his charging her with the extravagance of wasting a new gown on him, and he now perceived that the change lay deeper than any accident of dress. At the same time, he noticed that she betrayed her consciousness of it by a delicate, almost frightened blush. It was one of the compensations of Mrs. Lethbury's protracted childishness that she still blushed as prettily as at eighteen. Her body had been privileged not to outstrip her mind, and the two, as it seemed to Lethbury, were destined to travel together through an eternity of girlishness.

"I don't know what you mean," she said.

Since she never did, he always wondered at her bringing this out as a fresh grievance against him; but his wonder was unresentful, and he said good-humoredly: "You sparkle so that I thought you had on your diamonds."

She sighed and blushed again.

"It must be," he continued, "that you've been to a dressmaker's opening. You're absolutely brimming with illicit enjoyment."

She stared again, this time at the adjective. His adjectives always embarrassed her: their unintelligibleness savoured of impropriety.

"In short," he summed up, "you've been doing something that you're thoroughly ashamed of."

To his surprise she retorted: "I don't see why I should be ashamed of it!"

Lethbury leaned back with a smile of enjoyment. When there was nothing better going he always liked to listen to her explanations.

"Well—?" he said.

She was becoming breathless and ejaculatory. "Of course you'll laugh—you laugh at everything!"

"That rather blunts the point of my derision, doesn't it?" he interjected; but she pushed on without noticing:

"It's so easy to laugh at things."

"Ah," murmured Lethbury with relish, "that's Aunt Sophronia's, isn't it?"

Most of his wife's opinions were heirlooms, and he took a quaint pleasure in tracing their descent. She was proud of their age, and saw no reason for discarding them while they were still serviceable. Some, of course, were so fine that she kept them for state occasions, like her great-grandmother's Crown Derby; but from the lady known as Aunt Sophronia she had inherited a stout set of every-day prejudices that were practically as good as new; whereas her husband's, as she noticed, were always having to be replaced. In the early days she had fancied there might be a certain satisfaction in taxing him with the fact; but she had long since been silenced by the reply: "My dear, I'm not a rich man, but I never use an opinion twice if I can help it."

She was reduced, therefore, to dwelling on his moral deficiencies; and one of the most obvious of these was his refusal to take things seriously. On this occasion, however, some ulterior purpose kept her from taking up his taunt.

"I'm not in the least ashamed!" she repeated, with the air of shaking a banner to the wind; but the domestic atmosphere being calm, the banner drooped unheroically.

"That," said Lethbury judicially, "encourages me to infer that you ought to be, and that, consequently, you've been giving yourself the unusual pleasure of doing something I shouldn't approve of."

She met this with an almost solemn directness. "No," she said. "You won't approve of it. I've allowed for that."

"Ah," he exclaimed, setting down his liqueur-glass. "You've worked out the whole problem, eh?"

"I believe so."

"That's uncommonly interesting. And what is it?"

She looked at him quietly. "A baby."

If it was seldom given her to surprise him, she had attained the distinction for once.

"A baby?"

"Yes."

"A—human baby?"

"Of course!" she cried, with the virtuous resentment of the woman who has never allowed dogs in the house.

Lethbury's puzzled stare broke into a fresh smile. "A baby I shan't approve of? Well, in the abstract I don't think much of them, I admit. Is this an abstract baby?"

Again she frowned at the adjective; but she had reached a pitch of exaltation at which such obstacles could not deter her.

"It's the loveliest baby—" she murmured.

"Ah, then it's concrete. It exists. In this harsh world it draws its breath in pain—"

"It's the healthiest child I ever saw!" she indignantly corrected.

"You've seen it, then?"

Again the accusing blush suffused her. "Yes—I've seen it."

"And to whom does the paragon belong?"

And here indeed she confounded him. "To me—I hope," she declared.

He pushed his chair back with an articulate murmur. "To *you*—?"

"To *us*," she corrected.

"Good Lord!" he said. If there had been the least hint of hallucination in her transparent gaze—but no; it was as clear, as shallow, as easily fathomable as when he had first suffered the sharp surprise of striking bottom in it.

It occurred to him that perhaps she was trying to be funny: he knew that there is nothing more cryptic than the humor of the unhumorous.

"Is it a joke?" he faltered.

"Oh, I hope not. I want it so much to be a reality—"

He paused to smile at the limitations of a world in which jokes were not realities, and continued gently: "But since it is one already—"

"To us, I mean: to you and me. I want—" her voice wavered, and her eyes with it. "I have always wanted so dreadfully . . . it has been such a disappointment . . . not to . . ."

"I see," said Lethbury slowly.

But he had not seen before. It seemed curious now that he had never thought of her taking it in that way, had never surmised any hidden depths beneath her outspread obviousness. He felt as though he had touched a secret spring in her mind.

There was a moment's silence, moist and tremulous on her part, awkward and slightly irritated on his.

"You've been lonely, I suppose?" he began. It was odd, having suddenly to reckon with the stranger who gazed at him out of her trivial eyes.

"At times," she said.

"I'm sorry."

"It was not your fault. A man has so many occupations; and women who are clever—or very handsome—I suppose that's an occupation too. Sometimes I've felt that when dinner was ordered I had nothing to do till the next day."

"Oh," he groaned.

"It wasn't your fault," she insisted. "I never told you—but when I chose that rose-bud paper for the front-room upstairs, I always thought—"

"Well—?"

"It would be such a pretty paper—for a baby—to wake up in. That was years ago, of course; but it was rather an expensive paper . . . and it hasn't faded in the least . . ." she broke off incoherently.

"It hasn't faded?"

"No—and so I thought . . . as we don't use the room for anything . . . now that Aunt Sophronia is dead . . . I thought I might . . . you might . . . oh, Julian, if you could only have seen it just waking up in its crib!"

"Seen what—where? You haven't got a baby upstairs?"

"Oh, no—not yet," she said, with her rare laugh—the girlish bubbling of merriment that had seemed one of her chief graces in the early days. It occurred to him that he had not given her enough things to laugh about lately. But then she needed such very elementary things: she was as difficult to amuse as a savage. He concluded that he was not sufficiently simple.

"Alice," he said almost solemnly, "what *do* you mean?"

She hesitated a moment: he saw her gather her courage for a supreme effort. Then she said slowly, gravely, as though she were pronouncing a sacramental phrase:

"I'm so lonely without a little child—and I thought perhaps you'd let me adopt one . . . It's at the hospital . . . its mother is dead . . . and I could . . . pet it, and dress it, and do things for it . . . and it's such a good baby . . . you can ask any of the nurses . . . it would never, never bother you by crying . . ."

II

Lethbury accompanied his wife to the hospital in a mood of chastened wonder. It did not occur to him to oppose her wish. He knew, of course, that he would have to bear the brunt of the situation: the jokes at the club, the enquiries, the explanations. He saw himself in the comic role of the adopted father and welcomed it as an expiation. For in his rapid reconstruction of the past he found himself cutting a shabbier figure than he cared to admit. He had always been intolerant of stupid people, and it was his punishment to be convicted of stupidity. As his mind traversed the years between his marriage and this unexpected assumption of paternity, he saw, in the light of an overheated imagination, many signs of unwonted crassness. It was not that he had ceased to think his wife stupid: she *was* stupid, limited, inflexible; but there was a pathos in the struggles of her swaddled mind, in its blind reachings toward the primal emotions. He had always thought she would have been happier with a child; but he had thought it mechanically, because it had so often been thought before, because it was in the nature of things to think it of every woman, because his wife was so eminently one of a species that she fitted into all the generalizations of the sex. But he had regarded this generalization as merely typical of the triumph of tradition over experience. Maternity was no doubt the supreme function of primitive woman, the one end to which her whole organism tended; but the law of increasing complexity had operated in both sexes, and he had not seriously supposed that, outside the world of Christmas fiction and anecdotic art, such truisms had any special hold on the feminine imagination. Now he saw that the arts in question were kept alive by the vitality of the sentiments they appealed to.

Lethbury was in fact going through a rapid process of readjustment. His marriage had been a failure, but he had preserved toward his wife the exact fidelity of act that is sometimes supposed to excuse any divagation of feeling; so that, for years, the tie between them had consisted mainly in his abstaining from making love to other women. The abstention had not always been easy, for the world is surprisingly well-stocked with the kind of woman one ought to have married but did not; and Lethbury had not escaped the solicitation of such alternatives. His immunity had been purchased at the cost of taking refuge in the somewhat rarefied atmosphere of his perceptions; and his world being thus limited, he had given unusual care to its details, compensating himself for the narrowness of his horizon by the minute finish of his foreground. It was a world of fine shadings and the nicest proportions, where impulse seldom set a blundering foot, and the feast of reason was undisturbed by an intemperate flow of soul. To such a banquet his wife naturally remained uninvited. The diet would have disagreed with her, and she would probably have objected to the other guests. But Lethbury, miscalculating her needs, had hitherto supposed that he had made ample provision for them, and was consequently at liberty to enjoy his own fare without any reproach of mendicancy at his gates. Now he beheld her pressing a starved face against the windows of his life, and in his imaginative reaction he invested her with a pathos borrowed from the sense of his own shortcomings.

In the hospital the imaginative process continued with increasing force. He looked at his wife with new eyes. Formerly she had been to him a mere bundle of negations, a labyrinth of dead walls and bolted doors. There was nothing behind the walls, and the doors led no whither: he had sounded and listened often enough to be sure of that. Now he felt like a traveler who, exploring some ancient ruin, comes on an inner cell, intact amid the general dilapidation, and painted with images which reveal the forgotten uses of the building.

His wife stood by a white crib in one of the wards. In the crib lay a child, a year old, the nurse affirmed, but to Lethbury's eye a mere dateless fragment of humanity projected against a background of conjecture. Over this anonymous particle of life Mrs. Lethbury leaned, such ecstasy reflected in her face as strikes up, in Correggio's *Night-piece*, from the child's body to the mother's countenance. It was a light that irradiated and dazzled her. She looked up at an enquiry of Lethbury's, but as their glances met he perceived that she no longer saw him, that he had become as invisible to her as she had long been to him. He had to transfer his question to the nurse.

"What is the child's name?" he asked.

"We call her Jane," said the nurse.

III

Lethbury, at first, had resisted the idea of a legal adoption; but when he found that his wife could not be brought to regard the child as hers till it had been made so by process of law, he promptly withdrew his objection. On one point only he remained inflexible; and that was the changing of the waif's name. Mrs. Lethbury, almost at once, had expressed a wish to rechristen it: she fluctuated between Muriel and Gladys, deferring the moment of decision like a lady wavering between two bonnets. But Lethbury was unyielding. In the general surrender of his prejudices this one alone held out.

"But Jane is so dreadful," Mrs. Lethbury protested.

"Well, we don't know that *she* won't be dreadful. She may grow up a Jane." His wife exclaimed reproachfully. "The nurse says she's the loveliest—"

"Don't they always say that?" asked Lethbury patiently. He was prepared to be inexhaustibly patient now that he had reached a firm foothold of opposition.

"It's cruel to call her Jane," Mrs. Lethbury pleaded.

"It's ridiculous to call her Muriel."

"The nurse is *sure* she must be a lady's child."

Lethbury winced: he had tried, all along, to keep his mind off the question of antecedents.

"Well, let her prove it," he said, with a rising sense of exasperation. He wondered how he could ever have allowed himself to be drawn into such a ridiculous business; for the first time he felt fully the irony of it. He had visions of coming home in the afternoon to a house smelling of linseed and paregoric, and of being greeted by a chronic howl as he went up-stairs to dress for dinner. He had never been a club-man, but he saw himself becoming one now.

The worst of his anticipations were unfulfilled. The baby was surprisingly well and surprisingly quiet. Such infantile remedies as she absorbed were not potent enough to be perceived beyond the nursery; and when Lethbury could be induced to enter that sanctuary, there was nothing to jar his nerves in the mild pink presence of his adopted daughter. Jars there were, indeed: they were probably inevitable in the disturbed routine of the household; but they occurred between Mrs. Lethbury and the nurses, and Jane contributed to them only a placid stare which might have served as a rebuke to the combatants.

In the reaction from his first impulse of atonement, Lethbury noted with sharpened perceptions the effect of the change on his wife's character. He saw already the error of supposing that it could work any transformation in her. It simply magnified her existing qualities. She was like a dried sponge put in water: she expanded, but she did not change her shape. From the stand-point of scientific observation it was curious to see how her stored instincts responded to the pseudo-maternal call. She overflowed with the petty maxims of the occasion. One felt in her the epitome, the consummation, of centuries of animal maternity, so that this little woman, who screamed at a mouse and was nervous about burglars, came to typify the cave-mother rending her prey for her young.

It was less easy to regard philosophically the practical effects of her borrowed motherhood. Lethbury found with surprise that she was becoming assertive and definite. She no longer represented the negative side of his life; she showed, indeed, a tendency to inconvenient affirmations. She had gradually expanded her assumption of motherhood till it included his own share in the relation, and he suddenly found himself regarded as the father of Jane. This was a contingency he had not foreseen, and it took all his philosophy to accept it; but there were moments of compensation. For Mrs. Lethbury was undoubtedly happy for the first time in years; and the thought that he had tardily contributed to this end reconciled him to the irony of the means.

At first he was inclined to reproach himself for still viewing the situation from the outside, for remaining a spectator instead of a participant. He had been allured, for a moment, by the vision of several hands meeting over a cradle, as the whole body of domestic fiction bears witness to their doing; and the fact that no such conjunction took place he could explain only on the ground that it was a borrowed cradle. He did not dislike the little girl. She still remained to him a hypothetical presence, a query rather than a fact; but her nearness was not unpleasant, and there were moments when her tentative utterances, her groping steps, seemed to loosen the dry accretions enveloping his inner self. But even at such moments—moments which he invited and caressed—she did not bring him nearer to his wife. He now perceived that he had made a certain place in his life for Mrs. Lethbury, and that she no longer fitted into it. It was too late to enlarge the space, and so she overflowed and encroached. Lethbury struggled against the sense of submergence. He let down barrier after barrier, yielding privacy after privacy; but his wife's personality continued to dilate. She was no longer herself alone: she was herself and Jane. Gradually, in a monstrous fusion of identity, she became herself, himself and Jane; and instead of trying to adapt her to a spare crevice of his character, he found himself carelessly squeezed into the smallest compartment of the domestic economy.

IV

He continued to tell himself that he was satisfied if his wife was happy; and it was not till the child's tenth year that he felt a doubt of her happiness.

Jane had been a preternaturally good child. During the eight years of her adoption she had caused her foster-parents no anxiety beyond those connected with the usual succession of youthful diseases. But her unknown progenitors had given her a robust constitution, and she passed unperturbed through measles, chicken-pox and whooping-cough. If there was any suffering it was endured vicariously by Mrs. Lethbury, whose temperature rose and fell with the patient's, and who could not hear Jane sneeze without visions of a marble angel weeping over a broken column. But though Jane's prompt recoveries continued to belie such premonitions, though her existence continued to move forward on an even keel of good health and good conduct, Mrs. Lethbury's satisfaction showed no corresponding advance. Lethbury, at first, was disposed to add her disappointment to the long list of feminine inconsistencies with which the sententious observer of life builds up his favorable induction; but circumstances presently led him to take a kindlier view of the case.

Hitherto his wife had regarded him as a negligible factor in Jane's evolution. Beyond providing for his adopted daughter, and effacing himself before her, he was not expected to contribute to her well-being. But as time passed he appeared to his wife in a new light. It was he who was to educate Jane. In matters of the intellect, Mrs. Lethbury was the first to declare her deficiencies—to proclaim them, even, with a certain virtuous superiority. She said she did not pretend to be clever, and there was no denying the truth of the assertion. Now, however, she seemed less ready, not to own her limitations, but to glory in them. Confronted with the problem of Jane's instruction she stood in awe of the child.

"I have always been stupid, you know," she said to Lethbury with a new humility, "and I'm afraid I shan't know what is best for Jane. I'm sure she has a wonderfully good mind, and I should reproach myself if I didn't give her every opportunity." She looked at him helplessly. "You must tell me what ought to be done."

Lethbury was not unwilling to oblige her. Somewhere in his mental lumber-room there rusted a theory of education such as usually lingers among the impedimenta of the childless. He brought this out, refurbished it, and applied it to Jane. At first he thought his wife had not overrated the quality of the child's mind. Jane seemed extraordinarily intelligent. Her precocious definiteness of mind was encouraging to her inexperienced preceptor. She had no difficulty in fixing her attention, and he felt that every fact he imparted was being etched in metal. He helped his wife to engage the best teachers, and for a while continued to take an ex-official interest in his adopted daughter's studies. But gradually his interest waned. Jane's ideas did not increase with her acquisitions. Her young mind remained a mere receptacle for facts: a kind of cold-storage from which anything which had been put there could be taken out at a moment's notice, intact but congealed. She developed, moreover, an inordinate pride in the capacity of her mental storehouse, and a tendency to pelt her public with its contents. She was overheard to jeer at her nurse for not knowing when the Saxon Heptarchy had fallen, and she alternately dazzled and depressed Mrs. Lethbury by the wealth of her chronological allusions. She showed no interest in the significance of the facts she amassed: she simply collected dates as another child might have collected stamps or marbles. To her foster-mother she seemed a prodigy of wisdom; but Lethbury saw, with a secret movement of sympathy, how the aptitudes in which Mrs. Lethbury gloried were slowly estranging her from her child.

"She is getting too clever for me," his wife said to him, after one of Jane's historical flights, "but I am so glad that she will be a companion to you."

Lethbury groaned in spirit. He did not look forward to Jane's companionship. She was still a good little girl; but there was something automatic and formal in her goodness, as though it were a kind of moral calisthenics which she went through for the sake of showing her agility. An early consciousness of virtue had moreover constituted her the natural guardian and adviser of her elders. Before she was fifteen she had set about reforming the household. She took Mrs. Lethbury in hand first; then she extended her efforts to the servants, with consequences more disastrous to the domestic harmony; and lastly she applied herself to Lethbury. She proved to him by statistics that he smoked too much, and that it was injurious to the optic nerve to read in bed. She took him to task for not going to church more regularly, and pointed out to him the evils of desultory reading. She suggested that a regular course of study encourages mental concentration, and hinted that inconsecutiveness of thought is a sign of approaching age.

To her adopted mother her suggestions were equally pertinent. She instructed Mrs. Lethbury in an improved way of making beef stock, and called her attention to the unhygienic qualities of carpets. She poured out distracting facts about bacilli and vegetable mould, and demonstrated that curtains and picture-frames are a hot-bed of animal organisms. She learned by heart the nutritive ingredients of the principal articles of diet, and revolutionized the cuisine by an attempt to establish a scientific average between starch and phosphates. Four cooks left during this experiment, and Lethbury fell into the habit of dining at his dub.

Once or twice, at the outset, he had tried to check Jane's ardor; but his efforts resulted only in hurting his wife's feelings. Jane remained impervious, and Mrs. Lethbury resented any attempt to protect her from her daughter. Lethbury saw that she was consoled for the sense of her own inferiority by the thought of what Jane's intellectual companionship must be to him; and he tried to keep up the illusion by enduring with what grace he might the blighting edification of Jane's discourse.

V

As Jane grew up he sometimes avenged himself by wondering if his wife was still sorry that they had not called her Muriel. Jane was not ugly; she developed, indeed, a kind of categorical prettiness which might have been a projection of her mind. She had a creditable collection of features, but one had to take an inventory of them to find out that she was good-looking. The fusing grace had been omitted.

Mrs. Lethbury took a touching pride in her daughter's first steps in the world. She expected Jane to take by her complexion those whom she did not capture by her learning. But Jane's rosy freshness did not work any perceptible ravages. Whether the young men guessed the axioms on her lips and detected the encyclopædia in her eye, or whether they simply found no intrinsic interest in these features, certain it is, that, in spite of her mother's heroic efforts, and of incessant calls on Lethbury's purse, Jane, at the end of her first season, had dropped hopelessly out of the running. A few duller girls found her interesting, and one or two young men came to the house with the object of meeting other young women; but she was rapidly becoming one of the social supernumeraries who are asked out only because they are on people's lists.

The blow was bitter to Mrs. Lethbury; but she consoled herself with the idea that Jane had failed because she was too clever. Jane probably shared this conviction; at all events she betrayed no consciousness of failure. She had developed a pronounced taste for society, and went out, unweariedly and obstinately, winter after winter, while Mrs. Lethbury toiled in her wake, showering attentions on oblivious hostesses. To Lethbury there was something at once tragic and exasperating in the sight of their two figures, the one conciliatory, the other dogged, both pursuing with unabated zeal the elusive prize of popularity. He even began to feel a personal stake in the pursuit, not as it concerned Jane but as it affected his wife. He saw that the latter was the victim of Jane's disappointment: that Jane was not above the crude satisfaction of "taking it out" on her mother. Experience checked the impulse to come to his wife's defence; and when his resentment was at its height, Jane disarmed him by giving up the struggle.

Nothing was said to mark her capitulation; but Lethbury noticed that the visiting ceased and that the dressmaker's bills diminished. At the same time Mrs. Lethbury made it known that Jane had taken up charities; and before long Jane's conversation confirmed this announcement. At first Lethbury congratulated himself on the change; but Jane's domesticity soon began to weigh on him. During the day she was sometimes absent on errands of mercy; but in the evening she was always there. At first she and Mrs. Lethbury sat in the drawing-room together, and Lethbury smoked in the library; but presently Jane formed the habit of joining him there, and he began to suspect that he was included among the objects of her philanthropy.

Mrs. Lethbury confirmed the suspicion. "Jane has grown very serious minded lately," she said. "She imagines that she used to neglect you and she is trying to make up for it. Don't discourage her," she added innocently.

Such a plea delivered Lethbury helpless to his daughter's ministrations; and he found himself measuring the hours he spent with her by the amount of relief they must be affording her mother. There were even moments when he read a furtive gratitude in Mrs. Lethbury's eye.

But Lethbury was no hero, and he had nearly reached the limit of vicarious endurance when something wonderful happened. They never quite knew afterward how it had come about, or who first perceived it; but Mrs. Lethbury one day gave tremulous voice to their discovery.

"Of course," she said, "he comes here because of Elise." The young lady in question, a friend of Jane's, was possessed of attractions which had already been found to explain the presence of masculine visitors.

Lethbury risked a denial. "I don't think he does," he declared.

"But Elise is thought very pretty," Mrs. Lethbury insisted.

"I can't help that," said Lethbury doggedly.

He saw a faint light in his wife's eyes, but she remarked carelessly: "Mr. Budd would be a very good match for Elise."

"Lethbury could hardly repress a chuckle: he was so exquisitely aware that she was trying to propitiate the gods.

For a few weeks neither said a word; then Mrs. Lethbury once more reverted to the subject.

"It is a month since Elise went abroad," she said.

"Is it?"

"And Mr. Budd seems to come here just as often—"

"Ah," said Lethbury with heroic indifference; and his wife hastily changed the subject.

Mr. Winstanley Budd was a young man who suffered from an excess of manner. Politeness gushed from him in the driest season. He was always performing feats of drawingroom chivalry, and the approach of the most unobtrusive female threw him into attitudes which endangered the furniture. His features, being of the cherubic order, did not lend themselves to this role; but there were moments when he appeared to dominate them, to force them into compliance with an aquiline ideal. The range of Mr. Budd's social benevolence made its object hard to distinguish. He spread his cloak so indiscriminately that one could not always interpret the gesture, and Jane's impassive manner had the effect of increasing his demonstrations: she threw him into paroxysms of politeness.

At first he filled the house with his amenities; but gradually it became apparent that his most dazzling effects were directed exclusively to Jane. Lethbury and his wife held their breath and looked away from each other. They pretended not to notice the frequency of Mr. Budd's visits, they struggled against an imprudent inclination to leave the young people too much alone. Their conclusions were the result of indirect observation, for neither of them dared to be caught watching Mr. Budd: they behaved like naturalists on the trail of a rare butterfly.

In his efforts not to notice Mr. Budd, Lethbury centred his attentions on Jane; and Jane, at this crucial moment, wrung from him a reluctant admiration. While her parents went about dissembling their emotions, she seemed to have none to conceal. She betrayed neither eagerness nor surprise; so complete was her unconcern that there were moments when Lethbury feared it was obtuseness, when he could hardly help whispering to her that now was the moment to lower the net.

Meanwhile the velocity of Mr. Budd's gyrations increased with the ardor of courtship; his politeness became incandescent, and Jane found herself the centre of a pyrotechnical display culminating in the "set piece" of an offer of marriage.

Mrs. Lethbury imparted the news to her husband one evening after their daughter had gone to bed. The announcement was made and received with an air of detachment, as though both feared to be betrayed into unseemly exultation; but Lethbury, as his wife ended, could not repress the inquiry, "Have they decided on a day?"

Mrs. Lethbury's superior command of her features enabled her to look shocked. "What can you be thinking of? He only offered himself at five!"

"Of course—of course—" stammered Lethbury— "but nowadays people marry after such short engagements—"

"Engagement!" said his wife solemnly. "There is no engagement."

Lethbury dropped his cigar. "What on earth do you mean?"

"Jane is thinking it over."

"*Thinking it over?*"

"She has asked for a month before deciding."

Lethbury sank back with a gasp. Was it genius or was it madness? He felt incompetent to decide; and Mrs. Lethbury's next words showed that she shared his difficulty.

"Of course I don't want to hurry Jane—"

"Of course not," he acquiesced.

"But I pointed out to her that a young man of Mr. Budd's impulsive temperament might—might be easily discouraged—"

"Yes; and what did she say?"

"She said that if she was worth winning she was worth waiting for."

VI

The period of Mr. Budd's probation could scarcely have cost him as much mental anguish as it caused his would-be parents-in-law.

Mrs. Lethbury, by various ruses, tried to shorten the ordeal, but Jane remained inexorable; and each morning Lethbury came down to breakfast with the certainty of finding a letter of withdrawal from her discouraged suitor.

When at length the decisive day came, and Mrs. Lethbury, at its close, stole into the library with an air of chastened joy, they stood for a moment without speaking; then Mrs. Lethbury paid a fitting tribute to the proprieties by faltering out: "It will be dreadful to have to give her up—"

Lethbury could not repress a warning gesture; but even as it escaped him he realized that his wife's grief was genuine.

"Of course, of course," he said, vainly sounding his own emotional shallows for an answering regret. And yet it was his wife who had suffered most from Jane!

He had fancied that these sufferings would be effaced by the milder atmosphere of their last weeks together; but felicity did not soften Jane. Not for a moment did she relax her dominion: she simply widened it to include a new subject. Mr. Budd found himself under orders with the others; and a new fear assailed Lethbury as he saw Jane assume prenuptial control of her betrothed. Lethbury had never felt any strong personal interest in Mr. Budd; but as Jane's prospective husband the young man excited his sympathy. To his surprise he found that Mrs. Lethbury shared the feeling.

"I'm afraid he may find Jane a little exacting," she said, after an evening dedicated to a stormy discussion of the wedding arrangements. "She really ought to make some concessions. If he *wants* to be married in a black frock-coat instead of a dark gray one—" She paused and looked doubtfully at Lethbury.

"What can I do about it?" he said.

"You might explain to him—tell him that Jane isn't always—"

Lethbury made an impatient gesture. "What are you afraid of? His finding her out or his not finding her out?"

Mrs. Lethbury flushed. "You put it so dreadfully!"

Her husband mused for a moment; then he said with an air of cheerful hypocrisy: "After all, Budd is old enough to take care of himself."

But the next day Mrs. Lethbury surprised him. Late in the afternoon she entered the library, so breathless and inarticulate that he scented a catastrophe.

"I've done it!" she cried.

"Done what?"

"Told him." She nodded toward the door. "He's just gone. Jane is out, and I had a chance to talk to him alone."

Lethbury pushed a chair forward and she sank into it.

"What did you tell him? That she is *not* always—" Mrs. Lethbury lifted a tragic eye. "No; I told him that she always *is*—"

"Always *is*—?"

"Yes."

There was a pause. Lethbury made a call on his hoarded philosophy. He saw Jane suddenly reinstated in her evening sent by the library fire; but an answering chord in him thrilled at his wife's heroism.

"Well—what did he say?"

Mrs. Lethbury's agitation deepened. It was clear that the blow had fallen.

"He . . . he said . . . that we . . . had never understood Jane . . . or appreciated her . . ." The final syllables were lost in her handkerchief, and she left him marvelling at the mechanism of woman.

After that, Lethbury faced the future with an undaunted eye. They had done their duty—at least his wife had done hers—and they were reaping the usual harvest of ingratitude with a zest seldom accorded to such reaping. There was a marked change in Mr. Budd's manner, and his increasing coldness sent a genial glow through Lethbury's system. It was easy to bear with Jane in the light of Mr. Budd's disapproval.

There was a good deal to be borne in the last days, and the brunt of it fell on Mrs. Lethbury. Jane marked her transition to the married state by a seasonable but incongruous display of nerves. She became sentimental, hysterical and reluctant. She quarrelled with her betrothed and threatened to return the ring. Mrs. Lethbury had to intervene, and Lethbury felt the hovering sword of destiny. But the blow was suspended. Mr. Budd's chivalry was proof against all his bride's caprices and his devotion throve on her cruelty. Lethbury feared that he was too faithful, too enduring, and longed to urge him to vary his tactics. Jane presently reappeared with the ring on her finger, and consented to try on the wedding-dress; but her uncertainties, her reactions, were prolonged till the final day.

When it dawned, Lethbury was still in an ecstasy of apprehension. Feeling reasonably sure of the principal actors he had centered his fears on incidental possibilities. The clergyman might have a stroke, or the church might burn down, or there might be something wrong with the license. He did all that was humanly possible to avert such contingencies, but there remained that incalcuable factor known as the hand of God. Lethbury seemed to feel it groping for him.

At the altar it almost had him by the nape. Mr. Budd was late; and for five immeasurable minutes Lethbury and Jane faced a churchful of conjecture. Then the bridegroom appeared, flushed but chivalrous, and explaining to his father-in-law under cover of the ritual that he had torn his glove and had to go back for another.

"You'll be losing the ring next," muttered Lethbury; but Mr. Budd produced this article punctually, and a moment or two later was bearing its wearer captive down the aisle.

At the wedding-breakfast Lethbury caught his wife's eye fixed on him in mild disapproval, and understood that his hilarity was exceeding the bounds of fitness. He pulled himself together and tried to subdue his tone; but his jubilation bubbled over like a champagne-glass perpetually refilled. The deeper his draughts the higher it rose.

It was at the brim when, in the wake of the dispersing guests, Jane came down in her travelling-dress and fell on her mother's neck.

"I can't leave you!" she wailed, and Lethbury felt as suddenly sobered as a man under a douche. But if the bride was reluctant her captor was relentless.

Never had Mr. Budd been more dominant, more aquiline. Lethbury's last fears were dissipated as the young man snatched Jane from her mother's bosom and bore her off to the brougham.

The brougham rolled away, the last milliner's girl forsook her post by the awning, the red carpet was folded up, and the house door closed. Lethbury stood alone in the hall with his wife. As he turned toward her, he noticed the look of tired heroism in her eyes, the deepened lines of her face. They reflected his own symptoms too accurately not to appeal to him. The nervous tension had been horrible. He went up to her, and an answering impulse made her lay a hand on his arm. He held it there a moment.

"Let us go off and have a jolly little dinner at a restaurant," he proposed. There had been a time when such a suggestion would have surprised her to the verge of disapproval; but now she agreed to it at once.

"Oh, that would be so nice," she murmured with a great sigh of relief and assuagement.

Jane had fulfilled her mission after all: she had drawn them together at last.

About Rudyard Kipling

Beloved story teller and poet, Kipling was born in Bombay (Mumbai) India in 1865. His father taught there at The School of Art. He is best known for his writings about the British soldiers in India as well as his jungle stories for children. He was honored with the Nobel Prize for Literature in 1907. He and his family lived in East Sussex, England, until his death in 1936. His ashes were buried in Poets' Corner, Westminster Abbey next to his favorite writers, Charles Dickens and Thomas Hardy.

Wee Willie Winkie

"AN OFFICER AND A GENTLEMAN"

His full name was Percival William Williams, but he picked up the other name in a nursery-book, and that was the end of the christened titles. His mother's ayah called him Willie-Baba, but as he never paid the faintest attention to anything that the ayah said, her wisdom did not help matters.

His father was the Colonel of the 195th, and as soon as Wee Willie Winkie was old enough to understand what Military Discipline meant, Colonel Williams put him under it. There was no other way of managing the child. When he was good for a week, he drew good-conduct pay; and when he was bad, he was deprived of his good-conduct stripe. Generally he was bad, for India offers many chances of going wrong to little six-year-olds.

Children resent familiarity from strangers, and Wee Willie Winkie was a very particular child. Once he accepted an acquaintance, he was graciously pleased to thaw. He accepted Brandis, a subaltern of the 195th, on sight. Brandis was having tea at the Colonel's, and Wee Willie Winkie entered strong in the possession of a good-conduct badge won for not chasing the hens round the compound. He regarded Brandis with gravity for at least ten minutes, and then delivered himself of his opinion.

"I like you," said he slowly, getting off his chair and coming over to Brandis. "I like you. I shall call you Coppy, because of your hair. Do you mind being called Coppy? It is because of ve hair, you know."

Here was one of the most embarrassing of Wee Willie Winkie's peculiarities. He would look at a stranger for some time, and then, without warning or explanation, would give him a name. And the name stuck. No regimental penalties could break Wee Willie Winkie of this habit. He lost his good-conduct badge for christening the Commissioner's wife "Pobs"; but nothing that the Colonel could do made the Station forego the nickname, and Mrs. Collen remained "Pobs" till the end of her stay. So Brandis was christened "Coppy," and rose, therefore, in the estimation of the regiment.

If Wee Willie Winkie took an interest in any one, the fortunate man was envied alike by the mess and the rank and file. And in their envy lay no suspicion of self-interest. "The Colonel's son" was idolised on his own merits entirely. Yet Wee Willie Winkie was not lovely. His face was permanently freckled, as his legs were permanently scratched, and in spite of his mother's almost tearful remonstrances he had insisted upon having his long yellow locks cut short in the military fashion. "I want my hair like Sergeant Tummil's," said Wee Willie Winkie, and, his father abetting, the sacrifice was accomplished.

Three weeks after the bestowal of his youthful affections on Lieutenant Brandis—henceforward to be called "Coppy" for the sake of brevity—Wee Willie Winkie was destined to behold strange things and far beyond his comprehension.

Coppy returned his liking with interest. Coppy had let him wear for five rapturous minutes his own big sword-just as tall as Wee Willie Winkie. Coppy had promised him a terrier puppy; and Coppy had permitted him to witness the miraculous operation of shaving. Nay, more—Coppy had said that even he, Wee Willie Winkie, would rise in time to the ownership of a box of shiny knives, a silver soap-box, and a silver-handled "sputter-brush," as Wee Willie Winkie called it. Decidedly, there was no one except his father, who could give or take away good-conduct badges at pleasure, half so wise, strong, and valiant as Coppy with the Afghan and Egyptian medals on his breast. Why, then, should Coppy be guilty of the unmanly weakness of kissing—vehemently kissing—a "big girl," Miss Allardyce to wit? In the course of a morning ride Wee Willie Winkie had seen Coppy so doing, and, like the gentleman he was, had promptly wheeled round and cantered back to his groom, lest the groom should also see.

Under ordinary circumstances he would have spoken to his father, but he felt instinctively that this was a matter on which Coppy ought first to be consulted.

"Coppy," shouted Wee Willie Winkie, reining up outside that subaltern's bungalow early one morning—"I want to see you, Coppy!"

"Come in, young 'un," returned Coppy, who was at early breakfast in the midst of his dogs. "What mischief have you been getting into now?"

Wee Willie Winkie had done nothing notoriously bad for three days, and so stood on a pinnacle of virtue.

"I've been doing nothing bad," said he, curling himself into a long chair with a studious affectation of the Colonel's languor after a hot parade. He buried his freckled nose in a tea cup and, with eyes staring roundly over the rim, asked: "I say, Coppy, is it pwoper to kiss big girls?"

"By Jove! You're beginning early. Who do you want to kiss?"

"No one. My muvver's always kissing me if I don't stop her. If it isn't pwop-er, how was you kissing Major Allardyce's big girl last morning, by ve canal?"

Coppy's brow wrinkled. He and Miss Allardyce had with great craft managed to keep their engagement secret for a fortnight. There were urgent and imperative reasons why Major Allardyce should not know how matters stood for at least another month, and this small marplot had discovered a great deal too much.

"I saw you," said Wee Willie Winkie calmly. "But ve sais didn't see. I said, 'Hut jao!'"

"Oh, you had that much sense, you young Rip," groaned poor Coppy, half amused and half angry. "And how many people may you have told about it?"

"Only me myself. You didn't tell when I twied to wide ve buffalo ven my pony was lame; and I fought you wouldn't like."

"Winkie," said Coppy enthusiastically, shaking the small hand, "you're the best of good fellows. Look here, you can't understand all these things. One of these days—hang it, how can I make you see it!—I'm going to marry Miss Allardyce, and then she'll be Mrs. Coppy, as you say. If your young mind is so scandalised at the idea of kissing big girls, go and tell your father."

"What will happen?" said Wee Willie Winkie, who firmly believed that his father was omnipotent.

"I shall get into trouble," said Coppy, playing his trump card with an appealing look at the holder of the ace.

"Ven I won't," said Wee Willie Winkie briefly. "But my faver says it's un-man-ly to be always kissing, and I didn't fink you'd do vat, Coppy."

"I'm not always kissing, old chap. It's only now and then, and when you're bigger you'll do it too. Your father meant it's not good for little boys."

"Ah!" said Wee Willie Winkie, now fully enlightened. "It's like ve sputter-brush?"

"Exactly," said Coppy gravely.

"But I don't fink I'll ever want to kiss big girls, nor no one, 'cept my muvver. And I must vat, you know."

There was a long pause, broken by Wee Willie Winkie.

"Are you fond of vis big girl, Coppy?"

"Awfully!" said Coppy.

"Fonder van you are of Bell or ve Butcha—or me?"

"It's in a different way," said Coppy. "You see, one of these days Miss Allardyce will belong to me, but you'll grow up and command the Regiment and—all sorts of things. It's quite different, you see."

"Very well," said Wee Willie Winkie, rising. "If you're fond of ve big girl I won't tell any one. I must go now."

Coppy rose and escorted his small guest to the door, adding—"You're the best of little fellows, Winkie. I tell you what. In thirty days from now you can tell if you like—tell any one you like."

Thus the secret of the Brandis-Allardyce engagement was dependent on a little child's word. Coppy, who knew Wee Willie Winkie's idea of truth, was at ease, for he felt that he would not break promises. Wee Willie Winkie betrayed a special and unusual interest in Miss Allardyce, and, slowly revolving round that embarrassed young lady, was used to regard her gravely with unwinking eye. He was trying to discover why Coppy should have kissed her. She was not half so nice as his own mother. On the other hand, she was Coppy's property, and would in time belong to him. Therefore it behoved him to treat her with as much respect as Coppy's big sword or shiny pistol.

The idea that he shared a great secret in common with Coppy kept Wee Willie Winkie unusually virtuous for three weeks. Then the Old Adam broke out, and he made what he called a "camp-fire" at the bottom of the garden. How could he have foreseen that the flying sparks would have lighted the Colonel's little hay-rick and consumed a week's store for the horses? Sudden and swift was the punishment—deprivation of the good-conduct badge and, most sorrowful of all, two days' confinement to barracks—the house and verandah—coupled with the withdrawal of the light of his father's countenance.

He took the sentence like the man he strove to be, drew himself up with a quivering under-lip, saluted, and, once clear of the room, ran to weep bitterly in his nursery—called by him "my quarters." Coppy came in the afternoon and attempted to console the culprit.

"I'm under awwest," said Wee Willie Winkie mournfully, "and I didn't ought to speak to you."

Very early the next morning he climbed on to the roof of the house—that was not forbidden—and beheld Miss Allardyce going for a ride.

"Where are you going?" cried Wee Willie Winkie.

"Across the river," she answered, and trotted forward.

Now the cantonment in which the 195th lay was bounded on the north by a river—dry in the winter. From his earliest years, Wee Willie Winkie had been forbidden to go across the river, and had noted that even Coppy—the almost almighty Coppy—had never set foot beyond it. Wee Willie Winkie had once been read to, out of a big blue book, the history of the Princess and the Goblins—a most wonderful tale of a land where the Goblins were always warring with the children of men until they were defeated by one Curdie. Ever since that date it seemed to him that the bare black and purple hills across the river were inhabited by—Goblins, and, in truth, every one had said that there lived the Bad Men. Even in his own house the lower halves of the windows were covered with green paper on account of the Bad Men who might, if allowed clear view, fire into peaceful drawing-rooms and comfortable bedrooms. Certainly, beyond the river, which was the end of all the Earth, lived the Bad Men. And here was Major Allardyce's big girl, Coppy's property, preparing to venture into their borders! What would Coppy say if anything happened to her? If the Goblins ran off with her as they did with Curdie's Princess? She must at all hazards be turned back.

The house was still. Wee Willie Winkie reflected for a moment on the very terrible wrath of his father; and then—broke his arrest! It was a crime unspeakable. The low sun threw his shadow, very large and very black, on the trim garden-paths, as he went down to the stables and ordered his pony. It seemed to him in the hush of the dawn that all the big world had been bidden to stand still and look at Wee Willie Winkie guilty of mutiny. The drowsy sais gave him his mount, and, since the one great sin made all others insignificant, Wee Willie Winkie said that he was going to ride over to Coppy Sahib, and went out at a foot-pace, stepping on the soft mould of the flower-borders.

The devastating track of the pony's feet was the last misdeed that cut him off from all sympathy of Humanity. He turned into the road, leaned forward, and rode as fast as the pony could put foot to the ground in the direction of the river.

But the liveliest of twelve-two ponies can do little against the long canter of a Waler. Miss Allardyce was far ahead, had passed through the crops, beyond the Police-posts, when all the guards were asleep, and her mount was scattering the pebbles of the river-bed as Wee Willie Winkie left the cantonment and British India behind him. Bowed forward and still flogging, Wee Willie Winkie shot into Afghan territory, and could just see Miss Allardyce, a black speck, flickering across the stony plain. The reason of her wandering was simple enough. Coppy, in a tone of too-hastily-assumed authority, had told her overnight that she must not ride out by the river. And she had gone to prove her own spirit and teach Coppy a lesson.

Almost at the foot of the inhospitable hills, Wee Willie Winkie saw the Waler blunder and come down heavily. Miss Allardyce struggled clear, but her ankle had been severely twisted, and she could not stand. Having fully shown her spirit, she wept, and was surprised by the apparition of a white, wide-eyed child in khaki, on a nearly spent pony.

"Are you badly, badly hurted?" shouted Wee Willie Winkie, as soon as he was within range. "You didn't ought to be here."

"I don't know," said Miss Allardyce ruefully, ignoring the reproof. "Good gracious, child, what are you doing here?"

"You said you was going acwoss ve wiver," panted Wee Willie Winkie, throwing himself off his pony. "And nobody—not even Coppy—must go acwoss ve wiver, and I came after you ever so hard, but you wouldn't stop, and now you've hurted yourself, and Coppy will be angwy wiv me, and—I've bwoken my awwest! I've bwoken my awwest!"

The future Colonel of the 195th sat down and sobbed. In spite of the pain in her ankle the girl was moved.

"Have you ridden all the way from cantonments, little man? What for?"

"You belonged to Coppy. Coppy told me so!" wailed Wee Willie Winkie disconsolately. "I saw him kissing you, and he said he was fonder of you van Bell or ve Butcha or me. And so I came. You must get up and come back. You didn't ought to be here. Vis is a bad place, and I've bwoken my awwest."

"I can't move, Winkie," said Miss Allardyce, with a groan. "I've hurt my foot. What shall I do?"

She showed a readiness to weep anew, which steadied Wee Willie Winkie, who had been brought up to believe that tears were the depth of unmanliness. Still, when one is as great a sinner as Wee Willie Winkie, even a man may be permitted to break down.

"Winkie," said Miss Allardyce, "when you've rested a little, ride back and tell them to send out something to carry me back in. It hurts fearfully."

The child sat still for a little time and Miss Allardyce closed her eyes; the pain was nearly making her faint. She was roused by Wee Willie Winkie tying up the reins on his pony's neck and setting it free with a vicious cut of his whip that made it whicker. The little animal headed towards the cantonments.

"Oh, Winkie, what are you doing?"

"Hush!" said Wee Willie Winkie. "Vere's a man coming—one of ve Bad Men. I must stay wiv you. My faver says a man must always look after a girl. Jack will go home, and ven vey'll come and look for us. Vat's why I let him go."

Not one man but two or three had appeared from behind the rocks of the hills, and the heart of Wee Willie Winkie sank within him, for just in this manner were the Goblins wont to steal out and vex Curdie's soul. Thus had they played in Curdie's garden—he had seen the picture—and thus had they frightened the Princess's nurse. He heard them talking to each other, and recognised with joy the bastard Pushto that he had picked up from one of his father's grooms lately dismissed. People who spoke that tongue could not be the Bad Men. They were only natives after all.

They came up to the boulders on which Miss Allardyce's horse had blundered.

Then rose from the rock Wee Willie Winkie, child of the Dominant Race, aged six and three-quarters, and said briefly and emphatically "Jao!" The pony had crossed the river-bed.

The men laughed, and laughter from natives was the one thing Wee Willie Winkie could not tolerate. He asked them what they wanted and why they did not depart. Other men with most evil faces and crooked-stocked guns crept out of the shadows of the hills, till, soon, Wee Willie Winkie was face to face with an audience some twenty strong. Miss Allardyce screamed.

"Who are you?" said one of the men.

"I am the Colonel Sahib's son, and my order is that you go at once. You black men are frightening the Miss Sahib. One of you must run into cantonments and take the news that the Miss Sahib has hurt herself, and that the Colonel's son is here with her."

"Put our feet into the trap?" was the laughing reply. "Hear this boy's speech!"

"Say that I sent you—I, the Colonel's son. They will give you money."

"What is the use of this talk? Take up the child and the girl, and we can at least ask for the ransom. Ours are the villages on the heights," said a voice in the background.

These were the Bad Men—worse than Goblins—and it needed all Wee Willie Winkie's training to prevent him from bursting into tears. But he felt that to cry before a native, excepting only his mother's ayah, would be an infamy greater than any mutiny. Moreover, he, as future Colonel of the 195th, had that grim regiment at his back.

"Are you going to carry us away?" said Wee Willie Winkie, very blanched and uncomfortable.

"Yes, my little Sahib Bahadur," said the tallest of the men, "and eat you afterwards."

"That is child's talk," said Wee Willie Winkie. "Men do not eat men."

A yell of laughter interrupted him, but he went on firmly—"And if you do carry us away, I tell you that all my regiment will come up in a day and kill you all without leaving one. Who will take my message to the Colonel Sahib?"

Speech in any vernacular—and Wee Willie Winkie had a colloquial acquaintance with three—was easy to the boy who could not yet manage his "r's" and "th's" aright.

Another man joined the conference, crying: "O foolish men! What this babe says is true. He is the heart's heart of those white troops. For the sake of peace let them go both, for if he be taken, the regiment will break loose and gut the valley. Our villages are in the valley, and we shall not escape. That regiment are devils. They broke Khoda Yar's breast-bone with kicks when he tried to take the rifles; and if we touch this child they will fire and rape and plunder for a month, till nothing remains. Better to send a man back to take the message and get a reward. I say that this child is their God, and that they will spare none of us, nor our women, if we harm him."

It was Din Mahommed, the dismissed groom of the Colonel, who made the diversion, and an angry and heated discussion followed. Wee Willie Winkie, standing over Miss Allardyce, waited the upshot. Surely his "wegiment," his own "wegiment," would not desert him if they knew of his extremity.

The riderless pony brought the news to the 195th, though there had been consternation in the Colonel's household for an hour before. The little beast came in through the parade-ground in front of the main barracks, where the men were settling down to play Spoil-five till the afternoon. Devlin, the Colour-Sergeant of E Company, glanced at the empty saddle and tumbled through the barrack-rooms, kicking up each Room Corporal as he passed. "Up, you beggars! There's something happened to the Colonel's son," he shouted.

"He couldn't fall off! S'elp me, 'e couldn't fall off," blubbered a drummer-boy. "Go an' hunt acrost the river. He's over there if he's anywhere, an' maybe those Pathans have got 'im. For the love o' Gawd don't look for 'im in the nullahs! Let's go over the river."

"There's sense in Mott yet," said Devlin. "E Company, double out to the river—sharp!"

So E Company, in its shirt-sleeves mainly, doubled for the dear life, and in the rear toiled the perspiring Sergeant, adjuring it to double yet faster. The cantonment was alive with the men of the 195th hunting for Wee Willie Winkie, and the Colonel finally overtook E Company, far too exhausted to swear, struggling in the pebbles of the river-bed.

Up the hill under which Wee Willie Winkie's Bad Men were discussing the wisdom of carrying off the child and the girl, a look-out fired two shots.

"What have I said?" shouted Din Mahommed. "There is the warning! The pulton are out already and are coming across the plain! Get away! Let us not be seen with the boy."

The men waited for an instant, and then, as another shot was fired, withdrew into the hills, silently as they had appeared.

"The wegiment is coming," said Wee Willie Winkie confidently to Miss Allardyce, "and it's all wight. Don't cwy!"

He needed the advice himself, for ten minutes later, when his father came up, he was weeping bitterly with his head in Miss Allardyce's lap.

And the men of the 195th carried him home with shouts and rejoicings; and Coppy, who had ridden a horse into a lather, met him, and, to his intense disgust, kissed him openly in the presence of the men.

But there was balm for his dignity. His father assured him that not only would the breaking of arrest be condoned, but that the good-conduct badge would be restored as soon as his mother could sew it on his blouse-sleeve. Miss Allardyce had told the Colonel a story that made him proud of his son.

"She belonged to you, Coppy," said Wee Willie Winkie, indicating Miss Allardyce with a grimy forefinger. "I knew she didn't ought to go acwoss ve wiver, and I knew ve wegiment would come to me if I sent Jack home."

"You're a hero, Winkie," said Coppy—"a pukka hero!"

"I don't know what vat means," said Wee Willie Winkie, "but you mustn't call me Winkie any no more. I'm Percival Will'am Will'ams."

And in this manner did Wee Willie Winkie enter into his manhood.

About Saki

Hector Hugh Munro was born in 1870 in Akyab, Burma (Myanmar). His father was Inspector General of the Indian Imperial Police. When Hector was two years old his father sent him and his siblings to England to be raised by their grandparents. Munro became a journalist with the pen name Saki. His witty writings earned wide praise and he was recognized as a master storyteller. At the start of WWI, Saki volunteered as a trooper. While stationed in France in the battle of Ancre, hiding in a shell crater, he was killed by a German sniper. Saki was 46 years old.

The Toys of Peace

'Harvey,' said Eleanor Bope, handing her brother a cutting from a London morning paper* of the 19th of March, 'just read this about children's toys, please; it exactly carries out some of our ideas about influence and upbringing.'

'In the view of the National Peace Council,' ran the extract, 'there are grave objections to presenting our boys with regiments of fighting men, batteries of guns, and squadrons of "Dreadnoughts." Boys, the Council admits, naturally love fighting and all the panoply of war . . . but that is no reason for encouraging, and perhaps giving permanent form to, their primitive instincts. At the Children's Welfare Exhibition, which opens at Olympia in three weeks' time, the Peace Council will make an alternative suggestion to parents in the shape

*An actual extract from a London paper of March 1914.

of an exhibition of "peace toys." In front of a specially painted representation of the Peace Palace at The Hague will be grouped, not miniature soldiers but miniature civilians, not guns but ploughs and the tools of industry. . . . It is hoped that manufacturers may take a hint from the exhibit, which will bear fruit in the toy shops.'

'The idea is certainly an interesting and very well-meaning one,' said Harvey; 'whether it would succeed well in practice—'

'We must try,' interrupted his sister; 'you are coming down to us at Easter, and you always bring the boys some toys, so that will be an excellent opportunity for you to inaugurate the new experiment. Go about in the shops and buy any little toys and models that have special bearing on civilian life in its more peaceful aspects. Of course you must explain the toys to the children and interest them in the new idea. I regret to say that the "Siege of Adrianople" toy, that their Aunt Susan sent them, didn't need any explanation; they knew all the uniforms and flags, and even the names of the respective commanders, and when I heard them one day using what seemed to be the most objectionable language they said it was Bulgarian words of command; of course it *may* have been, but at any rate I took the toy away from them. Now I shall expect your Easter gifts to give quite a new impulse and direction to the children's minds; Eric is not eleven yet, and Bertie is only nine-and-a-half, so they are really at a most impressionable age.'

'There is primitive instinct to be taken into consideration, you know,' said Harvey doubtfully, 'and hereditary tendencies as well. One of their great-uncles fought in the most intolerant fashion at Inkerman—he was specially mentioned in dispatches, I believe—and their great-grandfather smashed all his Whig neighbours' hothouses when the great Reform Bill was passed. Still, as you say, they are at an impressionable age. I will do my best.'

On Easter Saturday Harvey Bope unpacked a large, promising-looking red cardboard box under the expectant eyes of his nephews. 'Your uncle has brought you the newest thing in toys,' Eleanor had said impressively, and youthful anticipation had been anxiously divided between Albanian soldiery and a Somali camel-corps. Eric was hotly in favour of the latter contingency. 'There would be Arabs on horseback,' he whispered; 'the Albanians have got jolly uniforms, and they fight all day long, and all night too, when there's a moon, but the country's rocky, so they've got no cavalry.'

A quantity of crinkly paper shavings was the first thing that met the view when the lid was removed; the most exciting toys always began like that. Harvey pushed back the top layer and drew forth a square, rather featureless building.

'It's a fort!' exclaimed Bertie.

'It isn't, it's the palace of the Mpret of Albania,' said Eric, immensely proud of his knowledge of the exotic title; 'it's got no windows, you see, so that passers-by can't fire in at the Royal Family.'

'It's a municipal dust-bin,' said Harvey hurriedly; 'you see all the refuse and litter of a town is collected there, instead of lying about and injuring the health of the citizens.'

In an awful silence he disinterred a little lead figure of a man in black clothes.

'That,' he said, 'is a distinguished civilian, John Stuart Mill. He was an authority on political economy.'

'Why?' asked Bertie.

'Well, he wanted to be; he thought it was a useful thing to be.'

Bertie gave an expressive grunt, which conveyed his opinion that there was no accounting for tastes.

Another square building came out, this time with windows and chimneys.

'A model of the Manchester branch of the Young Women's Christian Association,' said Harvey.

'Are there any lions?' asked Eric hopefully. He had been reading Roman history and thought that where you found Christians you might reasonably expect to find a few lions.

'There are no lions,' said Harvey. 'Here is another civilian, Robert Raikes, the founder of Sunday schools, and here is a model of a municipal wash-house. These little round things are loaves baked in a sanitary bakehouse. That lead figure is a sanitary inspector, this one is a district councillor, and this one is an official of the Local Government Board.'

'What does he do?' asked Eric wearily.

'He sees to things connected with his Department,' said Harvey. 'This box with a slit in it is a ballot-box. Votes are put into it at election times.'

'What is put into it at other times?' asked Bertie.

'Nothing. And here are some tools of industry, a wheelbarrow and a hoe, and I think these are meant for hop-poles. This is a model beehive, and that is a ventilator, for ventilating sewers. This seems to be another municipal dust-bin—no, it is a model of a school of art and a public library. This little lead figure is Mrs Hemans, a poetess, and this is Rowland Hill, who introduced the system of penny postage. This is Sir John Herschel, the eminent astrologer.'

'Are we to play with these civilian figures?' asked Eric.

'Of course,' said Harvey, 'these are toys; they are meant to be played with.'

'But how?'

It was rather a poser. 'You might make two of them contest a seat in Parliament,' said Harvey, 'and have an election—'

'With rotten eggs, and free fights, and ever so many broken heads!' exclaimed Eric.

'And noses all bleeding and everybody drunk as can be,' echoed Bertie, who had carefully studied one of Hogarth's pictures.

'Nothing of the kind,' said Harvey, 'nothing in the least like that. Votes will be put in the ballot-box, and the Mayor will count them—the district councillor will do for the Mayor—and he will say which has received the most votes, and then the two candidates will thank him for presiding, and each will say that the contest has been conducted throughout in the pleasantest and most straightforward fashion, and they part with expressions of mutual esteem. There's a jolly game for you boys to play. I never had such toys when I was young.'

'I don't think we'll play with them just now,' said Eric, with an entire absence of the enthusiasm that his uncle had shown; 'I think perhaps we ought to do a little of our holiday task. It's history this time; we've got to learn up something about the Bourbon period in France.'

'The Bourbon period,' said Harvey, with some disapproval in his voice.

'We've got to know something about Louis the Fourteenth,' continued Eric; 'I've learnt the names of all the principal battles already.'

This would never do. 'There were, of course, some battles fought during his reign,' said Harvey, 'but I fancy the accounts of them were much exaggerated; news was very unreliable in those days, and there were practically no war correspondents, so generals and commanders could magnify every little skirmish they engaged in till they reached the proportions of decisive battles. Louis was really famous, now, as a landscape gardener; the way he laid out Versailles was so much admired that it was copied all over Europe.'

'Do you know anything about Madame Du Barry?' asked Eric; 'didn't she have her head chopped off?'

'She was another great lover of gardening,' said Harvey evasively; 'in fact,

I believe the well-known rose Du Barry was named after her, and now I think you had better play for a little and leave your lessons till later.'

Harvey retreated to the library and spent some thirty or forty minutes in wondering whether it would be possible to compile a history, for use in elementary schools, in which there should be no prominent mention of battles, massacres, murderous intrigues, and violent deaths. The York and Lancaster period and the Napoleonic era would, he admitted to himself, present considerable difficulties, and the Thirty Years' War would entail something of a gap if you left it out altogether. Still, it would be something gained if, at a highly impressionable age, children could be got to fix their attention on the invention of calico printing instead of the Spanish Armada or the Battle of Waterloo.

It was time, he thought, to go back to the boys' room, and see how they were getting on with their peace toys. As he stood outside the door he could hear Eric's voice raised in command; Bertie chimed in now and again with a helpful suggestion.

'That is Louis the Fourteenth,' Eric was saying, 'that one in knee-breeches, that Uncle said invented Sunday schools. It isn't a bit like him, but it'll have to do.'

'We'll give him a purple coat from my paintbox by and by,' said Bertie.

'Yes, an' red heels. That is Madame de Maintenon, that one he called Mrs Hemans. She begs Louis not to go on this expedition, but he turns a deaf ear. He takes Marshal Saxe with him, and we must pretend that they have thousands of men with them. The watchword is *Qui vive*? and the answer is *L'etat c'est moi*—that was one of his favourite remarks, you know. They land at Manchester in the dead of night, and a Jacobite conspirator gives them the keys of the fortress.'

Peeping in through the doorway Harvey observed that the municipal dust-bin had been pierced with holes to accommodate the muzzles of imaginary cannon, and now represented the principal fortified position in Manchester; John Stuart Mill had been dipped in red ink, and apparently stood for Marshal Saxe.

'Louis orders his troops to surround the Young Women's Christian Association and seize the lot of them. "Once back at the Louvre and the girls are mine," he exclaims. We must use Mrs Hemans again for one of the girls; she says "Never," and stabs Marshal Saxe to the heart.'

'He bleeds dreadfully,' exclaimed Bertie, splashing red ink liberally over the façade of the Association building.

'The soldiers rush in and avenge his death with the utmost savagery. A hundred girls are killed'—here Bertie emptied the remainder of the red ink over the devoted building—'and the surviving five hundred are dragged off to the French ships. "I have lost a Marshal," says Louis, "but I do not go back empty-handed."'

Harvey stole away from the room, and sought out his sister.

'Eleanor,' he said, 'the experiment—'

'Yes?'

'Has failed. We have begun too late.'

About Virginia Woolf

Adeline Virginia Stephen was born in 1882 in Kensington, London. She was educated at home by her parents and their learned friends. In 1912 she married the writer Leonard Woolf. They were members of the intellectual circle called The Bloomsbury Group that flourished in the interwar period. A modernist writer for the 20th century, Virginia produced her most important works in that time. Plagued by bouts of mental illness, she committed suicide by drowning in 1941 at the age of 59.

Solid Objects

The only thing that moved upon the vast semicircle of the beach was one small black spot. As it came nearer to the ribs and spine of the stranded pilchard boat, it became apparent from a certain tenuity in its blackness that this spot possessed four legs; and moment by moment it became more unmistakable that it was composed of the persons of two young men. Even thus in outline against the sand there was an unmistakable vitality in them; an indescribable vigour in the approach and withdrawal of the bodies, slight though it was, which proclaimed some violent argument issuing from the tiny mouths of the little round heads. This was corroborated on closer view by the repeated lunging of a walking-stick on the right-hand side. 'You mean to tell me . . . You actually believe . . .' thus the walking-stick on the right-hand side next the waves seemed to be asserting as it cut long straight stripes upon the sand.

'Politics be damned!' issued clearly from the body on the left-hand side, and, as these words were uttered, the mouths, noses, chins, little moustaches, tweed caps, rough boots, shooting coats, and check stockings of the two speakers became clearer and clearer; the smoke of their pipes went up into the air; nothing was so solid, so living, so hard, red, hirsute, and virile as these two bodies for miles and miles of sea and sandhill.

They flung themselves down by the six ribs and spine of the black pilchard boat. You know how the body seems to shake itself free from an argument, and to apologize for a mood of exaltation; flinging itself down and expressing in the looseness of its attitude a readiness to take up with something new—whatever it may be that comes next to hand. So Charles, whose stick had been slashing the beach for half a mile or so, began skimming flat pieces of slate over the water; and John, who had exclaimed 'Politics be damned!' began burrowing his fingers down, down, into the sand. As his hand went further and further beyond the wrist, so that he had to hitch his sleeve a little higher, his eyes lost their intensity, or rather the background of thought and experience which gives an inscrutable depth to the eyes of grown people disappeared, leaving only the clear transparent surface, expressing nothing but wonder, which the eyes of young children display. No doubt the act of burrowing in the sand had something to do with it. He remembered that, after digging for a little, the water oozes round your finger-tips; the hole then becomes a moat; a well; a spring; a secret channel to the sea. As he was choosing which of these things to make it, still working his fingers in the water, they curled round something hard—a full drop of solid matter—and gradually dislodged a large irregular lump, and brought it to the surface. When the sand coating was wiped off, a green tint appeared. It was a lump of glass, so thick as to be almost opaque; the smoothing of the sea had completely worn off any edge or shape, so that it was impossible to say whether it had been bottle, tumbler or window-pane; it was nothing but glass; it was almost a precious stone. You had only to enclose it in a rim of gold, or pierce it with a wire, and it became a jewel; part of a necklace, or a dull, green light upon a finger. Perhaps after all it was really a gem; something worn by a dark Princess trailing her finger in the water as she sat in the stern of the boat and listened to the slaves singing as they rowed her across the Bay. Or the oak sides of a sunk Elizabethan treasure-chest had split apart, and, rolled over and over, over and over, its emeralds had come at last to shore. John turned it in his hands; he held it to the light; he held it so that its irregular mass blotted out the body and extended right arm of his friend. The green thinned and thickened slightly as it was held against the sky or against the body. It pleased him; it puzzled him; it was so hard, so concentrated, so definite an object compared with the vague sea and the hazy shore.

Now a sigh disturbed him—profound, final, making him aware that his friend Charles had thrown all the flat stones within reach, or had come to the conclusion that it was not worth while to throw them. They ate their sandwiches side by side. When they had done, and were shaking themselves and rising to their feet, John took the lump of glass and looked at it in silence. Charles looked at it too. But he saw immediately that it was not flat, and filling his pipe he said with the energy that dismisses a foolish strain of thought:

'To return to what I was saying—'

He did not see, or if he had seen would hardly have noticed, that John, after looking at the lump for a moment, as if in hesitation, slipped it inside his pocket. That impulse, too, may have been the impulse which leads a child to pick up one pebble on a path strewn with them, promising it a life of warmth and security upon the nursery mantelpiece, delighting in the sense of power and benignity which such an action confers, and believing that the heart of the stone leaps with joy when it sees itself chosen from a million like it, to enjoy this bliss instead of a life of cold and wet upon the high road. 'It might so easily have been any other of the millions of stones, but it was I, I, I!'

Whether this thought or not was in John's mind, the lump of glass had its place upon the mantelpiece, where it stood heavy upon a little pile of bills and letters and served not only as an excellent paper-weight, but also as a natural stopping place for the young man's eyes when they wandered from his book. Looked at again and again half consciously by a mind thinking of something else, any object mixes itself so profoundly with the stuff of thought that it loses its actual form and recomposes itself a little differently in an ideal shape which haunts the brain when we least expect it. So John found himself attracted to the windows of curiosity shops when he was out walking, merely because he saw something which reminded him of the lump of glass. Anything, so long as it was an object of some kind, more or less round, perhaps with a dying flame deep sunk in its mass, anything—china, glass, amber, rock, marble—even the smooth oval egg of a prehistoric bird would do. He took, also, to keeping his eyes upon the ground, especially in the neighbourhood of waste land where the household refuse is thrown away. Such objects often occurred there—thrown away, of no use to anybody, shapeless, discarded. In a few months he had collected four or five specimens that took their place upon the mantelpiece. They were useful, too, for a man who is standing for Parliament upon the brink of a brilliant career has any number of papers to keep in order—addresses to constituents, declarations of policy, appeals for subscriptions, invitations to dinner, and so on.

One day, starting from his rooms in the Temple to catch a train in order to address his constituents, his eyes rested upon a remarkable object lying half-hidden in one of those little borders of grass which edge the bases of vast legal buildings. He could only touch it with the point of his stick through the railings; but he could see that it was a piece of china of the most remarkable shape, as nearly resembling a starfish as anything—shaped, or broken accidentally, into five irregular but unmistakable points. The colouring was mainly blue, but green stripes or spots of some kind overlaid the blue, and lines of crimson gave it a richness and lustre of the most attractive kind. John was determined to possess it; but the more he pushed, the further it receded. At length he was forced to go back to his rooms and improvise a wire ring attached to the end of a stick, with which, by dint of great care and skill, he finally drew the piece of china within reach of his hands. As he seized hold of it he exclaimed in triumph. At that moment the clock struck. It was out of the question that he should keep his appointment. The meeting was held without him. But how had the piece of china been broken into this remarkable shape? A careful examination put it beyond doubt that the star shape was accidental, which made it all the more strange, and it seemed unlikely that there should be another such in existence. Set at the opposite end of the mantelpiece from the lump of glass that had been dug from the sand, it looked like a creature from another world—freakish and fantastic as a harlequin. It seemed to be pirouetting through space, winking light like a fitful star. The contrast between the china so vivid and alert, and the glass so mute and contemplative, fascinated him, and wondering and amazed he asked himself how the two came to exist in the same world, let alone to stand upon the same narrow strip of marble in the same room. The question remained unanswered.

He now began to haunt the places which are most prolific of broken china, such as pieces of waste land between railway lines, sites of demolished houses, and commons in the neighbourhood of London. But china is seldom thrown from a great height; it is one of the rarest of human actions. You have to find in conjunction a very high house, and a woman of such reckless impulse and passionate prejudice that she flings her jar or pot straight from the window without thought of who is below. Broken china was to be found in plenty, but broken in some trifling domestic accident, without purpose or character. Nevertheless, he was often astonished, as he came to go into the question more deeply, by the immense variety of shapes to be found in London alone, and there was still more cause for wonder and speculation in the differences of qualities and designs. The finest specimens he would bring home and place upon his mantelpiece, where, however, their duty was more and more of an ornamental nature, since papers needing a weight to keep them down became scarcer and scarcer.

He neglected his duties, perhaps, or discharged them absent-mindedly or his constituents when they visited him were unfavourably impressed by the appearance of his mantelpiece. At any rate he was not elected to represent them in Parliament, and his friend Charles, taking it much to heart and hurrying to condole with him, found him so little cast down by the disaster that he could only suppose that it was too serious a matter for him to realize all at once.

In truth, John had been that day to Barnes Common, and there under a furze bush had found a very remarkable piece of iron. It was almost identical with the glass in shape, massy and globular, but so cold and heavy, so black and metallic, that it was evidently alien to the earth and had its origin in one of the dead stars or was itself the cinder of a moon. It weighed his pocket down; it weighed the mantelpiece down; it radiated cold. And yet the meteorite stood upon the same ledge with the lump of glass and the star-shaped china.

As his eyes passed from one to another, the determination to possess objects that even surpassed these tormented the young man. He devoted himself more and more resolutely to the search. If he had not been consumed by ambition and convinced that one day some newly-discovered rubbish heap would reward him, the disappointments he had suffered, let alone the fatigue and derision, would have made him give up the pursuit. Provided with a bag and a long stick fitted with an adaptable hook, he ransacked all deposits of earth; raked beneath matted tangles of scrub; searched all alleys and spaces between walls where he had learned to expect to find objects of this kind thrown away. As his standard became higher and his taste more severe the disappointments were innumerable, but always some gleam of hope, some piece of china or glass curiously marked or broken lured him on. Day after day passed. He was no longer young. His career—that is his political career—was a thing of the past. People gave up visiting him. He was too silent to be worth asking to dinner. He never talked to anyone about his serious ambitions; their lack of understanding was apparent in their behaviour.

He leaned back in his chair now and watched Charles lift the stones on the mantelpiece a dozen times and put them down emphatically to mark what he was saying about the conduct of the Government, without once noticing their existence.

'What was the truth of it, John?' asked Charles suddenly, turning and facing him. 'What made you give it up like that all in a second?'

'I've not given it up,' John replied.

'But you've not the ghost of a chance now,' said Charles roughly.

'I don't agree with you there,' said John with conviction. Charles looked at him and was profoundly uneasy; the most extraordinary doubts possessed him; he had a queer sense that they were talking about different things. He looked round to find some relief for his horrible depression, but the disorderly appearance of the room depressed him still further. What was that stick, and the old carpet bag hanging against the wall? And then those stones? Looking at John, something fixed and distant in his expression alarmed him. He knew only too well that his mere appearance upon a platform was out of the question.

'Pretty stones,' he said as cheerfully as he could; and saying that he had an appointment to keep, he left John—forever.

About D. H. Lawrence

David Herbert Richards Lawrence was born in 1885 in the coal mining town of Eastwood in Nottinghamshire, England. He was the first local student to win a scholarship to Nottinghamshire High School. Poet, playwright, novelist, and social critic, he saw the dehumanizing effects of modernity and industrialization. Best known for his sensuous novels, *Lady Chatterley's Lover* and others, he endured persecution and censorship in his lifetime. He died in 1970. His ashes are interred in Taos, New Mexico.

The Rocking-Horse Winner

There was a woman who was beautiful, who started with all the advantages, yet she had no luck. She married for love, and the love turned to dust. She had bonny children, yet she felt they had been thrust upon her, and she could not love them. They looked at her coldly, as if they were finding fault with her. And hurriedly she felt she must cover up some fault in herself. Yet what it was that she must cover up she never knew. Nevertheless, when her children were present, she always felt the center of her heart go hard. This troubled her, and in her manner she was all the more gentle and anxious for her children, as if she loved them very much. Only she herself knew that at the center of her heart was a hard little place that could not feel love, no, not for anybody. Everybody else said of her: "She is such a good mother. She adores her children." Only she herself, and her children themselves, knew it was not so. They read it in each other's eyes.

There were a boy and two little girls. They lived in a pleasant house, with a garden, and they had discreet servants, and felt themselves superior to anyone in the neighborhood.

Although they lived in style, they felt always an anxiety in the house. There was never enough money. The mother had a small income, and the father had a small income, but not nearly enough for the social position which they had to keep up. The father went into town to some office. But though he had good prospects, these prospects never materialized. There was always the grinding sense of the shortage of money, though the style was always kept up.

At last the mother said: "I will see if *I* can't make something." But she did not know where to begin. She racked her brains, and tried this thing and the other, but could not find anything successful. The failure made deep lines come into her face. Her children were growing up, they would have to go to school. There must be more money, there must be more money. The father, who was always very handsome and expensive in his tastes, seemed as if he never *would* be able to do anything worth doing. And the mother, who had a great belief in herself, did not succeed any better, and her tastes were just as expensive.

And so the house came to be haunted by the unspoken phrase: *There must be more money! There must be more money!* The children could hear it all the time though nobody said it aloud. They heard it at Christmas, when the expensive and splendid toys filled the nursery. Behind the shining modern rocking horse, behind the smart doll's house, a voice would start whispering: "There *must* be more money! There *must* be more money!" And the children would stop playing, to listen for a moment. They would look into each other's eyes, to see if they had all heard. And each one saw in the eyes of the other two that they too had heard. "There *must* be more money! There *must* be more money!"

It came whispering from the springs of the still-swaying rocking horse, and even the horse, bending his wooden, champing head, heard it. The big doll, sitting so pink and smirking in her new pram, could hear it quite plainly, and seemed to be smirking all the more self-consciously because of it. The foolish puppy, too, that took the place of the teddy bear, he was looking so extraordinarily foolish for no other reason but that he heard the secret whisper all over the house: "There *must* be more money!"

Yet nobody ever said it aloud. The whisper was everywhere, and therefore no one spoke it. Just as no one ever says: "We are breathing!" in spite of the fact that breath is coming and going all the time.

"Mother," said the boy Paul one day, "why don't we keep a car of our own? Why do we always use Uncle's, or else a taxi?"

"Because we're the poor members of the family," said the mother.

"But why *are* we, Mother?"

"Well—I suppose," she said slowly and bitterly, "it's because your father has no luck."

The boy was silent for some time.

"Is luck money, Mother?" he asked rather timidly.

"No, Paul. Not quite. It's what causes you to have money."

"Oh!" said Paul vaguely. "I thought when Uncle Oscar said *filthy lucker*, it meant money."

"*Filthy lucre* does mean money," said the mother. "But it's lucre, not luck."

"Oh!" said the boy. "Then what is luck, Mother?"

"It's what causes you to have money. If you're lucky you have money. That's why it's better to be born lucky than rich. If you're rich, you may lose your money. But if you're lucky, you will always get more money."

"Oh! Will you? And is Father not lucky?"

"Very unlucky, I should say," she said bitterly.

The boy watched her with unsure eyes.

"Why?" he asked.

"I don't know. Nobody ever knows why one person is lucky and another unlucky."

"Don't they? Nobody at all? Does *nobody* know?"

"Perhaps God. But He never tells."

"He ought to, then. And aren't you lucky either, Mother?"

"I can't be, if I married an unlucky husband."

"But by yourself, aren't you?"

"I used to think I was, before I married. Now I think I am very unlucky indeed."

"Why?"

"Well—never mind! Perhaps I'm not really," she said. The child looked at her, to see if she meant it. But he saw, by the lines of her mouth, that she was only trying to hide something from him.

"Well, anyhow," he said stoutly, "I'm a lucky person."

"Why?" said his mother, with a sudden laugh.

He stared at her. He didn't even know why he had said it.

"God told me," he asserted, brazening it out.

"I hope He did, dear!" she said, again with a laugh, but rather bitter.

"He did, Mother!"

"Excellent!" said the mother.

The boy saw she did not believe him; or; rather, that she paid no attention to his assertion. This angered him somewhat, and made him want to compel her attention.

He went off by himself, vaguely, in a childish way, seeking for the clue to "luck." Absorbed, taking no heed of other people, he went about with a sort of stealth, seeking inwardly for luck. He wanted luck, he wanted it, he wanted it. When the two girls were playing dolls in the nursery, he would sit on his big rocking horse, charging madly into space, with a frenzy that made the little girls peer at him uneasily. Wildly the horse careered, the waving dark hair of the boy tossed, his eyes had a strange glare in them. The little girls dared not speak to him.

When he had ridden to the end of his mad little journey, he climbed down and stood in front of his rocking horse, staring fixedly into its lowered face. Its red mouth was slightly open, its big eye was wide and glassy-bright.

Now! he could silently command the snorting steed. Now, take me to where there is luck! Now take me!

And he would slash the horse on the neck with the little whip he had asked Uncle Oscar for. He *knew* the horse could take him to where there was luck, if only he forced it. So he would mount again, and start on his furious ride, hoping at last to get there. He knew he could get there.

"You'll break your horse, Paul!" said the nurse.

"He's always riding like that! I wish he'd leave off!" said his elder sister Joan.

But he only glared down on them in silence. Nurse gave him up. She could make nothing of him. Anyhow he was growing beyond her.

One day his mother and his uncle Oscar came in when he was on one of his furious rides. He did not speak to them.

"Hallo, you young jockey! Riding a winner?" said his uncle.

"Aren't you growing too big for a rocking horse? You're not a very little boy any longer, you know," said his mother.

But Paul only gave a blue glare from his big, rather close-set eyes. He would speak to nobody when he was in full tilt. His mother watched him with an anxious expression on her face.

At last he suddenly stopped forcing his horse into the mechanical gallop, and slid down.

"Well, I got there!" he announced fiercely, his blue eyes still flaring, and his sturdy long legs straddling apart.

"Where did you get to?" asked his mother.

"Where I wanted to go," he flared back at her.

"That's right, son!" said Uncle Oscar. "Don't you stop till you get there. What's the horse's name?"

"He doesn't have a name," said the boy.

"Gets on without all right?" asked the uncle.

"Well, he has different names. He was called Sansovino last week."

"Sansovino, eh? Won the Ascot. How did you know his name?"

"He always talks about horse races with Bassett," said Joan.

The uncle was delighted to find that his small nephew was posted with all the racing news. Bassett, the young gardener, who had been wounded in the left foot in the war and had got his present job through Oscar Cresswell, whose batman he had been, was a perfect blade of the "turf." He lived in the racing events, and the small boy lived with him.

Oscar Cresswell got it all from Bassett.

"Master Paul comes and asks me, so I can't do more than tell him, sir," said Bassett, his face terribly serious, as if he were speaking of religious matters.

"And does he ever put anything on a horse he fancies?"

"Well—I don't want to give him away—he's a young sport, a fine sport, sir. Would you mind asking him himself? He sort of takes a pleasure in it, and perhaps he'd feel I was giving him away, sir, if you don't mind."

Bassett was serious as a church.

The uncle went back to his nephew and took him off for a ride in the car.

"Say, Paul, old man, do you ever put anything on a horse?" the uncle asked.

The boy watched the handsome man closely.

"Why, do you think I oughtn't to?" he parried.

"Not a bit of it! I thought perhaps you might give me a tip for the Lincoln."

The car sped on into the country, going down to Uncle Oscar's place in Hampshire.

"Honor bright?" said the nephew.

"Honor bright, son!" said the uncle.

"Well, then, Daffodil."

"Daffodil! I doubt it, sonny. What about Mirza?"

"I only know the winner," said the boy. "That's Daffodil."

"Daffodil, eh?"

There was a pause. Daffodil was an obscure horse comparatively.

"Uncle!"

"Yes, son?"

"You won't let it go any further, will you? I promised Bassett."

"Bassett be damned, old man! What's he got to do with it?"

"We're partners. We've been partners from the first. Uncle, he lent me my first five shillings, which I lost. I promised him, honor bright, it was only between me and him; only you gave me that ten-shilling note I started winning with, so I thought you were lucky. You won't let it go any further, will you?"

The boy gazed at his uncle from those big, hot, blue eyes, set rather close together. The uncle stirred and laughed uneasily.

"Right you are, son! I'll keep your tip private. Daffodil, eh? How much are you putting on him?"

"All except twenty pounds," said the boy. "I keep that in reserve."

The uncle thought it a good joke.

"You keep twenty pounds in reserve, do you, you young romancer? What are you betting, then?"

"I'm betting three hundred," said the boy gravely. "But it's between you and me, Uncle Oscar! Honor bright?"

The uncle burst into a roar of laughter.

"It's between you and me all right, you young Nat Gould,"* he said, laughing. "But where's your three hundred?"

"Bassett keeps it for me. We're partners."

"You are, are you! And what is Bassett putting on Daffodil?"

"He won't go quite as high as I do, I expect. Perhaps he'll go a hundred and fifty."

"What, pennies?" laughed the uncle.

"Pounds," said the child, with a surprised look at his uncle. "Bassett keeps a bigger reserve than l do."

Between wonder and amusement Uncle Oscar was silent. He pursued the matter no further, but he determined to take his nephew with him to the Lincoln races.

"Now, son," he said, "I'm putting twenty on Mirza, and I'll put five for you on any horse you fancy. What's your pick?"

"Daffodil, Uncle."

"No, not the fiver on Daffodil!"

"I should if it was my own fiver," said the child.

"Good! Good! Right you are! A fiver for me and a fiver for you on Daffodil."

---

*Nathaniel Gould (1857–1919), an English novelist and sports columnist who wrote novels about horse racing.

The child had never been to a race meeting before, and his eyes were blue fire. He pursed his mouth tight, and watched. A Frenchman just in front had put his money on Lancelot. Wild with excitement, he flailed his arms up and down, yelling *"Lancelot! Lancelot!"* in his French accent.

Daffodil came in first, Lancelot second, Mirza third. The child, flushed and with eyes blazing, was curiously serene. His uncle brought him four five-pound notes, four to one.

"What am I to do with these?" he cried, waving them before the boy's eyes.

"I suppose we'll talk to Bassett," said the boy. "I expect I have fifteen hundred now; and twenty in reserve; and this twenty."

His uncle studied him for some moments.

"Look here, son!" he said. "You're not serious about Bassett and that fifteen hundred, are you?"

"Yes, I am. But it's between you and me, Uncle. Honor bright!"

"Honor bright all right, son! But I must talk to Bassett."

"If you'd like to be a partner, Uncle, with Bassett and me, we could all be partners. Only, you'd have to promise, honor bright, Uncle, not to let it go beyond us three. Bassett and I are lucky, and you must be lucky, because it was your ten shillings I started winning with . . ."

Uncle Oscar took both Bassett and Paul into Richmond Park for an afternoon, and there they talked.

"It's like this, you see, sir," Bassett said. "Master Paul would get me talking about racing events, spinning yarns, you know, sir. And he was always keen on knowing if I'd made or if I'd lost. It's about a year since, now, that I put five shillings on Blush of Dawn for him—and we lost. Then the luck turned, with that ten shillings he had from you, that we put on Singhalese. And since then, it's been pretty steady, all things considering. What do you say, Master Paul?"

"We're all right when we're sure," said Paul. "It's when we're not quite sure that we go down."

"Oh, but we're careful then," said Bassett.

"But when are you *sure*?" Uncle Oscar smiled.

"It's Master Paul, sir," said Bassett, in a secret, religious voice. "It's as if he had it from heaven. Like Daffodil, now, for the Lincoln. That was as sure as eggs."

"Did you put anything on Daffodil?" asked Oscar Cresswell.

"Yes, sir. I made my bit."

"And my nephew?"

Bassett was obstinately silent, looking at Paul.

"I made twelve hundred, didn't I, Bassett? I told Uncle I was putting three hundred on Daffodil."

"That's right," said Bassett, nodding.

"But where's the money?" asked the uncle.

"I keep it safe locked up, sir. Master Paul he can have it any minute he likes to ask for it."

"What, fifteen hundred pounds?"

"And twenty! And *forty*, that is, with the twenty he made on the course."

"It's amazing!" said the uncle.

"If Master Paul offers you to be partners, sir, I would, if I were you; if you'll excuse me," said Bassett.

Oscar Cresswell thought about it.

"I'll see the money," he said.

They drove home again, and sure enough, Bassett came round to the garden house with fifteen hundred pounds in notes. The twenty pounds reserve was left with Joe Glee, in the Turf Commission deposit.

"You see, it's all right, Uncle, when I'm *sure*! Then we go strong, for all we're worth. Don't we, Bassett?"

"We do that, Master Paul."

"And when are you sure?" said the uncle, laughing.

"Oh, well, sometimes I'm *absolutely* sure, like about Daffodil," said the boy; "and sometimes I have an idea; and sometimes I haven't even an idea, have I, Bassett? Then we're careful, because we mostly go down."

"You do, do you! And when you're sure, like about Daffodil, what makes you sure, sonny?"

"Oh, well, I don't know," said the boy uneasily. "I'm sure, you know, Uncle; that's all."

"It's as if he had it from heaven, sir," Bassett reiterated.

"I should say so!" said the uncle.

But he became a partner. And when the Leger was coming on, Paul was "sure" about Lively Spark, which was a quite inconsiderable horse. The boy insisted on putting a thousand on the horse, Bassett went for five hundred, and Oscar Cresswell two hundred. Lively Spark came in first, and the betting had been ten to one against him. Paul had made ten thousand.

"You see," he said, "I was absolutely sure of him."

Even Oscar Cresswell had cleared two thousand.

"Look here, son," he said, "this sort of thing makes me nervous."

"It needn't, Uncle! Perhaps I shan't be sure again for a long time."

"But what are you going to do with your money?" asked the uncle.

"Of course," said the boy. "I started it for Mother. She said she had no luck, because Father is unlucky, so I thought if *I* was lucky, it might stop whispering."

"What might stop whispering?"

"Our house. I *hate* our house for whispering."

"What does it whisper?"

"Why—why"—the boy fidgeted— "why, I don't know. But it's always short of money, you know, Uncle."

"I know it, son, I know it."

"You know people send Mother writs, don't you, Uncle?"

"I'm afraid I do," said the uncle.

"And then the house whispers, like people laughing at you behind your back. It's awful, that is! I thought if I was lucky. . . ."

"You might stop it," added the uncle.

The boy watched him with big blue eyes, that had an uncanny cold fire in them, and he said never a word.

"Well, then!" said the uncle. "What are we doing?"

"I shouldn't like Mother to know I was lucky," said the boy.

"Why not, son?"

"She'd stop me."

"I don't think she would."

"Oh!"—and the boy writhed in an odd way— "I *don't* want her to know, Uncle."

"All right, son! We'll manage it without her knowing."

They managed it very easily. Paul, at the other's suggestion, handed over five thousand pounds to his uncle, who deposited it with the family lawyer, who was then to inform Paul's mother that a relative had put five thousand pounds into his hands, which sum was to be paid out a thousand pounds at a time, on the mother's birthday, for the next five years.

"So she'll have a birthday present of a thousand pounds for five successive years," said Uncle Oscar. "I hope it won't make it all the harder for her later."

Paul's mother had her birthday in November. The house had been "whispering" worse than ever lately, and, even in spite of his luck, Paul could not bear up against it. He was very anxious to see the effect of the birthday letter, telling his mother about the thousand pounds.

When there were no visitors, Paul now took his meals with his parents, as he was beyond the nursery control. His mother went into town nearly every day. She had discovered that she had an odd knack of sketching furs and dress materials, so she worked secretly in the studio of a friend who was the chief artist for the leading drapers. She drew the figures of ladies in furs and ladies in silk and sequins for the newspaper advertisements. This young woman artist earned several thousand pounds a year, but Paul's mother only made several hundreds, and she was again dissatisfied. She so wanted to be first in something, and she did not succeed, even in making sketches for drapery advertisements.

She was down to breakfast on the morning of her birthday. Paul watched her face as she read her letters. He knew the lawyer's letter. As his mother read it, her face hardened and became more expressionless. Then a cold, determined look came on her mouth. She hid the letter under the pile of others, and said not a word about it.

"Didn't you have anything nice in the post for your birthday, Mother?" said Paul.

"Quite moderately nice," she said, her voice cold and absent.

She went away to town without saying more.

But in the afternoon Uncle Oscar appeared. He said Paul's mother had had a long interview with the lawyer, asking if the whole five thousand could not be advanced at once, as she was in debt.

"What do you think, Uncle?" said the boy.

"I leave it to you, son."

"Oh, let her have it, then! We can get some more with the other," said the boy.

"A bird in the hand is worth two in the bush, laddie!" said Uncle Oscar.

"But I'm sure to *know* for the Grand National; or the Lincolnshire; or else the Derby. I'm sure to know for *one* of them," said Paul.

So Uncle Oscar signed the agreement, and Paul's mother touched the whole five thousand. Then something very curious happened. The voices in the house suddenly went mad, like a chorus of frogs on a spring evening. There were certain new furnishings, and Paul had a tutor. He was *really* going to Eton, his father's school, in the following autumn. There were flowers in the winter, and a blossoming of the luxury Paul's mother had been used to. And yet the voices in the house, behind the sprays of mimosa and blossom, and from under the piles of iridescent cushions, simply trilled and screamed in a sort of ecstasy: "There *must* be more money! Oh-h-h; there *must* be more money. Oh, now, now-w! Now-w-w—there *must* be more money!—more than ever! More than ever!"

It frightened Paul terribly. He studied away at his Latin and Greek. But his intense hours were spent with Bassett. The Grand National had gone by; he had not "known," and had lost a hundred pounds. Summer was at hand. He was in agony for the Lincoln. But even for the Lincoln he didn't "know," and he lost fifty pounds. He became wild-eyed and strange, as if something were going to explode in him.

"Let it alone, son! Don't you bother about it!" urged Uncle Oscar. But it was as if the boy couldn't really hear what his uncle was saying.

"I've got to know for the Derby! I've got to know for the Derby!" the child reiterated, his big blue eyes blazing with a sort of madness.

His mother noticed how overwrought he was.

"You'd better go to the seaside. Wouldn't you like to go now to the seaside, instead of waiting? I think you'd better," she said, looking down at him anxiously, her heart curiously heavy because of him.

But the child lifted his uncanny blue eyes. "I couldn't possibly go before the Derby, Mother!" he said. "I couldn't possibly!"

"Why not?" she said, her voice becoming heavy when she was opposed. "Why not? You can still go from the seaside to see the Derby with your uncle Oscar, if that's what you wish. No need for you to wait here. Besides, I think you care too much about these races. It's a bad sign. My family has been a gambling family, and you won't know till you grow up how much damage it has done. But it has done damage. I shall have to send Bassett away, and ask Uncle Oscar not to talk racing to you, unless you promise to be reasonable about it; go away to the seaside and forget it. You're all nerves!"

"I'll do what you like, Mother, so long as you don't send me away till after the Derby," the boy said.

"Send you away from where? Just from this house?"

"Yes," he said, gazing at her.

"Why, you curious child, what makes you care about this house so much, suddenly? I never knew you loved it."

He gazed at her without speaking. He had a secret within a secret, something he had not divulged, even to Bassett or to his uncle Oscar.

But his mother, after standing undecided and a little bit sullen for some moments, said:

"Very well, then! Don't go to the seaside till after the Derby, if you don't wish it. But promise me you won't let your nerves go to pieces. Promise you won't think so much about horse racing and *events*, as you call them!"

"Oh, no," said the boy casually. "I won't think much about them, Mother. You needn't worry. I wouldn't worry, Mother, if I were you."

"If you were me and I were you," said his mother, "I wonder what we *should* do!"

"But you know you needn't worry, Mother, don't you?" the boy repeated.

"I should be awfully glad to know it," she said wearily.

"Oh, well you *can*, you know. I mean, you *ought* to know you needn't worry," he insisted.

"Ought I? Then I'll see about it," she said.

Paul's secret of secrets was his wooden horse, that which had no name. Since he was emancipated from a nurse and a nursery governess, he had had his rocking horse removed to his own bedroom at the top of the house.

"Surely, you're too big for a rocking horse!" his mother had remonstrated.

"Well, you see, Mother, till I can have a *real* horse, I like to have *some* sort of animal about," had been his quaint answer.

"Do you feel he keeps you company?" She laughed.

"Oh, yes! He's very good, he always keeps me company, when I'm there," said Paul.

So the horse, rather shabby, stood in an arrested prance in the boy's bedroom.

The Derby was drawing near, and the boy grew more and more tense. He hardly heard what was spoken to him, he was very frail, and his eyes were really uncanny. His mother had sudden strange seizures of uneasiness about him. Sometimes, for half an hour, she would feel a sudden anxiety about him that was almost anguish. She wanted to rush to him at once, and know he was safe.

Two nights before the Derby, she was at a big party in town, when one of her rushes of anxiety about her boy, her firstborn, gripped her heart till she could hardly speak. She fought with the feeling, might and main, for she believed in common sense. But it was too strong. She had to leave the dance and go downstairs to telephone to the country. The children's nursery governess was terribly surprised and startled at being rung up in the night.

"Are the children all right, Miss Wilmot?"

"Oh, yes, they are quite all right."

"Master Paul? Is he all right?"

"He went to bed as right as a trivet. Shall I run up and look at him?"

"No," said Paul's mother reluctantly. "No! Don't trouble. It's all right. Don't sit up. We shall be home fairly soon." She did not want her son's privacy intruded upon.

"Very good," said the governess.

It was about one o'clock when Paul's mother and father drove up to their house. All was still. Paul's mother went to her room and slipped off her white fur cloak. She had told her maid not to wait up for her. She heard her husband downstairs, mixing a whisky and soda.

And then, because of the strange anxiety at her heart, she stole upstairs to her son's room. Noiselessly she went along the upper corridor. Was there a faint noise? What was it?

She stood, with arrested muscles, outside his door, listening. There was a strange, heavy, and yet not loud noise. Her heart stood still. It was a soundless noise, yet rushing and powerful. Something huge, in violent, hushed motion. What was it? What in God's name was it? She ought to know. She felt that she knew the noise. She knew what it was.

Yet she could not place it. She couldn't say what it was. And on and on it went, like a madness.

Softly, frozen with anxiety and fear, she turned the door handle.

The room was dark. Yet in the space near the window, she heard and saw something plunging to and fro. She gazed in fear and amazement.

Then suddenly she switched on the light, and saw her son, in his green pajamas, madly surging on the rocking horse. The blaze of light suddenly lit him up, as he urged the wooden horse, and lit her up, as she stood, blonde, in her dress of pale green and crystal, in the doorway.

"Paul!" she cried. "Whatever are you doing?"

"It's Malabar!" he screamed, in a powerful, strange voice. "It's Malabar!"

His eyes blazed at her for one strange and senseless second, as he ceased urging his wooden horse. Then he fell with a crash to the ground, and she, all her tormented motherhood flooding upon her, rushed to gather him up.

But he was unconscious, and unconscious he remained, with some brain fever. He talked and tossed, and his mother sat stonily by his side.

"Malabar! It's Malabar! Bassett, Bassett, I *know*! It's Malabar!"

So the child cried, trying to get up and urge the rocking horse that gave him his inspiration.

"What does he mean by Malabar?" asked the heart-frozen mother.

"I don't know," said the father stonily.

"What does he mean by Malabar?" she asked her brother Oscar.

"It's one of the horses running for the Derby," was the answer.

And, in spite of himself, Oscar Cresswell spoke to Bassett, and himself put a thousand on Malabar: at fourteen to one.

The third day of the illness was critical: they were waiting for a change. The boy, with his rather long, curly hair, was tossing ceaselessly on the pillow. He never slept nor regained consciousness, and his eyes were like blue stones. His mother sat, feeling her heart had gone, turned actually into a stone.

In the evening, Oscar Cresswell did not come, but Bassett sent a message, saying could he come up for one moment, just one moment? Paul's mother was very angry at the intrusion, but on second thought she agreed. The boy was the same. Perhaps Bassett might bring him to consciousness.

The gardener, a shortish fellow with a little brown mustache, and sharp little brown eyes, tiptoed into the room, touched his imaginary cap to Paul's mother, and stole to the bedside, staring with glittering, smallish eyes at the tossing, dying child.

"Master Paul!" he whispered. "Master Paul! Malabar came in first all right, a clean win. I did as you told me. You've made over seventy thousand pounds, you have; you've got over eighty thousand. Malabar came in all right, Master Paul."

"Malabar! Malabar! Did I say Malabar, Mother? Did I say Malabar? Do you think I'm lucky, Mother? I knew Malabar, didn't I? Over eighty thousand pounds! I call that lucky, don't you, Mother? Over eighty thousand pounds! I knew, didn't I know I knew? Malabar came in all right. If I ride my horse till I'm sure, then I tell you, Bassett, you can go as high as you like. Did you go for all you were worth, Bassett?"

"I went a thousand on it, Master Paul."

"I never told you, Mother, that if I can ride my horse, and *get there*, then I'm absolutely sure—oh, absolutely! Mother, did I ever tell you? I *am* lucky!"

"No, you never did," said the mother.

But the boy died in the night.

And even as he lay dead, his mother heard her brother's voice saying to her: "My God, Hester, you're eighty-odd thousand to the good, and a poor devil of a son to the bad. But, poor devil, poor devil, he's best gone out of a life where he rides his rocking horse to find a winner."

About Edna Ferber

Born in Kalamazoo, Michigan, in 1885, Ferber and her family moved to Appleton, Wisconsin, when Edna was 12. There she received her education and attended Lawrence University. She wrote for several newspapers before publishing her first novel. In 1925 *So Big* won the Pulitzer Prize for Fiction. She moved to New York and wrote stories and novels: *Giant, Show Boat, Cimarron,* and more. A member of the famed Algonquin Roundtable, she enjoyed New York and died there in 1968 at age 82.

The Afternoon of a Faun

Though he rarely heeded its summons—cagy boy that he was—the telephone rang oftenest for Nick. Because of the many native noises of the place, the telephone had a special bell that was a combination buzz and ring. It sounded above the roar of outgoing cars, the splash of the hose, the sputter and hum of the electric battery in the rear. Nick heard it, unheeding. A voice—Smitty's or Mike's or Elmer's—answering its call. Then, echoing through the gray, vaulted spaces of the big garage: "Nick! Oh, Ni-ick!"

From the other side of the great cement-floored enclosure, or in muffled tones from beneath a car: "Whatcha want?"

"Dame on the wire."

"I ain't in."

The obliging voice again, dutifully repeating the message: "He ain't in . . .

Well, it's hard to say. He might be in in a couple hours and then again he might not be back till late. I guess he's went to Hammond on a job—" (Warming to his task now.) "Say, won't I do?...Who's fresh! Aw, say, *lady*!"

You'd think, after repeated rebuffs of this sort, she could not possibly be so lacking in decent pride as to leave her name for Smitty or Mike or Elmer to bandy about. But she invariably did, baffled by Nick's elusiveness. She was likely to be any one of a number. Miss Bauers phoned: Will you tell him, please? (A nasal voice, and haughty, with the hauteur that seeks to conceal secret fright.) Tell him it's important. Miss Ahearn phoned: Will you tell him, please? Just say Miss Ahearn. A-h-e-a-r-n. Miss Olson: Just Gertie. But oftenest Miss Bauers.

Cupid's messenger, wearing grease-grimed overalls and the fatuous grin of the dalliant male, would transmit his communication to the uneager Nick.

"'S wonder you wouldn't answer the phone onct yourself. Says you was to call Miss Bauers any time you come in between one and six at Hyde Park—wait a min't'—yeh—Hyde Park 6079, and any time after six at—"

"Wha' d she want?"

"Well, how the hell should *I* know! Says call Miss Bauers any time between one and six at Hyde Park 6—"

"Swell chanst. *Swell* chanst!"

Which explains why the calls came oftenest for Nick. He was so indifferent to them. You pictured the patient and persistent Miss Bauers, or the oxlike Miss Olson, or Miss Ahearn, or just Gertie hovering within hearing distance of the telephone listening, listening—while one o'clock deepened to six—for the call that never came; plucking up fresh courage at six until six o'clock dragged on to bedtime. When next they met: "I bet you was there all the time. Pity you wouldn't answer a call when a person leaves their name. You could of give me a ring. I bet you was there all the time."

"Well, maybe I was."

Bewildered, she tried to retaliate with the boomerang of vituperation.

How could she know? How could she know that this slim, slick young garage mechanic was a woodland creature in disguise—a satyr in store clothes—a wild thing who perversely preferred to do his own pursuing? How could Miss Bauers know—she who cashiered in the Green Front Grocery and Market on Fifty-third Street? Or Miss Olson, at the Rialto ticket window? Or the Celtic, emotional Miss Ahearn, the manicure? Or Gertie the goof? They knew nothing of mythology; of pointed ears and pug noses and goat's feet. Nick's ears, to their fond gaze, presented an honest red surface protruding from either side of his head. His feet, in tan laced shoes, were ordinary feet, a little more than ordinarily expert, perhaps, in the convolutions of the dance at Englewood Masonic Hall, which is part of Chicago's vast South Side. No; a faun, to Miss Bauers, Miss Olson, Miss Ahearn, and just Gertie, was one of those things in the Lincoln Park Zoo.

Perhaps, sometimes, they realized, vaguely, that Nick was different. When, for example, they tried—and failed—to picture him looking interestedly at one of those three-piece bedroom sets glistening like pulled taffy in the window of the instalment furniture store, while they, shy yet proprietary, clung to his arm and eyed the price ticket. Now $98.50. You couldn't see Nick interested in bedroom sets, in price tickets, in any of those settled, fixed, everyday things. He was fluid, evasive, like quicksilver, though they did not put it thus.

Miss Bauers, goaded to revolt, would say pettishly: "You're like a mosquito, that's what. Person never knows from one minute to the other where you're at."

"Yeh," Nick would retort. "When you know where a mosquito's at, what do you do to him? Plenty. I ain't looking to be squashed."

Miss Ahearn, whose public position (the Hygienic Barber Shop. Gent's manicure, 50c.) offered unlimited social opportunities, would assume a gay indifference. "They's plenty boys begging to take me out every hour in the day. Swell lads, too. I ain't waiting round for any greasy mechanic like you. Don't think it. Say, lookit your nails! They'd queer you with me, let alone what else all is wrong with you."

In answer Nick would put one hand—one broad, brown, steel-strong hand with its broken discolored nails—on Miss Ahearn's arm, in its flimsy georgette sleeve. Miss Ahearn's eyelids would flutter and close, and a little shiver would run with icy-hot feet all over Miss Ahearn.

Nick was like that.

Nick's real name wasn't Nick at all—or scarcely at all. His last name was Nicholas, and his parents, long before they became his parents, traced their origin to some obscure Czechoslovakian province—long before we became so glib with our Czechoslovakia. His first name was Dewey, knowing which you automatically know the date of his birth. It was a patriotic but unfortunate choice on the part of his parents. The name did not fit him; was too mealy; not debonair enough. Nick. Nicky in tenderer moments (Miss Bauers, Miss Olson, Miss Ahearn, just Gertie, et al.).

His method with women was firm and somewhat stern, but never brutal. He never waited for them if they were late. Any girl who assumed that her value was enhanced in direct proportion to her tardiness in keeping an engagement with Nick found herself standing disconsolate on the corner of Fifty-third and Lake trying to look as if she were merely waiting for the Lake Park car and not peering wistfully up and down the street in search of a slim, graceful, hurrying figure that never came.

It is difficult to convey in words the charm that Nick possessed. Seeing him, you beheld merely a medium-sized young mechanic in reasonably grimed garage clothes when working; and in tight pants, tight coat, silk shirt, long-visored green cap when at leisure. A rather pallid skin due to the nature of his work. Large deft hands, a good deal like the hands of a surgeon, square, blunt-fingered, spatulate. Indeed, as you saw him at work, a wire-netted electric bulb held in one hand, the other plunged deep into the vitals of the car on which he was engaged, you thought of a surgeon performing a major operation. He wore one of those round skullcaps characteristic of his craft (the brimless crown of an old felt hat). He would deftly remove the transmission case and plunge his hand deep into the car's guts, feeling expertly about with his engine-wise fingers as a surgeon feels for liver, stomach, gall bladder, intestines, appendix. When he brought up his hands, all dripping with grease (which is the warm blood of the car), he invariably had put his finger on the sore spot.

All this, of course, could not serve to endear him to the girls. On the contrary, you would have thought that his hands alone, from which he could never quite free the grease and grit, would have caused some feeling of repugnance among the lily-fingered. But they, somehow, seemed always to be finding an excuse to touch him: his tie, his hair, his coat sleeve. They seemed even to derive a vicarious thrill from holding his hat or cap when on an outing. They brushed imaginary bits of lint from his coat lapel. They tried on his seal ring, crying: "Oo, lookit, how big it is for me, even my thumb!" He called this "pawing a guy over"; and the lint ladies he designated as "thread pickers."

No; it can't be classified, this powerful draw he had for them. His conversation furnished no clue. It was commonplace conversation, limited, even dull. When astonished, or impressed, or horrified, or amused, he said: "Ken yuh feature that!" When emphatic or confirmatory, he said: "You *tell* 'em!"

It wasn't his car and the opportunities it furnished for drives, both country and city. That motley piece of mechanism represented such an assemblage of unrelated parts as could only have been made to coordinate under Nick's expert guidance. It was out of commission more than half the time, and could never be relied upon to furnish a holiday. Both Miss Bauers and Miss Ahearn had twelve-cylinder opportunities that should have rendered them forever unfit for travel in Nick's one-lung vehicle of locomotion.

It wasn't money. Though he was generous enough with what he had, Nick couldn't be generous with what he hadn't. And his wage at the garage was $40 a week. Miss Ahearn's silk stockings cost $4.50.

His unconcern should have infuriated them, but it served to pique. He wasn't actually as unconcerned as he appeared, but he had early learned that effort in their direction was unnecessary. Nick had little imagination; a gorgeous selfishness; a tolerantly contemptuous liking for the sex. Naturally, however, his attitude toward them had been somewhat embittered by being obliged to watch their method of driving a car in and out of the Ideal Garage doorway. His own manipulation of the wheel was nothing short of wizardry.

He played the harmonica.

Each Thursday afternoon was Nick's half day off. From twelve until seven-thirty he was free to range the bosky highways of Chicago. When his car—he called it "the bus"—was agreeable, he went awheel in search of amusement. The bus being indisposed, he went afoot. He rarely made plans in advance; usually was accompanied by some successful telephonee. He rather liked to have a silken skirt beside him fluttering and flirting in the breeze as he broke the speed regulations.

On this Thursday afternoon in July he had timed his morning job to a miraculous nicety so that at the stroke of twelve his workaday garments dropped from him magically, as though he were a male (and reversed) Cinderella. There was a wash room and a rough sort of sleeping room containing two cots situated in the second story of the Ideal Garage. Here Nick shed the loose garments of labor for the fashionably tight habiliments of leisure. Private chauffeurs whose employers housed their cars in the Ideal Garage used this nook for a lounge and smoker. Smitty, Mike, Elmer, and Nick snatched stolen siestas there in the rare absences of the manager. Sometimes Nick spent the night there when forced to work overtime. His home life, at best, was a sketchy affair. Here chauffeurs, mechanics, washers lolled at ease exchanging soft-spoken gossip, motor chat, speculation, comment, and occasional verbal obscenity. Each possessed a formidable knowledge of that neighborhood section of Chicago known as Hyde Park. This knowledge was not confined to car costs and such impersonal items, but included meals, scandals, relationships, finances, love affairs, quarrels, peccadillos. Here Nick often played his harmonica, his lips sweeping the metal length of it in throbbing rendition of such sure-fire sentimentality as The Long, Long Trail, or Mammy, while the others talked, joked, kept time with tapping feet or wagging heads.

Today the hot little room was empty except for Nick, shaving before the cracked mirror on the wall, and old Elmer, reading a scrap of yesterday's newspaper as he lounged his noon hour away. Old Elmer was thirty-seven, and Nicky regarded him as an octogenarian. Also, old Elmer's conversation bored Nick to the point of almost sullen resentment. Old Elmer was a family man. His talk was all of his family—the wife, the kids, the flat. A garrulous person, lank, pasty, dish-faced, and amiable. His half day off was invariably spent tinkering about the stuffy little flat—painting, nailing up shelves, mending a broken window shade, puttying a window, playing with his pasty little boy, aged sixteen months, and his pasty little girl, aged three years. Next day he regaled his fellow workers with elaborate recitals of his holiday hours.

"Believe me, that kid's a caution. Sixteen months old, and what does he do yesterday? He unfastens the ketch on the back-porch gate. We got a gate on the back porch, see." (This frequent "see" which interlarded Elmer's verbiage was not used in an interrogatory way, but as a period, and by way of emphasis. His voice did not take the rising inflection as he uttered it.) "What does he do, he opens it. I come home, and the wife says to me: 'Say, you better get busy and fix a new ketch on that gate to the back porch. Little Elmer, first thing I know, he'd got it open today and was crawling out almost.' Say, can you beat that for a kid sixteen months—"

Nick had finished shaving, had donned his clean white soft shirt. His soft collar fitted to a miracle about his strong throat. Nick's sartorial effects were a triumph—on forty a week. "Say, can't you talk about nothing but that kid of yours? I bet he's a bum specimen at that. Runt, like his pa."

Elmer flung down his newspaper in honest indignation as Nick had wickedly meant he should. "Is that so! Why, we was wrastling round—me and him, see—last night on the floor, and what does he do, he raises his mitt and hands me a wallop in the stomick it like to knock the wind out of me. That's all. Sixteen months—"

"Yeh. I suppose this time next year he'll be boxing for money."

Elmer resumed his paper. "What do *you* know." His tone mingled pity with contempt.

Nick took a last critical survey of the cracked mirror's reflection and found it good. "Nothing, only this: you make me sick with your kids and your missus and your place. Say, don't you never have no fun?"

"Fun! Why, say, last Sunday we was out to the beach, and the kid swum out first thing you know—"

"Oh, shut up!" He was dressed now. He slapped his pockets. Harmonica. Cigarettes. Matches. Money. He was off, his long-visored cloth cap pulled jauntily over his eyes.

Elmer, bearing no rancor, flung a last idle query: "Where you going?"

"How should I know? Just bumming around. Bus is outa commission, and I'm outa luck."

He clattered down the stairs, whistling.

Next door for a shine at the Greek bootblack's. Enthroned on the dais, a minion at his feet, he was momentarily monarchial. How's the boy? Good? Same here. Down, his brief reign ended. Out into the bright noon-day glare of Fifty-third Street.

A fried-egg sandwich. Two blocks down and into the white-tiled lunch-room. He took his place in the row perched on stools in front of the white slab, his feet on the railing, his elbows on the counter. Four white-aproned vestals with blotchy skins performed rites over the steaming nickel urns, slid dishes deftly along the slick surface of the white slab, mopped up moisture with a sly gray rag. No nonsense about them. This was the rush hour. Hungry men from the shops and offices and garages of the district were bent on food (not badinage). They ate silently, making a dull business of it. Coffee? What kinda pie do you want? No fooling here. "Hello, Jessie."

As she mopped the slab in front of him you noticed a slight softening of her features, intent so grimly on her task. "What's yours?"

"Bacon-and-egg sandwich. Glass of milk. Piece of pie. Blueberry."

Ordinarily she would not have bothered. But with him: "The blueberry ain't so good today, I noticed. Try the peach?"

"All right." He looked at her. She smiled. Incredibly, the dishes ordered seemed to leap out at her from nowhere. She crashed them down on the glazed white surface in front of him. The bacon-and-egg sandwich was served open-faced, an elaborate confection. Two slices of white bread, side by side. On one reposed a fried egg, hard, golden, delectable, indigestible. On the other three crisp curls of bacon. The ordinary order held two curls only. A dish so rich in calories as to make it food sufficient for a day. Jessie knew nothing of calories, nor did Nick. She placed a double order of butter before him—two yellow pats, moisture-beaded. As she scooped up his milk from the can you saw that the glass was but three-quarters filled. From a deep crock she ladled a smaller scoop and filled the glass to the top. The deep crock held cream. Nick glanced up at her again. Again Jessie smiled. A plain damsel, Jessie, and capable. She went on about her business. What's yours? Coffee with? White or rye? No nonsense about her. And yet: "Pie all right?"

"Yeh. It's good."

She actually blushed.

He finished, swung himself off the stool, nodded to Jessie. She stacked his dishes with one lean, capable hand, mopped the slab with the other, but as she made for the kitchen she flung a glance at him over her shoulder.

"Day off?"

"Yeh."

"Some folks has all the luck."

He grinned. His teeth were strong and white and even. He walked toward the door with his light quick step, paused for a toothpick as he paid his check, was out again into the July sunlight. Her face became dull again.

Well, not one o'clock. Guessed he'd shoot a little pool. He dropped into Moriarty's cigar store. It was called a cigar store because it dealt in magazines, newspapers, soft drinks, golf balls, cigarettes, pool, billiards, chocolates, chewing gum, and cigars. In the rear of the store were four green-topped tables, three for pool and one for billiards. He hung about aimlessly, watching the game at the one occupied table. The players were slim young men like himself, their clothes replicas of his own, their faces lean and somewhat hard. Two of them dropped out. Nick took a cue from the rack, shed his tight coat. They played under a glaring electric light in the heat of the day, yet they seemed cool, aloof, immune from bodily discomfort. It was a strangely silent game and as mirthless as that of the elfin bowlers in Rip Van Winkle. The slim-waisted shirted figures bent plastically over the table in the graceful postures of the game. You heard only the click of the balls, an occasional low-voiced exclamation. A solemn crew, and unemotional.

Now and then: "What's all the shootin' fur?"

"In she goes."

Nick, winner, tired of it in less than an hour. He bought a bottle of some acidulous drink just off the ice and refreshed himself with it, drinking from the bottle's mouth. He was vaguely restless, dissatisfied. Out again into the glare of two o'clock Fifty-third Street. He strolled up a block toward Lake Park Avenue. It was hot. He wished the bus wasn't sick. Might go in swimming, though. He considered this idly. Hurried steps behind him. A familiar perfume wafted to his senses. A voice nasal yet cooing. Miss Bauers. Miss Bauers on a pleasure bent, palpably, being attired in the briefest of silks, white-strapped slippers, white silk stockings, scarlet hat. The Green Front Grocery and Market closed for a half day each Thursday afternoon during July and August. Nicky had not availed himself of the knowledge.

"Well, if it ain't Nicky! I just seen you come out of Moriarty's as I was passing." (She had seen him go in an hour before and had waited a patient hour in the drug store across the street.) "What you doing around loose this hour the day, anyway?"

I'm off 'safternoon."

"Are yuh? So'm I." Nicky said nothing. Miss Bauers shifted from one plump silken leg to the other. "What you doing?"

"Oh, nothing much."

"So'm I. Let's do it together." Miss Bauers employed the direct method.

"Well," said Nick, vaguely. He didn't object particularly. And yet he was conscious of some formless program forming mistily in his mind—a program that did not include the berouged, bepowdered, plump, and silken Miss Bauers.

"I phoned you this morning, Nicky. Twice."

"Yeh?"

"They said you wasn't in."

"Yeh?"

A hard young woman, Miss Bauers, yet simple: powerfully drawn toward this magnetic and careless boy; powerless to forge chains strong enough to hold him. "Well, how about Riverview? I ain't been this summer."

"Oh, that's so darn far. Take all day getting there, pretty near."

"Not driving, it wouldn't."

"I ain't got the bus. Busted."

His apathy was getting on her nerves. "How about a movie, then?" Her feet hurt. It was hot.

His glance went up the street toward the Harper, down the street toward the Hyde Park. The sign above the Harper offered Mother o' Mine. The lettering above the Hyde Park announced Love's Sacrifice.

"Gawd, no," he made decisive answer.

Miss Bauers's frazzled nerves snapped. "You make me sick! Standing there. Nothing don't suit you. Say, I ain't so crazy to go round with you. Cheap guy! Prob'ly you'd like to go over to Wooded Island or something, in Jackson Park, and set on the grass and feed the squirrels. That'd be a treat for me, that would." She laughed a high, scornful tear-near laugh.

"Why—say—" Nick stared at her, and yet she felt he did not see her.

A sudden peace came into his face—the peace of a longing fulfilled. He turned his head. A Lake Park Avenue street car was roaring its way toward them. He took a step toward the roadway. "I got to be going."

Fear flashed its flame into Miss Bauers's pale blue eyes. "Going! How do you mean, going? Going where?"

"I got to be going." The car had stopped opposite them. His young face was stern, implacable. Miss Bauers knew she was beaten, but she clung to hope tenaciously, piteously. "I got to see a party, see?"

"You never said anything about it in the first place. Pity you wouldn't say so in the first place. Who you got to see, anyway?" She knew it was useless to ask. She knew she was beating her fists against a stone wall, but she must needs ask notwithstanding: "Who you got to see?"

"I got to see a party. I forgot." He made the car step in two long strides; had swung himself up. "So long!" The car door slammed after him. Miss Bauers, in her unavailing silks, stood disconsolate on the hot street corner.

He swayed on the car platform until Sixty-third Street was reached. There he alighted and stood a moment at the curb surveying idly the populous corner. He purchased a paper bag of hot peanuts from a vender's glittering scarlet and nickel stand, and crossed the street into the pathway that led to Jackson Park, munching as he went. In an open space reserved for games some boys were playing baseball with much hoarse hooting and frenzied action. He drew near to watch. The ball, misdirected, sailed suddenly toward him. He ran backward at its swift approach, leaped high, caught it, and with a long curving swing, so easy as to appear almost effortless, sent it hurtling back. The lad on the pitcher's mound made as if to catch it, changed his mind, dodged, started after it.

The boy at bat called to Nick: "Heh, you! Wanna come on and pitch?"

Nick shook his head and went on.

He wandered leisurely along the gravel path that led to the park golf shelter. The wide porch was crowded with golfers and idlers. A foursome was teed up at the first tee. Nick leaned against a porch pillar waiting for them to drive. That old boy had pretty good practise swing. . . . Stiff, though. . . . Lookit that dame. Je's! I bet she takes fifteen shots before she ever gets on to the green. . . . There, that kid had pretty good drive. Must of been hundred and fifty, anyway. Pretty good for a kid.

Nick, in the course of his kaleidoscopic career, had been a caddie at thirteen in tom shirt and flapping knickers. He had played the smooth, expert, scornful game of the caddie with a natural swing from the lithe waist and a follow-through that was the envy of the muscle-bound men who watched him. He hadn't played in years. The game no longer interested him. He entered the shelter lunchroom. The counters were lined with lean, brown, hungry men and lean, brown, hungry women. They were eating incredible dishes considering that the hour was 3 P.M. and the day a hot one. Corned-beef hash with a poached egg on top; wieners and potato salad; meat pies; hot roast beef sandwiches; steaming cups of coffee in thick white ware; watermelon. Nick slid a leg over a stool as he had done earlier in the afternoon. Here, too, the Hebes were of stern stuff, as their needs must be to serve these ravenous hordes of club swingers who swarmed upon them from dawn to dusk. Their task it was to wait upon the golfing male, which is man at his simplest—reduced to the least common denominator and shorn of all attraction for the female eye and heart. They represented merely hungry mouths, weary muscles, reaching fists. The waitresses served them as a capable attendant serves another woman's child—efficiently and without emotion.

"Blueberry pie à la mode," said Nick—"with strawberry ice cream."

Inured as she was to the horrors of gastronomic miscegenation, the waitress—an old girl—recoiled at this.

"Say, I don't think you'd like that. They don't mix so very good. Why don't you try the peach pie instead with the strawberry ice cream—if you want strawberry?" He looked so young and cool and fresh.

"Blueberry," repeated Nick sternly, and looked her in the eye. The old waitress laughed a little and was surprised to find herself laughing. "'S for you to say." She brought him the monstrous mixture, and he devoured it to the last chromatic crumb.

"Nothing the matter with that," he remarked as she passed, dishladen.

She laughed again tolerantly, almost tenderly. "Good thing you're young." Her busy glance lingered a brief moment on his face. He sauntered out.

Now he took the path to the right of the shelter, crossed the road, struck the path again, came to a rustic bridge that humped high in the middle, spanning a cool green stream, willow-bordered. The cool green stream was an emerald chain that threaded its way in a complete circlet about the sylvan spot known as Wooded Island, relic of World's Fair days.

The little island lay, like a thing under enchantment, silent, fragrant, golden, green, exquisite. Squirrels and blackbirds, rabbits and pigeons mingled in Æsopian accord. The air was warm and still, held by the encircling trees and shrubbery. There was not a soul to be seen. At the far north end the two Japanese model houses, survivors of the exposition, gleamed white among the trees.

Nick stood a moment. His eyelids closed, languorously. He stretched his arms out and up deliciously, bringing his stomach in and his chest out. He took off his cap and stuffed it into his pocket. He strolled across the thick cool nap of the grass, deserting the pebble path. At the west edge of the island a sign said: "No One Allowed in the Shrubbery." Ignoring it, Nick parted the branches, stopped and crept, reached the bank that sloped down to the cool green stream, took off his coat, and lay relaxed upon the ground. Above him the tree branches made a pattern against the sky. Little ripples lipped the shore. Scampering velvet-footed things, feathered things, winged things made pleasant stir among the leaves. Nick slept.

He awoke in half an hour refreshed. He lay there, thinking of nothing—a charming gift. He found a stray peanut in his pocket and fed it to a friendly squirrel. His hand encountered the cool metal of his harmonica. He drew out the instrument, placed his coat, folded, under his head, crossed his knees, one leg swinging idly, and began to play rapturously. He was perfectly happy. He played Gimme Love, whose jazz measures are stolen from Mendelssohn's Spring Song. He did not know this. The leaves rustled. He did not turn his head.

"Hello, Pan!" said a voice. A girl came down the slope and seated herself beside him. She was not smiling.

Nick removed the harmonica from his lips and wiped his mouth with the back of his hand. "Hello who?"

"Hello, Pan."

"Wrong number, lady," Nick said, and again applied his lips to the mouth organ. The girl laughed then, throwing back her head. Her throat was long and slim and brown. She clasped her knees with her arms and looked at Nick amusedly. Nick thought she was a kind of homely little thing.

"Pan," she explained, "was a pagan deity. He played pipes in the woods."

"'S all right with me," Nick ventured, bewildered but amiable. He wished she'd go away. But she didn't. She began to take off her shoes and stockings. She went down to the water's edge, then, and paddled her feet. Nick sat up, outraged. "Say, you can't do that."

She glanced back at him over her shoulder. "Oh, yes, I can. It's so hot."

She wriggled her toes ecstatically.

The leaves rustled again, briskly, unmistakably this time. A heavy tread. A rough voice. 'Say, looka here! Get out of there, you! What the—" A policeman, red-faced, wroth. "You can't do that! Get outa here!"

It was like a movie, Nick thought.

The girl turned her head. "Oh, now, Mr. Elwood," she said.

"Oh, it's you, miss," said the policeman. You would not have believed it was the same policeman. He even giggled. "Thought you was away."

"I was. In fact, I am, really. I just got sick of it and ran away for a day. Drove. Alone. The family'll be wild."

"All the way?" said the policeman, incredulously. "Say, I thought that looked like your car standing out there by the road; but I says no, she ain't in town." He looked sharply at Nick, whose face had an Indian composure, though his feelings were mixed. "Who's this?"

"He's a friend of mine. His name's Pan." She was drying her feet with an inadequate rose-colored handkerchief. She crept crabwise up the bank, and put on her stockings and slippers.

"Why'n't you come out and set on a bench?" suggested the policeman, worriedly.

The girl shook her head. "In Arcadia we don't sit on benches. I should think you'd know that. Go on away, there's a dear. I want to talk to this—to Pan."

He persisted. "What'd your pa say, I'd like to know!" The girl shrugged her shoulders. Nick made as though to rise. He was worried. A nut, that's what. She pressed him down with a hard brown hand.

"Now it's all right. He's going. Old Fuss!" The policeman stood a brief moment longer. Then the foliage rustled again. He was gone. The girl sighed, happily. "Play that thing some more, will you? You're a wiz at it, aren't you?"

"I'm pretty good," said Nick, modestly. Then the outrageousness of her conduct struck him afresh. "Say, who're you, anyway?"

"My name's Berry—short for Bernice. . . . What's yours, Pan?"

"Nick—that is—Nick."

"Ugh, terrible! I'll stick to Pan. What d'you do when you're not Panning?" Then, at the bewilderment in his face: "What's your job?"

"I work in the Ideal Garage. Say, you're pretty nosey, ain't you?"

"Yes, pretty. . . . That accounts for your nails, h'm?" She looked at her own brown paws. "'Bout as bad as mine. I drove one hundred and fifty miles today."

"Ya-as, you did!"

"I did! Started at six. And I'll probably drive back tonight."

"You're crazy!"

"I know it," she agreed, "and it's wonderful. . . . Can you play the Tommy Toddle?"

"Yeh. It's kind of hard, though, where the runs are. I don't get the runs so very good." He played it. She kept time with head and feet. When he had finished and wiped his lips:

"Elegant!" She took the harmonica from him, wiped it brazenly on the much-abused, rose-colored handkerchief and began to play, her cheeks puffed out, her eyes round with effort. She played the Tommy Toddle, and her runs were perfect. Nick's chagrin was swallowed by his admiration and envy.

"Say, kid, you got more wind than a factory whistle. Who learned you to play?"

She struck her chest with a hard brown fist. "Tennis. . . . Tim taught me."

"Who's Tim?"

"The—a chauffeur."

Nick leaned closer. "Say, do you ever go to the dances at Englewood Masonic Hall?"

"I never have."

"Jah like to go some time?"

"I'd love it." She grinned up at him, her teeth flashing white in her brown face.

"It's swell here," he said, dreamily. "Like the woods?"

"Yes."

"Winter, when it's cold and dirty, I think about how it's here summers. It's like you could take it out of your head and look at it whenever you wanted to."

"Endymion."

"Huh?"

"A man said practically the same thing the other day. Name of Keats."

"Yeh?"

"He said: 'A thing of beauty is a joy forever.'"

"That's one way putting it," he agreed, graciously.

Unsmilingly she reached over with one slim forefinger, as if compelled, and touched the blond hairs on Nick's wrist. Just touched them. Nick remained motionless. The girl shivered a little, deliciously. She glanced at him shyly. Her lips were provocative. Thoughtlessly, blindly, Nick suddenly flung an arm about her, kissed her. He kissed her as he had never kissed Miss Bauers—as he had never kissed Miss Ahearn, Miss Olson, or just Gertie. The girl did not scream, or push him away, or slap him, or protest, or giggle as would have the above-mentioned young ladies. She sat breathing rather fast, a tinge of scarlet showing beneath the tan.

"Well, Pan," she said, low-voiced, "you're running true to form, anyway." She eyed him appraisingly. "Your appeal is in your virility, I suppose. Yes."

"My what?"

She rose. "I've got to go."

Panic seized him. "Say, don't drive back tonight, huh? Wherever it is you've got to go. You ain't driving back tonight?"

She made no answer; parted the bushes, was out on the gravel path in the sunlight, a slim, short-skirted, almost childish figure. He followed. They crossed the bridge, left the island, reached the roadway almost in silence. At the side of the road was a roadster. Its hood was the kind that conceals power. Its lamps were two giant eyes rimmed in precious metal. Its line spelled strength. Its body was foreign. Nick's engine-wise eyes saw these things at a glance.

"That your car?"

"Yes."

"Gosh!"

She unlocked it, threw in the clutch, shifted, moved. "Say!" was wrung from Nick helplessly. She waved at him. "Good-by, Pan." He stared, stricken. She was off swiftly, silently; flashed around a corner; was hidden by the trees and shrubs.

He stood a moment. He felt bereaved, cheated. Then a little wave of exaltation shook him. He wanted to talk to someone. "Gosh!" he said again. He glanced at his wrist. Five-thirty. He guessed he'd go home. He guessed he'd go home and get one of Ma's dinners. One of Ma's dinners and talk to Ma. The Sixty-third Street car. He could make it and back in plenty time.

Nick lived in that section of Chicago known as Englewood, which is not so sylvan as it sounds, but appropriate enough for a faun. Not only that; he lived in S. Green Street, Englewood. S. Green Street, near Seventieth, is almost rural with its great elms and poplars, its frame cottages, its back gardens. A neighborhood of thrifty, foreign-born fathers and mothers, many children, tree-lined streets badly paved. Nick turned in at a two-story brown frame cottage. He went around to the back. Ma was in the kitchen.

Nick's presence at the evening meal was an uncertain thing. Sometimes he did not eat at home for a week, excepting only his hurried early breakfast. He rarely spent an evening at home, and when he did used the opportunity for making up lost sleep. Pa never got home from work until after six. Nick liked his dinner early and hot. On his rare visits his mother welcomed him like one of the Gracchi. Mother and son understood each other wordlessly, having much in common. You would not have thought it of her (forty-six bust, forty waist, measureless hips), but Ma was a nymph at heart. Hence Nick.

"Hello, Ma!" She was slamming expertly about the kitchen.

"Hello, yourself," said Ma. Ma had a line of slang gleaned from her numerous brood. It fell strangely from her lips. Ma had never quite lost a tinge of foreign accent, though she had come to America when a girl. A hearty, zestful woman, savoring life with gusto, undiminished by child-bearing and hard work. "Eating home, Dewey?" She alone used his given name.

"Yeh, but I gotta be back by seven-thirty. Got anything ready?"

"Dinner ain't, but I'll get you something. Plenty. Platter ham and eggs and a quick fry. Cherry cobbler's done. I'll fix you some." (Cherry cobbler is shortcake with a soul.)

He ate enormously at the kitchen table, she hovering over him.

"What's the news, Dewey?"

"Ain't none." He ate in silence. Then: "How old was you when you married Pa?"

"Me? Say, I wasn't no more'n a kid. I gotta laugh when I think of it."

"What was Pa earning?"

She laughed a great hearty laugh, dipping a piece of bread sociably in the ham fat on the platter as she stood by the table, just to bear him company.

"Say, earn! If he'd of earned what you was earning now, we'd of thought we was millionaires. Time Etty was born he was pulling down thirteen a week, and we saved on it." She looked at him suddenly, sharply. "Why?"

"Oh, I was just wondering."

"Look what good money he's getting now! If I was you, I wouldn't stick around no old garage for what they give you. You could get a good job in the works with Pa; first thing you know you'd be pulling down big money. You're smart like that with engines. . . . Takes a lot of money nowadays for feller to get married."

"You *tell* 'em," agreed Nick. He looked up at her, having finished eating. His glance was almost tender. "How'd you come to marry Pa, anyway? You and him's so different."

The nymph in Ma leaped to the surface and stayed there a moment, sparkling, laughing, dimpling. "Oh, I dunno. I kept running away and he kept running after. Like that."

He looked up again quickly at that. "Yeh. That's it. Fella don't like to have no girl chasing him all the time. Say, he likes to do the chasing himself. Ain't that the truth?"

"You *tell* 'em!" agreed Ma. A great jovial laugh shook her. Heavy-footed now, but light of heart.

Suddenly: "I'm thinking; of going to night school. Learn something. I don't know nothing."

"You do, too, Dewey!"

"Aw, wha'd I know? I never had enough schooling. Wished I had."

"Who's doings was it? You wouldn't stay. Wouldn't go no more than sixth reader and quit. Nothing wouldn't get you to go."

He agreed gloomily. "I know it. I don't know what nothing is. Uh—Arcadia—or—now—vitality or nothing."

"Oh, that comes easy," she encouraged him, "when you begin once."

He reached for her hand gratefully. "You're a swell cook, Ma." He had a sudden burst of generosity, of tenderness. "Soon's the bus is fixed I'll take you joy-riding over to the lake."

Ma always wore a boudoir cap of draggled lace and ribbon for motoring. Nick almost never offered her a ride. She did not expect him to.

She pushed him playfully. "Go on! You got plenty young girls to take riding, not your ma."

"Oh, girls!" he said, scornfully. Then in another tone: "Girls."

He was off. It was almost seven. Pa was late. He caught a car back to Fifty-third Street. Elmer was lounging in the cool doorway of the garage. Nick, in sheer exuberance of spirits, squared off, doubled his fists, and danced about Elmer in a semicircle, working his arms as a prizefighter does, warily. He jabbed at Elmer's jaw playfully.

"What you been doing," inquired that long-suffering gentleman, "makes you feel so good? Where you been?"

"Oh, nowheres. Bumming round. Park."

He turned in the direction of the stairway. Elmer lounged after him. "Oh, say, dame's been calling you for the last hour and a half. Like to busted the phone. Makes me sick."

"Aw, Bauers."

"No, that wasn't the name. Name's Mary or Berry, or something like that. A dozen times, I betcha. Says you was to call her as soon as you come in. Drexel 47—wait a min't'—yeh—that's right—Drexel 473—"

"Swell chanst," said Nick. Suddenly his buoyancy was gone. His shoulders drooped. His cigarette dangled limp. Disappointment curved his lips, burdened his eyes. "*Swell* chanst!"

About Katherine Mansfield

Katherine Mansfield Beauchamp was born to a socially prominent family in Wellington, New Zealand, in 1888. Her pen name was Katherine Mansfield. Her father sent her to London at age 15 to study the cello. There she met D. H. Lawrence and Virginia Woolf and decided that writing would be her career. Her many short stories established her as a prominent modernist writer. Contracting tuberculosis in 1918, she sought treatments in France and died there in 1923, age 34.

The Garden-Party

And after all the weather was ideal. They could not have had a more perfect day for a garden-party if they had ordered it. Windless, warm, the sky without a cloud. Only the blue was veiled with a haze of light gold, as it is sometimes in early summer. The gardener had been up since dawn, mowing the lawns and sweeping them, until the grass and the dark flat rosettes where the daisy plants had been seemed to shine. As for the roses, you could not help feeling they understood that roses are the only flowers that impress people at garden-parties; the only flowers that everybody is certain of knowing. Hundreds, yes, literally hundreds, had come out in a single night; the green bushes bowed down as though they had been visited by archangels.

Breakfast was not yet over before the men came to put up the marquee.

"Where do you want the marquee put, Mother?"

"My dear child, it's no use asking me. I'm determined to leave everything to you children this year. Forget I am your mother. Treat me as an honoured guest."

But Meg could not possibly go and supervise the men. She had washed her hair before breakfast, and she sat drinking her coffee in a green turban, with a dark wet curl stamped on each cheek. Jose, the butterfly, always came down in a silk petticoat and kimono jacket.

"You'll have to go, Laura; you're the artistic one."

Away Laura flew, still holding her piece of bread-and-butter. It's so delicious to have an excuse for eating out of doors, and besides, she loved having to arrange things; she always felt she could do it so much better than anybody else.

Four men in their shirt-sleeves stood grouped together on the garden path. They carried staves covered with rolls of canvas, and they had big tool-bags slung on their backs. They looked impressive. Laura wished now that she had not got the bread-and-butter, but there was nowhere to put it, and she couldn't possibly throw it away. She blushed and tried to look severe and even a little bit short-sighted as she came up to them.

"Good morning," she said, copying her mother's voice. But that sounded so fearfully affected that she was ashamed, and stammered like a little girl, "Oh—er—have you come—is it about the marquee?"

"That's right, miss," said the tallest of the men, a lanky, freckled fellow, and he shifted his tool-bag, knocked back his straw hat, and smiled down at her. "That's about it."

His smile was so easy, so friendly that Laura recovered. What nice eyes he had, small, but such a dark blue! And now she looked at the others, they were smiling too. "Cheer up, we won't bite," their smile seemed to say. How very nice workmen were! And what a beautiful morning! She mustn't mention the morning; she must be businesslike. The marquee.

"Well, what about the lily-lawn? Would that do?"

And she pointed to the lily-lawn with the hand that didn't hold the bread-and-butter. They turned, they stared in the direction. A little fat chap thrust out his under-lip, and the tall fellow frowned.

"I don't fancy it," said he. "Not conspicuous enough. You see with a thing like a marquee," and he turned to Laura in his easy way, "you want to put it somewhere where it'll give you a bang slap in the eye, if you follow me."

Laura's upbringing made her wonder for a moment whether it was quite respectful of a workman to talk to her of bangs slap in the eye. But she did quite follow him.

"A corner of the tennis-court," she suggested. "But the band's going to be in one corner."

"H'm, going to have a band, are you?" said another of the workmen. He was pale. He had a haggard look as his dark eyes scanned the tennis-court. What was he thinking?

"Only a very small band," said Laura gently. Perhaps he wouldn't mind so much if the band was quite small. But the tall fellow interrupted.

"Look here, miss, that's the place. Against those trees. Over there. That'll do fine."

Against the karakas.* Then the karaka-trees would be hidden. And they were so lovely, with their broad, gleaming leaves, and their clusters of yellow fruit. They were like trees you imagined growing on a desert island, proud, solitary, lifting their leaves and fruits to the sun in a kind of silent splendour. Must they be hidden by a marquee?

---

* An evergreen tree with large glossy leaves.

They must. Already the men had shouldered their staves and were making for the place. Only the tall fellow was left. He bent down, pinched a spring of lavender, put his thumb and forefinger to his nose and snuffed up the smell. When Laura saw that gesture she forgot all about the karakas in her wonder at him caring for things like that—caring for the smell of lavender. How many men that she knew would have done such a thing? Oh, how extraordinarily nice workmen were, she thought. Why couldn't she have workmen for friends rather than the silly boys she danced with and who came to Sunday night supper? She would get on much better with men like these.

It's all the fault, she decided, as the tall fellow drew something on the back of an envelope, something that was to be looped up or left to hang, of these absurd class distinctions. Well, for her part, she didn't feel them. Not a bit, not an atom. . . . And now there came the chock-chock of wooden hammers. Some one whistled, some one sang out, "Are you right there, matey?" "Matey!" The friendliness of it, the—the—Just to prove how happy she was, just to show the tall fellow how at home she felt, and how she despised stupid conventions. Laura took a big bite of her bread-and-butter as she stared at the little drawing. She felt just like a work-girl.

"Laura, Laura, where are you? Telephone, Laura!" a voice cried from the house.

"Coming!" Away she skimmed, over the lawn, up the path, up the steps, across the veranda, and into the porch. In the hall her father and Laurie were brushing their hats ready to go to the office.

"I say, Laura," said Laurie very fast, "you might just give a squiz* at my coat before this afternoon. See if it wants pressing."

* Australian slang, meaning a quick, close look.

"I will," said she. Suddenly she couldn't stop herself. She ran at Laurie and gave him a small, quick squeeze. "Oh, I do love parties, don't you?" gasped Laura.

"Ra-ther," said Laurie's warm, boyish voice, and he squeezed his sister too, and gave her a gentle push. "Dash off to the telephone, old girl."

The telephone. "Yes, yes; oh yes. Kitty? Good morning, dear. Come to lunch? Do, dear. Delighted of course. It will only be a very scratch meal—just the sandwich crusts and broken meringue-shells and what's left over. Yes, isn't it a perfect morning? Your white? Oh, I certainly should. One moment—hold the line. Mother's calling." And Laura sat back. "What, mother? Can't hear."

Mrs. Sheridan's voice floated down the stairs. "Tell her to wear that sweet hat she had on last Sunday."

"Mother says you're to wear that *sweet* hat you had on last Sunday. Good. One o'clock. Bye-bye."

Laura put back the receiver, flung her arms over her head, took a deep breath, stretched, and let them fall. "Huh," she sighed, and the moment after the sigh she sat up quickly. She was still, listening. All the doors in the house seemed to be open. The house was alive with soft, quick steps and running voices. The green baize door that led to the kitchen regions swung open and shut with a muffled thud. And now there came a long, chuckling absurd sound. It was the heavy piano being moved on its stiff castors. But the air! If you stopped to notice, was the air always like this? Little faint winds were playing chase, in at the tops of the windows, out at the doors. And there were two tiny spots of sun, one on the inkpot, one on a silver photograph frame, playing too. Darling little spots. Especially the one on the inkpot lid. It was quite warm. A warm little silver star. She could have kissed it.

The front door bell pealed, and there sounded the rustle of Sadie's print skirt on the stairs. A man's voice murmured; Sadie answered, careless, "I'm sure I don't know. Wait. I'll ask Mrs. Sheridan."

"What is it, Sadie?" Laura came into the hall.

"It's the florist, Miss Laura."

It was, indeed. There, just inside the door, stood a wide, shallow tray full of pots of pink lilies. No other kind. Nothing but lilies—canna lilies, big pink flowers, wide open, radiant, almost frighteningly alive on bright crimson stems.

"O-oh, Sadie!" said Laura, and the sound was like a little moan. She crouched down as if to warm herself at the blaze of lilies; she felt they were in her fingers, on her lips, growing in her breast.

"It's some mistake," she said faintly. "Nobody ever ordered so many. Sadie, go and find mother."

But at that moment Mrs. Sheridan joined them.

"It's quite right," she said calmly. "Yes, I ordered them. Aren't they lovely?" She pressed Laura's arm. "I was passing the shop yesterday, and I saw them in the window. And I suddenly thought for once in my life I shall have enough canna lilies. The garden-party will be a good excuse."

"But I thought you said you didn't mean to interfere," said Laura. Sadie had gone. The florist's man was still outside at his van. She put her arm round her mother's neck and gently, very gently she bit her mother's ear.

"My darling child, you wouldn't like a logical mother, would you? Don't do that. Here's the man."

He carried more lilies still, another whole tray.

"Bank them up, just inside the door, on both sides of the porch, please," said Mrs. Sheridan. "Don't you agree, Laura?"

"Oh, I *do* mother."

In the drawing-room Meg, Jose, and good little Hans had at last succeeded in moving the piano.

"Now, if we put this chesterfield against the wall and move everything out of the room except the chairs, don't you think?"

"Quite."

"Hans, move these tables into the smoking-room, and bring a sweeper to take these marks off the carpet and—one moment, Hans—" Jose loved giving orders to the servants, and they loved obeying her. She always made them feel they were taking part in some drama. "Tell mother and Miss Laura to come here at once."

"Very good, Miss Jose."

She turned to Meg. "I want to hear what the piano sounds like, just in case I'm asked to sing this afternoon. Lets try over 'This life is Weary.'"

Pom! Ta-ta-ta *Tee*-ta! The piano burst out so passionately that Jose's face changed. She clasped her hands. She looked mournfully and enigmatically at her mother and Laura as they came in.

> This Life is *Wee*-ary,
> A Tear—a Sigh.
> A Love that *Chan*-ges,
>   This Life is *Wee*-ary,
> A tear—a Sigh.
> A Love that *Chan*-ges,
> And then . . . Good-bye!

But at the word "Good-bye," and although the piano sounded more desperate than ever, her face broke into a brilliant dreadfully unsympathetic smile.

"Aren't I in a good voice, mummy?" she beamed.

> This Life is *Wee*-ary,
> Hope comes to Die.
> A Dream—a *Wa*-kening.

But now Sadie interrupted them. "What is it, Sadie?"

"If you please, m'm, cook says have you got the flags for the sandwiches?"

"The flags for the sandwiches, Sadie?" echoed Mrs. Sheridan dreamily. And the children knew by her face that she hadn't got them. "Let me see." And she said to Sadie firmly, "Tell cook I'll let her have them in ten minutes."

Sadie went.

"Now, Laura," said her mother quickly. "Come with me into the smoking-room. I've got the names somewhere on the back of an envelope. You'll have to write them out for me. Meg, go upstairs this minute and take that wet thing off your head. Jose, run and finish dressing this instant. Do you hear me, children, or shall I have to tell your father when he comes home to-night? And—and, Jose pacify cook if you do go into the kitchen, will you? I'm terrified of her this morning."

The envelope was found at last behind the dining-room clock, though how it had got there Mrs. Sheridan could not imagine.

"One of you children must have stolen it out of my bag, because I remember vividly—cream cheese and lemon-curd. Have you done that?"

"Yes,"

"Egg and—" Mrs. Sheridan held the envelope away from her. "It looks like mice. It can't be mice, can it?"

"Olive, pet," said Laura, looking over her shoulder.

"Yes, of course, olive. What a horrible combination it sounds. Egg and olive."

They were finished at last, and Laura took them off to the kitchen. She found Jose there pacifying the cook, who did not look at all terrifying.

"I have never seen such exquisite sandwiches," said Jose's rapturous voice. "How many kinds did you say there were, cook? Fifteen?"

"Fifteen, Miss Jose."

"Well, cook, I congratulate you."

Cook swept up crusts with the long sandwich knife, and smiled broadly.

"Godber's has come," announced Sadie, issuing out of the pantry. She had seen the man pass the window.

That meant the cream puffs had come. Godber's were famous for their cream puffs. Nobody ever thought of making them at home.

"Bring them in and put them on the table, my girl," ordered cook.

Sadie brought them in and went back to the door. Of course Laura and Jose were far too grown-up to really care about such things. All the same, they couldn't help agreeing that the puffs looked very attractive. Very. Cook began arranging them, shaking off the extra icing sugar.

"Don't they carry one back to all one's parties?" said Laura.

"I suppose they do," said practical Jose, who never liked to be carried back. "They look beautifully light and feathery, I must say."

"Have one each, my dears," said cook in her comfortable voice. "Yer ma won't know."

Oh, impossible. Fancy cream puffs so soon after breakfast. The very idea made one shudder. All the same, two minutes later Jose and Laura were licking their fingers with that absorbed inward look that only comes from whipped cream.

"Let's go into the garden, out by the back way," suggested Laura. "I want to see how the men are getting on with the marquee. They're such awfully nice men."

But the back door was blocked by cook, Sadie, Godber's man, and Hans.

Something had happened.

"Tuk-tuk-tuk," clucked cook like an agitated hen. Sadie had her hand clapped to her cheek as though she had toothache. Hans's face was screwed up in the effort to understand. Only Godber's man seemed to be enjoying himself; it was his story.

"What's the matter? What's happened?"

"There's been a horrible accident," said Cook. "A man killed."

"A man killed! Where? How? When?"

But Godber's man wasn't going to have his story snatched from under his very nose.

"Know those little cottages just below here, miss?" Know them? Of course, she knew them. "Well, there's a young chap living there, name of Scott, a carter. His horse shied at a traction-engine, corner of Hawke Street this morning; and he was thrown out on the back of his head. Killed."

"Dead!" Laura stared at Godber's man.

"Dead when they picked him up," said Godber's man with relish. "They were taking the body home as I come up here." And he said to the cook, "He's left a wife and five little ones."

"Jose, come here." Laura caught hold of her sister's sleeve and dragged her through the kitchen to the other side of the green baize door. There she paused and leaned against it. "Jose!" she said, horrified, "however are we going to stop everything?"

"Stop everything, Laura!" cried Jose in astonishment. "What do you mean?"

"Stop the garden-party, of course." Why did Jose pretend?

But Jose was still more amazed. "Stop the garden-party? My dear Laura, don't be so absurd. Of course we can't do anything of the kind. Nobody expects us to. Don't be so extravagant."

"But we can't possibly have a garden-party with a man dead just outside the front gate."

That really was extravagant, for the little cottages were in a lane to themselves at the very bottom of a steep rise that led up to the house. A broad road ran between. True, they were far too near. They were the greatest possible eyesore, and they had no right to be in that neighbourhood at all. They were little mean dwellings painted a chocolate brown. In the garden patches there were nothing but cabbage stalks, sick hens, and tomato cans. The very smoke coming out of their chimneys was poverty-stricken. Little rags and shreds of smoke so unlike the great silvery plumes that uncurled from the Sheridans' chimneys. Washerwomen lived in the lane and sweeps and a cobbler, and a man whose house-front was studded all over with minute bird-cages. Children swarmed. When the Sheridans were little they were forbidden to set foot there because of the revolting language and of what they might catch. But since they were grown up, Laura and Laurie on their prowls sometimes walked through. It was disgusting and sordid. They came out with a shudder. But still one must go everywhere; one must see everything. So through they went.

"And just think of what the band would sound like to that poor woman," said Laura.

"Oh, Laura!" Jose began to be seriously annoyed. "If you're going to stop a band playing every time some one has an accident, you'll lead a very strenuous life. I'm every bit as sorry about it as you. I feel just as sympathetic." Her eyes hardened. She looked at her sister just as she used to when they were little and fighting together. "You won't bring a drunken workman back to life by being sentimental," she said softly.

"Drunk! Who said he was drunk?" Laura turned furiously on Jose. She said, just as they had used to say on those occasions, "I'm going straight up to tell mother."

"Do, dear," cooed Jose.

"Mother, can I come into your room?" Laura turned the big glass door-knob.

"Of course, child. Why, what's the matter? What's given you such a colour?" And Mrs. Sheridan turned round from her dressing-table. She was trying on a new hat.

"Mother, a man's been killed," began Laura.

"*Not* in the garden?" interrupted her mother.

"No, no!"

"Oh, what a fright you gave me!" Mrs. Sheridan sighed with relief, and took off the big hat and held it on her knees.

"But listen, mother," said Laura. Breathless, half-choking, she told the dreadful story. "Of course, we can't have our party, can we?" she pleaded. "The band and everybody arriving. They'd hear us, mother, they're nearly neighbours!"

To Laura's astonishment her mother behaved just like Jose, it was harder to bear because she seemed amused. She refused to take Laura seriously.

"But, my dear child, use your common sense. It's only by accident we've heard of it. If some one had died there normally—and I can't understand how they keep alive in those poky little holes—we should still be having our party, shouldn't we?"

Laura had to say "yes" to that, but she felt it was all wrong. She sat down on her mother's sofa and pinched the cushion frill.

"Mother, isn't it really terribly heartless of us?" she asked.

"Darling!" Mrs. Sheridan got up and came over to her, carrying the hat. Before Laura could stop her she had popped it on. "My child!" said her mother, "that hat is yours. It's made for you. It's much too young for me. I have never seen you look such a picture. Look at yourself!" And she held up her hand-mirror.

"But, mother," Laura began again. She couldn't look at herself; she turned aside.

This time Mrs. Sheridan lost patience just as Jose had done.

"You are being very absurd, Laura," she said coldly. "People like that don't expect sacrifices from us. And it's not very sympathetic to spoil everybody's enjoyment as you're doing now."

"I don't understand," said Laura, and she walked quickly out of the room into her own bedroom. There, quite by chance, the first thing she saw was this charming girl in the mirror, in her black hat trimmed with gold daisies, and a long black velvet ribbon. Never had she imagined she could look like that. Is mother right? she thought. And now she hoped her mother was right. Am I being extravagant? Perhaps it was extravagant. Just for a moment she had another glimpse of that poor woman and those little children, and the body being carried into the house. But it all seemed blurred, unreal, like a picture in the newspaper. I'll remember it again after the party's over, she decided. And somehow that seemed quite the best plan. . . .

Lunch was over by half-past one. By half-past two they were all ready for the fray. The green-coated band had arrived and was established in a corner of the tennis-court.

"My dear!" trilled Kitty Maitland, "aren't they too like frogs for words? You ought to have arranged them round the pond with the conductor in the middle on a leaf."

Laurie arrived and hailed them on his way to dress. At the sight of him Laura remembered the accident again. She wanted to tell him. If Laurie agreed with the others, then it was bound to be all right. And she followed him into the hall.

"Laurie!"

"Hallo!" He was half-way upstairs, but when he turned round and saw Laura he suddenly puffed out his cheeks and goggled his eyes at her. "My word, Laura; You do look stunning," said Laurie. "What an absolutely topping hat!"

Laura said faintly "Is it?" and smiled up at Laurie, and didn't tell him after all.

Soon after that people began coming in streams. The band struck up; the hired waiters ran from the house to the marquee. Wherever you looked there were couples strolling, bending to the flowers, greeting, moving on over the lawn. They were like bright birds that had alighted in the Sheridans' garden for this one afternoon, on their way to—where? Ah, what happiness it is to be with people who all are happy, to press hands, press cheeks, smile into eyes.

"Darling Laura, how well you look!"

"What a becoming hat, child!"

"Laura, you look quite Spanish. I've never seen you look so striking."

And Laura, glowing, answered softly, "Have you had tea? Won't you have an ice? The passion-fruit ices really are rather special." She ran to her father and begged him. "Daddy darling, can't the band have something to drink?"

And the perfect afternoon slowly ripened, slowly faded, slowly its petals closed.

"Never a more delightful garden-party . . ." "The greatest success . . ." "Quite the most . . ."

Laura helped her mother with the good-byes. They stood side by side in the porch till it was all over.

"All over, all over, thank heaven," Mrs. Sheridan. "Round up the others, Laura. Let's go and have some fresh coffee. I'm exhausted. Yes, it's been very successful. But oh, these parties, these parties! Why will you children insist on giving parties!" And they all of them sat down in the deserted marquee.

"Have a sandwich, daddy dear. I wrote the flag."

"Thanks." Mr. Sheridan took a bite and the sandwich was gone. He took another. "I suppose you didn't hear of a beastly accident that happened to-day?" he said.

"My dear," said Mrs. Sheridan, holding up her hand, "we did. It nearly ruined the party. Laura insisted we should put it off."

"Oh mother!" Laura didn't want to be teased about it.

"It was a horrible affair all the same," said Mr. Sheridan. "The chap was married too. Lived just below in the lane, and leaves a wife and half a dozen kiddies, so they say."

An awkward little silence fell. Mrs. Sheridan fidgeted with her cup. Really, it was very tactless of father . . .

Suddenly she looked up. There on the table were all those sandwiches, cakes, puffs, all uneaten, all going to be wasted. She had one of her brilliant ideas.

"I know," she said. "Let's make up a basket. Let's send that poor creature some of this perfectly good food. At any rate, it will be the greatest treat for the children. Don't you agree? And she's sure to have neighbours calling in and so on. What a point to have it all ready prepared. Laura!" She jumped up. "Get me the big basket out of the stairs cupboard."

"But, mother, do you really think it's a good idea?" said Laura.

Again, how curious, she seemed to be different from them all. To take scraps from their party. Would the poor woman really like that?

"Of course!" What's the matter with you to-day? An hour or two ago you were insisting on us being sympathetic, and now—"

Oh, well! Laura ran for the basket. It was filled, it was heaped by her mother.

"Take it yourself, darling," said she. "Run down just as you are. No, wait, take the arum lilies too. People of that class are so impressed by arum lilies."

"The stems will ruin her lace frock," said practical Jose.

So they would. Just in time. "Only the basket, then. And, Laura!"— her mother followed her out of the marquee—"don't on any account—"

"What, mother?"

No, better not push such ideas into the child's head! "Nothing! Run along."

It was just growing dusky as Laura shut their garden gates. A big dog ran by like a shadow. The road gleamed white, and down below in the hollow the little cottages were in deep shade. How quiet it seemed after the afternoon. Here she was going down the hill to somewhere where a man lay dead, and she couldn't realize it. Why couldn't she? She stopped a minute. And it seemed to her that kisses, voices, tinkling spoons, laughter, the smell of crushed grass were somehow inside her. She had no room for anything else. How strange! She looked up at the pale sky, and all she thought was, "Yes, it was the most successful party."

Now the broad road was crossed. The lane began, smoky and dark. Women in shawls and men's tweed caps hurried by. Men hung over the palings; the children played in the doorways. A low hum came from the mean little cottages. In some of them there was a flicker of light, and a shadow, crab-like, moved across the window. Laura bent her head and hurried on. She wished now she had put on a coat. How her frock shone! And the big hat with the velvet streamer—if only it was another hat! Were the people looking at her! They must be. It was a mistake to have come; she knew all along it was a mistake. Should she go back even now?

No, too late. This was the house. It must be. A dark knot of people stood outside. Beside the gate an old, old woman with a crutch sat in a chair, watching. She had her feet on a newspaper. The voices stopped as Laura drew near. The group parted. It was as though she was expected, as though they had known she was coming here.

Laura was terribly nervous. Tossing the velvet ribbon over her shoulder, she said to a woman standing by, "Is this Mrs. Scott's house?" and the woman, smiling queerly, said, "It is, my lass."

Oh, to be away from this! She actually said, "Help me, God," as she walked up the tiny path and knocked. To be away from those staring eyes, or to be covered up in anything, one of those women's shawls even. I'll just leave the basket and go, she decided. I shan't even wait for it to be emptied.

Then the door opened. A little woman in black showed in the gloom.

Laura said, "Are you Mrs. Scott?" But to her horror the woman answered, "Walk in please, miss," and she was shut in the passage.

"No," said Laura, "I don't want to come in. I only want to leave this basket. Mother sent—"

The little woman in the gloomy passage seemed not to have heard her. "Step this way, please, miss," she said in an oily voice, and Laura followed her.

She found herself in a wretched little low kitchen, lighted by a smoky lamp. There was a woman sitting before the fire.

"Em," said the little creature who had let her in. "Em! It's a young lady." She turned to Laura. She said meaningly, "I'm 'er sister, Miss. You'll excuse 'er, won't you?"

"Oh, but of course!" said Laura. "Please, please don't disturb her. I—I only want to leave—"

But at that moment the woman at the fire turned round. Her face, puffed up, red, with swollen eyes and swollen lips, looked terrible. She seemed as though she couldn't understand why Laura was there. What did it mean? Why was this stranger standing in the kitchen with a basket? What was it all about? And the poor face puckered up again.

"All right, my dear," said the other. "I'll thenk the young lady."

And again she began, "You'll excuse her, miss, I'm sure," and her face, swollen too, tried an oily smile.

Laura only wanted to get out, to get away. She was back in the passage. The door opened. She walked straight through into the bedroom, where the dead man was lying.

"You'd like a look at 'im, wouldn't you?" said Em's sister, and she brushed past Laura over to the bed. "Don't be afraid, my lass,"—and now her voice sounded fond and sly, and fondly she drew down the sheet— "'e looks a picture. There's nothing to show. Come along my dear."

Laura came.

There lay a young man, fast asleep—sleeping so soundly, so deeply, that he was far, far away from them both. Oh, so remote, so peaceful. He was dreaming. Never wake him up again. His head was sunk in the pillow, his eyes were closed; they were blind under the closed eyelids. He was given up to his dream. What did garden-parties and baskets and lace frocks matter to him? He was far from all those things. He was wonderful, beautiful. While they were laughing and while the band was playing, this marvel had come to the lane. Happy . . . happy . . . All is well, said the sleeping face. This is just as it should be. I am content.

But all the same you had to cry, and she couldn't go out of the room without saying something to him. Laura gave a loud childish sob.

"Forgive my hat," she said.

And this time she didn't wait for Em's sister. She found her way out of the door, down the path, past all those dark people. At the corner of the lane she met Laurie.

He stepped out of the shadow. "Is that you, Laura?"

"Yes."

"Mother was getting anxious. Was it all right?"

"Yes, quite. Oh, Laurie!" She took his arm, she pressed up against him.

"I say, you're not crying, are you?" asked her brother.

Laura shook her head. She was.

Laurie put his arm round her shoulder. "Don't cry," he said in his warm, loving voice. "Was it awful?"

"No," sobbed Laura. "It was simply marvellous. But, Laurie—" She stopped, she looked at her brother. "Isn't life," she stammered, "isn't life—" But what life was she couldn't explain. No matter. He quite understood.

"*Isn't* it, darling?" said Laurie.

About F. Scott Fitzgerald

Francis Scott Key Fitzgerald, named for his famous second cousin thrice removed, was born in St. Paul, Minnesota, in 1896. He entered Princeton University at age 17, dedicating himself to a writing career. Fitzgerald wrote countless short stories and acclaimed novels that established him as one of America's greatest writers and chronicler of 'The Jazz Age' of the 1920's. Later, financial strain and alcoholism brought on a heart attack and death in 1940 at age 44. Recognition of his literary greatness came after his death.

The Diamond as Big as the Ritz

John T. Unger came from a family that had been well known in Hades—a small town on the Mississippi River—for several generations. John's father had held the amateur golf championship through many a heated contest; Mrs. Unger was known "from hot-box to hot-bed" as the local phrase went, for her political addresses; and young John T. Unger, who had just turned sixteen, had danced all the latest dances from New York before he put on long trousers. And now, for a certain time, he was to be away from home. That respect for a New England education which is the bane of all provincial places, which drains them yearly of their most promising young men, had seized upon his parents. Nothing would suit them but that he should go to St. Midas' School near Boston—Hades was too small to hold their darling and gifted son.

Now in Hades—as you know if you ever have been there—the names of the more fashionable preparatory schools and colleges mean very little. The inhabitants have been so long out of the world that, though they make a show of keeping up to date in dress and manners and literature, they depend to a great extent on hearsay, and a function that in Hades would be considered elaborate would doubtless be hailed by a Chicago beef-princess as "perhaps a little tacky."

John T. Unger was on the eve of departure. Mrs. Unger, with maternal fatuity, packed his trunks full of linen suits and electric fans, and Mr. Unger presented his son with an asbestos pocket-book stuffed with money.

"Remember, you are always welcome here," he said. "You can be sure, boy, that we'll keep the home fires burning."

"I know," answered John huskily.

"Don't forget who you are and where you come from," continued his father proudly, "and you can do nothing to harm you. You are an Unger—from Hades."

So the old man and the young shook hands and John walked away with tears streaming from his eyes. Ten minutes later he had passed outside the city limits, and he stopped to glance back for the last time. Over the gates the old-fashioned Victorian motto seemed strangely attractive to him. His father had tried time and time again to have it changed to something with a little more push and verve about it, such as "Hades—Your Opportunity," or else a plain "Welcome" sign set over a hearty handshake pricked out in electric lights. The old motto was a little depressing, Mr. Unger had thought—but now . . .

St. Midas' School is half an hour from Boston in a Rolls-Pierce motor-car. The actual distance will never be known, for no one, except John T. Unger, had ever arrived there save in a Rolls-Pierce and probably no one ever will again. St. Midas' is the most expensive and the most exclusive boys' preparatory school in the world.

John's first two years there passed pleasantly. The fathers of all the boys were money-kings and John spent his summers visiting at fashionable resorts. While he was very fond of all the boys he visited, their fathers struck him as being much of a piece, and in his boyish way he often wondered at their exceeding sameness. When he told them where his home was they would ask jovially, "Pretty hot down there?" and John would muster a faint smile and answer, "It certainly is." His response would have been heartier had they not all made this joke—at best varying it with, "Is it hot enough for you down there?" which he hated just as much.

In the middle of his second year at school, a quiet, handsome boy named Percy Washington had been put in John's form. The newcomer was pleasant in his manner and exceedingly well dressed even for St. Midas', but for some reason he kept aloof from the other boys. The only person with whom he was intimate was John T. Unger, but even to John he was entirely uncommunicative concerning his home or his family. That he was wealthy went without saying, but beyond a few such deductions John knew little of his friend, so it promised rich confectionery for his curiosity when Percy invited him to spend the summer at his home "in the West." He accepted, without hesitation.

It was only when they were in the train that Percy became, for the first time, rather communicative. One day while they were eating lunch in the dining-car and discussing the imperfect characters of several of the boys at school, Percy suddenly changed his tone and made an abrupt remark.

"My father," he said, "is by far the richest man in the world."

"Oh," said John, politely. He could think of no answer to make to this confidence. He considered "That's very nice," but it sounded hollow and was on the point of saying, "Really?" but refrained since it would seem to question Percy's statement. And such an astounding statement could scarcely be questioned.

"By far the richest," repeated Percy.

"I was reading in the *World Almanac*," began John, " that there was one man in America with an income of over five million a year and four men with incomes of over three million a year, and—"

"Oh, they're nothing," Percy's mouth was a half-moon of scorn. "Catchpenny capitalists, financial small-fry, petty merchants and money-lenders. My father could buy them out and not know he'd done it."

"But how does he—"

"Why haven't they put down *his* income tax? Because he doesn't pay any. At least he pays a little one—but he doesn't pay any on his *real* income."

"He must be very rich," said John simply. "I'm glad. I like very rich people.

"The richer a fella is, the better I like him." There was a look of passionate frankness upon his dark face. "I visited the Schnlitzer-Murphys last Easter. Vivian Schnlitzer-Murphy had rubies as big as hen's eggs, and sapphires that were like globes with lights inside them—"

"I love jewels," agreed Percy enthusiastically. "Of course I wouldn't want any one at school to know about it, but I've got quite a collection myself. I used to collect them instead of stamps."

"And diamonds," continued John eagerly. "The Schnlitzer-Murphys had diamonds as big as walnuts—"

"That's nothing." Percy had leaned forward and dropped his voice to a low whisper. "That's nothing at all. My father has a diamond bigger than the Ritz-Carlton Hotel."

II

The Montana sunset lay between two mountains like a gigantic bruise from which dark arteries spread themselves over a poisoned sky. An immense distance under the sky crouched the village of Fish, minute, dismal, and forgotten. There were twelve men, so it was said, in the village of Fish, twelve sombre and inexplicable souls who sucked a lean milk from the almost literally bare rock upon which a mysterious populatory force had begotten them. They had become a race apart, these twelve men of Fish, like some species developed by an early whim of nature, which on second thought had abandoned them to struggle and extermination.

Out of the blue-black bruise in the distance crept a long line of moving lights upon the desolation of the land, and the twelve men of Fish gathered like ghosts at the shanty depot to watch the passing of the seven o'clock train, the Transcontinental Express from Chicago. Six times or so a year the Transcontinental Express, through some inconceivable jurisdiction, stopped at the village of Fish, and when this occurred a figure or so would disembark, mount into a buggy that always appeared from out of the dusk, and drive off toward the bruised sunset. The observation of this pointless and preposterous phenomenon had become a sort of cult among the men of Fish. To observe, that was all; there remained in them none of the vital quality of illusion which would make them wonder or speculate, else a religion might have grown up around these mysterious visitations. But the men of Fish were beyond all religion—the barest and most savage tenets of even Christianity could gain no foothold on that barren rock—so there was no altar, no priest, no sacrifice; only each night at seven the silent concourse by the shanty depot, a congregation who lifted up a prayer of dim, anaemic wonder.

On this June night, the Great Brakeman, whom, had they deified any one, they might well have chosen as their celestial protagonist, had ordained that the seven o'clock train should leave its human (or inhuman) deposit at Fish. At two minutes after seven Percy Washington and John T. Unger disembarked, hurried past the spellbound, the agape, the fearsome eyes of the twelve men of Fish, mounted into a buggy which had obviously appeared from nowhere, and drove away.

After half an hour, when the twilight had coagulated into dark, the silent negro who was driving the buggy hailed an opaque body somewhere ahead of them in the gloom. In response to his cry, it turned upon them a luminous disk which regarded them like a malignant eye out of the unfathomable night. As they came closer, John saw that it was the taillight of an immense automobile, larger and more magnificent than any he had ever seen. Its body was of gleaming metal richer than nickel and lighter than silver, and the hubs of the wheels were studded with iridescent geometric figures of green and yellow—John did not dare to guess whether they were glass or jewel.

Two negroes, dressed in glittering livery such as one sees in pictures of royal processions in London, were standing at attention beside the car and as the two young men dismounted from the buggy they were greeted in some language which the guest could not understand, but which seemed to be an extreme form of the Southern negro's dialect.

"Get in," said Percy to his friend, as their trunks were tossed to the ebony roof of the limousine. "Sorry we had to bring you this far in that buggy, but of course it wouldn't do for the people on the train or those Godforsaken fellas in Fish to see this automobile."

"Gosh! What a car!" This ejaculation was provoked by its interior. John saw that the upholstery consisted of a thousand minute and exquisite tapestries of silk, woven with jewels and embroideries, and set upon a background of cloth of gold. The two armchair seats in which the boys luxuriated were covered with stuff that resembled duvetyn, but seemed woven in numberless colors of the ends of ostrich feathers.

"What a car!" cried John again, in amazement.

"This thing?" Percy laughed. "Why, it's just an old junk we use for a station wagon."

By this time they were gliding along through the darkness toward the break between the two mountains.

"We'll be there in an hour and a half," said Percy, looking at the clock. "I may as well tell you it's not going to be like anything you ever saw before."

If the car was any indication of what John would see, he was prepared to be astonished indeed. The simple piety prevalent in Hades has the earnest worship of and respect for riches as the first article of its creed—had John felt otherwise than radiantly humble before them, his parents would have turned away in horror at the blasphemy.

They had now reached and were entering the break between the two mountains and almost immediately the way became much rougher.

"If the moon shone down here, you'd see that we're in a big gulch," said Percy, trying to peer out of the window. He spoke a few words into the mouthpiece and immediately the footman turned on a searchlight and swept the hillsides with an immense beam.

"Rocky, you see. An ordinary car would be knocked to pieces in half an hour. In fact, it'd take a tank to navigate it unless you knew the way. You notice we're going uphill now."

They were obviously ascending, and within a few minutes the car was crossing a high rise, where they caught a glimpse of a pale moon newly risen in the distance. The car stopped suddenly and several figures took shape out of the dark beside it—these were negroes also. Again the two young men were saluted in the same dimly recognizable dialect; then the negroes set to work and four immense cables dangling from overhead were attached with hooks to the hubs of the great jeweled wheels. At a resounding "Hey-yahl" John felt the car being lifted slowly from the ground—up and up—clear of the tallest rocks on both sides — then higher, until he could see a wavy, moonlit valley stretched out before him in sharp contrast to the quagmire of rocks that they had just left. Only on one side was there still rock—and then suddenly there was no rock beside them or anywhere around.

It was apparent that they had surmounted some immense knife-blade of stone, projecting perpendicularly into the air. In a moment they were going down again, and finally with a soft bump they were landed upon the smooth earth.

"The worst is over," said Percy, squinting out the window. "It's only five miles from here, and our own road—tapestry brick—all the way. This belongs to us. This is where the United States ends, father says."

"Are we in Canada?"

"We are not. We're in the middle of the Montana Rockies. But you are now on the only five square miles of land in the country that's never been surveyed."

"Why hasn't it? Did they forget it?"

"No," said Percy, grinning, "they tried to do it three times. The first time my grandfather corrupted a whole department of the State survey; the second time he had the official maps of the United States tinkered with—that held them for fifteen years. The last time was harder. My father fixed it so that their compasses were in the strongest magnetic field ever artificially set up. He had a whole set of surveying instruments made with a slight defection that would allow for this territory not to appear, and he substituted them for the ones that were to be used. Then he had a river deflected and he had what looked like a village built up on its banks—so that they'd see it, and think it was a town ten miles farther up the valley. There's only one thing my father's afraid of," he concluded, "only one thing in the world that could be used to find us out."

"What's that?"

Percy sank his voice to a whisper.

"Aeroplanes," he breathed. "We've got half a dozen anti-aircraft guns and we've arranged it so far—but there've been a few deaths and a great many prisoners. Not that we mind *that*, you know, father and I, but it upsets mother and the girls, and there's always the chance that some time we won't be able to arrange it."

Shreds and tatters of chinchilla, courtesy clouds in the green moon's heaven, were passing the green moon like precious Eastern stuffs paraded for the inspection of some Tartar khan. It seemed to John that it was day, and that he was looking at some lads sailing above him in the air, showering down tracts and patent medicine circulars, with their messages of hope for despairing, rockbound hamlets. It seemed to him that he could see them look down out of the clouds and stare—and stare at whatever there was to stare at in this place whither he was bound—What then? Were they induced to land by some insidious device there to be immured far from patent medicines and from tracts until the judgment day—or, should they fail to fall into the trap, did a quick puff of smoke and the sharp round of a splitting shell bring them drooping to earth—and "upset" Percy's mother and sisters. John shook his head and the wraith of a hollow laugh issued silently from his parted lips. What desperate transaction lay hidden here? What a moral expedient of a bizarre Croesus? What terrible and golden mystery? . . .

The chinchilla clouds had drifted past now and outside the Montana night was bright as day. The tapestry brick of the road was smooth to the tread of the great tires as they rounded a still, moonlit lake; they passed into darkness for a moment, a pine grove, pungent and cool, then they came out into a broad avenue of lawn and John's exclamation of pleasure was simultaneous with Percy's taciturn "We're home."

Full in the light of the stars, an exquisite chateau rose from the borders of the lake, climbed in marble radiance half the height of an adjoining mountain, then melted in grace, in perfect symmetry, in translucent feminine languor, into the massed darkness of a forest of pine. The many towers, the slender tracery of the sloping parapets, the chiselled wonder of a thousand yellow windows with their oblongs and hectagons and triangles of golden light, the shattered softness of the intersecting planes of star-shine and blue shade, all trembled on John's spirit like a chord of music. On one of the towers, the tallest, the blackest at its base, an arrangement of exterior lights at the top made a sort of floating fairy-land—and as John gazed up in warm enchantment the faint acciaccare sound of violins drifted down in a rococo harmony that was like nothing he had ever heard before. Then in a moment the car stopped before wide, high marble steps around which the night air was fragrant with a host of flowers. At the top of the steps two great doors swung silently open and amber light flooded out upon the darkness, silhouetting the figure of an exquisite lady with black, high-piled hair, who held out her arms toward them.

"Mother," Percy was saying, "this is my friend, John Unger, from Hades."

Afterward John remembered that first night as a daze of many colors, of quick sensory impressions, of music soft as a voice in love, and of the beauty of things, lights and shadows, and motions and faces. There was a white-haired man who stood drinking a many-hued cordial from a crystal thimble set on a golden stem. There was a girl with a flowery face, dressed like Titania with braided sapphires in her hair. There was a room where the solid, soft gold of the walls yielded to the pressure of his hand, and a room that was like a platonic conception of the ultimate prison—ceiling, floor, and all, it was lined with an unbroken mass of diamonds, diamonds of every size and shape, until, lit with tall violet lamps in the corners, it dazzled the eyes with a whiteness that could be compared only with itself, beyond human wish or dream.

Through a maze of these rooms the two boys wandered. Sometimes the floor under their feet would flame in brilliant patterns from lighting below, patterns of barbaric dashing colors, of pastel delicacy, of sheer whiteness, or of subtle and intricate mosaic, surely from some mosque on the Adriatic Sea. Sometimes beneath layers of thick crystal he would see blue or green water swirling, inhabited by vivid fish and growths of rainbow foliage. Then they would be treading on furs of every texture and color or along corridors of palest ivory, unbroken as though carved complete from the gigantic tusks of dinosaurs extinct before the age of man . . .

Then a hazily remembered transition, and they were at dinner—where each plate was of two almost imperceptible layers of solid diamond between which was curiously worked a filigree of emerald design, a shaving sliced from green air. Music, plangent and unobtrusive, drifted down through far corridors—his chair, feathered and curved insidiously to his back, seemed to engulf and overpower him as he drank his first glass of port. He tried drowsily to answer a question that had been asked him, but the honeyed luxury that clasped his body added to the illusion of sleep—jewels, fabrics, wines, and metals blurred before his eyes into a sweet mist . . .

"Yes," he replied with a polite effort, "it certainly is hot enough for me down there."

He managed to add a ghostly laugh; then, without movement, without resistance, he seemed to float off and away, leaving an iced dessert that was pink as a dream . . . He fell asleep.

When he awoke he knew that several hours had passed. He was in a great quiet room with ebony walls and a dull illumination that was too faint, too subtle, to be called a light. His young host was standing over him.

"You fell asleep at dinner," Percy was saying. "I nearly did, too—it was such a treat to be comfortable again after this year of school. Servants undressed and bathed you while you were sleeping."

"Is this a bed or a cloud?" sighed John. "Percy, Percy — before you go, I want to apologize."

"For what?"

"For doubting you when you said you had a diamond as big as the Ritz-Carlton Hotel."

Percy smiled.

"I thought you didn't believe me. It's thata mountain, you know."

"What mountain?" "The mountain the chateau rests on. It's not very big for a mountain. But except for fifty feet of sod and gravel on top it's solid diamond. One diamond, one cubic mile without a flaw. Aren't you listening? Say—"

But John T. Unger had again fallen asleep.

III

Morning. As he awoke he perceived drowsily that the room had at the same moment become dense with sunlight. The ebony panels of one wall had slid aside on a sort of track, leaving his chamber half open to the day. A large negro in a white uniform stood beside his bed.

"Good-evening," muttered John, summoning his brains from the wild places.

"Good-morning, sir. Are you ready for your bath, sir? Oh, don't get up—I'll put you in, if you'll just unbutton your pajamas—there. Thank you, sir."

John lay quietly as his pajamas were removed—he was amused and delighted; he expected to be lifted like a child by this black Gargantua who was tending him, but nothing of the sort happened; instead he felt the bed tilt up slowly on its side—he began to roll, startled at first, in the direction of the wall, but when he reached the wall its drapery gave way, and sliding two yards farther down a fleecy incline he plumped gently into water the same temperature as his body.

He looked about him. The runway or rollway on which he had arrived had folded gently back into place. He had been projected into another chamber and was sitting in a sunken bath with his head just above the level of the floor. All about him, lining the walls of the room and the sides and bottom of the bath itself, was a blue aquarium, and gazing through the crystal surface on which he sat, he could see fish swimming among amber lights and even gliding without curiosity past his outstretched toes, which were separated from them only by the thickness of the crystal. From overhead, sunlight came down through sea-green glass.

"I suppose, sir, that you'd like hot rosewater and soapsuds this morning, sir—and perhaps cold salt water to finish."

The negro was standing beside him.

"Yes," agreed John, smiling inanely, "as you please." Any idea of ordering this bath according to his own meagre standards of living would have been priggish and not a little wicked.

The negro pressed a button and a warm rain began to fall, apparently from overhead, but really, so John discovered after a moment, from a fountain arrangement near by. The water turned to a pale rose color and jets of liquid soap spurted into it from four miniature walrus heads at the corners of the bath. In a moment a dozen little paddle-wheels, fixed to the sides, had churned the mixture into a radiant rainbow of pink foam which enveloped him softly with its delicious lightness, and burst in shining, rosy bubbles here and there about him.

"Shall I turn on the moving-picture machine, sir?" suggested the negro deferentially. "There's a good one-reel comedy in this machine to-day, or I can put in a serious piece in a moment, if you prefer it."

"No, thanks," answered John, politely but firmly. He was enjoying his bath too much to desire any distraction. But distraction came. In a moment he was listening intently to the sound of flutes from just outside, flutes dripping a melody that was like a waterfall, cool and green as the room itself, accompanying a frothy piccolo, in play more fragile than the lace of suds that covered and charmed him.

After a cold salt-water bracer and a cold fresh finish, he stepped out and into a fleecy robe, and upon a couch covered with the same material he was rubbed with oil, alcohol, and spice. Later he sat in a voluptuous chair while he was shaved and his hair was trimmed.

"Mr. Percy is waiting in your sitting-room," said the negro, when these operations were finished. "My name is Gygsum, Mr. Unger, sir. I am to see to Mr. Unger every morning."

John walked out into the brisk sunshine of his living-room, where he found breakfast waiting for him and Percy, gorgeous in white kid knickerbockers, smoking in an easy chair.

IV

This is the story of the Washington family as Percy sketched it for John during breakfast.

The father of the present Mr. Washington had been a Virginian, a direct descendant of George Washington, and Lord Baltimore. At the close of the Civil War he was a twenty-five-year-old Colonel with a played-out plantation and about a thousand dollars in gold.

Fitz-Norman Culpepper Washington, for that was the young Colonel's name, decided to present the Virginia estate to his younger brother and go West. He selected two dozen of the most faithful blacks, who, of course, worshipped him, and bought twenty-five tickets to the West, where he intended to take out land in their names and start a sheep and cattle ranch.

When he had been in Montana for less than a month and things were going very poorly indeed, he stumbled on his great discovery. He had lost his way when riding in the hills, and after a day without food he began to grow hungry. As he was without rifle, he was forced to pursue a squirrel, and in the course of the pursuit he noticed that it was carrying something shiny in its mouth. Just before it vanished into its hole—for Providence did not intend that this squirrel should alleviate his hunger—it dropped its burden. Sitting down to consider the situation Fitz-Norman's eye was caught by a gleam in the grass beside him. In ten seconds he had completely lost his appetite and gained one hundred thousand dollars. The squirrel, which had refused with annoying persistence to become food, had made him a present of a large and perfect diamond.

Late that night he found his way to camp and twelve hours later all the males among his darkies were back by the squirrel hole digging furiously at the side of the mountain. He told them he had discovered a rhinestone mine, and, as only one or two of them had ever seen a small diamond before, they believed him, without question. When the magnitude of his discovery became apparent to him, he found himself in a quandary. The mountain was *a* diamond — it was literally nothing else but solid diamond. He filled four saddle bags full of glittering samples and started on horseback for St. Paul. There he managed to dispose of half a dozen small stones—when he tried a larger one a storekeeper fainted and Fitz-Norman was arrested as a public disturber. He escaped from jail and caught the train for New York, where he sold a few medium-sized diamonds and received in exchange about two hundred thousand dollars in gold. But he did not dare to produce any exceptional gems—in fact, he left New York just in time. Tremendous excitement had been created in jewelry circles, not so much by the size of his diamonds as by their appearance in the city from mysterious sources. Wild rumors became current that a diamond mine had been discovered in the Catskills, on the Jersey coast, on Long Island, beneath Washington Square. Excursion trains, packed with men carrying picks and shovels, began to leave New York hourly, bound for various neighboring El Dorados. But by that time young Fitz-Norman was on his way back to Montana.

By the end of a fortnight he had estimated that the diamond in the mountain was approximately equal in quantity to all the rest of the diamonds known to exist in the world. There was no valuing it by any regular computation, however, for it was *one solid diamond*—and if it were offered for sale not only would the bottom fall out of the market, but also, if the value should vary with its size in the usual arithmetical progression, there would not be enough gold in the world to buy a tenth part of it. And what could any one do with a diamond that size?

It was an amazing predicament. He was, in one sense, the richest man that ever lived—and yet was he worth anything at all? If his secret should transpire there was no telling to what measures the Government might resort in order to prevent a panic, in gold as well as in jewels. They might take over the claim immediately and institute a monopoly.

There was no alternative—he must market his mountain in secret. He sent South for his younger brother and put him in charge of his colored following—darkies who had never realized that slavery was abolished. To make sure of this, he read them a proclamation that he had composed, which announced that General Forrest had reorganized the shattered Southern armies and defeated the North in one pitched battle. The negroes believed him implicitly. They passed a vote declaring it a good thing and held revival services immediately.

Fitz-Norman himself set out for foreign parts with one hundred thousand dollars and two trunks filled with rough diamonds of all sizes. He sailed for Russia in a Chinese junk and six months after his departure from Montana he was in St. Petersburg. He took obscure lodgings and called immediately upon the court jeweller, announcing that he had a diamond for the Czar. He remained in St. Petersburg for two weeks, in constant danger of being murdered, living from lodging to lodging, and afraid to visit his trunks more than three or four times during the whole fortnight.

On his promise to return in a year with larger and finer stones, he was allowed to leave for India. Before he left, however, the Court Treasurers had deposited to his credit, in American banks, the sum of fifteen million dollars—under four different aliases.

He returned to America in 1868, having been gone a little over two years. He had visited the capitals of twenty-two countries and talked with five emperors, eleven kings, three princes, a shah, a khan, and a sultan. At that time Fitz-Norman estimated his own wealth at one billion dollars. One fact worked consistently against the disclosure of his secret. No one of his larger diamonds remained in the public eye for a week before being invested with a history of enough fatalities, amours, revolutions, and wars to have occupied it from the days of the first Babylonian Empire.

From 1870 until his death in 1900, the history of Fitz-Norman Washington was a long epic in gold. There were side issues, of course—he evaded the surveys, he married a Virginia lady, by whom he had a single son, and he was compelled, due to a series of unfortunate complications, to murder his brother, whose unfortunate habit of drinking himself into an indiscreet stupor had several times endangered their safety. But very few other murders stained these happy years of progress and expansion.

Just before he died he changed his policy, and with all but a few million dollars of his outside wealth bought up rare minerals in bulk, which he deposited in the safety vaults of banks all over the world, marked as bric-à-brac. His son, Braddock Tarleton Washington, followed this policy on an even more tensive scale. The minerals were converted into the rarest of all elements—radium—so that the equivalent of a billion dollars in gold could be placed in a receptacle no bigger than a cigar box.

When Fitz-Norman had been dead three years, his son, Braddock, decided that the business had gone far enough. The amount of wealth that he and his father had taken out of the mountain was beyond all exact computation. He kept a note-book in cipher in which he set down the approximate quantity of radium in each of the thousand banks he patronized, and recorded the alias under which it was held. Then he did a very simple thing—he sealed up the mine.

He sealed up the mine. What had been taken out of it would support all the Washingtons yet to be born in unparalleled luxury for generations. His one care must be the protection of his secret, lest in the possible panic attendant on its discovery he should be reduced with all the property-holders in the world to utter poverty.

This was the family among whom John T. Unger was staying. This was the story he heard in his silver-walled living-room the morning after his arrival.

V

After breakfast, John found his way out the great marble entrance, and looked curiously at the scene before him. The whole valley, from the diamond mountain to the steep granite cliff five miles away, still gave off a breath of golden haze which hovered idly above the fine sweep of lawns and lakes and gardens. Here and there clusters of elms made delicate groves of shade, contrasting strangely with the tough masses of pine forest that held the hills in a grip of dark-blue green. Even as John looked he saw three fawns in single file patter out from one clump about a half mile away and disappear with awkward gayety into the black-ribbed half-light of another. John would not have been surprised to see a goat-foot piping his way among the trees or to catch a glimpse of pink nymph-skin and flying yellow hair between the greenest of the green leaves.

In some such cool hope he descended the marble steps, disturbing faintly the sleep of two silky Russian wolfhounds at the bottom, and set off along a walk of white and blue brick that seemed to lead in no particular direction.

He was enjoying himself as much as he was able. It is youth's felicity as well as its insufficiency that it can never live in the present, but must always be measuring up the day against its own radiantly imagined future—flowers and gold, girls and stars, they are only prefigurations and prophecies of that incomparable, unattainable young dream.

John rounded a soft corner where the massed rosebushes filled the air with heavy scent, and struck off across a park toward a patch of moss under some trees. He had never lain upon moss, and he wanted to see whether it was really soft enough to justify the use of its name as an adjective. Then he saw a girl coming toward him over the grass. She was the most beautiful person he had ever seen.

She was dressed in a white little gown that came just below her knees, and a wreath of mignonettes clasped with blue slices of sapphire bound up her hair. Her pink bare feet scattered the dew before them as she came. She was younger than John—not more than sixteen.

"Hello," she cried softly, "I'm Kismine."

She was much more than that to John already. He advanced toward her, scarcely moving as he drew near lest he should tread on her bare toes.

"You haven't met me," said her soft voice. Her blue eyes added, "Oh, but you've missed a great deal!". . . "You met my sister, Jasmine, last night. I was sick with lettuce poisoning," went on her soft voice, and her eyes continued, "and when I'm sick I'm sweet—and when I'm well."

"You have made an enormous impression on me," said John's eyes, "and I'm not so slow myself"—"How do you do?" said his voice. "I hope you're better this morning."—"You darling," added his eyes tremulously.

John observed that they had been walking along the path. On her suggestion they sat down together upon the moss, the softness of which he failed to determine.

He was critical about women. A single defect—a thick ankle, a hoarse voice, a glass eye—was enough to make him utterly indifferent. And here for the first time in his life he was beside a girl who seemed to him the incarnation of physical perfection.

"Are you from the East?" asked Kismine with charming interest.

"No," answered John simply. "I'm from Hades."

Either she had never heard of Hades, or she could think of no pleasant comment to make upon it, for she did not discuss it further.

"I'm going East to school this fall," she said. "D'you think I'll like it? I'm going to New York to Miss Bulge's. It's very strict, but you see over the weekends I'm going to live at home with the family in our New York house, because father heard that the girls had to go walking two by two."

"Your father wants you to be proud," observed John.

"We are," she answered, her eyes shining with dignity. "None of us has ever been punished. Father said we never should be. Once when my sister Jasmine was a little girl she pushed him down-stairs and he just got up and limped away.

"Mother was—well, a little startled," continued Kismine, "when she heard that you were from—from where you *are* from, you know. She said that when she was a young girl—but then, you see, she's a Spaniard and old-fashioned."

"Do you spend much time out here?" asked John, to conceal the fact that he was somewhat hurt by this remark. It seemed an unkind allusion to his provincialism.

"Percy and Jasmine and I are here every summer, but next summer Jasmine is going to Newport. She's coming out in London a year from this fall. She'll be presented at court."

"Do you know," began John hesitantly, "you're much more sophisticated than I thought you were when I first saw you?"

"Oh, no, I'm not," she exclaimed hurriedly. "Oh, I wouldn't think of being. I think that sophisticated young people are terribly common, don't you? I'm not at all, really. If you say I am, I'm going to cry."

She was so distressed that her lip was trembling. John was impelled to protest:

"I didn't mean that; I only said it to tease you."

"Because I wouldn't mind if I *were*," she persisted "but I'm *not*. I'm very innocent and girlish. I never smoke, or drink, or read anything except poetry. I know scarcely any mathematics or chemistry. I dress *very* simply—in fact,

I scarcely dress at all. I think sophisticated is the last thing you can say about me. I believe that girls ought to enjoy their youths in a wholesome way."

"I do too," said John heartily.

Kismine was cheerful again. She smiled at him, and a still-born tear dripped from the corner of one blue eye.

"I like you," she whispered, intimately. "Are you going to spend all your time with Percy while you're here, or will you be nice to me? Just think—I'm absolutely fresh ground. I've never had a boy in love with me in all my life. I've never been allowed even to *see* boys alone—except Percy. I came all the way out here into this grove hoping to run into you, where the family wouldn't be around."

Deeply flattered, John bowed from the hips as he had been taught at dancing school in Hades.

"We'd better go now," said Kismine sweetly. "I have to be with mother at eleven. You haven't asked me to kiss you once. I thought boys always did that nowadays."

John drew himself up proudly.

"Some of them do," he answered, "but not me. Girls don't do that sort of thing—in Hades."

Side by side they walked back toward the house.

VI

John stood facing Mr. Braddock Washington in the full sunlight. The elder man was about forty with a proud, vacuous face, intelligent eyes, and a robust figure. In the mornings he smelt of horses—the best horses. He carried a plain walking-stick of gray birch with a single large opal for a grip. He and Percy were showing John around.

"The slaves' quarters are there." His walking-stick indicated a cloister of marble on their left that ran in graceful Gothic along the side of the mountain. "In my youth I was distracted for a while from the business of life by a period of absurd idealism. During that time they lived in luxury. For instance, I equipped every one of the rooms with a tile bath."

"I suppose," ventured John, with an ingratiating laugh, "that they used the bathtubs to keep coal in. Mr. Schnlitzer-Murphy told me that once he—"

"The opinions of Mr. Schnlitzer-Murphy are of little importance, I should imagine," interrupted Braddock Washington, coldly. "My slaves did not keep coal in their bathtubs. They had orders to bathe every day, and they did. If they hadn't I might have ordered a sulphuric acid shampoo. I discontinued the baths for quite another reason. Several of them caught cold and died. Water is not good for certain races—except as a beverage."

John laughed, and then decided to nod his head in sober agreement. Braddock Washington made him uncomfortable.

"All these negroes are descendants of the ones my father brought North with him. There are about two hundred and fifty now. You notice that they've lived so long apart from the world that their original dialect has become an almost indistinguishable patois. We bring a few of them up to speak English —my secretary and two or three of the house servants.

"This is the golf course," he continued, as they strolled along the velvet winter grass. "It's all a green, you see—no fairway, no rough, no hazards."

He smiled pleasantly at John.

"Many men in the cage, father?" asked Percy suddenly.

Braddock Washington stumbled, and let forth an involuntary curse.

"One less than there should be," he ejaculated darkly—and then added after a moment, "We've had difficulties."

"Mother was telling me," exclaimed Percy, "that Italian teacher—"

"A ghastly error," said Braddock Washington angrily. "But of course there's a good chance that we may have got him. Perhaps he fell somewhere in the woods or stumbled over a cliff. And then there's always the probability that if he did get away his story wouldn't be believed. Nevertheless, I've had two dozen men looking for him in different towns around here."

"And no luck?"

"Some. Fourteen of them reported to my agent that they'd each killed a man answering to that description, but of course it was probably only the reward they were after—"

He broke off. They had come to a large cavity in the earth about the circumference of a merry-go-round and covered by a strong iron grating. Braddock Washington beckoned to John, and pointed his cane down through the grating. John stepped to the edge and gazed. Immediately his ears were assailed with a wild clamor from below.

"Come on down to Hell!"

"Hello, kiddo, how's the air up there?"

"Hey! Throw us a rope!"

"Got an old doughnut, Buddy, or a couple of second-hand sandwiches?"

"Say, fella, if you'll push down that guy you're with, we'll show you a quick disappearance scene."

"Paste him one for me, will you?"

It was too dark to see clearly into the pit below, but John could tell from the coarse optimism and rugged vitality of the remarks and voices that they proceeded from middle-class Americans of the more spirited type. Then Mr. Washington put out his cane and touched a button in the grass, and the scene below sprang into light.

"These are some adventurous mariners who had the misfortune to discover El Dorado," he remarked.

Below them there had appeared a large hollow in the earth shaped like the interior of a bowl. The sides were steep and apparantly of polished glass, and on its slightly concave surface stood about two dozen men clad in the half costume, half uniform, of aviators. Their upturned faces, lit with wrath, with malice, with despair, with cynical humor, were covered with long growths of beard, but with the exception of a few who had pined perceptibly away, they seemed to be a well-fed, healthy lot.

Braddock Washington drew a garden chair to the edge of the pit and sat down.

"Well, how are you, boys?" he inquired genially.

A chorus of execration in which all joined except a few too dispirited to cry out, rose up into the sunny air, but Braddock Washington heard it with unruffled composure. When its last echo had died away he spoke again.

"Have you thought up a way out of your difficulty?"

From here and there among them a remark floated up.

"We decided to stay here for love!"

"Bring us up there and we'll find us a way!"

Braddock Washington waited until they were again quiet. Then he said:

"I've told you the situation. I don't want you here. I wish to heaven I'd never seen you. Your own curiosity got you here, and any time that you can think of a way out which protects me and my interests I'll be glad to consider it. But so long as you confine your efforts to digging tunnels—yes, I know about the new one you've started—you won't get very far. This isn't as hard on you as you make it out, with all your howling for the loved ones at home. If you were the type who worried much about the loved ones at home, you'd never have taken up aviation."

A tall man moved apart from the others, and held up his hand to call his captor's attention to what he was about to say.

"Let me ask you a few questions!" he cried. "You pretend to be a fair-minded man."

"How absurd. How could a man of *my* position be fair-minded toward *you*? You might as well speak of a Spaniard being fair-minded toward a piece of steak."

At this harsh observation the faces of the two dozen steaks fell, but the tall man continued:

"All right!" he cried. "We've argued this out before. You're not a humanitarian and you're not fair-minded, but you're human—at least you say you are—and you ought to be able to put yourself in our place for long enough to think how—how—how—"

"How what?" demanded Washington, coldly.

"—how unnecessary—"

"Not to me."

"Well,—how cruel—"

"We've covered that. Cruelty doesn't exist where self-preservation is involved. You've been soldiers: you know that. Try another."

"Well, then, how stupid."

"There," admitted Washington, "I grant you that. But try to think of an alternative. I've offered to have all or any of you painlessly executed if you wish. I've offered to have your wives, sweethearts, children, and mothers kidnapped and brought out here. I'll enlarge your place down there and feed and clothe you the rest of your lives. If there was some method of producing permanent amnesia I'd have all of you operated on and released immediately, somewhere outside of my preserves. But that's as far as my ideas go."

"How about trusting us not to peach on you?" cried someone.

"You don't proffer that suggestion seriously," said Washington, with an expression of scorn. "I did take out one man to teach my daughter Italian. Last week he got away."

A wild yell of jubilation went up suddenly from two dozen throats and a pandemonium of joy ensued. The prisoners clog-danced and cheered and yodled and wrestled with one another in a sudden up-rush of animal spirits. They even ran up the glass sides of the bowl as far as they could, and slid back to the bottom upon the natural cushions of their bodies. The tall man started a song in which they all joined—

"Oh, we'll hang the kaiser
On a sour apple tree—"

Braddock Washington sat in inscrutable silence until the song was over.

"You see," he remarked, when he could gain a modicum of attention, "I bear you no ill-will. I like to see you enjoying yourselves. That's why I didn't tell you the whole story at once. The man—what was his name? Critchtichiello?—was shot by some of my agents in fourteen different places."

Not guessing that the places referred to were cities, the tumult of rejoicing subsided immediately.

"Nevertheless," cried Washington with a touch of anger, "he tried to run away. Do you expect me to take chances with any of you after an experience like that?"

Again a series of ejaculations went up.

"Sure!"

"Would your daughter like to learn Chinese?"

"Hey, I can speak Italian! My mother was a wop."

"Maybe she'd like t'learna speak N'Yawk!"

"If she's the little one with the big blue eyes I can teach her a lot of things better than Italian."

"I knew some Irish songs—and I could hammer brass once't."

Mr. Washington reached forward suddenly with his cane and pushed the button in the grass so that the picture below went out instantly, and there remained only that great dark mouth covered dismally with the black teeth of the grating.

"Hey!" called a single voice from below, "you ain't goin' away without givin' us your blessing?"

But Mr. Washington, followed by the two boys, was already strolling on toward the ninth hole of the golf course, as though the pit and its contents were no more than a hazard over which his facile iron had triumphed with ease.

VII

July under the lee of the diamond mountain was a month of blanket nights and of warm, glowing days. John and Kismine were in love. He did not know that the little gold football (inscribed with her legend *Pro deo et patria et St. Mida*) which he had given her rested on a platinum chain next to her bosom. But it did. And she for her part was not aware that a large sapphire which had dropped one day from her simple coiffure was stowed away tenderly in John's jewel box.

Late one afternoon when the ruby and ermine music room was quiet, they spent an hour there together. He held her hand and she gave him such a look that he whispered her name aloud. She bent toward him—then hesitated.

"Did you say 'Kismine'?" she asked softly, "or—"

She had wanted to be sure. She thought she might have misunderstood.

Neither of them had ever kissed before, but in the course of an hour it seemed to make little difference.

The afternoon drifted away. That night when a last breath of music drifted down from the highest tower, they each lay awake, happily dreaming over the separate minutes of the day. They had decided to be married as soon as possible.

VIII

Every day Mr. Washington and the two young men went hunting or fishing in the deep forests or played golf around the somnolent course—games which John diplomatically allowed his host to win—or swam in the mountain coolness of the lake. John found Mr. Washington a somewhat exacting personality—utterly uninterested in any ideas or opinions except his own. Mrs. Washington was aloof and reserved at all times. She was apparently indifferent to her two daughters, and entirely absorbed in her son Percy, with whom she held interminable conversations in rapid Spanish at dinner.

Jasmine, the elder daughter, resembled Kismine in appearance—except that she was somewhat bow-legged, and terminated in large hands and feet—but was utterly unlike her in temperament. Her favorite books had to do with poor girls who kept house for widowed fathers. John learned from Kismine that Jasmine had never recovered from the shock and disappointment caused her by the termination of the World War, just as she was about to start for Europe as a canteen expert. She had even pined away for a time, and Braddock Washington had taken steps to promote a new war in the Balkans—but she had seen a photograph of some wounded Serbian soldiers and lost interest in the whole proceedings. But Percy and Kismine seemed to have inherited the arrogant attitude in all its harsh magnificence from their father. A chaste and consistent selfishness ran like a pattern through their every idea.

John was enchanted by the wonders of the château and the valley. Braddock Washington, so Percy told him, had caused to be kidnapped a landscape gardener, an architect, a designer of state settings, and a French decadent poet left over from the last century. He had put his entire force of negroes at their disposal, guaranteed to supply them with any materials that the world could offer, and left them to work out some ideas of their own. But one by one they had shown their uselessness. The decadent poet had at once begun bewailing his separation from the boulevards in spring—he made some vague remarks about spices, apes, and ivories, but said nothing that was of any practical value. The stage designer on his part wanted to make the whole valley a series of tricks and sensational effects—a state of things that the Washingtons would soon have grown tired of. And as for the architect and the landscape gardener, they thought only in terms of convention. They must make this like this and that like that.

But they had, at least, solved the problem of what was to be done with them—they all went mad early one morning after spending the night in a single room trying to agree upon the location of a fountain, and were now confined comfortably in an insane asylum at Westport, Connecticut.

"But," inquired John curiously, "who did plan all your wonderful reception rooms and halls, and approaches and bathrooms—?"

"Well," answered Percy, "I blush to tell you, but it was a moving-picture fella. He was the only man we found who was used to playing with an unlimited amount of money, though he did tuck his napkin in his collar and couldn't read or write."

As August drew to a close John began to regret that he must soon go back to school. He and Kismine had decided to elope the following June.

"It would be nicer to be married here," Kismine confessed, "but of course I could never get father's permission to marry you at all. Next to that I'd rather elope. It's terrible for wealthy people to be married in America at present—they always have to send out bulletins to the press saying that they're going to be married in remnants, when what they mean is just a peck of old second-hand pearls and some used lace worn once by the Empress Eugenie."

"I know," agreed John fervently. "When I was visiting the Schnlitzer-Murphys, the eldest daughter, Gwendolyn, married a man whose father owns half of West Virginia. She wrote home saying what a tough struggle she was carrying on on his salary as a bank clerk—and then she ended up saying that 'Thank God, I have four good maids anyhow, and that helps a little.'"

"It's absurd," commented Kismine. "Think of the millions and millions of people in the world, laborers and all, who get along with only two maids."

One afternoon late in August a chance remark of Kismine's changed the face of the entire situation, and threw John into a state of terror.

They were in their favorite grove, and between kisses John was indulging in some romantic forebodings which he fancied added poignancy to their relations.

"Sometimes I think we'll never marry," he said sadly. "You're too wealthy, too magnificent. No one as rich as you are can be like other girls. I should marry the daughter of some well-to-do wholesale hardware man from Omaha or Sioux City, and be content with her half-million."

"I knew the daughter of a wholesale hardware man once," remarked Kismine. "I don't think you'd have been contented with her. She was a friend of my sister's. She visited here."

"Oh, then you've had other guests?" exclaimed John in surprise.

Kismine seemed to regret her words.

"Oh, yes," she said hurriedly, "we've had a few."

"But aren't you—wasn't your father afraid they'd talk outside?"

"Oh, to some extent, to some extent," she answered. "Let's talk about something pleasanter."

But John's curiosity was aroused.

"Something pleasanter!" he demanded. "What's unpleasant about that? Weren't they nice girls?"

To his great surprise Kismine began to weep.

"Yes—th—that's the—the whole t-trouble. I grew qu-quite attached to some of them. So did Jasmine, but she kept inv-viting them anyway. I couldn't under*stand* it."

A dark suspicion was born in John's heart.

"Do you mean that they *told*, and your father had them—removed?"

"Worse than that," she muttered brokenly. "Father took no chances—and Jasmine kept writing them to come, and they had *such* a good time!"

She was overcome by a paroxysm of grief.

Stunned with the horror of this revelation, John sat there open-mouthed feeling the nerves of his body twitter like so many sparrows perched upon his spinal column.

"Now, I've told you, and I shouldn't have," she said, calming suddenly and drying her dark blue eyes.

"Do you mean to say that your father had them *murdered* before they left?"

She nodded.

"In August usually—or early in September. It's only natural for us to get all the pleasure out of them that we can first."

"How abominable! How—why, I must be going crazy! Did you really admit that—"

"I did," interrupted Kismine, shrugging her shoulders. "We can't very well imprison them like those aviators, where they'd be a continual reproach to us every day. And it's always been made easier for Jasmine and me, because father had it done sooner than we expected. In that way we avoided any farewell scene—"

"So you murdered them! Uh!" cried John.

"It was done very nicely. They were drugged while they were asleep—and their families were always told that they died of scarlet fever in Butte."

"But—I fail to understand why you kept on inviting them!"

"I didn't," burst out Kismine. "I never invited one. Jasmine did. And they always had a very good time. She'd give them the nicest presents toward the last. I shall probably have visitors too—I'll harden up to it. We can't let such an inevitable thing as death stand in the way of enjoying life while we have it. Think how lonesome it'd be out here if we never had *any* one. Why, father and mother have sacrificed some of their best friends just as we have."

"And so," cried John accusingly, "and so you were letting me make love to you and pretending to return it, and talking about marriage, all the time knowing perfectly well that I'd never get out of here alive—"

"No," she protested passionately. "Not any more. I did at first. You were here. I couldn't help that, and I thought your last days might as well be pleasant for both of us. But then I fell in love with you, and—I'm honestly sorry you're going to—going to be put away—though I'd rather you'd be put away than ever kiss another girl."

"Oh, you would, would you?" cried John ferociously.

"Much rather. Besides, I've always heard that a girl can have more fun with a man whom she knows she can never marry. Oh, why did I tell you? I've probably spoiled your whole good time now, and we were really enjoying things when you didn't know it. I knew it would make things sort of depressing for you."

"Oh, you did, did you?" John's voice trembled with anger. "I've heard about enough of this. If you haven't any more pride and decency than to have an affair with a fellow that you know isn't much better than a corpse, I don't want to have any more to do with you!"

"You're not a corpse!" she protested in horror. "You're not a corpse! I won't have you saying that I kissed a corpse!"

"I said nothing of the sort!"

"You did! You said I kissed a corpse!"

"I didn't!"

Their voices had risen, but upon a sudden interruption they both subsided into immediate silence. Footsteps were coming along the path in their direction, and a moment later the rose bushes were parted displaying Braddock Washington, whose intelligent eyes set in his good-looking vacuous face were peering in at them.

"Who kissed a corpse?" he demanded in obvious disapproval.

"Nobody," answered Kismine quickly. "We were just joking."

"What are you two doing here, anyhow?" he demanded gruffly. "Kismine, you ought to be—to be reading or playing golf with your sister. Go read! Go play golf! Don't let me find you here when I come back!"

Then he bowed at John and went up the path.

"See?" said Kismine crossly, when he was out of hearing. "You've spoiled it all. We can never meet any more. He won't let me meet you. He'd have you poisoned if he thought we were in love."

"We're not, any more!" cried John fiercely, "so he can set his mind at rest upon that. Moreover, don't fool yourself that I'm going to stay around here.

Inside of six hours I'll be over those mountains if I have to gnaw a passage through them, and on my way East."

They had both got to their feet, and at this remark Kismine came close and put her arm through his.

"I'm going, too."

"You must be crazy—"

"Of course I'm going," she interrupted impatiently.

"You most certainly are not. You—"

"Very well," she said quietly, "we'll catch up with father now and talk it over with him."

Defeated, John mustered a sickly smile.

"Very well, dearest," he agreed, with pale and unconvincing affection, "we'll go together."

His love for her returned and settled placidly on his heart. She was his—she would go with him to share his dangers. He put his arms about her and kissed her fervently. After all she loved him; she had saved him, in fact.

Discussing the matter, they walked slowly back toward the château. They decided that since Braddock Washington had seen them together they had best depart the next night. Nevertheless, John's lips were unusually dry at dinner, and he nervously emptied a great spoonful of peacock soup into his left lung. He had to be carried into the turquoise and sable card-room and pounded on the back by one of the under-butlers, which Percy considered a joke.

IX

Long after midnight John's body gave a nervous jerk, and he sat suddenly upright, staring into the veils of somnolence that draped the room. Through the squares of blue darkness that were his open windows, he heard a faint far-away sound that died upon a bed of wind before identifying itself on his memory, clouded with uneasy dreams. But the sharp noise that had succeeded it was nearer, was just outside the room—the click of a turned knob, a footstep, a whisper, he could not tell; a hard lump gathered in the pit of his stomach, and his whole body ached in the moment that he strained agonizingly to hear. Then one of the veils seemed to dissolve, and he saw a vague figure standing by the door, a figure only faintly limned and blocked in upon the darkness, mingled so with the folds of the drapery as to seem distorted, like a reflection seen in a dirty pane of glass.

With sudden movement of fright or resolution John pressed the button by his bedside, and the next moment he was sitting in the great sunken bath of the adjoining room, waked into alertness by the shock of the cold water which half filled it.

He sprang out, and his wet pajamas scattering a heavy trickle of water behind him, ran for the aquamarine door which he knew led out onto the ivory landing of the second floor. The door opened noiselessly. A single crimson lamp burning in a great dome above lit the magnificent sweep of the carved stairways with a poignant beauty. For a moment John hesitated, appalled by the silent splendor massed about him, seeming to envelop in its gigantic folds and contours the solitary drenched little figure shivering upon the ivory landing. Then simultaneously two things happened. The door of his own sitting-room swung open, precipitating three naked negroes into the hall—and, as John swayed in wild terror toward the stairway, another door slid back in the wall on the other side of the corridor, and John saw Braddock Washington standing in the lighted lift, wearing a fur coat and a pair of riding boots which reached to his knees and displayed, above, the glow on his rose-colored pajamas.

On the instant the three negroes—John had never seen any of them before, and it flashed through his mind that they must be professional executioners—paused in their movement toward John, and turned expectantly to the man in the lift, who burst out with an imperious command:

"Get in here! All three of you! Quick as hell!"

Then, within the instant, the three negroes darted into the cage, the oblong of light was blotted out as the lift door slid shut, and John was again alone in the hall. He slumped weakly down against an ivory stair.

It was apparent that something portentous had occurred, something which, for the moment at least, had postponed his own petty disaster. What was it? Had the negroes risen in revolt? Had the aviators forced aside the iron bars of the grating? Or had the men of Fish stumbled blindly through the hills and gazed with bleak, joyless eyes upon the gaudy valley? John did not know. He heard a faint whir of air as the lift whizzed up again, and then a moment later, as it descended. It was probable that Percy was hurrying to his father's assistance, and it occurred to John that this was his opportunity to join Kismine and plan an immediate escape. He waited until the lift had been silent for several minutes; shivering a little with the night cool that whipped in through his wet pajamas, he returned to his room and dressed himself quickly. Then he mounted a long flight of stairs and turned down the corridor carpeted with Russian sable which led to Kismine's suite.

The door of her sitting-room was open and the lamps were lighted. Kismine, in an angora kimono, stood near the window of the room in a listening attitude, and as John entered noiselessly, she turned toward him.

"Oh, it's you!" she whispered, crossing the room to him. "Did you hear them?"

"I heard your father's slaves in my—"

"No," she interrupted excitedly. "Aeroplanes!"

"Aeroplanes? Perhaps that was the sound that woke me."

"There's at least a dozen. I saw one a few moments ago dead against the moon. The guard back by the cliff fired his rifle and that's what roused father. We're going to open on them right away."

"Are they here on purpose?"

"Yes—it's that Italian who got away—"

Simultaneously with her last word, a succession of sharp cracks tumbled in through the open window. Kismine uttered a little cry, took a penny with fumbling fingers from a box on her dresser, and ran to one of the electric lights. In an instant the entire château was in darkness—she had blown out the fuse.

"Come on!" she cried to him. "We'll go up to the roof garden, and watch it from there!"

Drawing a cape about her, she took his hand, and they found their way out the door. It was only a step to the tower lift, and as she pressed the button that shot them upward he put his arms around her in the darkness and kissed her mouth. Romance had come to John Unger at last. A minute later they had stepped out upon the star-white platform. Above, under the misty moon, sliding in and out of the patches of cloud that eddied below it, floated a dozen dark-winged bodies in a constant circling course. From here and there in the alley flashes of fire leaped toward them, followed by sharp detonations. Kismine clapped her hands with pleasure, which a moment later turned to dismay as the aeroplanes, at some pre-arranged signal, began to release their bombs and the whole of the valley became a panorama of deep reverberate sound and lurid light.

Before long the aim of the attackers became concentrated upon the points where the anti-aircraft guns were situated, and one of them was almost immediately reduced to a giant cinder to lie smouldering in a park of rose bushes.

"Kismine," begged John, "you'll be glad when I tell you that this attack came on the eve of my murder. If I hadn't heard that guard shoot off his gun back by the pass I should now be stone dead—"

"I can't hear you!" cried Kismine, intent on the scene before her. "You'll have to talk louder!"

"I simply said," shouted John, "that we'd better get out before they begin to shell the château!"

Suddenly the whole portico of the negro quarters cracked asunder, a geyser of flame shot up from under the colonnades, and great fragments of jagged marble were hurled as far as the borders of the lake.

"There go fifty thousand dollars' worth of slaves," cried Kismine, "at pre-war prices. So few Americans have any respect for property."

John renewed his efforts to compel her to leave. The aim of the aeroplanes was becoming more precise minute by minute, and only two of the anti-aircraft guns were still retaliating. It was obvious that the garrison, encircled with fire, could not hold out much longer.

"Come on!" cried John, pulling Kismine's arm, "we've got to go. Do you realize that those aviators will kill you without question if they find you?"

She consented reluctantly.

"We'll have to wake Jasmine!" she said, as they hurried toward the lift. Then she added in a sort of childish delight: "We'll be poor, won't we? Like people in books. And I'll be an orphan and utterly free. Free and poor! What fun!" She stopped and raised her lips to him in a delighted kiss.

"It's impossible to be both together," said John grimly. "People have found that out. And I should choose to be free as preferable of the two. As an extra caution you'd better dump the contents of your jewel box into your pockets."

Then minutes later the two girls met John in the dark corridor and they descended to the main floor of the château. Passing for the last time through the magnificence of the splendid halls, they stood for a moment out on the terrace, watching the burning negro quarters and the flaming embers of two planes which had fallen on the other side of the lake. A solitary gun was still keeping up a sturdy popping, and the attackers seemed timorous about descending lower, but sent their thunderous fireworks in a circle around it, until any chance shot might annihilate its Ethiopian crew.

John and the two sisters passed down the marble steps, turned sharply to the left, and began to ascend a narrow path that wound like a garter around the diamond mountain. Kismine knew a heavily wooded spot half-way up where they could lie concealed and yet be able to observe the wild night in the valley—finally to make an escape, when it should be necessary, along a secret path laid in a rocky gully.

X

It was three o'clock when they attained their destination. The obliging and phlegmatic Jasmine fell off to sleep immediately, leaning against the trunk of a large tree, while John and Kismine sat, his arm around her, and watched the desperate ebb and flow of the dying battle among the ruins of a vista that had been a garden spot that morning. Shortly after four o'clock the last remaining gun gave out a clanging sound and went out of action in a swift tongue of red smoke. Though the moon was down, they saw the flying bodies were circling closer to the earth. When the planes had made certain that the beleaguered possessed no further resources, they would land and the dark and glittering reign of the Washingtons would be over.

With the cessation of the firing the valley grew quiet. The embers of the two aeroplanes glowed like the eyes of some monster crouching in the grass. The château stood dark and silent, beautiful without light as it had been beautiful in the sun, while the woody rattles of Nemesis filled the air above with a growing and receding complaint. Then John perceived that Kismine, like her sister, had fallen sound asleep.

It was long after four when he became aware of footsteps along the path they had lately followed, and he waited in breathless silence until the persons to whom they belonged had passed the vantage-point he occupied. There was a faint stir in the air now that was not of human origin, and the dew was cold; he knew that the dawn would break soon. John waited until the steps had gone a safe distance up the mountain and were inaudible. Then he followed. About half-way to the steep summit the trees fell away and a hard saddle of rock spread itself over the diamond beneath. Just before he reached this point he slowed down his pace, warned by an animal sense that there was life just ahead of him. Coming to a high boulder, he lifted his head gradually above its edge. His curiosity was rewarded; this is what he saw:

Braddock Washington was standing there motionless, silhouetted against the gray sky without sound or sign of life. As the dawn came up out of the east, lending a cold green color to the earth, it brought the solitary figure into insignificant contrast with the new day.

While John watched, his host remained for a few moments absorbed in some inscrutable contemplation; then he signalled to the two negroes who crouched at his feet to lift the burden which lay between them. As they struggled upright, the first yellow beam of the sun struck through the innumerable prisms of an immense and exquisitely chiselled diamond—and a white radiance was kindled that glowed upon the air like a fragment of the morning star. The bearers staggered beneath its weight for a moment—then their rippling muscles caught and hardened under the wet shine of the skins and the three figures were again motionless in their defiant impotency before the heavens.

After a while the white man lifted his head and slowly raised his arms in a gesture of attention, as one who would call a great crowd to hear—but there was no crowd, only the vast silence of the mountain and the sky, broken by faint bird voices down among the trees. The figure on the saddle of rock began to speak ponderously and with an inextinguishable pride.

"You out there—" he cried in a trembling voice. "You—there—!" He paused, his arms still uplifted, his head held attentively as though there might be men coming down the mountain, but the mountain was bare of human life. There was only sky and a mocking flute of wind along the tree-tops. Could Washington be praying? For a moment John wondered. Then the illusion passed—there was something in the man's whole attitude antithetical to prayer.

"Oh, you above there!"

The voice was become strong and confident. This was no forlorn supplication. If anything, there was in it a quality of monstrous condescension.

"You there—"

Words too quickly uttered to be understood, flowing one into the other . . . John listened breathlessly, catching a phrase here and there, while the voice broke off, resumed, broke off again—now strong and argumentative, now colored with a slow, puzzled impatience. Then a conviction commenced to dawn on the single listener, and as realization crept over him a spray of quick blood rushed through his arteries. Braddock Washington was offering a bribe to God!

That was it—there was no doubt. The diamond in the arms of his slaves was some advance sample, a promise of more to follow.

That, John perceived after a time, was the thread running through his sentences. Prometheus Enriched was calling to witness forgotten sacrifices, forgotten rituals, prayers obsolete before the birth of Christ. For a while his discourse took the form of reminding God of this gift or that which Divinity had deigned to accept from men—great churches if he would rescue cities from the plague, gifts of myrrh and gold, of human lives and beautiful women and captive armies, of children and queens, of beasts of the forest and field, sheep and goats, harvests and cities, whole conquered lands that had been offered up in lust or blood for His appeasal, buying a meed's worth of alleviation from the Divine wrath—and now he, Braddock Washington, Emperor of Diamonds, king and priest of the age of gold, arbiter of splendor and luxury, would offer up a treasure such as princes before him had never dreamed of, offer it up not in suppliance, but in pride.

He would give to God, he continued, getting down to specifications, the greatest diamond in the world. This diamond would be cut with many more thousand facets than there were leaves on a tree, and yet the whole diamond would be shaped with the perfection of a stone no bigger than a fly. Many men would work upon it for many years. It would be set in a great dome of beaten gold, wonderfully carved and equipped with gates of opal and crusted sapphire. In the middle would be hollowed out a chapel presided over by an altar of iridescent, decomposing, ever-changing radium which would burn out the eyes of any worshipper who lifted up his head from prayer—and on this altar there would be slain for the amusement of the Divine Benefactor any victim He should choose, even though it should be the greatest and most powerful man alive.

In return he asked only a simple thing, a thing that for God would be absurdly easy—only that matters should be as they were yesterday at this hour and that they should so remain. So very simple! Let but the heavens open, swallowing these men and their aeroplanes—and then close again. Let him have his slaves once more, restored to life and well.

There was no one else with whom he had ever needed to treat or bargain.

He doubted only whether he had made his bribe big enough. God had His price, of course. God was made in man's image, so it had been said: He must have His price. And the price would be rare—no cathedral whose building consumed many years, no pyramid constructed by ten thousand workmen, would be like this cathedral, this pyramid.

He paused here. That was his proposition. Everything would be up to specifications and there was nothing vulgar in his assertion that it would be cheap at the price. He implied that Providence could take it or leave it.

As he approached the end his sentences became broken, became short and uncertain, and his body seemed tense, seemed strained to catch the slightest pressure or whisper of life in the spaces around him. His hair had turned gradually white as he talked, and now he lifted his head high to the heavens like a prophet of old—magnificently mad.

Then, asJohn stared in giddy fascination, it seemed to him that a curious phenomenon took place somewhere around him. It was as though the sky had darkened for an instant, as though there had been a sudden murmur in a gust of wind, a sound of far-away trumpets, a sighing like the rustle of a great silken robe—for a time the whole of nature round about partook of this darkness: the birds' song ceased; the trees were still, and far over the mountain there was a mutter of dull, menacing thunder.

That was all. The wind died along the tall grasses of the valley. The dawn and the day resumed their place in a time, and the risen sun sent hot waves of yellow mist that made its path bright before it. The leaves laughed in the sun, and their laughter shook the trees until each bough was like a girls' school in fairyland. God had refused to accept the bribe.

For another moment John watched the triumph of the day. Then, turning, he saw a flutter of brown down by the lake, then another flutter, then another, like the dance of golden angels alighting from the clouds. The aeroplanes had come to earth.

John slid off the boulder and ran down the side of the mountain to the clump of trees, where the two girls were awake and waiting for him. Kismine sprang to her feet, the jewels in her pockets jingling, a question on her parted lips, but instinct told John that there was no time for words. They must get off the mountain without losing a moment. He seized a hand of each, and in silence they threaded the tree-trunks, washed with light now and with the rising mist. Behind them from the valley came no sound at all, except the complaint of the peacocks far away and the pleasant undertone of morning.

When they had gone about half a mile, they avoided the park land and entered a narrow path that led over the next rise of ground. At the highest point of this they paused and turned around. Their eyes rested upon the mountainside they had just left—oppressed by some dark sense of tragic impendency.

Clear against the sky a broken, white-haired man was slowly descending the steep slope, followed by two gigantic and emotionless negroes, who carried a burden between them which still flashed and glittered in the sun. Half-way down two other figures joined them—John could see that they were Mrs. Washington and her son, upon whose arm she leaned. The aviators had clambered from their machines to the sweeping lawn in front of the château, and with rifles in hand were starting up the diamond mountain in skirmishing formation.

But the little group of five which had formed farther up and was engrossing all the watchers' attention had stopped upon a ledge of rock. The negroes stooped and pulled up what appeared to be a trap-door in the side of the mountain. Into this they all disappeared, the white-haired man first, then his wife and son, finally the two negroes, the glittering tips of whose jeweled head-dresses caught the sun for a moment before the trap-door descended and engulfed them all.

Kismine clutched John's arm.

"Oh," she cried wildly, "where are they going? What are they going to do?"

"It must be some underground way of escape—"

A little scream from the two girls interrupted his sentence.

"Don't you see?" sobbed Kismine hysterically. "The mountain is wired!"

Even as she spoke John put up his hands to shield his sight. Before their eyes the whole surface of the mountain had changed suddenly to a dazzling burning yellow, which showed up through the jacket of turf as light shows through a human hand. For a moment the intolerable glow continued, and then like an extinguished filament it disappeared, revealing a black waste from which blue smoke arose slowly, carrying off with it what remained of vegetation and of human flesh. Of the aviators there was left neither blood nor bone—they were consumed as completely as the five souls who had gone inside.

Simultaneously, and with an immense concussion, the château literally threw itself into the air, bursting into flaming fragments as it rose, and then tumbling back upon itself in a smoking pile that lay projecting half into the water of the lake. There was no fire—what smoke there was drifted off mingling with the sunshine, and for a few minutes longer a powdery dust of marble drifted from the great featureless pile that had once been the house of jewels. There was no more sound and three people were alone in the valley.

XI

At sunset John and his two companions reached the high cliff which had marked the boundaries of the Washingtons' dominion, and looking back found the valley tranquil and lovely in the dusk. They sat down to finish the food which Jasmine had brought with her in a basket.

"There!" she said, as she prepared the table-cloth and put the sandwiches in a neat pile upon it. "Don't they look tempting? I always think that food tastes better outdoors."

"With that remark," remarked Kismine, "Jasmine enters the middle class."

"Now," said John eagerly, "turn out your pocket and let's see what jewels you brought along. If you made a good selection we three ought to live comfortably all the rest of our lives."

Obediently Kismine put her hand in her pocket and tossed two handfuls of glittering stones before him.

"Not so bad!" cried John, enthusiastically. "They aren't very big, but—Hello!" His expression changed as he held one of them up to the declining sun. "Why, these aren't diamonds! There's something the matter!"

"By golly!" exclaimed Kismine, with a startled look. "What an idiot I am!"

"Why, these are rhinestones!" cried John.

"I know. She broke into a laugh. "I opened the wrong drawer. They belonged on the dress of a girl who visited Jasmine. I got her to give them to me in exchange for diamonds. I'd never seen anything but precious stones before."

"And this is what you brought?"

"I'm afraid so." She fingered the brilliants wistfully. "I think I like these better. I'm a little tired of diamonds."

"Very well," said John gloomily. "We'll have to live in Hades. And you will grow old telling incredulous women that you got the wrong drawer. Unfortunately your father's bank-books were consumed with him."

"Well, what's the matter with Hades?"

"If I come home with a wife at my age my father is just as liable as not to cut me off with a hot coal, as they say down there."

Jasmine spoke up.

"I love washing," she said quietly. "I have always washed my own handkerchiefs. I'll take in laundry and support you both."

"Do they have washwomen in Hades?" asked Kismine innocently.

"Of course, " answered John. "It's just like anywhere else."

"I thought—perhaps it was too hot to wear any clothes."

John laughed.

"Just try it!" he suggested. "They'll run you out before you're half started."

"Will father be there?" she asked.

John turned to her in astonishment.

"Your father is dead," he replied somberly. "Why should he go to Hades? You have it confused with another place that was abolished long ago."

After supper they folded up the table-cloth and spread their blankets for the night.

"What a dream it was," Kismine sighed, gazing up at the stars. "How strange it seems to be here with one dress and a penniless fiancé!

"Under the stars," she repeated. "I never noticed the stars before. I always thought of them as great big diamonds that belonged to some one. Now they frighten me. They make me feel that it was all a dream, all my youth."

"It *was* a dream," said John quietly. "Everybody's youth is a dream, a form of chemical madness."

"How pleasant then to be insane!"

"So I'm told," said John gloomily. "I don't know any longer. At any rate, let us love for a while, for a year or so, you and me. That's a form of divine drunkenness that we can all try. There are only diamonds in the whole world, diamonds and perhaps the shabby gift of disillusion. Well, I have that last and I will make the usual nothing of it." He shivered. "Turn up your coat collar, little girl, the night's full of chill and you'll get pneumonia. His was a great sin who first invented consciousness. Let us lose it for a few hours."

So wrapping himself in his blanket he fell off to sleep.

About Ernest Hemingway

Born in 1899 in Oak Park, Illinois, Hemingway was educated in local schools and became a reporter for *The Kansas City Star* before volunteering as an ambulance driver in WWI in Italy. After the war, with a group of expatriates in Paris, he was identified with the modernist writers called "The Lost Generation." He produced most of his work, seven novels and six short story collections, between the 1920's and 1950's and won a Pulitzer Prize in 1953 and the Nobel Prize in 1954. In 1961, with deteriorating physical and mental health, he committed suicide.

A Clean, Well-Lighted Place

It was late and every one had left the café except an old man who sat in the shadow the leaves of the tree made against the electric light. In the day time the street was dusty, but at night the dew settled the dust and the old man liked to sit late because he was deaf and now at night it was quiet and he felt the difference. The two waiters inside the café knew that the old man was a little drunk, and while he was a good client they knew that if he became too drunk he would leave without paying, so they kept watch on him.

"Last week he tried to commit suicide," one waiter said.

"Why?"

"He was in despair."

"What about?"

"Nothing."

"How do you know it was nothing?"

"He has plenty of money."

They sat together at a table that was close against the wall near the door of the café and looked at the terrace where the tables were all empty except where the old man sat in the shadow of the leaves of the tree that moved slightly in the wind. A girl and a soldier went by in the street. The street light shone on the brass number on his collar. The girl wore no head covering and hurried beside him.

"The guard will pick him up," one waiter said.

"What does it matter if he gets what he's after?"

"He had better get off the street now. The guard will get him. They went by five minutes ago."

The old man sitting in the shadow rapped on his saucer with his glass. The younger waiter went over to him.

"What do you want?"

The old man looked at him. "Another brandy," he said.

"You'll be drunk," the waiter said. The old man looked at him. The waiter went away.

"He'll stay all night," he said to his colleague. "I'm sleepy now. I never get into bed before three o'clock. He should have killed himself last week."

The waiter took the brandy bottle and another saucer from the counter inside the café and marched out to the old man's table. He put down the saucer and poured the glass full of brandy.

"You should have killed yourself last week," he said to the deaf man. The old man motioned with his finger. "A little more," he said. The waiter poured on into the glass so that the brandy slopped over and ran down the stem into the top saucer of the pile. "Thank you," the old man said. The waiter took the bottle back inside the café. He sat down at the table with his colleague again.

"He's drunk now," he said.

"He's drunk every night."

"What did he want to kill himself for?"

"How should I know."

"How did he do it?"

"He hung himself with a rope."

"Who cut him down?"

"His niece."

"Why did they do it?"

"Fear for his soul."

"How much money has he got?"

"He's got plenty."

"He must be eighty years old."

"Anyway I should say he was eighty."

"I wish he would go home. I never go to bed before three o'clock. What kind of hour is that to go to bed?"

"He stays up because he likes it."

"He's lonely. I'm not lonely. I have a wife waiting in bed for me."

"He had a wife once too."

"A wife would be no good to him now."

"You can't tell. He might be better with a wife."

"His niece looks after him. You said she cut him down."

"I know."

"I wouldn't want to be that old. An old man is a nasty thing."

"Not always. This old man is clean. He drinks without spilling. Even now, drunk. Look at him."

"I don't want to look at him. I wish he would go home. He has no regard for those who must work."

The old man looked from his glass across the square, then over at the waiters.

"Another brandy," he said, pointing to his glass. The waiter who was in a hurry came over.

"Finished," he said, speaking with that omission of syntax stupid people employ when talking to drunken people or foreigners. "No more tonight. Close now."

"Another," said the old man.

"No. Finished." The waiter wiped the edge of the table with a towel and shook his head.

The old man stood up, slowly counted saucers, took a leather coin purse from his pocket and paid for the drinks, leaving half a peseta tip.

The waiter watched him go down the street, a very old man walking unsteadily but with dignity.

"Why didn't you let him stay and drink?" the unhurried waiter asked. They were putting up the shutters. "It is not half-past two."

"I want to go home to bed."

"What is an hour?"

"More to me than to him."

"An hour is the same."

"You talk like an old man yourself. He can buy a bottle and drink at home."

"It's not the same."

"No, it is not," agreed the waiter with a wife. He did not wish to be unjust. He was only in a hurry.

"And you? You have no fear of going home before your usual hour?"

"Are you trying to insult me?"

"No, *hombre*, only to make a joke."

"No," the waiter who was in a hurry said, rising from pulling down the metal shutters. "I have confidence. I am all confidence."

"You have youth, confidence, and a job," the older waiter said. "You have everything."

"And what do you lack?"

"Everything but work."

"You have everything I have."

"No. I have never had confidence and I am not young."

"Come on. Stop talking nonsense and lock up."

"I am of those who like to stay late at the café," the older waiter said. "With all those who do not want to go to bed. With all those who need a light for the night."

"I want to go home and into bed."

"We are of two different kinds," the older waiter said. He was now dressed to go home. "It is not only a question of youth and confidence although those things are very beautiful. Each night I am reluctant to close up because there may be some one who needs the café."

"*Hombre*, there are *bodegas* open all night long."

"You do not understand. This is a clean and pleasant café. It is well lighted. The light is very good and also, now, there are shadows of the leaves."

"Good night," said the younger waiter.

"Good night," the other said. Turning off the electric light he continued the conversation with himself. It is the light of course but it is necessary that the place be clean and pleasant. You do not want music. Certainly you do not want music. Nor can you stand before a bar with dignity although that is all that is provided for these hours. What did he fear? It was not fear or dread. It was a nothing that he knew too well. It was all a nothing and a man was nothing too. It was only that and light was all it needed and a certain cleanness and order. Some lived in it and never felt it but he knew it all was *nada y pues nada y nada y pues nada.* Our *nada* who art in *nada*, *nada* be thy name thy kingdom *nada* thy will be *nada* in *nada* as it is in *nada*. Give us this *nada* our daily *nada* and *nada* us our *nada* as we *nada* our *nada*s and *nada* us not into *nada* but deliver us from *nada; pues nada*. Hail nothing full of nothing, nothing is with thee. He smiled and stood before a bar with a shining steam pressure coffee machine.

"What's yours?" asked the barman.

"*Nada*."

"*Otro loco más*," said the barman and turned away.

"A little cup," said the waiter.

The barman poured it for him.

"The light is very bright and pleasant but the bar is unpolished," the waiter said.

The barman liked at him but did not answer. It was too late at night for conversation.

"You want another *copita*?" the barman asked.

"No, thank you," said the waiter and went out. He disliked bars and *bodegas*. A clean, well-lighted café was a very different thing. Now, without thinking further, he would go home to his room. He would lie in the bed and finally, with daylight, he would go to sleep. After all, he said to himself, it is probably only insomnia. Many must have it.

About Elizabeth Bowen

This Anglo-Irish storyteller was born in Dublin in 1899. Later her parents acquired Bowen's Court in County Cork where Elizabeth summered. Her father's mental illness in 1907 prompted her mother to move with Elizabeth to Hythe in Kent, England. After studying in London, and mingling with The Bloomsbury Group, she chose a writing career, publishing her first short story collection in 1923. Her many stories and novels focus on relationships of the upper classes. She died of cancer in 1973.

Her Table Spread

Alban had few options on the subject of marriage; his attitude to women was negative, but in particular he was not attracted to Miss Cuffe. Coming down early for dinner, red satin dress cut low, she attacked the silence with loud laughter before he had spoken. He recollected having heard that she was abnormal—at twenty-five, of statuesque development, still detained in childhood. The two other ladies, in beaded satins, made entrances of a surprising formality. It occurred to him, his presence must constitute an occasion: they certainly sparkled. Old Mr Rossiter, uncle to Mrs Treye, came last, more sourly. They sat for some time without the addition of lamplight. Dinner was not announced; the ladies by remaining on guard, seemed to deprecate any question of its appearance. No sound came from other parts of the Castle.

Miss Cuffe was an heiress to whom the Castle belonged and whose guests they all were. But she carefully followed the movements of her aunt, Mrs Treye; her ox-eyes moved from face to face in happy submission rather than expectancy. She was continually preoccupied with attempts at gravity, as though holding down her skirts in a high wind. Mrs Treye and Miss Carbin combined to cover her excitement; still, their looks frequently stole from the company to the windows, of which there were too many. He received a strong impression someone outside was waiting to come in. At last, with a sigh they got up: dinner had been announced.

The Castle was built on high ground, commanding the estuary; a steep hill, with trees, continued above it. On fine days the view was remarkable, of almost Italian brilliance, with that constant reflection up from the water that even now prolonged the too-long day. Now, in continuous evening rain, the winding wooded line of the further shore could be seen and, nearer the windows, a smothered island with the stump of a watch-tower. Where the Castle stood, a higher tower had answered the island's. Later a keep, then wings, had been added; now the fine peaceful residence had French windows opening on to the terrace. Invasions from the water would henceforth be social, perhaps amorous. On the slope down from the terrace, trees began again; almost, but not quite concealing the destroyer. Alban, who knew nothing, had not yet looked down.

It was Mr Rossiter who first spoke of the destroyer—Alban meanwhile glancing along the table; the preparations had been stupendous. The destroyer had come today. The ladies all turned to Alban: the beads on their bosoms sparkled. So this was what they had here, under their trees. Engulfed by their pleasure, from now on he disappeared personally. Mr Rossiter, rising a note, continued. The estuary, it appeared, was deep, with a channel buoyed up it. By a term of the Treaty, English ships were permitted to anchor in these waters.

'But they've been afraid of the rain!' chimed in Valeria Cuffe.

'Hush,' said her aunt, 'that's silly. Sailors would be accustomed to getting wet.'

But, Miss Carbin reported, that spring there *had* already been one destroyer. Two of the officers had been seen dancing at the hotel at the head of the estuary.

'So,' said Alban, 'you are quite in the world.' He adjusted his glasses in her direction.

Miss Carbin—blonde, not forty, and an attachment of Mrs Treye's—shook her head despondently. 'We were all away at Easter. Wasn't it curious they should have come then? The sailors walked in the demesne but never touched the daffodils.'

'As though I should have cared!' claimed Valeria passionately.

'Morale too good,' stated Mr Rossiter.

'But next evening,' continued Miss Carbin, 'the officers did not go to the hotel. They climbed up here through the trees to the terrace—you see, they had no idea. Friends of ours were staying here at the Castle, and they apologized. Our friends invited them in to supper . . .'

'Did they accept?'

The three ladies said in a breath: 'Yes, they came.'

Valeria added urgently, 'So don't you *think*—?'

'So tonight we have a destroyer to greet you,' Mrs Treye said quickly to Alban. 'It is quite an event; the country people are coming down from the mountains. These waters are very lonely; the steamers have given up since the bad times; there is hardly a pleasure-boat. The weather this year has driven visitors right away.'

'You are beautifully remote.'

'Yes,' agreed Miss Carbin. 'Do you know much about the Navy? Do you think, for instance, that this is likely to be the same destroyer?'

'*Will they remember*?' Valeria's bust was almost on the table. But with a rustle Mrs Treye pressed Valeria's toe. For the dining-room also looked out across the estuary, and the great girl had not once taken her eyes from the window. Perhaps it was unfortunate that Mr Alban should have coincided with the destroyer. Perhaps it was unfortunate for Mr Alban too.

For he saw now he was less than half the feast; unappeased, the party sat looking through him, all grouped at an end of the table—to the other, chairs had been pulled up. Dinner was being served very slowly. Candles—possible to see from the water—were lit now; some wet peonies glistened. Outside, day still lingered hopefully. The bushes over the edge of the terrace were like heads—you could have sworn sometimes you saw them mounting, swaying in manly talk. Once, wound up in the rain, a bird whistled, seeming hardly a bird.

'Perhaps since then they have been to Greece, or Malta?'

'That would be the Mediterranean fleet,' said Mr Rossiter.

They were sorry to think of anything out in the rain tonight.

'The decks must be streaming,' said Miss Carbin.

Then Valeria, exclaiming 'Please excuse me!' pushed her chair in and ran from the room.

'She is impulsive,' explained Mrs Treye. 'Have you been to Malta, Mr Alban?'

In the drawing-room, empty of Valeria, the standard lamps had been lit. Through their ballet-skirt shades, rose and lemon, they gave out a deep, welcoming light. Alban, at the ladies' invitation, undraped the piano. He played, but they could see he was not pleased. It was obvious he had always been a civilian, and when he had taken his place on the piano-stool—which he twirled round three times, rather fussily—his dinner-jacket wrinkled across the shoulders. It was sad they should feel so indifferent, for he came from London. Mendelssohn was exasperating to them—they opened all four windows to let the music downhill. They preferred not to draw the curtains; the air, though damp, being pleasant tonight, they said.

The piano was damp, but Alban played almost all his heart out. He played out the indignation of years his mild manner concealed. He had failed to love; nobody did anything about this; partners at dinner gave him less than half their attention. He knew some spring had dried up at the root of the world. He was fixed in the dark rain, by an indifferent shore. He played badly, but they were unmusical. Old Mr Rossiter, who was not what he seemed, went back to the dining-room to talk to the parlour maid.

Valeria, glittering vastly, appeared in a window.

'Come *in*!' her aunt cried in indignation. She would die of a chill, childless, in fact unwedded; the Castle would have to be sold and where would they all be?

But—'Lights down there!' Valeria shouted above the music.

They had to run out for a moment, laughing and holding cushions over their bare shoulders. Alban left the piano; they looked boldly down from the terrace. Indeed, there they were: two lights like arc-lamps, blurred by rain and drawn down deep in reflection into the steady water. There were, too, ever so many portholes, all lit up.

'Perhaps they are playing bridge,' said Miss Carbin.

'Now I wonder if Uncle Robert ought to have called,' said Mrs Treye. 'Perhaps we have seemed remiss—one calls on a regiment.'

'Patrick could row him out tomorrow.'

'He hates the water.' She sighed. 'Perhaps they will be gone.'

'Let's go for a row now—let's go for a row with a lantern,' besought Valeria, jumping and pulling her aunt's elbow. They produced such indignation she disappeared again—wet satin skirts and all—into the bushes. The ladies could do no more: Alban suggested the rain might spot their dresses.

'They must lose a great deal, playing cards throughout an evening for high stakes,' Miss Carbin said with concern as they all sat down again.

'Yet, if you come to think of it, somebody must win.'

But the naval officers who so joyfully supped at Easter had been, Miss Carbin knew, a Mr Graves, and a Mr Garrett: *they* would certainly lose. 'At all events, it is better than dancing at the hotel; there would be nobody of their type.'

'There is nobody there at all.'

'I expect they are best where they are . . . Mr Alban, a Viennese waltz?'

He played while the ladies whispered, waving the waltz time a little distractedly. Mr Rossiter, coming back, momentously stood: they turned in hope: even the waltz halted. But he brought no news. 'You should call Valeria in. You can't tell who may be round the place. She's not fit to be out tonight.'

'Perhaps she's not out.'

'She is,' said Mr Rossiter crossly. 'I just saw her racing past the window with a lantern.'

Valeria's mind was made up: she was a princess. Not for nothing had she had the dining-room silver polished and all set out. She would pace around in red satin that swished behind, while Mr Alban kept on playing a loud waltz. They would be dazed at all she had to offer—also her new statues and the leopard-skin from the auction.

When he and she were married (she inclined a little to Mr Garrett) they would invite all the Navy up the estuary and give them tea. Her estuary would be filled up, like a regatta, with loud excited battleships tooting to one another and flags flying. The terrace would be covered with grateful sailors, leaving room for the band. She would keep the peacocks her aunt did not allow. His friends would be surprised to notice that Mr Garrett had meanwhile become an admiral, all gold. He would lead the other admirals into the Castle and say, while they wiped their feet respectfully: 'These are my wife's statues; she has given them to me. One is Mars, one is Mercury. We have a Venus, but she is not dressed. And wait till I show you our silver and gold plates . . .' The Navy would be unable to tear itself away.

She had been excited for some weeks at the idea of marrying Mr Alban, but now the lovely appearance of the destroyer put him out of her mind. He would not have done; he was not handsome. But she could keep him to play the piano on quiet afternoons.

Her friends had told her Mr Garrett was quite a Viking. She was so very familiar with his appearance that she felt sometimes they had already been married for years—though still, sometimes, he could not realize his good luck. She still had to remind him the island was hers too . . . Tonight, Aunt and darling Miss Carbin had so fallen in with her plans, putting on their satins and decorating the drawing-room, that the dinner became a betrothal feast. There was some little hitch about the arrival of Mr Garrett—she had heard that gentlemen sometimes could not tie their ties. And now he was late and would be discouraged. So she must now go halfway down to the water and wave a lantern.

But she put her two hands over the lantern, then smothered it in her dress. She had a panic. Supposing she should prefer Mr Graves?

She had heard Mr Graves was stocky, but very merry; when he came to supper at Easter he slid in the gallery. He would teach her to dance, and take her to Naples and Paris . . . Oh, dear, oh, dear, then they must fight for her;

that was all there was to it . . . She let the lantern out of her skirts and waved. Her fine arm with bangles went up and down, up and down, with the staggering light; the trees one by one jumped up from the dark, like savages.

Inconceivably, the destroyer took no notice.

Undisturbed by oars, the rain stood up from the water; not a light rose to peer, and the gramophone, though it remained very faint, did not cease or alter.

In mackintoshes, Mr Rossiter and Alban meanwhile made their way to the boat-house, Alban did not know why. 'If that goes on,' said Mr Rossiter, nodding towards Valeria's lantern, 'they'll fire one of their guns at us.'

'Oh, no. Why?' said Alban. He buttoned up, however, the collar of his mackintosh.

'Nervous as cats. It's high time that girl was married. She's a nice girl in many ways, too.'

'Couldn't we get the lantern away from her?' They stepped on a paved causeway and heard the water nibble the rocks.

'She'd scream the place down. She's of age now, you see.'

'But if—'

'Oh, she won't do that; I was having a bit of fun with you.' Chuckling equably, Mrs Treye's uncle unlocked and pulled open the boat-house door. A bat whistled out.

'Why are we here?'

'She might come for the boat; she's a fine oar,' said Mr Rossiter wisely. The place was familiar to him; he lit an oil-lamp and, sitting down on a trestle with a staunch air of having done what he could, reached a bottle of whisky out of the boat. He motioned the bottle to Alban. It's a wild night,' he said. 'Ah, well, we don't have these destroyers every day.'

'That seems fortunate.'

'Well, it is and it isn't.' Restoring the bottle to the vertical, Mr Rossiter continued: 'It's a pity you don't want a wife. You'd be the better for a wife, d'you see, a young fellow like you. She's got a nice character; she's a girl you could shape. She's got a nice income.' The bat returned from the rain and knocked round the lamp. Lowering the bottle frequently, Mr Rossiter talked to Alban (whose attitude remained negative) of women in general and the parlour maid in particular . . .

'*Bat*!' Alban squealed irrepressibly, and with his hand to his ear—where he still felt it—fled from the boat-house. Mr Rossiter's conversation continued. Alban's pumps squelched as he ran; he skidded along the causeway and balked at the upward steps. His soul squelched equally: he had been warned, he had been warned. He had heard they were all mad; he had erred out of headiness and curiosity. A degree of terror was agreeable to his vanity: by express wish he had occupied haunted rooms. Now he had no other pumps in this country, no idea where to buy them, and a ducal visit ahead. Also, wandering as it were among the apples and amphoras of an art school, he had blundered into the life room: woman revolved gravely.

'Hell,' he said to the steps, mounting, his mind blank to the outcome.

He was nerved for the jumping lantern, but half-way up to the Castle darkness was once more absolute. Her lantern had gone out; he could orientate himself—in spite of himself—by her sobbing. Absolute desperation. He pulled up so short that, for balance, he had to cling to a creaking tree.

'Hi!' she croaked. Then: 'You *are* there! I hear you!'

'Miss Cuffe—'

'How too bad you are! I never heard you rowing. I thought you were never coming—'

'Quietly, my dear girl.'

'Come up quickly. I haven't even seen you. Come up to the windows—'

'Miss Cuffe—'

'Don't you remember the way?' As sure but not so noiseless as a cat in the dark, Valeria hurried to him.

'Mr Garrett—' she panted. 'I'm Miss Cuffe. Where have you been? I've destroyed my beautiful red dress and they've eaten up your dinner. But we're still waiting. Don't be afraid; you'll soon be there now. I'm Miss Cuffe; this is my Castle—'

'Listen, it's I, Mr Alban—'

'Ssh, ssh, Mr Alban: *Mr Garrett has landed.*'

Her cry, his voice, some breath of the joyful intelligence, brought the others on to the terrace, blind with lamplight.

'Valeria?'

'Mr Garrett has landed!'

Mrs Treye said to Miss Carbin under her breath, 'Mr Garrett has come.'

Miss Carbin, half weeping with agitation, replied, 'We must go in.' But uncertain who was to speak next, or how to speak, they remained leaning over the darkness. Behind, through the windows, lamps spread great skirts of light, and Mars and Mercury, unable to contain themselves, stooped from their pedestals. The dumb keyboard shone like a ballroom floor.

Alban, looking up, saw their arms and shoulders under the bright rain. Close by, Valeria's fingers creaked on her warm wet satin. She laughed like a princess, magnificently justified. Their unseen faces were all three lovely, and, in the silence after the laughter, such a strong tenderness reached him that, standing there in full manhood, he was for a moment not exiled. For the moment, without moving or speaking, he stood, in the dark, in a flame, as though all three said: 'My darling . . .'

Perhaps it was best for them all that early, when next day first lightened the rain, the destroyer steamed out—below the extinguished Castle where Valeria lay with her arms wide, past the boat-house where Mr Rossiter lay insensible and the bat hung masked in its wings—down the estuary into the open sea.

About Frank O'Connor

Born Michael Francis O'Donovan in 1903, this Irish writer of more than 150 stories and memoirs was raised in Cork by an alcoholic father, Michael O'Donovan, and his loving and abused mother, Minnie O'Connor (whose name became his pen name), O'Connor fought with the Irish Republican Army in their war for independence and was imprisoned. Following his release he wrote many stories and was published by *The New Yorker* to critical acclaim, followed by invitations to lecture and teach. He suffered a stroke at Stanford University and later died in Dublin in 1966.

Guests of the Nation

I

At dusk the big Englishman, Belcher, would shift his long legs out of the ashes and say 'Well, chums, what about it?' and Noble and myself would say 'All right, chum' (for we had picked up some of their curious expressions), and the little Englishman, Hawkins, would light the lamp and bring out the cards. Sometimes Jeremiah Donovan would come up and supervise the game, and get excited over Hawkins' cards, which he always played badly, and shout at him, as if he was one of our own, 'Ah, you divil, why didn't you play the tray?'

But ordinarily Jeremiah was a sober and contented poor devil like the big Englishman, Belcher, and was looked up to only because he was a fair hand at documents, though he was slow even with them. He wore a small cloth hat and big gaiters over his long pants, and you seldom saw him with his hands out of his pockets. He reddened when you talked to him, tilting from toe to heel and back, and looking down all the time at his big farmer's feet. Noble and myself used to make fun of his broad accent, because we were both from the town.

I could not at the time see the point of myself and Noble guarding Belcher and Hawkins at all, for it was my belief that you could have planted that pair down anywhere from this to Claregalway and they'd have taken root there like a native weed. I never in my short experience saw two men take to the country as they did.

They were passed on to us by the Second Battalion when the search for them became too hot, and Noble and myself, being young, took them over with a natural feeling of responsibility, but Hawkins made us look like fools when he showed that he knew the country better than we did.

'You're the bloke they call Bonaparte,' he says to me. 'Mary Brigid O'Connell told me to ask what you'd done with the pair of her brother's socks you borrowed.'

For it seemed, as they explained it, that the Second had little evenings, and some of the girls of the neighbourhood turned up, and, seeing they were such decent chaps, our fellows could not leave the two Englishmen out. Hawkins learned to dance 'The Walls of Limerick', 'The Siege of Ennis' and 'The Waves of Tory' as well as any of them, though he could not return the compliment, because our lads at that time did not dance foreign dances on principle.

So whatever privileges Belcher and Hawkins had with the Second they just took naturally with us, and after the first couple of days we gave up all pretence of keeping an eye on them. Not that they could have got far, because they had accents you could cut with a knife, and wore khaki tunics and overcoats with civilian pants and boots, but I believe myself they never had any idea of escaping and were quite content to be where they were.

It was a treat to see how Belcher got off with the old woman in the house where we were staying. She was a great warrant to scold, and cranky even with us, but before ever she had a chance of giving our guests, as I may call them, a lick of her tongue, Belcher had made her his friend for life. She was breaking sticks, and Belcher who had not been more than ten minutes in the house, jumped up and went over to her.

'Allow me, madam,' he said, smiling his queer little smile. 'Please allow me,' and he took the hatchet from her. She was too surprised to speak, and after that, Belcher would be at her heels, carrying a bucket, a basket, or a load of turf. As Noble said, he got into looking before she leapt, and hot water, or any little thing she wanted, Belcher would have ready for her. For such a huge man (and though I am five foot ten myself I had to look up at him) he had an uncommon lack of speech. It took us a little while to get used to him, walking in and out like a ghost, without speaking. Especially because Hawkins talked enough for a platoon, it was strange to hear Belcher with his toes in the ashes come out with a solitary 'Excuse me, chum,' or 'That's right, chum.' His one and only passion was cards, and he was a remarkably good card player. He could have skinned myself and Noble, but whatever we lost to him, Hawkins lost to us, and Hawkins only played with the money Belcher gave him.

Hawkins lost to us because he had too much old gab, and we probably lost to Belcher for the same reason. Hawkins and Noble argued about religion into the early hours of the morning, and Hawkins worried the life out of Noble, who had a brother a priest, with a string of questions that would puzzle a cardinal. Even in treating of holy subjects, Hawkins had a deplorable tongue. I never met a man who could mix such a variety of cursing and bad language into any argument. He was a terrible man, and a fright to argue. He never did a stroke of work, and when he had no one else to argue with, he got stuck in the old woman.

He met his match in her, for when he tried to get her to complain profanely of the drought she gave him a great comedown by blaming it entirely on Jupiter Pluvius (a deity neither Hawkins nor I had ever heard of, though Noble said that among the pagans it was believed that he had something to do with the rain). Another day he was swearing at the capitalists for starting the German war when the old lady laid down her iron, puckered up her little crab's mouth and said: 'Mr Hawkins, you can say what you like about the war, and think you'll deceive me because I'm only a simple poor countrywoman, but I know what started the war. It was the Italian Count that stole the heathen divinity out of the temple of Japan. Believe me, Mr Hawkins, nothing but sorrow and want can follow people who disturb the hidden powers.'

A queer old girl, all right.

II

One evening we had our tea and Hawkins lit the lamp and we all sat into cards. Jeremiah Donovan came in too, and sat and watched us for a while, and it suddenly struck me that he had no great love for the two Englishmen. It came as a surprise to me because I had noticed nothing of it before.

Late in the evening a really terrible argument blew up between Hawkins and Noble about capitalists and priests and love of country.

'The capitalists pay the priests to tell you about the next world so that you won't notice what the bastards are up to in this,' said Hawkins.

'Nonsense, man!' said Noble, losing his temper. 'Before ever a capitalist was thought of people believed in the next world.'

Hawkins stood up as though he was preaching.

'Oh, they did, did they?' he said with a sneer. 'They believed all the things you believe—isn't that what you mean? And you believe God created Adam, and Adam created Shem and Shem created Jehoshophat. You believe all that silly old fairytale about Eve and Eden and the apple. Well listen to me, chum! If you're entitled to a silly belief like that, I'm entitled to my own silly belief—which is that the first thing your God created was a bleeding capitalist, with morality and Rolls-Royce complete. Am I right, chum?' he says to Belcher.

'You're right, chum,' says Belcher with a smile, and he got up from the table to stretch his long legs into the fire and stroke his moustache. So, seeing that Jeremiah Donovan was going, and that there was no knowing when the argument about religion would be over, I went out with him. We strolled down to the village together, and then he stopped, blushing and mumbling, and said I should be behind, keeping guard. I didn't like the tone he took with me, and anyway I was bored with life in the cottage, so I replied by asking what the hell we wanted to guard them for at all.

He looked at me in surprise and said: 'I thought you knew we were keeping them as hostages.'

'Hostages?' I said.

'The enemy have prisoners belonging to us, and now they're talking of shooting them,' he said. 'If they shoot our prisoners, we'll shoot theirs.'

'Shoot Belcher and Hawkins?' I said.

'What else did you think we were keeping them for?' he asked.

'Wasn't it very unforeseen of you not to warn Noble and myself of that in the beginning?' I said.

'How was it?' he said. 'You might have known that much.'

'We could not know it, Jeremiah Donovan,' I said. 'How could we when they were on our hands so long?'

'The enemy have our prisoners as long and longer,' he said.

'That's not the same thing at all,' said I.

'What difference is there?' said he.

I couldn't tell him, because I knew he wouldn't understand. If it was only an old dog that you had to take to the vet's, you'd try and not get too fond of him, but Jeremiah Donovan was not a man who would ever be in danger of that.

'And when is this to be decided?' I said.

'We might hear tonight,' he said. 'Or tomorrow or the next day at latest. So if it's only hanging round that's a trouble to you, you'll be free soon enough.'

It was not the hanging round that was a trouble to me at all by this time. I had worse things to worry about. When I got back to the cottage the argument was still on. Hawkins was holding forth in his best style, maintaining that there was no next world, and Noble saying that there was; but I could see that Hawkins had had the best of it.

'Do you know what, chum?' he was saying with a saucy smile. 'I think you're just as big a bleeding unbeliever as I am. You say you believe in the next world, and you know just as much about the next world as I do, which is sweet damn-all. What's heaven? You don't know. Where's heaven? You don't know. You know sweet damn-all! I ask you again, do they wear wings?'

'Very well, then,' said Noble. 'They do. Is that enough for you? They do wear wings.'

'Where do they get them then? Who makes them? Have they a factory for wings? Have they a sort of store where you hand in your chit and take your bleeding wings?'

'You're an impossible man to argue with,' said Noble. 'Now, listen to me—' And they were off again.

It was long after midnight when we locked up and went to bed. As I blew out the candle I told Noble. He took it very quietly. When we'd been in bed about an hour he asked if I thought we should tell the Englishmen. I didn't, because I doubted if the English would shoot our men. Even if they did, the Brigade officers, who were always up and down to the Second Battalion and knew the Englishmen well, would hardly want to see them plugged. 'I think so too,' said Noble. 'It would be great cruelty to put the wind up them now.'

'It was very unforeseen of Jeremiah Donovan, anyhow,' said I.

It was next morning that we found it so hard to face Belcher and Hawkins. We went about the house all day, scarcely saying a word. Belcher didn't seem to notice; he was stretched into the ashes as usual, with his usual look of waiting in quietness for something unforeseen to happen, but Hawkins noticed it and put it down to Noble being beaten in the argument of the night before.

'Why can't you take the discussion in the proper spirit?' he said severely. 'You and your Adam and Eve! I'm a Communist, that's what I am. Communist or Anarchist, it all comes to much the same thing.' And he went round the house, muttering when the fit took him: 'Adam and Eve! Adam and Eve! Nothing better to do with their time than pick bleeding apples!'

III

I don't know how we got through that day, but I was very glad when it was over, the tea things were cleared away, and Belcher said in his peaceable way: 'Well, chums, what about it?' We sat round the table and Hawkins took out the cards, and just then I heard Jeremiah Donovan's footsteps on the path and a dark presentiment crossed my mind. I rose from the table and caught him before he reached the door.

'What do you want?' I asked.

'I want those two soldier friends of yours,' he said, getting red.

'Is that the way, Jeremiah Donovan?' I asked.

'That's the way. There were four of our lads shot this morning, one of them a boy of sixteen.'

'That's bad,' I said.

At that moment Noble followed me out, and the three of us walked down the path together, talking in whispers. Feeney, the local intelligence officer, was standing by the gate.

'What are you going to do about it?' I asked Jeremiah Donovan.

'I want you and Noble to get them out; tell them they're being shifted again; that'll be the quietest way.'

'Leave me out of that,' said Noble, under his breath.

Jeremiah Donovan looked at him hard.

'All right,' he says. 'You and Feeney get a few tools from the shed and dig a hole by the far end of the bog. Bonaparte and myself will be after you. Don't let anyone see you with the tools. I wouldn't like it to go beyond ourselves.'

We saw Feeney and Noble go round to the shed and went in ourselves. I left Jeremiah Donovan to do the explanations. He told them that he had orders to send them back to the Second Battalion. Hawkins let out a mouthful of curses, and you could see that though Belcher didn't say anything, he was a bit upset too. The old woman was for having them stay in spite of us, and she didn't stop advising them until Jeremiah Donovan lost his temper and turned on her. He had a nasty temper, I noticed. It was pitch dark in the cottage by this time, but no one thought of lighting the lamp, and in the darkness the two Englishmen fetched their topcoats and said goodbye to the old woman.

'Just as a man makes a home of a bleeding place, some bastard at headquarters thinks you're too cushy and shunts you off,' said Hawkins, shaking her hand.

'A thousand thanks, madam,' said Belcher. 'A thousand thanks for everything'—as though he'd made it up.

We went round to the back of the house and down towards the bog. It was only then that Jeremiah Donovan told them. He was shaking with excitement.

'There were four of our fellows shot in Cork this morning and now you are to be shot as a reprisal.'

'What are you talking about?' snaps Hawkins. 'It's bad enough being mucked about as we are without having to put up with your funny jokes.'

'It isn't a joke,' said Donovan. 'I'm sorry, Hawkins, but it's true,' and begins on the usual rigmarole about duty and how unpleasant it is. I never noticed that people who talk a lot about duty find it much of a trouble to them.

'Oh, cut it out!' said Hawkins.

'Ask Bonaparte,' said Donovan, seeing that Hawkins wasn't taking him seriously. 'Isn't it true, Bonaparte?'

'It is,' I said, and Hawkins stopped.

'Ah, for Christ's sake, chum!'

'I mean it, chum,' I said.

'You don't sound as if you meant it.'

'If he doesn't mean it, I do,' said Donovan, working himself up.

'What have you against me, Jeremiah Donovan?'

'I never said I had anything against you. But why did your people take out four of your prisoners and shoot them in cold blood?'

He took Hawkins by the arm and dragged him on, but it was impossible to make him understand that we were in earnest. I had the Smith and Wesson in my pocket and I kept fingering it and wondering what I'd do if they put up a fight for it or ran, and wishing to God they'd do one or the other. I knew if they did run for it, that I'd never fire on them. Hawkins wanted to know was Noble in it, and when we said yes, he asked us why Noble wanted to plug him. Why did any of us want to plug him? What had he done to us? Weren't we all chums? Didn't we understand him and didn't he understand us? Did we imagine for an instant that he'd shoot us for all the so-and-so officers in the so-and-so British Army?

By this time we'd reached the bog, and I was so sick I couldn't even answer him. We walked along the edge of it in the darkness, and every now and then Hawkins would call a halt and begin all over again, as if he was wound up, about our being chums, and I knew that nothing but the sight of the grave would convince him that we had to do it. And all the time I was hoping that something would happen; that they'd run for it or that Noble would take over the responsibility from me. I had the feeling that it was worse on Noble than on me.

IV

At last we saw the lantern in the distance and made towards it. Noble was carrying it and Feeney was standing somewhere in the darkness behind him, and the picture of them so still and silent in the bogland brought it home to me that we were in earnest, and banished the last bit of hope I had.

Belcher, on recognising Noble, said: 'Hallo, chum,' in his quiet way, but Hawkins flew at him at once, and the argument began all over again, only this time Noble had nothing to say for himself and stood with his head down, holding the lantern between his legs.

It was Jeremiah Donovan who did the answering. For the twentieth time, as though it was haunting his mind, Hawkins asked if anybody thought he'd shoot Noble.

'Yes, you would,' said Jeremiah Donovan.

'No, I wouldn't, damn you!'

'You would, because you'd know you'd be shot for not doing it.'

'I wouldn't, not if I was to be shot twenty times over. I wouldn't shoot a pal. And Belcher wouldn't—isn't that right, Belcher?'

'That's right, chum,' Belcher said, but more by way of answering the question than of joining in the argument. Belcher sounded as though whatever unforeseen thing he'd always been waiting for had come at last.

'Anyway, who says Noble would be shot if I wasn't? What do you think I'd do if I was in his place, out in the middle of a blasted bog?'

'What would you do?' asked Donovan.

'I'd go with him wherever he was going, of course. Share my last bob with him and stick by him through thick and thin. No one can ever say of me that I let down a pal.'

'We've had enough of this,' said Jeremiah Donovan, cocking his revolver. 'Is there any message you want to send?'

'No, there isn't.'

'Do you want to say your prayers?'

Hawkins came out with a cold-blooded remark that even shocked me and turned on Noble again.

'Listen to me, Noble,' he said. 'You and me are chums. You can't come over to my side, so I'll come over to your side. That show you I mean what I say?

Give me a rifle and I'll go along with you and the other lads.'

Noble answered him. We knew that was no way out.

'Hear what I'm saying?' he said. 'I'm through with it. I'm a deserter or anything else you like. I don't believe in your stuff, but it's no worse than mine. That satisfy you?'

Noble raised his head, but Donovan began to speak and he lowered it again without replying.

'For the last time, have you any messages to send?' said Donovan in a cold, excited sort of voice.

'Shut up, Donovan! You don't understand me, but these lads do. They're not the sort to make a pal and kill a pal. They're not the tools of any capitalist.'

I alone of the crowd saw Donovan raise his Webley to the back of Hawkins's neck, and as he did so I shut my eyes and tried to pray. Hawkins had begun to say something else when Donovan fired, and as I opened my eyes at the bang, I saw Hawkins stagger at the knees and lie out flat at Noble's feet, slowly and as quiet as a kid falling asleep, with the lantern-light on his lean legs and bright farmer's boots. We all stood very still, watching him settle out in the last agony.

Then Belcher took out a handkerchief and began to tie it about his own eyes (in our excitement we'd forgotten to do the same for Hawkins), and, seeing it wasn't big enough, turned and asked for the loan of mine. I gave it to him, and he knotted the two together and pointed with his foot at Hawkins.

'He's not quite dead,' he said. 'Better give him another.'

Sure enough, Hawkins's left knee was beginning to rise. I bent down and put my gun to his head; then recollecting myself, I got up again. Belcher understood what was in my mind.

'Give him his first,' he said. 'I don't mind. Poor bastard, we don't know what's happening to him now.'

I knelt and fired. By this time I didn't seem to know what I was doing. Belcher, who was fumbling a bit awkwardly with the handkerchiefs, came out with a laugh as he heard the shot. It was the first time I had heard him laugh and it sent a shudder down my back; it sounded so unnatural.

'Poor bugger!' he said quietly. 'And last night he was so curious about it all. It's very queer, chums, I always think. Now he knows as much about it as they'll ever let him know, and last night he was all in the dark.'

Donovan helped him to tie the handkerchiefs about his eyes. 'Thanks, chum,' he said. Donovan asked if there were any messages he wanted sent.

'No, chum,' he said. 'Not for me. If any of you would like to write to Hawkins's mother, you'll find a letter from her in his pocket. He and his mother were great chums. But my missus left me eight years ago. Went away with another fellow and took the kid with her. I like the feeling of a home, as you may have noticed, but I couldn't start another again after that.'

It was an extraordinary thing, but in those few minutes Belcher said more than in all the weeks before. It was just as if the sound of the shot had started a flood of talk in him and he could go on the whole night like that, quite happily, talking about himself. We stood around like fools now that he couldn't see us any longer. Donovan looked at Noble, and Noble shook his head. Then Donovan raised his Webley, and at that moment Belcher gave his queer laugh again. He may have thought we were talking about him, or perhaps he noticed the same thing I'd noticed and couldn't understand it.

'Excuse me, chums,' he said. 'I feel I'm talking the hell of a lot, and so silly, about my being so handy about a house and things like that. But this thing came on me suddenly. You'll forgive me, I'm sure.'

'You don't want to say a prayer?' asked Donovan.

'No, chum,' he said. 'I don't think it would help. I'm ready, and you boys want to get it over.'

'You understand that we're only doing our duty?' said Donovan.

Belcher's head was raised like a blind man's, so that you could only see his chin and the top of his nose in the lantern-light.

'I never could make out what duty was myself,' he said. 'I think you're all good lads, if that's what you mean. I'm not complaining.'

Noble, just as if he couldn't bear any more of it, raised his fist at Donovan, and in a flash Donovan raised his gun and fired. The big man went over like a sack of meal, and this time there was no need for a second shot.

I don't remember much about the burying, but that it was worse than all the rest because we had to carry them to the grave. It was all mad lonely with nothing but a patch of lantern-light between ourselves and the dark, and birds hooting and screeching all round, disturbed by the guns. Noble went through Hawkins's belongings to find the letter from his mother, and then joined his hands together. He did the same with Belcher. Then, when we'd filled in the grave, we separated from Jeremiah Donovan and Feeney and took our tools back to the shed. All the way we didn't speak a word. The kitchen was dark and cold as we'd left it, and the old woman was sitting over the hearth, saying her beads. We walked past her into the room, and Noble struck a match to light the lamp. She rose quietly and came to the doorway with all her cantankerousness gone.

'What did ye do with them?' she asked in a whisper, and Noble started so that the match went out in his hand.

'What's that?' he asked without turning round.

'I heard ye,' she said.

'What did you hear?' asked Noble.

'I heard ye. Do you think I didn't hear ye, putting the spade back in the houseen?'

Noble struck another match and this time the lamp lit for him.

'Was that what ye did to them?' she asked.

Then, by God, in the very doorway, she fell on her knees and began praying, and after looking at her for a minute or two Noble did the same by the fireplace. I pushed my way out past her and left them at it. I stood at the door, watching the stars and listening to the shrieking of the birds dying out over the bogs. It is so strange what you feel at times like that you can't describe it. Noble says he saw everything ten times the size, as though there were nothing in the whole world but that little patch of bog with the two Englishmen stiffening into it, but with me it was as if the patch of bog where the Englishmen were was a million miles away, and even Noble and the old woman, mumbling behind me, and the birds and the bloody stars were all far away, and I was somehow very small and very lost and lonely like a child astray in the snow. And anything that happened to me afterwards, I never felt the same about again.

About Morley Callaghan

Born in 1903 and raised and educated in Toronto, Canada, Callaghan wrote for the Toronto *Daily Star* where he met and befriended Ernest Hemingway. Callaghan's first collection of short stories was published in 1929. He went to Paris and joined with the modernist expats there. An infamous boxing match between him and Hemingway, he knocking Hemingway to the mat, is recalled in Callaghan's memoir, *That Summer in Paris*. Callaghan produced countless stories to critical acclaim until his death at the age of 87, outliving most of his writing friends.

Last Spring They Came Over

Alfred Bowles came to Canada from England and got a job on a Toronto paper. He was a young fellow with clear, blue eyes and heavy pimples on the lower part of his face, the son of a Baptist minister whose family was too large for his salary. He got thirty dollars a week on the paper and said it was surprisingly good screw to start. For five a week he got an attic room in a brick house painted brown on Mutual Street. He ate his meals in a quick-lunch near the office. He bought a cane and a light-gray fedora.

He wasn't a good reporter but was inoffensive and obliging. After he had been working two weeks the fellows took it for granted he would be fired in a little while and were nice to him, liking the way the most trifling occurrences surprised him. He was happy to carry his cane on his arm and wear the fedora at a jaunty angle, quite the reporter. He liked to explain that he was doing well. He wrote home about it.

When they put him doing night police he felt important, phoning the fire department, hospitals, and police stations, trying to be efficient. He was getting along all right. It was disappointing when after a week the assistant city editor, Mr H. J. Brownson, warned him to phone his home if anything important happened, and he would have another man cover it. But Bowles got to like hearing the weary, irritable voice of the assistant city editor called from his bed at three o'clock in the morning. He liked to politely call Mr Brownson as often and as late as possible, thinking it a bit of good fun.

Alfred wrote long letters to his brother and to his father, the Baptist minister using a typewriter, carefully tapping the keys, occasionally laughing to himself. In a month's time he had written six letters describing the long city room, the fat belly of the city editor, and the bad words the night editor used when speaking of the Orangemen.

The night editor took a fancy to him because of the astounding puerility of his political opinions. Alfred was always willing to talk pompously of the British Empire policing the world and about all Catholics being aliens, and the future of Ireland and Canada resting with the Orangemen. He flung his arms wide and talked in the hoarse voice of a bad actor, but no one would have thought of taking him seriously. He was merely having a dandy time. The night editor liked him because he was such a nice boy.

Then Alfred's brother came out from the Old Country, and got a job on the same paper. Some of the men started talking about cheap cockney labourers crowding the good guys out of the jobs, but Harry Bowles was frankly glad to get the thirty a week. It never occurred to him that he had a funny idea of good money. With his first pay he bought a derby hat, a pair of spats, and a cane, but even though his face was clear and had a good colour he never looked as nice as his younger brither because his heavy nose curved up at the end. The landlady on Mutual Street moved a double bed into Alfred's room and Harry slept with his brother.

The days passed with many good times together. At first it was awkward that Alfred should be working at night and his brother in the day-time, but Harry was pleased to come down to the office every night at eleven and they went down the street to the hotel that didn't bother about Prohibition. They drank a few glasses of good beer. It became a kind of rite that had to be performed carefully. Harry would put his left foot and Alfred his right foot on the rail and leaning an elbow on the bar they would slowly survey the zigzag line of frothing glasses the length of the long bar. Men jostled them for a place at the foot-rail.

And Alfred said: 'Well, a bit of luck.'

Harry grinning and raising his glass said: 'Righto.'

'It's the stuff that heals.'

'Down she goes.'

'It helps the night along.'

'Fill them up again.'

'Toodleoo.'

Then they would walk out of the crowded bar-room, vaguely pleased with themselves. Walking slowly and erectly along the street they talked with assurance, a mutual respect for each other's opinion making it merely an exchange of information. They talked of the Englishman in Canada, comparing his lot with that of the Englishman in South Africa and India. They had never travelled but to ask what they knew of strange lands would have made one feel uncomfortable; it was better to take it for granted that the Bowles boys knew all about the ends of the earth and had judged them carefully, for in their eyes was the light of far-away places. Once in a while, after walking a block or two, one of the brothers would say he would damn well like to see India and the other would say it would be simply topping.

After work and on Sundays they took a look at the places they had heard about in the city. One Sunday they got up in good time and took the boat to Niagara. Their father had written asking if they had seen the Falls and would they send some souvenirs. That day they had as nice a time as a man would want to have, Standing near the pipe-rail a little way from the hotel that overlooks the Falls they watched the water-line just before the drop, smooth as a long strip of bevelled glass, and Harry compared it favourably with a cataract in the Himalayas and a giant waterfall in Africa, just above the Congo. They took a car along the gorge and getting off near the whirlpool, picked out a little hollow near a big rock at the top of the embankment where the grass was lush and green. They stretched themselves out with hats tilted over their eyes for sunshades. The river whirled below. They talked about the funny ways of Mr Brownson and his short fat legs and about the crazy women who fainted at the lifted hand of the faith healer who was in the city for the week. They liked the distant rumble of the Falls. They agreed to try and save a lot of money and go west to the Pacific in a year's time. They never mentioned trying to get a raise in pay.

Afterwards they each wrote home about the trip, sending the souvenirs.

Neither one was doing well on the paper, Harry wasn't much good because he hated writing the plain copy and it was hard for him to be strictly accurate. He liked telling a good tale but it never occurred to him that he was deliberately lying. He imagined a thing and straightway felt it to be true. But it never occurred to Alfred to depart from the truth. He was accurate but lazy, never knowing when he was really working. He was taken off night police and for two weeks helped a man do courts at the City Hall. He got to know the boys at the press gallery, who smiled at his naïve sincerity and thought him a decent chap, without making up their minds about him. Every noon-hour Harry came to the press gallery and the brothers, sitting at typewriters, wrote long letters all about the country and the people, anything interesting, and after exchanging letters, tilted back in their swivel chairs, laughing out loud. Heaven only knows who got the letters in the long run. Neither one when in the press gallery seemed to write anything for the paper.

Some of the men tried kidding Alfred, teasing him about women, asking if he found the girls in this country to his liking; but he seemed to enjoy it more than they did. Seriously he explained that he had never met a girl in this country, but they looked very nice. Once Alfred and Bun Brophy, a red-headed fellow with a sharp tongue who did City Hall for the paper, were alone in the gallery. Brophy had in his hands a big picture of five girls in masquerade costumes. Without explaining that he loved one of the girls Brophy asked Bowles which of the lot was the prettiest.

'You want me to settle that,' said Alfred, grinning and waving his pipe. He very deliberately selected a demure little girl with a shy smile.

Brophy was disappointed. 'Don't you think this one is pretty?'—a colourful, bold-looking girl.

'Well, she's all right in her way, but she's too vivacious. I'll take this one. I like them kittenish,' Alfred said.

Brophy wanted to start an argument but Alfred said it was neither here nor there. He really didn't like women.

'You mean to say you never step out?' Brophy said.

'I've never seemed to mix with them,' he said, adding that the whole business didn't matter because he liked boys much better.

The men in the press room heard about it and some suggested nasty things to Alfred. It was hard to tease him when he wouldn't be serious. Sometimes they asked if he took Harry out walking in the evenings. Brophy called them the heavy lovers. The brothers didn't mind because they thought the fellows were having a little fun.

In the fall Harry was fired. The editor in a nice note said that he was satisfied Mr H. W. Bowles could not adapt himself to their methods. But everyone wondered why he hadn't been fired sooner. He was no good on the paper.

The brothers smiled, shrugged their shoulders and went on living together. Alfred still had his job. Every noon-hour in the City Hall press room they were together, writing letters.

Time passed and the weather got cold. Alfred's heavy coat came from the Old Country and he gave his vest and a thin sweater to Harry, who had only a light spring coat. As the weather got colder Harry buttoned his coat higher up on his throat and even though he looked cold he was neat as a pin with his derby and cane.

Then Alfred lost his job. The editor, disgusted called him a fool. For the first time since coming over last spring he felt hurt, something inside him was hurt and he told his brother about it, wanting to know why people acted in such a way. He said he had been doing night police. On the way over to No. 1 station very late Thursday night he had met two men from other papers. They told him about a big fire earlier in the evening just about the time when Alfred was accustomed to going to the hotel to have a drink with his brother. They were willing to give all the details and Alfred thankfully shook hands with them and hurried back to the office to write the story. Next morning the assistant city editor phoned Alfred and asked how it was the morning papers missed the story. Alfred tried to explain but Mr Brownson said he was a damn fool for not phoning the police and making sure instead of trying to make the paper look like a pack of fools printing a fake story. The fellows who had kidded him said that too. Alfred kept asking his brother why the fellows had to do it. He seemed to be losing a good feeling for people.

Still the brothers appeared at noontime in the press room. They didn't write so many letters. They were agreeable, cheerful, on good terms with everybody. Bun Brophy every day asked how they were doing and they felt at home there. Harry would stand for a while watching the checker game always in progress, knowing that if he stood staring intently at the black and red squares, watching every deliberate move, he would be asked to sit in when it was necessary that one of the players make the rounds in the hall. Once Brophy gave Harry his place and walked over to the window where Alfred stood watching the fleet of automobiles arranged in a square in the courtyard. The police wagon with a load of drunks was backing toward the cells.

'Say, Alfie, I often wonder how you guys manage,' he said.

'Oh, first rate.'

'Well, you ought to be in a bad way by now.'

'Oh no, we have solved the problem,' said Alfred in a grand way, grinning, as if talking about the British Empire.

He was eager to tell how they did it. There was a store in their block where a package of tobacco could be got for five cents; they did their own cooking and were able to live on five dollars a week.

'What about coming over and having tea with us sometimes?' Alfred said. He was decidedly on his uppers but he asked Brophy to visit them and have tea.

Brophy, abashed, suggested the three of them go over to the café and have a little toast. Harry talked volubly on the way over and while having coffee.

He was really a better taker than his brother. They sat in an arm-chair lunch, gripped the handles of their thick mugs, and talked about religion. The brothers were sons of a Baptist minister but never thought of going to church. It seemed that Brophy had travelled a lot during war-time and afterward in Asia Minor and India. He was telling about a great golden temple of the Sikhs at Amritsar and Harry listened carefully, asking many questions. Then they talked about newspapers until Harry started talking about the East, slowly feeling his way. All of a sudden he told about standing on a height of land near Amritsar, looking down at a temple. It couldn't have been so but he would have it that Brophy and he had seen the same temple and he described the country in the words Brophy had used. When he talked that way you actually believed that he had seen the temple.

Alfred liked listening to his brother but he said finally: 'Religion is a funny business. I tell you it's a funny business.' And for the time being no one would have thought of talking seriously about religion. Alfred had a casual way of making a cherished belief or opinion seem unimportant, a way of dismissing even the bright yarns of his brother.

After that afternoon in the café Brophy never saw Harry. Alfred came often to the City Hall but never mentioned his brother. Someone said maybe Harry had a job but Alfred laughed and said no such luck in this country, explaining casually that Harry had a bit of a cold and was resting up. In the passing days Alfred came only once in a while to the City Hall, writing his letter without enthusiasm.

The press men would have tried to help the brothers if they had heard Harry was sick. They were entirely ignorant of the matter. On a Friday afternoon at three-thirty Alfred came into the gallery and, smiling apologetically, told Brophy that his brother was dead; the funeral was to be in three-quarters of an hour; would he mind coming? It was pneumonia, he added. Brophy, looking hard at Alfred, put on his hat and coat and they went out.

It was a poor funeral. The hearse went on before along the way to the Anglican cemetery that overlooks the ravine. One old cab followed behind. There had been a heavy fall of snow in the morning, and the slush of the pavement was thick. Alfred and Brophy sat in the old cab, silent. Alfred was leaning forward, his chin resting on his hands, the cane acting as a support, and the heavy pimples stood out on the lower part of his white face. Brophy was uncomfortable and chilly but he mopped his shining forehead with a big handkerchief. The window was open and the air was cold and damp.

Alfred politely asked how Mrs Brophy was doing. Then he asked about Mr Brownson.

'Oh, he's fine,' Brophy said. He wanted to close the window but it would have been necessary to move Alfred so he sat huddled in the corner, shivering.

Alfred asked suddenly if funerals didn't leave a bad taste in the mouth and Brophy, surprised, started talking absently about that golden temple of the Sikhs in India. Alfred appeared interested until they got to the cemetery. He said suddenly he would have to take a look at the temple one fine day.

They buried Harry Bowles in a grave in the paupers' section on a slippery slope of the hill. The earth was hard and chunky and it thumped down on the coffin case. It snowed a little near the end.

On the way along the narrow, slippery foot-path up the hill Alfred thanked Brophy for being thoughtful enough to come to the funeral. There was little to say. They shook hands and went different ways.

After a day or two Alfred again appeared in the press room. He watched the checker game, congratulated the winner and then wrote home. The men were sympathetic and said it was too bad about his brother. And he smiled cheerfully and said they were good fellows. In a little while he seemed to have convinced them that nothing important had really happened.

His last cent must have gone to the undertaker, for he was particular about paying bills, but he seemed to get along all right. Occasionally he did a little work for the paper, a story from a night assignment when the editor thought the staff was being overworked.

One afternoon at two-thirty in the press gallery Brophy saw the last of Alfred, who was sucking his pipe, his feet up on a desk, wanting to be amused. Brophy asked if anything had turned up. In a playful, resigned tone, his eye on the big clock, Alfred said he had until three to join the Air Force. They wouldn't take him, he said unless he let them know by three.

Brophy said, 'How will you like that?'

'I don't fancy it.'

'But you're going through.'

'Well, I'm not sure. Something else may come along.' It was a quarter to three and he was sitting there waiting for a job to turn up before three.

No one saw him after that, but he didn't join the Air Force. Someone in the gallery said that wherever he went he probably wrote home as soon as he got there.

About John Cheever

Born in 1912 in Quincy, Massachusetts, John was the son of a prosperous shoe salesman. But the failing shoe industry and the Great Depression left the family in financial straits. Cheever dropped out of school and began writing in earnest, selling a story, *Buffalo*, to *The New Yorker* for $45. Soon his stories drew critical and popular attention. As he recorded suburban life in the 1950's, he was called "The Chekhov of the Suburbs." He won the Pulitzer Prize in 1979 and the National Medal for Literature from the Academy of Arts and Letters just six weeks before his death in 1982.

The Country Husband

To begin at the beginning, the airplane from Minneapolis in which Francis Weed was travelling East ran into heavy weather. The sky had been a hazy blue, with the clouds below the plane lying so close together that nothing could be seen of the earth. Then mist began to form outside the windows, and they flew into a white cloud of such density that it reflected the exhaust fires. The color of the cloud darkened to gray, and the plane began to rock. Francis had been in heavy weather before, but he had never been shaken up so much. The man in the seat beside him pulled a flask out of his pocket and took a drink. Francis smiled at his neighbor, but the man looked away; he wasn't sharing his painkiller with anyone. The plane had begun to drop and flounder wildly. A child was crying. The air in the cabin was overheated and stale, and Francis' left foot went to sleep. He read a little from a paper book that he had bought at the airport, but the violence of the storm divided his attention. It was black outside the ports. The exhaust fires blazed and shed sparks in the dark, and, inside, the shaded lights, the stuffiness, and the window curtains gave the cabin an atmosphere of intense and misplaced domesticity. Then the lights flickered and went out. "You know what I've always wanted to do?" the man beside Francis said suddenly. "I've always wanted to buy a farm in New Hampshire and raise beef cattle." The stewardess announced that they were going to make an emergency landing. All but the child saw in their minds the spreading wings of the Angel of Death. The pilot could be heard singing faintly, "I've got sixpence, jolly, jolly sixpence. I've got sixpence to last me all my life . . ." There was no other sound.

The loud groaning of the hydraulic valves swallowed up the pilot's song, and there was a shrieking high in the air, like automobile brakes, and the plane hit flat on its belly in a cornfield and shook them so violently that an old man up forward howled, "Me kidneys! Me kidneys!" The stewardess flung open the door, and someone opened an emergency door at the back, letting in the sweet noise of their continuing mortality—the idle splash and smell of a heavy rain. Anxious for their lives, they filed out of the doors and scattered over the cornfield in all directions, praying that the thread would hold. It did. Nothing happened. When it was clear that the plane would not burn or explode, the crew and the stewardess gathered the passengers together and led them to the shelter of a barn. They were not far from Philadelphia, and in a little while a string of taxis took them into the city. "It's just like the Marne," someone said, but there was surprisingly little relaxation of that suspiciousness with which many Americans regard their fellow-travellers.

In Philadelphia, Francis Weed got a train to New York. At the end of that journey, he crossed the city and caught, just as it was about to pull out, the commuting train that he took five nights a week to his home in Shady Hill.

He sat with Trace Bearden. "You know, I was in that plane that just crashed outside Philadelphia," he said. "We came down in a field . . ." He had travelled faster than the newspapers or the rain, and the weather in New York was sunny and mild. It was a day in late September, as fragrant and shapely as an apple. Trace listened to the story, but how could he get excited? Francis had no powers that would let him re-create a brush with death—particularly in the atmosphere of a commuting train, journeying through a sunny countryside where already, in the slum gardens, there were signs of harvest. Trace picked up his newspaper, and Francis was left alone with his thoughts. He said good night to Trace on the platform at Shady Hill and drove in his second-hand Volkswagen up to the Blenhollow neighborhood, where he lived.

The Weeds' Dutch Colonial house was larger than it appeared to be from the driveway. The living room was spacious and divided like Gaul into three parts. Around an ell to the left as one entered from the vestibule was the long table, laid for six, with candles and a bowl of fruit in the center. The sounds and smells that came from the open kitchen door were appetizing, for Julia Weed was a good cook. The largest part of the living room centered around a fireplace. On the right were some bookshelves and a piano. The room was polished and tranquil, and from the windows that opened to the west there was some late-summer sunlight, brilliant and as clear as water. Nothing here was neglected; nothing had not been burnished. It was not the kind of household where, after prying open a stuck cigarette box, you would find an old shirt button and a tarnished nickel. The hearth was swept, the roses on the piano were reflected in the polish of the broad top, and there was an album of Schubert waltzes on the rack. Louisa Weed, a pretty girl of nine, was looking out the western windows. Her younger brother Henry was standing beside her. Her still younger brother, Toby, was studying the figures of some tonsured monks drinking beer on the polished brass of the wood box. Francis, taking off his hat and putting down his paper, was not consciously pleased with the scene; he was not that reflective. It was his element, his creation, and he returned to it with that sense of lightness and strength with which any creature returns to its home. "Hi, everybody," he said. "The plane from Minneapolis . . ."

Nine times out of ten, Francis would be greeted with affection, but tonight the children are absorbed in their own antagonisms. Francis has not finished his sentence about the plane crash before Henry plants a kick in Louisa's behind. Louisa swings around, saying, "*Damn* you!" Francis makes the mistake of scolding Louisa for bad language before he punishes Henry. Now Louisa turns on her father and accuses him of favoritism. Henry is always right; she is persecuted and lonely; her lot is hopeless. Francis turns to his son, but the boy has justification for the kick—she hit him first; she hit him on the ear, which is dangerous. Louisa agrees with this passionately. She hit him on the ear, and she *meant* to hit him on the ear, because he messed up her china collection. Henry says that this is a lie. Little Toby turns away from the wood box to throw in some evidence for Louisa. Henry claps his hand over little Toby's mouth. Francis separates the two boys but accidentally pushes Toby into the wood box. Toby begins to cry. Louisa is already crying. Just then, Julia Weed comes into that part of the room where the table is laid. She is a pretty, intelligent woman, and the white in her hair is premature. She does not seem to notice the fracas. "Hello, darling," she says serenely to Francis. "Wash your hands, everyone. Dinner is ready." She strikes a match and lights the six candles in this vale of tears.

This simple announcement, like the war cries of the Scottish chieftains, only refreshes the ferocity of the combatants. Louisa gives Henry a blow on the shoulder. Henry, although he seldom cries, has pitched nine innings and is tired. He bursts into tears. Little Toby discovers a splinter in his hand and begins to howl. Francis says loudly that he has been in a plane crash and that he is tired. Julia appears again, from the kitchen, and, still ignoring the chaos, asks Francis to go upstairs and tell Helen that everything is ready. Francis is happy to go; it is like getting back to headquarters company. He is planning to tell his oldest daughter about the airplane crash, but Helen is lying on her bed reading a *True Romance* magazine, and the first thing Francis does is to take the magazine from her hand and remind Helen that he has forbidden her to buy it. She did not buy it, Helen replies. It was given to her by her best friend, Bessie Black. Everybody reads *True Romance*. Bessie Black's father reads *True Romance*. There isn't a girl in Helen's class who doesn't read *True Romance*. Francis expresses his detestation of the magazine and then tells her dinner is ready—although from the sounds downstairs it doesn't seem so. Helen follows him down the stairs. Julia has sealed herself in the candlelight and spread a napkin over her lap. Neither Louisa nor Henry has come to the table. Little Toby is still howling, lying face down on the floor. Francis speaks to him gently: "Daddy was in a plane crash this afternoon, Toby. Don't you want to hear about it?" Toby goes on crying. "If you don't come to the table now, Toby," Francis says, "I'll have to send you to bed without any supper." The little boy rises, gives a cutting look, flies up the stairs to his bedroom, and slams the door. "Oh dear," Julia says, and starts to go after him. Francis says that she will spoil him. Julia says that Toby is ten pounds underweight and has to be encouraged to eat. Winter is coming, and he will spend the cold months in bed unless he has his dinner. Julia goes upstairs. Francis sits down at the table with Helen. Helen is suffering from the dismal feeling of having read too intently on a fine day, and she gives her father and the room a jaded look. She doesn't understand about the plane crash, because there wasn't a drop of rain in Shady Hill.

Julia returns with Toby, and they all sit down and are served. "Do I have to look at that big, fat slob?" Henry says, of Louisa. Everybody but Toby enters into this skirmish, and it rages up and down the table for five minutes. Toward the end, Henry puts his napkin over his head and, trying to eat that way, spills spinach all over his shirt. Francis asks Julia if the children couldn't have their dinner earlier. Julia's guns are loaded for this. She can't cook two dinners and lay two tables. She paints with lightning strokes that panorama of drudgery in which her youth, her beauty, and her wit have been lost. Francis says he must be understood; he was nearly killed in an airplane crash, and he doesn't like to come home every night to a battlefield. Now Julia is deeply committed. Her voice trembles. He doesn't come home every night to a battlefield. The accusation is stupid and mean. Everything was tranquil until he arrived. She stops speaking, puts down her knife and fork, and looks into her plate as if it is a gulf. She begins to cry. "Poor Mummy!" Toby says, and when Julia gets up from the table, drying her tears with a napkin, Toby goes to her side. "Poor Mummy," he says. "Poor Mummy!" And they climb the stairs together. The other children drift away from the battlefield, and Francis goes into the back garden for a cigarette and some air.

It was a pleasant garden, with walks and flower beds and places to sit. The sunset had nearly burned out, but there was still plenty of light. Put into a thoughtful mood by the crash and the battle, Francis listened to the evening sounds of Shady Hill. "Varmits! Rascals!" old Mr. Nixon shouted to the squirrels in his bird-feeding station. "Avaunt and quit my sight!" A door slammed. Someone was playing tennis on the Babcocks' court; someone was cutting grass. Then Donald Goslin, who lived at the corner, began to play the "Moonlight Sonata." He did this nearly every night. He threw tempo out the window and played it *rubato* from beginning to end, like an outpouring of tearful petulance, lonesomeness, and self-pity—of everything it was Beethoven's greatness not to know. The music rang up and down the street beneath the trees like an appeal for love, for tenderness, aimed at some lonely housemaid—some fresh-faced, homesick girl from Galway, looking at old snapshots in her third-floor room. "Here, Jupiter, here, Jupiter," Francis called to the Mercers' retriever. Jupiter crashed through the tomato vines with the remains of a felt hat in his mouth.

Jupiter was an anomaly. His retrieving instincts and his high spirits were out of place in Shady Hill. He was as black as coal, with a long, alert, intelligent, rakehell face. His eyes gleamed with mischief, and he held his head high. It was the fierce, heavily collared dog's head that appears in heraldry, in tapestry, and that used to appear on umbrella handles and walking sticks. Jupiter went where he pleased, ransacking wastebaskets, clotheslines, garbage pails, and shoebags. He broke up garden parties and tennis matches, and got mixed up in the processional at Christ's Church on Sunday, barking at the men in red dresses. He crashed through old Mr. Nixon's rose garden two or three times a day, cutting a wide swath through the Condesa de Sastagos, and as soon as Donald Goslin lighted his barbecue fire on Thursday nights, Jupiter would get the scent. Nothing the Goslins did could drive him away. Sticks and stones and rude commands only moved him to the edge of the terrace, where he remained, with his gallant and heraldic muzzle, waiting for Donald Goslin to turn his back and reach for the salt. Then he would spring onto the terrace, lift the steak lightly off the fire, and run away with the Goslins' dinner. Jupiter's days were numbered. The Wrightsons' German gardener or the Farquarsons' cook would soon poison him. Even old Mr. Nixon might put some arsenic in the garbage that Jupiter loved. "Here, Jupiter, Jupiter!" Francis called, but the dog pranced off, shaking the hat in his white teeth. Looking in at the windows of his house, Francis saw that Julia had come down and was blowing out the candles.

Julia and Francis Weed went out a great deal. Julia was well liked and gregarious, and her love of parties sprang from a most natural dread of chaos and loneliness. She went through her morning mail with real anxiety, looking for invitations, and she usually found some, but she was insatiable, and if she had gone out seven nights a week, it would not have cured her of a reflective look—the look of someone who hears distant music—for she would always suppose that there was a more brilliant party somewhere else. Francis limited her to two week-night parties, putting a flexible interpretation on Friday, and rode through the weekend like a dory in a gale. The day after the airplane crash, the Weeds were to have dinner with the Farquarsons.

Francis got home late from town, and Julia got the sitter while he dressed, and then hurried him out of the house. The party was small and pleasant, and Francis settled down to enjoy himself. A new maid passed the drinks. Her hair was dark, and her face was round and pale and seemed familiar to Francis. He had not developed his memory as a sentimental faculty. Wood smoke, lilac, and other such perfumes did not stir him, and his memory was something like his appendix—a vestigial repository. It was not his limitation at all to be unable to escape the past; it was perhaps his limitation that he had escaped it so successfully. He might have seen the maid at other parties, he might have seen her taking a walk on Sunday afternoons, but in either case he would not be searching his memory now. Her face was, in a wonderful way, a moon face—Norman or Irish—but it was not beautiful enough to account for his feeling that he had seen her before, in circumstances that he ought to be able to remember. He asked Nellie Farquarson who she was. Nellie said that the maid had come through an agency, and that her home was Trénon, in Normandy—a small place with a church and a restaurant that Nellie had once visited. While Nellie talked on about her travels abroad, Francis realized where he had seen the woman before. It had been at the end of the war. He had left a replacement depot with some other men and taken a three-day pass in Trénon. On their second day, they had walked out to a crossroads to see the public chastisement of a young woman who had lived with the German commandant during the Occupation.

It was a cool morning in the fall. The sky was overcast, and poured down onto the dirt crossroads a very discouraging light. They were on high land and could see how like one another the shapes of the clouds and the hills were as they stretched off toward the sea. The prisoner arrived sitting on a three-legged stool in a farm cart. She stood by the cart while the mayor read the accusation and the sentence. Her head was bent and her face was set in that empty half smile behind which the whipped soul is suspended. When the mayor was finished, she undid her hair and let it fall across her back. A little man with a gray mustache cut off her hair with shears and dropped it on the ground. Then, with a bowl of soapy water and a straight razor, he shaved her skull clean. A woman approached and began to undo the fastenings of her clothes, but the prisoner pushed her aside and undressed herself. When she pulled her chemise over her head and threw it on the ground, she was naked. The women jeered; the men were still. There was no change in the falseness or the plaintiveness of the prisoner's smile. The cold wind made her white skin rough and hardened the nipples of her breasts. The jeering ended gradually, put down by the recognition of their common humanity. One woman spat on her, but some inviolable grandeur in her nakedness lasted through the ordeal. When the crowd was quiet, she turned—she had begun to cry—and, with nothing on but a pair of worn black shoes and stockings, walked down the dirt road alone away from the village. The round white face had aged a little, but there was no question but that the maid who passed his cocktails and later served Francis his dinner was the woman who had been punished at the crossroads.

The war seemed now so distant and that world where the cost of partisanship had been death or torture so long ago. Francis had lost track of the men who had been with him in Vésey. He could not count on Julia's discretion. He could not tell anyone. And if he had told the story now, at the dinner table, it would have been a social as well as a human error. The people in the Farquarsons' living room seemed united in their tacit claim that there had been no past, no war—that there was no danger or trouble in the world. In the recorded history of human arrangements, this extraordinary meeting would have fallen into place, but the atmosphere of Shady Hill made the memory unseemly and impolite. The prisoner withdrew after passing the coffee, but the encounter left Francis feeling languid; it had opened his memory and his senses, and left them dilated. He had Julia drive home when the party ended, and Julia went into the house. Francis stayed in the car to take the sitter home.

Expecting to see Mrs. Henlein, the old lady who usually stayed with the children, he was surprised when a young girl opened the door and came out onto the lighted stoop. She stayed in the light to count her textbooks. She was frowning and beautiful. Now, the world is full of beautiful young girls, but Francis saw here the difference between beauty and perfection. All those endearing flaws, moles, birthmarks, and healed wounds were missing, and he experienced in his consciousness that moment when music breaks glass, and felt a pang of recognition as strange, deep, and wonderful as anything in his life. It hung from her frown, from an impalpable darkness in her face—a look that impressed him as a direct appeal for love. When she had counted her books, she came down the steps and opened the car door. In the light, he saw that her cheeks were wet. She got in and shut the door.

"You're new," Francis said.

"Yes. Mrs. Henlein is sick. I'm Anne Murchison."

"Did the children give you any trouble?"

"Oh, no, no." She turned and smiled at him unhappily in the dim dashboard light. Her light hair caught on the collar of her jacket, and she shook her head to set it loose.

"You've been crying."

"Yes."

"I hope it was nothing that happened in our house."

"No, no, it was nothing that happened in your house." Her voice was bleak. "It's no secret. Everybody in the village knows. Daddy's an alcoholic, and he just called me from some saloon and gave me a piece of his mind. He thinks I'm immoral. He called just before Mrs. Weed came back."

"I'm sorry."

"Oh, *Lord*!" She gasped and began to cry. She turned toward Francis, and he took her in his arms and let her cry on his shoulder. She shook in his embrace, and this movement accentuated his sense of the fineness of her flesh and bone. The layers of their clothing felt thin, and when her shuddering began to diminish, it was so much like a paroxysm of love that Francis lost his head and pulled her roughly against him. She drew away. "I live on Belleview Avenue," she said. "You go down Lansing Street to the railroad bridge."

"All right." He started the car.

"You turn left at the traffic light . . . Now you turn right here and go straight on toward the tracks."

The road Francis took brought him out of his own neighborhood, across the tracks, and toward the river, to a street where the near-poor lived, in houses whose peaked gables and trimmings of wooden lace conveyed the purest feelings of pride and romance, although the houses themselves could not have offered much privacy or comfort, they were all so small. The street was dark, and, stirred by the grace and beauty of the troubled girl, he seemed, in turning in to it, to have come into the deepest part of some submerged memory. In the distance, he saw a porch light burning. It was the only one, and she said that the house with the light was where she lived. When he stopped the car, he could see beyond the porch light into a dimly lighted hallway with an old-fashioned clothes tree. "Well, here we are," he said, conscious that a young man would have said something different.

She did not move her hands from the books, where they were folded, and she turned and faced him. There were tears of lust in his eyes. Determinedly—not sadly—he opened the door on his side and walked around to open hers. He took her free hand, letting his fingers in between hers, climbed at her side the two concrete steps, and went up a narrow walk through a front garden where dahlias, marigolds, and roses—things that had withstood the light frosts—still bloomed, and made a bittersweet smell in the night air. At the steps, she freed her hand and then turned and kissed him swiftly. Then she crossed the porch and shut the door. The porch light went out, then the light in the hall. A second later, a light went on upstairs at the side of the house, shining into a tree that was still covered with leaves. It took her only a few minutes to undress and get into bed, and then the house was dark.

Julia was asleep when Francis got home. He opened a second window and got into bed to shut his eyes on that night, but as soon as they were shut—as soon as he had dropped off to sleep—the girl entered his mind, moving with perfect freedom through its shut doors and filling chamber after chamber with her light, her perfume, and the music of her voice. He was crossing the Atlantic with her on the old *Mauretania* and, later, living with her in Paris. When he woke from this dream, he got up and smoked a cigarette at the open window. Getting back into bed, he cast around in his mind for something he desired to do that would injure no one, and he thought of skiing. Up through the dimness in his mind rose the image of a mountain deep in snow. It was late in the day. Wherever his eyes looked, he saw broad and heartening things. Over his shoulder, there was a snow-filled valley, rising into wooded hills where the trees dimmed the whiteness like a sparse coat of hair. The cold deadened all sound but the loud, iron clanking of the lift machinery. The light on the trails was blue, and it was harder than it had been a minute or two earlier to pick the turns, harder to judge—now that the snow was all deep blue—the crust, the ice, the bare spots, and the deep piles of dry powder. Down the mountain he swung, matching his speed against the contours of a slope that had been formed in the first ice age, seeking with ardor some simplicity of feeling and circumstance. Night fell then, and he drank a Martini with some old friend in a dirty country bar.

In the morning, Francis' snow-covered mountain was gone, and he was left with his vivid memories of Paris and the *Mauretania*. He had been bitten gravely. He washed his body, shaved his jaws, drank his coffee, and missed the seven-thirty-one. The train pulled out just as he brought his car to the station, and the longing he felt for the coaches as they drew stubbornly away from him reminded him of the humors of love. He waited for the eight-two, on what was now an empty platform. It was a clear morning; the morning seemed thrown like a gleaming bridge of light over his mixed affairs. His spirits were feverish and high. The image of the girl seemed to put him into a relationship to the world that was mysterious and enthralling. Cars were beginning to fill up the parking lot, and he noticed that those that had driven down from the high land above Shady Hill were white with hoarfrost. This first clear sign of autumn thrilled him. An express train—a night train from Buffalo or Albany—came down the tracks between the platforms, and he saw that the roofs of the foremost cars were covered with a skin of ice. Struck by the miraculous physicalness of everything, he smiled at the passengers in the dining car, who could be seen eating eggs and wiping their mouths with napkins as they travelled. The sleeping-car compartments, with their soiled bed linen, trailed through the fresh morning like a string of rooming-house windows. Then he saw an extraordinary thing; at one of the bedroom windows sat an unclothed woman of exceptional beauty, combing her golden hair. She passed like an apparition through Shady Hill, combing and combing her hair, and Francis followed her with his eyes until she was out of sight. Then old Mrs. Wrightson joined him on the platform and began to talk.

"Well, I guess you must be surprised to see me here the third morning in a row," she said, "but because of my window curtains I'm becoming a regular commuter. The curtains I bought on Monday I returned on Tuesday, and the curtains I bought on Tuesday I'm returning today. On Monday, I got exactly what I wanted—it's a wool tapestry with roses and birds—but when I got them home, I found they were the wrong length. Well, I exchanged them yesterday, and when I got them home, I found they were still the wrong length. Now I'm praying to high Heaven that the decorator will have them in the right length, because you know my house, you *know* my living-room windows, and you can imagine what a problem they present. I don't know what to do with them."

"I know what to do with them," Francis said.

"What?"

"Paint them black on the inside, and shut up."

There was a gasp from Mrs. Wrightson, and Francis looked down at her to be sure that she knew he meant to be rude. She turned and walked away from him, so damaged in spirit that she limped. A wonderful feeling enveloped him, as if light were being shaken about him, and he thought again of Venus combing and combing her hair as she drifted through the Bronx. The realization of how many years had passed since he had enjoyed being deliberately impolite sobered him. Among his friends and neighbors, there were brilliant and gifted people—he saw that—but many of them, also, were bores and fools, and he made the mistake of listening to them all with equal attention. He had confused a lack of discrimination with Christian love, and the confusion seemed general and destructive. He was grateful to the girl for this bracing sensation of independence. Birds were singing—cardinals and the last of the robins. The sky shone like enamel. Even the smell of ink from his morning paper honed his appetite for life, and the world that was spread out around him was plainly a paradise.

If Francis had believed in some hierarchy of love—in spirits armed with hunting bows, in the capriciousness of Venus and Eros—or even in magical potions, philtres, and stews, in scapulae and quarters of the moon, it might have explained his susceptibility and his feverish high spirits. The autumnal loves of middle age are well publicized, and he guessed that he was face to face with one of these, but there was not a trace of autumn in what he felt. He wanted to sport in the green woods, scratch where he itched, and drink from the same cup.

His secretary, Miss Rainey, was late that morning—she went to a psychiatrist three mornings a week—and when she came in, Francis wondered what advice a psychiatrist would have for him. But the girl promised to bring back into his life something like the sound of music. The realization that this music might lead him straight to a trial for statutory rape at the county courthouse collapsed his happiness. The photograph of his four children laughing into the camera on the beach at Gay Head reproached him. On the letterhead of his firm there was a drawing of the "Laocoōn," and the figure of the priest and his sons in the coils of the snake appeared to him to have the deepest meaning.

He had lunch with Pinky Trabert, who told him a couple of dirty stories. At a conversational level, the mores of his friends were robust and elastic, but he knew that the moral card house would come down on them all—on Julia and the children as well—if he got caught taking advantage of a babysitter. Looking back over the recent history of Shady Hill for some precedent, he found there was none. There was no turpitude; there had not been a divorce since he lived there; there had not even been a breath of scandal. Things seemed arranged with more propriety even than in the Kingdom of Heaven. After leaving Pinky, Francis went to a jeweller's and bought the girl a bracelet. How happy this clandestine purchase made him, how stuffy and comical the jeweller's clerks seemed, how sweet the women who passed at his back smelled! On Fifth Avenue, passing Atlas with his shoulders bent under the weight of the world, Francis thought of the strenuousness of containing his physicalness within the patterns he had chosen.

He did not know when he would see the girl next. He had the bracelet in his inside pocket when he got home. Opening the door of his house, he found her in the hall. Her back was to him, and she turned when she heard the door close. Her smile was open and loving. Her perfection stunned him like a fine day—a day after a thunderstorm. He seized her and covered her lips with his, and she struggled but she did not have to struggle for long, because just then little Gertrude Flannery appeared from somewhere and said, "Oh, Mr. Weed . . ."

Gertrude was a stray. She had been born with a taste for exploration, and she did not have it in her to center her life with her affectionate parents. People who did not know the Flannerys concluded from Gertrude's behavior that she was the child of a bitterly divided family, where drunken quarrels were the rule. This was not true. The fact that little Gertrude's clothing was ragged and thin was her own triumph over her mother's struggle to dress her warmly and neatly. Garrulous, skinny, and unwashed, she drifted from house to house around the Blenhollow neighborhood, forming and breaking alliances based on an attachment to babies, animals, children her own age, adolescents, and sometimes adults. Opening your front door in the morning, you would find Gertrude sitting on your stoop. Going into the bathroom to shave, you would find Gertrude using the toilet. Looking into your son's crib, you would find it empty, and, looking further, you would find that Gertrude had pushed him in his baby carriage into the next village. She was helpful, pervasive, honest, hungry, and loyal. She never went home of her own choice. When the time to go arrived, she was indifferent to all its signs. "Go home, Gertrude," people could be heard saying in one house or another, night after night. "Go home, Gertrude." "It's time for you to go home now, Gertrude." "You had better go home and get your supper, Gertrude." "I told you to go home twenty minutes ago, Gertrude." "Your mother will be worrying about you, Gertrude." "Go home, Gertrude, go home."

There are times when the lines around the human eye seem like shelves of eroded stone and when the staring eye itself strikes us with such a wilderness of animal feeling that we are at a loss. The look Francis gave the little girl was ugly and queer, and it frightened her. He reached into his pocket—his hands were shaking—and took out a quarter. "Go home, Gertrude, go home, and don't tell anyone, Gertrude. Don't—" He choked and ran into the living room as Julia called down to him from upstairs to hurry and dress.

The thought that he would drive Anne Murchison home later that night ran like a golden thread through the events of the party that Francis and Julia went to, and he laughed uproariously at dull jokes, dried a tear when Mabel Mercer told him about the death of her kitten, and stretched, yawned, sighed, and grunted like any other man with a rendezvous at the back of his mind. The bracelet was in his pocket. As he sat talking, the smell of grass was in his nose, and he was wondering where he would park the car. Nobody lived in the old Parker mansion, and the driveway was used as a lover's lane. Townsend Street was a dead end, and he could park there, beyond the last house. The old lane that used to connect Elm Street to the riverbanks was overgrown, but he had walked there with his children, and he could drive his car deep enough into the brushwoods to be concealed.

The Weeds were the last to leave the party, and their host and hostess spoke of their own married happiness while they all four stood in the hallway saying good night. "She's my girl," their host said, squeezing his wife. "She's my blue sky. After sixteen years, I still bite her shoulders. She makes me feel like Hannibal crossing the Alps."

The Weeds drove home in silence. Francis brought his car up to the driveway and sat still, with the motor running. "You can put the car in the garage," Julia said as she got out. "I told the Murchison girl she could leave at eleven. Someone drove her home." She shut the door, and Francis sat in the dark. He would be spared nothing then, it seemed, that a fool was not spared: ravening, lewdness, jealousy, this hurt to his feelings that put tears in his eyes, even scorn—for he could see clearly the image he now presented, his arms spread over the steering wheel and his head buried in them for love. Francis had been a dedicated Boy Scout when he was young, and, remembering the precepts of his youth, he left his office early the next afternoon and played some round-robin squash, but, with his body toned up by exercise and a shower, he realized that he might better have stayed at his desk. It was a frosty night when he got home. The air smelled sharply of change. When he stepped into the house, he sensed an unusual stir. The children were in their best clothes, and when Julia came down she was wearing a lavender dress and her diamond sunburst. She explained the stir: Mr. Hubber was coming at seven to take their photograph for the Christmas card. She had put out Francis' blue suit and a tie with some color in it, because the picture was going to be in color this year. Julia was light-hearted at the thought of being photographed for Christmas. It was the kind of ceremony she enjoyed.

Francis went upstairs to change his clothes. He was tired from the day's work and tired with longing, and sitting on the edge of the bed had the effect of deepening his weariness. He thought of Anne Murchison, and the physical need to express himself, instead of being restrained by the pink lamps on Julia's dressing table, engulfed him. He went to Julia's desk, took a piece of writing paper, and began to write on it. "Dear Anne, I love you, I love you, I love you . . ." No one would see the letter, and he used no restraint. He used phrases like "Heavenly bliss," and "love nest." He salivated, sighed, and trembled. When Julia called him to come down, the abyss between his fantasy and the practical world opened so wide that he felt it affect the muscles of his heart.

Julia and the children were on the stoop, and the photographer and his assistant had set up a double battery of floodlights to show the family and architectural beauty of the entrance to their house. People who had come home on a late train slowed their cars to see the Weeds being photographed for their Christmas card. A few waved and called to the family. It took half an hour of smiling and wetting their lips before Mr. Hubber was satisfied. The heat of the lights made an unfresh smell in the frosty air, and when they were turned off, they lingered on the retina of Francis' eyes.

Later that night, while Francis and Julia were drinking their coffee in the living room, the doorbell rang. Julia answered the door and let in Clayton Thomas. He had come to pay her for some theatre tickets that she had given his mother some time ago, and that Helen Thomas had scrupulously insisted on paying for, though Julia had asked her not to. Julia invited him in to have a cup of coffee. "I won't have any coffee," Clayton said, "but I will come in for a minute." He followed her into the living room, said good evening to Francis, and sat down awkwardly in a chair.

Clayton's father had been killed in the war, and the young man's fatherlessness surrounded him like an element. This may have been conspicuous in Shady Hill because the Thomases were the only family that lacked a piece; all the other marriages were intact and productive. Clayton was in his second or third year of college, and he and his mother lived alone in a large house which she hoped to sell. Clayton had once made some trouble. Years ago, he had stolen some money and run away; he had got to California before they caught up with him. He was tall and homely, wore horn-rimmed glasses, and spoke in a deep voice.

"When do you go back to college, Clayton?" Francis asked.

"I'm not going back," Clayton said. "Mother doesn't have the money, and there's no sense in all this pretense. I'm going to get a job, and if we sell the house, we'll take an apartment in New York."

"Won't you miss Shady Hill?" Julia asked.

"No," Clayton said. "I don't like it."

"Why not?" Francis asked.

"Well, there's a lot here I don't approve of," Clayton said gravely. "Things like the club dances. Last Saturday night, I looked in toward the end and saw Mr. Granner trying to put Mrs. Minot into the trophy case. They were both drunk. I disapprove of so much drinking."

"It was Saturday night," Francis said.

"And all the dovecotes are phony," Clayton said. "And the way people clutter up their lives. I've thought about it a lot, and what seems to me to be really wrong with Shady Hill is that it doesn't have any future. So much energy is spent in perpetuating the place—in keeping out undesirables, and so forth—that the only idea of the future anyone has is just more and more commuting trains and more parties. I don't think that's healthy. I think people ought to be able to dream big dreams about the future. I think people ought to be able to dream great dreams."

"It's too bad you couldn't continue with college," Julia said.

"I wanted to go to divinity school," Clayton said.

"What's your church?" Francis asked.

"Unitarian, Theosophist, Transcendentalist, Humanist," Clayton said.

"Wasn't Emerson a transcendentalist?" Julia asked.

"I mean the English transcendentalists," Clayton said. "All the American transcendentalists were goops."

"What kind of a job do you expect to get?" Francis asked.

"Well, I'd like to work for a publisher," Clayton said, "but everyone tells me there's nothing doing. But it's the kind of thing I'm interested in. I'm writing a long verse play about good and evil. Uncle Charlie might get me into a bank, and that would be good for me. I need the discipline. I have a long way to go in forming my character. I have some terrible habits. I talk too much. I think I ought to take vows of silence. I ought to try not to speak for a week, and discipline myself. I've thought of making a retreat at one of the Episcopalian monasteries, but I don't like Trinitarianism."

"Do you have any girl friends?" Francis asked.

"I'm engaged to be married," Clayton said. "Of course, I'm not old enough or rich enough to have my engagement observed or respected or anything, but I bought a simulated emerald for Anne Murchison with the money I made cutting lawns this summer. We're going to be married as soon as she finishes school."

Francis recoiled at the mention of the girl's name. Then a dingy light seemed to emanate from his spirit, showing everything—Julia, the boy, the chairs—in their true colorlessness. It was like a bitter turn of the weather.

"We're going to have a large family," Clayton said. "Her father's a terrible rummy, and I've had my hard times, and we want to have lots of children. Oh, she's wonderful, Mr. and Mrs. Weed, and we have so much in common. We like all the same things. We sent out the same Christmas card last year without planning it, and we both have an allergy to tomatoes, and our eyebrows grow together in the middle. Well, good night."

Julia went to the door with him. When she returned, Francis said that Clayton was lazy, irresponsible, affected, and smelly. Julia said that Francis seemed to be getting intolerant; the Thomas boy was young and should be given a chance. Julia had noticed other cases where Francis had been short-tempered. "Mrs. Wrightson has asked everyone in Shady Hill to her anniversary party but us," she said.

"I'm sorry. Julia."

"Do you know why they didn't ask us?"

"Why?"

"Because you insulted Mrs. Wrightson."

"Then you know about it?"

"June Masterson told me. She was standing behind you."

Julia walked in front of the sofa with a small step that expressed, Francis knew, a feeling of anger.

"I did insult Mrs. Wrightson, Julia, and I meant to. I've never liked her parties, and I'm glad she's dropped us."

"What about Helen?"

"How does Helen come into this?"

"Mrs. Wrightson's the one who decides who goes to the assemblies."

"You mean she can keep Helen from going to the dances?"

"Yes."

"I hadn't thought of that."

"Oh, I knew you hadn't thought of it," Julia cried, thrusting hilt-deep into this chink of his armor. "And it makes me furious to see this kind of stupid thoughtlessness wreck everyone's happiness."

"I don't think I've wrecked anyone's happiness."

"Mrs. Wrightson runs Shady Hill and has run it for the last forty years. I don't know what makes you think that in a community like this you can indulge every impulse you have to be insulting, vulgar, and offensive."

"I have very good manners," Francis said, trying to give the evening a turn toward the light.

"Damn you, Francis Weed!" Julia cried, and the spit of her words struck him in the face. "I've worked hard for the social position we enjoy in this place, and I won't stand by and see you wreck it. You must have understood when you settled here that you couldn't expect to live like a bear in a cave."

"I've got to express my likes and dislikes."

"You can conceal your dislikes. You don't have to meet everything head-on, like a child. Unless you're anxious to be a social leper. It's no accident that we get asked out a great deal. It's no accident that Helen has so many friends. How would you like to spend your Saturday nights at the movies? How would you like to spend your Sundays raking up dead leaves? How would you like it if your daughter spent the assembly nights sitting at her window, listening to the music from the club? How would you like it—" He did something then that was, after all, not so unaccountable, since her words seemed to raise up between them a wall so deadening that he gagged: He struck her full in the face. She staggered and then, a moment later, seemed composed. She went up the stairs to their room. She didn't slam the door. When Francis followed, a few minutes later, he found her packing a suitcase.

"Julia, I'm very sorry."

"It doesn't matter," she said. She was crying.

"Where do you think you're going?"

"I don't know. I just looked at a timetable. There's an eleven-sixteen into New York. I'll take that."

"You can't go, Julia."

"I can't stay. I know that."

"I'm sorry about Mrs. Wrightson, Julia, and I'm—"

"It doesn't matter about Mrs. Wrightson. That isn't the trouble."

"What is the trouble?"

"You don't love me."

"I do love you, Julia."

"No, you don't."

"Julia, I do love you, and I would like to be as we were—sweet and bawdy and dark—but now there are so many people."

"You hate me."

"I don't hate you, Julia."

"You have no idea of how much you hate me. I think it's subconscious. You don't realize the cruel things you've done."

"What cruel things, Julia?"

"The cruel acts your subconscious drives you to in order to express your hatred of me."

"What, Julia?"

"I've never complained."

"Tell me."

"You don't know what you're doing."

"Tell me."

"Your clothes."

"What do you mean?"

"I mean the way you leave your dirty clothes around in order to express your subconscious hatred of me."

"I don't understand."

"I mean your dirty socks and your dirty pajamas and your dirty underwear and your dirty shirts!" She rose from kneeling by the suitcase and faced him, her eyes blazing and her voice ringing with emotion. "I'm talking about the fact that you've never learned to hang up anything. You just leave your clothes all over the floor where they drop, in order to humiliate me. You do it on purpose!" She fell on the bed, sobbing.

"Julia, darling!" he said, but when she felt his hand on her shoulder she got up.

"Leave me alone," she said. "I have to go." She brushed past him to the closet and came back with a dress. "I'm not taking any of the things you've given me," she said. "I'm leaving my pearls and the fur jacket."

"Oh, Julia!" Her figure, so helpless in its self-deceptions, bent over the suitcase made him nearly sick with pity. She did not understand how desolate her life would be without him. She didn't understand the hours that working women have to keep. She didn't understand that most of her friendships existed within the framework of their marriage, and that without this she would find herself alone. She didn't understand about travel, about hotels, about money. "Julia, I can't let you go! What you don't understand, Julia, is that you've come to be dependent on me."

She tossed her head back and covered her face with her hands. "Did you say that *I* was dependent on *you*?" she asked. "Is that what you said? And who is it that tells you what time to get up in the morning and when to go to bed at night? Who is it that prepares your meals and picks up your dirty closet and invites your friends to dinner? If it weren't for me, your neckties would be greasy and your clothing would be full of moth holes. You were alone when I met you, Francis Weed, and you'll be alone when I leave. When Mother asked you for a list to send out invitations to our wedding, how many names did you have to give her? Fourteen!"

"Cleveland wasn't my home, Julia."

"And how many of your friends came to the church? Two!"

"Cleveland wasn't my home, Julia."

"Since I'm not taking the fur jacket," she said quietly, "you'd better put it back into storage. There's an insurance policy on the pearls that comes due in January. The name of the laundry and the maid's telephone number—all those things are in my desk. I hope you won't drink too much, Francis. I hope that nothing bad will happen to you. If you do get into serious trouble, you can call me."

"Oh my darling, I can't let you go!" Francis said. "I can't let you go, Julia!" He took her in his arms.

"I guess I'd better stay and take care of you for a little while longer," she said.

Riding to work in the morning, Francis saw the girl walk down the aisle of the coach. He was surprised; he hadn't realized that the school she went to was in the city, but she was carrying books, she seemed to be going to school. His surprise delayed his reaction, but then he got up clumsily and stepped into the aisle. Several people had come between them, but he could see her ahead of him, waiting for someone to open the car door, and then, as the train swerved, putting out her hand to support herself as she crossed the platform into the next car. He followed her through that car and halfway through another before calling her name— "Anne! Anne!"—but she didn't turn. He followed her into still another car, and she sat down in an aisle seat. Coming up to her, all his feelings warm and bent in her direction, he put his hand on the back of her seat—even this touch warmed him and, leaning down to speak to her, he saw that it was not Anne. It was an older woman wearing glasses. He went on deliberately into another car, his face red with embarrassment and the much deeper feeling of having his good sense challenged; for if he couldn't tell one person from another, what evidence was there that his life with Julia and the children had as much reality as his dreams of iniquity in Paris or the litter, the grass smell, and the cave-shaped trees in Lovers' Lane.

Late that afternoon, Julia called to remind Francis that they were going out for dinner. A few minutes later, Trace Bearden called. "Look, fellar," Trace said. "I'm calling for Mrs. Thomas. You know? Clayton, that boy of hers, doesn't seem able to get a job, and I wondered if you could help. If you'd call Charlie Bell—I know he's indebted to you—and say a good word for the kid, I think Charlie would—"

"Trace, I hate to say this," Francis said, "but I don't feel that I can do anything for that boy. The kid's worthless. I know it's a harsh thing to say, but it's a fact. Any kindness done for him would backfire in everybody's face. He's just a worthless kid, Trace, and there's nothing to be done about it. Even if we got him a job, he wouldn't be able to keep it for a week. I know that to be a fact. It's an awful thing, Trace, and I know it is, but instead of recommending that kid, I'd feel obliged to warn people against him—people who knew his father and would naturally want to step in and do something. I'd feel obliged to warn them. He's a thief . . ."

The moment this conversation was finished, Miss Rainey came in and stood by his desk. "I'm not going to be able to work for you any more, Mr. Weed," she said. "I can stay until the seventeenth if you need me, but I've been offered a whirlwind of a job, and I'd like to leave as soon as possible."

She went out, leaving him to face alone the wickedness of what he had done to the Thomas boy. His children in their photograph laughed and laughed, glazed with all the bright colors of summer, and he remembered that they had met a bagpiper on the beach that day and he had paid the piper a dollar to play them a battle song of The Black Watch. The girl would be at the house when he got home. He would spend another evening among his kind neighbors, picking and choosing dead-end streets, car tracks, and the driveways of abandoned houses. There was nothing to mitigate his feeling—nothing that laughter or a game of softball with the children would change—and, thinking back over the plane crash, the Farquarsons' new maid, and Anne Murchison's difficulties with her drunken father, he wondered how he could have avoided arriving at just where he was. He was in trouble. He had been lost once in his life, coming back from a trout stream in the north woods, and he had now the same bleak realization that no amount of cheerfulness or hopefulness or valor or perseverance could help him find, in the gathering dark, the path that he'd lost. He smelled the forest. The feeling of bleakness was intolerable, and he saw clearly that he had reached the point where he would have to make a choice.

He could go to a psychiatrist, like Miss Rainey; he could go to church and confess his lusts; he could go to a Danish massage parlor in the West Seventies that had been recommended by a salesman; he could rape the girl or trust that he would somehow be prevented from doing this; or he could get drunk. It was his life, his boat, and, like every other man, he was made to be the father of thousands, and what harm could there be in a tryst that would make them both feel more kindly toward the world? This was the wrong train of thought, and he came back to the first, the psychiatrist. He had the telephone number of Miss Rainey's doctor, and he called and asked for an immediate appointment. He was insistent with the doctor's secretary—it was his manner in business—and when she said that the doctor's schedule was full for the next few weeks, Francis demanded an appointment that day and was told to come at five.

The psychiatrist's office was in a building that was used mostly by doctors and dentists, and the hallways were filled with the candy smell of mouthwash and memories of pain. Francis' character had been formed upon a series of private resolves—resolves about cleanliness, about going off the high diving board or repeating any other feat that challenged his courage, about punctuality, honesty, and virtue. To abdicate the perfect loneliness in which he had made his most vital decisions shattered his concept of character and left him now in a condition that felt like shock. He was stupefied. The scene for his *miserere mei Deus* was, like the waiting room of so many doctors' offices, a crude token gesture toward the sweets of domestic bliss: a place arranged with antiques, coffee tables, potted plants, and etchings of snow-covered bridges and geese in flight, although there were no children, no marriage bed, no stove, even, in this travesty of a house, where no one had ever spent the night and where the curtained windows looked straight onto a dark air shaft. Francis gave his name and address to a secretary and then saw, at the side of the room, a policeman moving toward him. "Hold it, hold it," the policeman said. "Don't move. Keep your hands where they are."

"I think it's all right, Officer," the secretary began "I think it will be—"

"Let's make sure," the policeman said, and he began to slap Francis' clothes, looking for what—pistols, knives, an icepick? Finding nothing, he went off, and the secretary began a nervous apology: "When you called on the telephone, Mr. Weed, you seemed very excited, and one of the doctor's patients has been threatening his life, and we have to be careful. If you want to go in now?" Francis pushed open a door connected to an electrical chime, and in the doctor's lair sat down heavily, blew his nose into a handkerchief, searched in his pockets for cigarettes, for matches, for something, and said hoarsely, with tears in his eyes, "I'm in love, Dr. Herzog."

It is a week or ten days later in Shady Hill. The seven-fourteen has come and gone, and here and there dinner is finished and the dishes are in the dishwashing machine. The village hangs, morally and economically, from a thread; but it hangs by its thread in the evening light. Donald Goslin has begun to worry the "Moonlight Sonata" again. *Marcato ma sempre pianissimo!* He seems to be wringing out a wet bath towel, but the housemaid does not heed him. She is writing a letter to Arthur Godfrey. In the cellar of his house, Francis Weed is building a coffee table. Dr. Herzog recommended woodwork as a therapy, and Francis finds some true consolation in the simple arithmetic involved and in the holy smell of new wood. Francis is happy. Upstairs, little Toby is crying, because he is tired. He puts off his cowboy hat, gloves, and fringed jacket, unbuckles the belt studded with gold and rubies, the silver bullets and holsters, slips off his suspenders, his checked shirt, and Levis, and sits on the edge of his bed to pull off his high boots. Leaving this equipment in a heap, he goes to the closet and takes his space suit off a nail. It is a struggle for him to get into the long tights, but he succeeds. He loops the magic cape over his shoulders and, climbing onto the footboard of his bed, he spreads his arms and flies the short distance to the floor, landing with a thump that is audible to everyone in the house but himself.

"Go home, Gertrude, go home," Mrs. Masterson says. "I told you to go home an hour ago, Gertrude. It's way past your suppertime, and your mother will be worried. Go home!" A door on the Babcocks' terrace flies open, and out comes Mrs. Babcock without any clothes on, pursued by her naked husband. (Their children are away at boarding school, and their terrace is screened by a hedge.) Over the terrace they go and in at the kitchen door, as passionate and handsome a nymph and satyr as you will find on any wall in Venice. Cutting the last of the roses in her garden, Julia hears old Mr. Nixon shouting at the squirrels in his bird-feeding station. "Rapscallions! Varmits! Avaunt and quit my sight!" A miserable cat wanders into the garden, sunk in spiritual and physical discomfort. Tied to its head is a small straw hat—a doll's hat—and it is securely buttoned into a doll's dress, from the skirts of which protrudes its long, hairy tail. As it walks, it shakes its feet, as if it had fallen into water.

"Here, pussy, pussy, pussy!" Julia calls. "Here, pussy, here, poor pussy!" But the cat gives her a skeptical look and stumbles away in its skirts. The last to come is Jupiter. He prances through the tomato vines, holding in his generous mouth the remains of an evening slipper. Then it is dark; it is a night where kings in golden suits ride elephants over the mountains.

About Shirley Jackson

She claimed to be born in 1919 but birth records show that she was born in 1916. This popular American writer of horror stories is thought to have influenced a new generation of contemporary writers such as Stephen King. Her work, in the tradition of Hawthorne and Poe, attracted wide audiences and raised controversy with critics and the public. She and her husband, critic Stanley Edgar Hyman, raised four children in North Bennington, Vermont, where she died of heart failure in 1965 at age 48.

The Lottery

The morning of June 27th was clear and sunny, with the fresh warmth of a full-summer day; the flowers were blossoming profusely and the grass was richly green. The people of the village began to gather in the square, between the post office and the bank, around ten o'clock; in some towns there were so many people that the lottery took two days and had to be started on June 26th, but in this village, where there were only about three hundred people, the whole lottery took less than two hours, so it could begin at ten o'clock in the morning and still be through in time to allow the villagers to get home for noon dinner.

The children assembled first, of course. School was recently over for the summer, and the feeling of liberty sat uneasily on most of them; they tended to gather quietly for a while before they broke into boisterous play, and their talk was still of the classroom and the teacher, of books and reprimands. Bobby Martin had already stuffed his pockets full of stones, and the other boys soon followed his example, selecting the smoothest and roundest stones; Bobby and Harry Jones and Dickie Delacroix—the villagers pronounced this name "Dellacroy"—eventually made a great pile of stones in one corner of the square and guarded it against the raids of the other boys. The girls stood aside, talking among themselves, looking over their shoulders at the boys, and the very small children rolled in the dust or clung to the hands of their older brothers or sisters.

Soon the men began to gather, surveying their own children, speaking of planting and rain, tractors and taxes. They stood together, away from the pile of stones in the corner, and their jokes were quiet and they smiled rather than laughed. The women, wearing faded house dresses and sweaters, came shortly after their menfolk. They greeted one another and exchanged bits of gossip as they went to join their husbands. Soon the women, standing by their husbands, began to call to their children, and the children came reluctantly, having to be called four or five times. Bobby Martin ducked under his mother's grasping hand and ran, laughing, back to the pile of stones. His father spoke up sharply, and Bobby came quickly and took his place between his father and his oldest brother.

The lottery was conducted—as were the square dances, the teen-age club, the Halloween program—by Mr. Summers, who had time and energy to devote to civic activities. He was a round-faced, jovial man and he ran the coal business, and people were sorry for him, because he had no children and his wife was a scold. When he arrived in the square, carrying the black wooden box, there was a murmur of conversation among the villagers, and he waved and called, "Little late today, folks." The postmaster, Mr. Graves, followed him, carrying a three-legged stool, and the stool was put in the center of the square and Mr. Summers set the black box down on it. The villagers kept their distance, leaving a space between themselves and the stool, and when Mr. Summers said, "Some of you fellows want to give me a hand?" there was a hesitation before two men, Mr. Martin and his oldest son, Baxter, came forward to hold the box steady on the stool while Mr. Summers stirred up the papers inside it.

The original paraphernalia for the lottery had been lost long ago, and the black box now resting on the stool had been put into use even before Old Man Warner, the oldest man in town, was born. Mr. Summers spoke frequently to the villagers about making a new box, but no one liked to upset even as much tradition as was represented by the black box. There was a story that the present box had been made with some pieces of the box that had preceded it, the one that had been constructed when the first people settled down to make a village here. Every year, after the lottery, Mr. Summers began talking again about a new box, but every year the subject was allowed to fade off without anything's being done. The black box grew shabbier each year; by now it was no longer completely black but splintered badly along one side to show the original wood color, and in some places faded or stained.

Mr. Martin and his oldest son, Baxter, held the black box securely on the stool until Mr. Summers had stirred the papers thoroughly with his hand. Because so much of the ritual had been forgotten or discarded, Mr. Summers had been successful in having slips of paper substituted for the chips of wood that had been used for generations. Chips of wood, Mr. Summers had argued, had been all very well when the village was tiny, but now that the population was more than three hundred and likely to keep on growing, it was necessary to use something that would fit more easily into the black box. The night before the lottery, Mr. Summers and Mr. Graves made up the slips of paper and put them in the box, and it was then taken to the safe of Mr. Summers' coal company and locked up until Mr. Summers was ready to take it to the square next morning. The rest of the year, the box was put away, sometimes one place, sometimes another; it had spent one year in Mr. Graves's barn and another year underfoot in the post office, and sometimes it was set on a shelf in the Martin grocery and left there.

There was a great deal of fussing to be done before Mr. Summers declared the lottery open. There were the lists to make up—of heads of families, heads of households in each family, members of each household in each family. There was the proper swearing-in of Mr. Summers by the postmaster, as the official of the lottery; at one time, some people remembered, there had been a recital of some sort, performed by the official of the lottery, a perfunctory, tuneless chant that had been rattled off duly each year; some people believed that the official of the lottery used to stand just so when he said or sang it, others believed that he was supposed to walk among the people, but years and years ago this part of the ritual had been allowed to lapse. There had been, also, a ritual salute, which the official of the lottery had had to use in addressing each person who came up to draw from the box, but this also had changed with time, until now it was felt necessary only for the official to speak to each person approaching. Mr. Summers was very good at all this; in his clean white shirt and blue jeans, with one hand resting carelessly on the black box, he seemed very proper and important as he talked interminably to Mr. Graves and the Martins.

Just as Mr. Summers finally left off talking and turned to the assembled villagers, Mrs. Hutchinson came hurriedly along the path to the square, her sweater thrown over her shoulders, and slid into place in the back of the crowd. "Clean forgot what day it was," she said to Mrs. Delacroix, who stood next to her, and they both laughed softly. "Thought my old man was out back stacking wood," Mrs. Hutchinson went on, "and then I looked out the window and the kids was gone, and then I remembered it was the twenty-seventh and came a-running." She dried her hands on her apron, and Mrs. Delacroix said, "You're in time, though. They're still talking away up there."

Mrs. Hutchinson craned her neck to see through the crowd and found her husband and children standing near the front. She tapped Mrs. Delacroix on the arm as a farewell and began to make her way through the crowd. The people separated good-humoredly to let her through; two or three people said, in voices just loud enough to be heard across the crowd, "Here comes your Missus, Hutchinson," and "Bill, she made it after all." Mrs. Hutchinson reached her husband, and Mr. Summers, who had been waiting, said cheerfully, "Thought we were going to have to get on without you, Tessie." Mrs. Hutchinson said, grinning, "Wouldn't have me leave m'dishes in the sink, now, would you, Joe?," and soft laughter ran through the crowd as the people stirred back into position after Mrs. Hutchinson's arrival.

"Well, now," Mr. Summers said soberly, "guess we better get started, get this over with, so's we can go back to work. Anybody ain't here?"

"Dunbar," several people said. "Dunbar, Dunbar."

Mr. Summers consulted his list. "Clyde Dunbar," he said. "That's right. He's broke his leg, hasn't he? Who's drawing for him?"

"Me, I guess," a woman said, and Mr. Summers turned to look at her. "Wife draws for her husband," Mr. Summers said. "Don't you have a grown boy to do it for you, Janey?" Although Mr. Summers and everyone else in the village knew the answer perfectly well, it was the business of the official of the lottery to ask such questions formally. Mr. Summers waited with an expression of polite interest while Mrs. Dunbar answered.

"Horace's not but sixteen yet," Mrs. Dunbar said regretfully. "Guess I gotta fill in for the old man this year."

"Right," Mr. Summers said. He made a note on the list he was holding. Then he asked, "Watson boy drawing this year?"

A tall boy in the crowd raised his hand. "Here," he said. "I'm drawing for m'mother and me." He blinked his eyes nervously and ducked his head as several voices in the crowd said things like "Good fellow, Jack," and "Glad to see your mother's got a man to do it."

"Well," Mr. Summers said, "guess that's everyone. Old Man Warner make it?"

"Here," a voice said, and Mr. Summers nodded.

A sudden hush fell on the crowd as Mr. Summers cleared his throat and looked at the list. "All ready?" he called. "Now, I'll read the names—heads of families first—and the men come up and take a paper out of the box. Keep the paper folded in your hand without looking at it until everyone has had a turn. Everything clear?"

The people had done it so many times that they only half listened to the directions; most of them were quiet, wetting their lips, not looking around. Then Mr. Summers raised one hand high and said, "Adams." A man disengaged himself from the crowd and came forward. "Hi, Steve," Mr. Summers said, and Mr. Adams said, "Hi, Joe." They grinned at one another humorlessly and nervously. Then Mr. Adams reached into the black box and took out a folded paper. He held it firmly by one corner as he turned and went hastily back to his place in the crowd, where he stood a little apart from his family, not looking down at his hand.

"Allen," Mr. Summers said. "Anderson . . . Bentham."

"Seems like there's no time at all between lotteries any more," Mrs. Delacroix said to Mrs. Graves in the back row. "Seems like we got through with the last one only last week."

"Time sure goes fast," Mrs. Graves said.

"Clark . . . Delacroix."

"There goes my old man," Mrs. Delacroix said. She held her breath while her husband went forward.

"Dunbar," Mr. Summers said, and Mrs. Dunbar went steadily to the box while one of the women said, "Go on, Janey," and another said, "There she goes."

"We're next," Mrs. Graves said. She watched while Mr. Graves came around from the side of the box, greeted Mr. Summers gravely, and selected a slip of paper from the box. By now, all through the crowd there were men holding the small folded papers in their large hands, turning them over and over nervously. Mrs. Dunbar and her two sons stood together, Mrs. Dunbar holding the slip of paper.

"Harburt . . . Hutchinson."

"Get up there, Bill," Mrs. Hutchinson said, and the people near her laughed.

"Jones."

"They do say," Mr. Adams said to Old Man Warner, who stood next to him, "that over in the north village they're talking of giving up the lottery."

Old Man Warner snorted. "Pack of crazy fools," he said. "Listening to the young folks, nothing's good enough for *them*. Next thing you know, they'll be wanting to go back to living in caves, nobody work any more, live *that* way for a while. Used to be a saying about 'Lottery in June, corn be heavy soon.' First thing you know, we'd all be eating stewed chickweed and acorns. There's *always* been a lottery," he added petulantly. "Bad enough to see young Joe Summers up there joking with everybody."

"Some places have already quit lotteries," Mrs. Adams said.

"Nothing but trouble in *that*," Old Man Warner said stoutly. "Pack of young fools." "Martin." And Bobby Martin watched his father go forward. "Overdyke . . . Percy."

"I wish they'd hurry," Mrs. Dunbar said to her older son. "I wish they'd hurry."

"They're almost through," her son said.

"You get ready to run tell Dad," Mrs. Dunbar said.

Mr. Summers called his own name and then stepped forward precisely and selected a slip from the box. Then he called, "Warner."

"Seventy-seventh year I been in the lottery," Old Man Warner said as he went through the crowd. "Seventy-seventh time."

"Watson." The tall boy came awkwardly through the crowd. Someone said, "Don't be nervous, Jack," and Mr. Summers said, "Take your time, son."

"Zanini."

After that, there was a long pause, a breathless pause, until Mr. Summers, holding his slip of paper in the air, said, "All right, fellows." For a minute, no one moved, and then all the slips of paper were opened. Suddenly, all the women began to speak at once, saying, "Who is it?," "Who's got it?," "Is it the Dunbars?," "Is it the Watsons?" Then the voices began to say, "It's Hutchinson. It's Bill." "Bill Hutchinson's got it."

"Go tell your father," Mrs. Dunbar said to her older son.

People began to look around to see the Hutchinsons. Bill Hutchinson was standing quiet, staring down at the paper in his hand. Suddenly, Tessie Hutchinson shouted to Mr. Summers, "You didn't give him time enough to take any paper he wanted. I saw you. It wasn't fair!"

"Be a good sport, Tessie," Mrs. Delacroix called, and Mrs. Graves said, "All of us took the same chance."

"Shut up, Tessie," Bill Hutchinson said.

"Well, everyone," Mr. Summers said, "that was done pretty fast, and now we've got to be hurrying a little more to get done in time." He consulted his next list. "Bill," he said, "you draw for the Hutchinson family. You got any other households in the Hutchinsons?" "There's Don and Eva," Mrs. Hutchinson yelled. "Make *them* take their chance!"

"Daughters draw with their husbands' families, Tessie," Mr. Summers said gently. "You know that as well as anyone else."

"It wasn't *fair*," Tessie said.

"I guess not, Joe," Bill Hutchinson said regretfully. "My daughter draws with her husband's family, that's only fair. And I've got no other family except the kids."

"Then, as far as drawing for families is concerned, it's you," Mr. Summers said in explanation, "and as far as drawing for households is concerned, that's you, too. Right?"

"Right," Bill Hutchinson said.

"How many kids, Bill?" Mr. Summers asked formally.

"Three," Bill Hutchinson said. "There's Bill, Jr., and Nancy, and little Dave. And Tessie and me."

"All right, then," Mr. Summers said. "Harry, you got their tickets back?"

Mr. Graves nodded and held up the slips of paper. "Put them in the box, then," Mr. Summers directed. "Take Bill's and put it in."

"I think we ought to start over," Mrs. Hutchinson said, as quietly as she could. "I tell you it wasn't *fair*. You didn't give him time enough to choose. *Every*body saw that."

Mr. Graves had selected the five slips and put them in the box, and he dropped all the papers but those onto the ground, where the breeze caught them and lifted them off.

"Listen, everybody," Mrs. Hutchinson was saying to the people around her.

"Ready, Bill?" Mr. Summers asked, and Bill Hutchinson, with one quick glance around at his wife and children, nodded.

"Remember," Mr. Summers said, "take the slips and keep them folded until each person has taken one. Harry, you help little Dave." Mr. Graves took the hand of the little boy, who came willingly with him up to the box. "Take a paper out of the box, Davy," Mr. Summers said. Davy put his hand into the box and laughed. "Take just *one* paper," Mr. Summers said. "Harry, you hold it for him." Mr. Graves took the child's hand and removed the folded paper from the tight fist and held it while little Dave stood next to him and looked up at him wonderingly.

"Nancy next," Mr. Summers said. Nancy was twelve, and her school friends breathed heavily as she went forward, switching her skirt, and took a slip daintily from the box. "Bill,Jr.," Mr. Summers said, and Billy, his face red and his feet overlarge, nearly knocked the box over as he got a paper out. "Tessie," Mr. Summers said. She hesitated for a minute, looking around defiantly, and then set her lips and went up to the box. She snatched a paper out and held it behind her.

"Bill," Mr. Summers said, and Bill Hutchinson reached into the box and felt around, bringing his hand out at last with the slip of paper in it.

The crowd was quiet. A girl whispered, "I hope it's not Nancy," and the sound of the whisper reached the edges of the crowd.

"It's not the, way it used to be," Old Man Warner said clearly. "People ain't the way they used to be."

"All right," Mr. Summers said. "Open the papers. Harry, you open little Dave's."

Mr. Graves opened the slip of paper and there was a general sigh through the crowd as he held it up and everyone could see that it was blank. Nancy and Bill,Jr., opened theirs at the same time, and both beamed and laughed, turning around to the crowd and holding their slips of paper above their heads.

"Tessie," Mr. Summers said. There was a pause, and then Mr. Summers looked at Bill Hutchinson, and Bill unfolded his paper and showed it. It was blank.

"It's Tessie," Mr. Summers said, and his voice was hushed. "Show us her paper, Bill."

Bill Hutchinson went over to his wife and forced the slip of paper out of her hand. It had a black spot on it, the black spot Mr. Summers had made the night before with the heavy pencil in the coal-company office. Bill Hutchinson held it up, and there was a stir in the crowd.

"All right, folks," Mr. Summers said. "Let's finish quickly."

Although the villagers had forgotten the ritual and lost the original black box, they still remembered to use stones. The pile of stones the boys had made earlier was ready; there were stones on the ground with the blowing scraps of paper that had come out of the box. Mrs. Delacroix selected a stone so large she had to pick it up with both hands and turned to Mrs. Dunbar. "Come on," she said. "Hurry up."

Mrs. Dunbar had small stones in both hands, and she said, gasping for breath, "I can't run at all. You'll have to go ahead and I'll catch up with you."

The children had stones already, and someone gave little Davy Hutchinson a few pebbles.

Tessie Hutchinson was in the center of a cleared space by now, and she held her hands out desperately as the villagers moved in on her. "It isn't fair," she said. A stone hit her on the side of the head.

Old Man Warner was saying, "Come on, come on, everyone." Steve Adams was in the front of the crowd of villagers, with Mrs. Graves beside him.

"It isn't fair, it isn't right," Mrs. Hutchinson screamed, and then they were upon her.

About Mavis Gallant

She was born in Montreal, Canada, in 1922 as Mavis Leslie Young. In 1940 she married John Gallant, and took his name, although they divorced in 1947. Dedicated to a writing career, she left Montreal in 1950 and settled in Paris, where she spent most of her life writing short stories, many of them published in *The New Yorker* and in numerous celebrated collections. Named a Foreign Honorary Member of the American Academy of Arts and Letters in1989 and Commander of the Order of Canada in 1993, she remained a Canadian citizen. She died in Paris in 2014 at age 91.

The Ice Wagon Going Down the Street

Now that they are out of world affairs and back where they started, Peter Frazier's wife says, 'Everybody else did well in the international thing except us.'

'You have to be crooked,' he tells her.

'Or smart. Pity we weren't.'

It is Sunday morning. They sit in the kitchen, drinking their coffee, slowly, remembering the past. They say the names of people as if they were magic. Peter thinks, *Agnes Brusen*, but there are hundreds of other names. As a private married joke, Peter and Sheilah wear the silk dressing gowns they bought in Hong Kong. Each thinks the other a peacock, rather splendid, but they pretend the dressing gowns are silly and worn in fun.

Peter and Sheilah and their two daughters, Sandra and Jennifer, are visiting Peter's unmarried sister, Lucille. They have been Lucille's guests seventeen weeks, ever since they returned to Toronto from the Far East. Their big old steamer trunk blocks a corner of the kitchen, making a problem of the refrigerator door; but even Lucille says the trunk may as well stay where it is, for the present. The Fraziers' future is so unsettled; everything is still in the air.

Lucille has given her bedroom to her two nieces, and sleeps on a camp cot in the hall. The parents have the living-room divan. They have no privileges here; they sleep after Lucille has seen the last television show that interests her. In the hall closet their clothes are crushed by winter overcoats. They know they are being judged for the first time. Sandra and Jennifer are waiting for Sheilah and Peter to decide. They are waiting to learn where these exotic parents will fly to next. What sort of climate will Sheilah consider? What job will Peter consent to accept? When the parents are ready, the children will make a decision of their own. It is just possible that Sandra and Jennifer will choose to stay with their aunt.

The peacock parents are watched by wrens. Lucille and her nieces are much the same—sandy-coloured, proudly plain. Neither of the girls has the father's insouciance or the mother's appearance—her height, her carriage, her thick hair, and sky-blue eyes. The children are more cautious than their parents; more Canadian. When they saw their aunt's apartment they had been away from Canada nine years, ever since they were two and four; and Jennifer, the elder, said, 'Well, now we're home.' Her voice is nasal and flat. Where did she learn that voice? And why should this be home? Peter's answer to anything about his mystifying children is, 'It must be in the blood.'

On Sunday morning Lucille takes her nieces to church. It seems to be the only condition she imposes on her relations: the children must be decent. The girls go willingly, with their new hats and purses and gloves and coral bracelets and strings of pearls. The parents, ramshackle, sleepy, dim in the brain because it is Sunday, sit down to their coffee and privacy and talk of the past.

'We weren't crooked,' says Peter. 'We weren't even smart.'

Sheilah's head bobs up; she is no drowner. It is wrong to say they have nothing to show for time. Sheilah has the Balenciaga. It is a black afternoon dress, stiff and boned at the waist; long for the fashions of now, but neither Sheilah nor Peter would change a thread. The Balenciaga is their talisman, their treasure; and after they remember it they touch hands and think that the years are not behind them but hazy and marvellous and still to be lived.

The first place they went to was Paris. In the early fifties the pick of the international jobs was there. Peter had inherited the last scrap of money he knew he was ever likely to see, and it was enough to get them over: Sheilah and Peter and the babies and the steamer trunk. To their joy and astonishment they had money in the bank. They said to each other, 'It should last a year.' Peter was fastidious about the new job; he hadn't come all this distance to accept just anything. In Paris he met Hugh Taylor, who was earning enough smuggling gasoline to keep his wife in Paris and a girl in Rome. That impressed Peter, because he remembered Taylor as a sour scholarship student without the slightest talent for life. Taylor had a job, of course. He hadn't said to himself, I'll go over to Europe and smuggle gasoline. It gave Peter an idea; he saw the shape of things. First you catch your fish. Later, at an international party, he met Johnny Hertzberg, who told him Germany was the place. Hertzberg said that anyone who came out of Germany broke now was too stupid to be here, and deserved to be back home at a desk. Peter nodded, as if he had already thought of that. He began to think about Germany. Paris was fine for a holiday, but it had been picked clean. Yes, Germany. His money was running low. He thought about Germany quite a lot.

That winter was moist and delicate; so fragile that they daren't speak of it now. There seemed to be plenty of everything and plenty of time. They were living the dream of a marriage, the fabric uncut, nothing slashed or spoiled. All winter they spent their money, and went to parties, and talked about Peter's future job. It lasted four months. They spent their money, lived in the future, and were never as happy again.

After four months they were suddenly moved away from Paris, but not to Germany—to Geneva. Peter thinks it was because of the incident at the Trudeau wedding at the Ritz. Paul Trudeau was a French Canadian Peter had known at school and in the Navy. Trudeau had turned into a snob, proud of his career and his Paris connections. He tried to make the difference felt, but Peter thought the difference was only for strangers. At the wedding reception Peter lay down on the floor and said he was dead. He held a white azalea in a brass pot on his chest, and sang, 'Oh, hear us when we cry to Thee for those in peril on the sea.' Sheilah bent over him and said, 'Pete, darling, get up. Pete, listen, every single person who can do something for you is in this room. If you love me, you'll get up.'

'I do love you,' he said, ready to engage in a serious conversation. 'She's so beautiful,' he told a second face. 'She's nearly as tall as I am. She was a model in London. I met her over in London in the war. I met her there in the war.' He lay on his back with the azalea on his chest, explaining their history. A waiter took the brass pot away, and after Peter had been hauled to his feet he knocked the waiter down. Trudeau's bride, who was freshly out of an Ursuline convent, became hysterical; and even though Paul Trudeau and Peter were old acquaintances, Trudeau never spoke to him again. Peter says now that French Canadians always have that bit of spite. He says Trudeau asked the Embassy to interfere. Luckily, back home there were still a few people to whom the name 'Frazier' meant something, and it was to these people that Peter appealed. He wrote letters saying that a French-Canadian combine was preventing his getting a decent job; and could anything be done? No one answered directly, but it was clear that what they settled for was exile to Geneva: a season of meditation and remorse, as he explained to Sheilah, and it was managed tactfully, through Lucille. Lucille wrote that a friend of hers, May Fergus, now a secretary in Geneva, had heard about a job. The job was filing pictures in the information service of an international agency in the Palais des Nations. The pay was so-so, but Lucille thought Peter must be getting fed up doing nothing.

Peter often asks his sister now who put her up to it—what important person told her to write that letter suggesting Peter go to Geneva?

'Nobody,' says Lucille. 'I mean, nobody in the way *you* mean. I really did have this girl friend working there, and I knew you must be running through your money pretty fast in Paris.'

'It must have been somebody pretty high up,' Peter says. He looks at his sister admiringly, as he has often looked at his wife.

Peter's wife had loved him in Paris. Whatever she wanted in marriage she found that winter, there. In Geneva, where Peter was a file clerk and they lived in a furnished flat, she pretended they were in Paris and life was still the same. Often, when the children were at supper, she changed as though she and Peter were dining out. She wore the Balenciaga, and put candles on the card table where she and Peter ate their meal. The neckline of the dress was soiled with make-up. Peter remembers her dabbing on the make-up with a wet sponge. He remembers her in the kitchen, in the soiled Balenciaga, patting on the make-up with a filthy sponge. Behind her, at the kitchen table, Sandra and Jennifer, in buttonless pajamas and bunny slippers, ate their supper of marmalade sandwiches and milk. When the children were asleep, the parents dined solemnly, ritually, Sheilah sitting straight as a queen.

It was a mysterious period of exile, and he had to wait for signs, or signals, to know when he was free to leave. He never saw the job any other way. He forgot he had applied for it. He thought he had been sent to Geneva because of a misdemeanor and had to wait to be released. Nobody pressed him at work. His immediate boss had resigned, and he was alone for months in a room with two desks. He read the *Herald-Tribune*, and tried to discover how things were here—how the others ran their lives on the pay they were officially getting. But it was a closed conspiracy. He was not dealing with adventures now but civil servants waiting for pension day. No one ever answered his questions. They pretended to think his questions were a form of wit. His only solace in exile was the few happy weekends he had in the late spring and early summer. He had met another old acquaintance, Mike Burleigh. Mike was a serious liberal who had married a serious heiress. The Burleighs had two guest lists. The first was composed of stuffy people they felt obliged to entertain, while the second was made up of their real friends, the friends they wanted. The real friends strove hard to become stuffy and dull and thus achieve the first guest list, but few succeeded. Peter went on the first list straight away. Possibly Mike didn't understand, at the beginning, why Peter was pretending to be a file clerk. Peter had such an air—he might have been sent by a universal inspector to see how things in Geneva were being run.

Every Friday in May and June and part of July, the Fraziers rented a sky-blue Fiat and drove forty miles east of Geneva to the Burleighs' summer house. They brought the children, a suitcase, the children's tattered picture books, and a token bottle of gin. This, in memory, is a period of water and water birds, swans, roses, and singing birds. The children were small and still belonged to them. If they remember too much, their mouths water, their stomachs hurt. Peter says, 'it was fine while it lasted.' Enough. While it lasted Sheilah and Madge Burleigh were close. They abandoned their husbands and spent long summer afternoons comparing their mothers and praising each other's skin and hair. To Madge, and not to Peter, Sheilah opened her Liverpool childhood with the words 'rat poor'. Peter heard about it later, from Mike. The women's friendship seemed to Peter a bad beginning. He trusted women but not with each other. It lasted ten weeks. One Sunday, Madge said she needed the two bedrooms the Fraziers usually occupied for a party of sociologists from Pakistan, and that was the end. In November, the Fraziers heard that the summer house had been closed, and that the Burleighs were in Geneva, in their winter flat; they gave no sign. There was no help for it, and no appeal.

Now Peter began firing letters to anyone who had ever known his late father. He was living in a mild yellow autumn. Why does he remember the streets of the city dark, and the windows everywhere black with rain? He remembers being with Sheilah and the children as if they clung together while just outside their small shelter it rained and rained. The children slept in the bedroom of the flat because the window gave on the street and they could breathe air. Peter and Sheilah had the living-room couch. Their window was not a real window but a square on a well of cement. The flat seemed damp as a cave. Peter remembers steam in the kitchen, pools under the sink, sweat on the pipes. Water streamed on him from the children's clothes, washed and dripping overhead. The trunk, upended in the children's room, was not quite unpacked. Sheilah had not signed her name to this life; she had not given in. Once Peter heard her drop her aitches. 'You kids are lucky,' she said to the girls. 'I never 'ad so much as a sit-down meal. I ate chips out of a paper or I 'ad a butty out on the stairs.' He never asked her what a butty was. He thinks it means bread and cheese.

The day he heard 'You kids are lucky' he understood they were becoming in fact something they had only *appeared* to be until now—the shabby civil servant and his brood. If he had been European he would have ridden to work on a bicycle, in the uniform of his class and condition. He would have worn a tight coat, a turned collar, and a dirty tie. He wondered then if coming here had been a mistake, and if he should not, after all, still be in a place where his name meant something. Surely Peter Frazier should live where 'Frazier' counts? In Ontario even now when he says 'Frazier' an absent look comes over his hearer's face, as if its owner were consulting an interior guide. What is Frazier? What does it mean? Oil? Power? Politics? Wheat? Real estate? The creditors had the house sealed when Peter's father died. His aunt collapsed with a heart attack in somebody's bachelor apartment, leaving three sons and a widower to surmise they had never known her. Her will was a disappointment. None of that generation left enough. One made it: the granite Presbyterian immigrants from Scotland. Their children, a generation of daunted women and maiden men, held still. Peter's father's crowd spent: they were not afraid of their fathers, and their grandfathers were old. Peter and his sister and his cousins lived on the remains. They were left the rinds of income, of notions, and the memories of ideas rather than ideas intact. If Peter can choose his reincarnation, let him be the oppressed son of a Scottish parson. Let Peter grow up on cuffs and iron principles. Let him make the fortune! Let him flee the manse! When he was small his patrimony was squandered under his nose. He remembers people dancing in his father's house. He remembers seeing and nearly understanding adultery in a guest room, among a pile of wraps. He thought he had seen a murder; he never told. He remembers licking glasses wherever he found them—on window sills, on stairs, in the pantry. In his room he listened while Lucille read Beatrix Potter. The bad rabbit stole the carrot from the good rabbit without saying please, and downstairs was the noise of the party—the roar of the crouched lion. When his father died he saw the chairs upside down and the bailiff's chalk marks. Then the doors were sealed.

He has often tried to tell Sheilah why he cannot be defeated. He remembers his father saying, 'Nothing can touch us,' and Peter believed it and still does. It has prevented his taking his troubles too seriously. 'Nothing can be as bad as this,' he will tell himself. 'It is happening to me.' Even in Geneva, where his status was file clerk, where he sank and stopped on the level of the men who never emigrated, the men on the bicycles—even there he had a manner of strolling to work as if his office were a pastime, and his real life a secret so splendid he could share it with no one except himself.

In Geneva Peter worked for a woman—a girl. She was a Norwegian from a small town in Saskatchewan. He supposed they had been put together because they were Canadians; but they were as strange to each other as if 'Canadian' meant any number of things, or had no real meaning. Soon after Agnes Brusen came to the office she hung her framed university degree on the wall. It was one of the gritty, prideful gestures that stand for push, toil, and family sacrifice. He thought, then, that she must be one of a family of immigrants for whom education is everything. Hugh Taylor had told him that in some families the older children never marry until the youngest have finished school. Sometimes every second child is sacrificed and made to work for the education of the next born. Those who finish college spend years paying back. They are white-hot Protestants, and they live with a load of work and debt and obligation. Peter placed his new colleague on scraps of information. He had never been in the West.

She came to the office on a Monday morning in October. The office was overheated and painted cream. It contained two desks, the filing cabinets, a map of the world as it had been in 1945, and the Charter of the United Nations left behind by Agnes Brusen's predecessor. (She took down the Charter without asking Peter if he minded, with the impudence of gesture you find in women who wouldn't say boo to a goose; and then she hung her college degree on the nail where the Charter had been.) Three people brought her in—a whole committee. One of them said, 'Agnes, this is Pete Frazier. Pete, Agnes Brusen. Pete's Canadian, too, Agnes. He knows all about the office, so ask him anything.'

Of course he knew all about the office: he knew the exact spot where the cord of the venetian blind was frayed, obliging one to give an extra tug to the right.

The girl might have been twenty-three: no more. She wore a brown tweed suit with bone buttons, and a new silk scarf and new shoes. She clutched an unscratched brown purse. She seemed dressed in going-away presents. She said, 'Oh, I never smoke,' with a convulsive movement of her hand, when Peter offered his case. He was courteous, hiding his disappointment. The people he worked with had told him a Scandinavian girl was arriving, and he had expected a stunner. Agnes was a mole: she was small and brown, and round-shouldered as if she had always carried parcels or younger children in her arms. A mole's profile was turned when she said goodbye to her committee. If she had been foreign, ill-favoured though she was, he might have flirted a little, just to show that he was friendly; but their being Canadian, and suddenly left together, was a sexual damper. He sat down and lit his own cigarette. She smiled at him, questioningly, he thought, and sat as if she had never seen a chair before. He wondered if his smoking was annoying her. He wondered if she was fidgety about drafts, or allergic to anything, and whether she would want the blind up or down. His social compass was out of order because the others couldn't tell Peter and Agnes apart. There was a world of difference between them, yet it was she who had been brought in to sit at the larger of the two desks.

While he was thinking this she got up and walked around the office, almost on tiptoe, opening the doors of closets and pulling out the filing trays. She looked inside everything except the drawers of Peter's desk. (In any case, Peter's desk was locked. His desk is locked wherever he works. In Geneva he went into Personnel one morning, early, and pinched his application form. He had stated on the form that he had seven years' experience in public relations and could speak French, German, Spanish, and Italian. He has always collected anything important about himself—anything useful. But he can never get on with the final act, which is getting rid of the information. He has kept papers about for years, a constant source of worry.)

'I know this looks funny, Mr Ferris,' said the girl. 'I'm not really snooping or anything. I just can't feel easy in a new place unless I know where everything is. In a new place everything seems so hidden.'

If she had called him 'Ferris' and pretended not to know he was Frazier, it could only be because they had sent her here to spy on him and see if he had repented and was fit for a better place in life. 'You'll be all right here,' he said. 'Nothing's hidden. Most of us haven't got brains enough to have secrets. This is Rainbow Valley.' Depressed by the thought that they were having him watched now, he passed his hand over his hair and looked outside to the lawn and the parking lot and the peacocks someone gave the Palais des Nations years ago. The peacocks love no one. They wander about the parked cars looking elderly, bad-tempered, mournful, and lost.

Agnes had settled down again. She folded her silk scarf and placed it just so, with her gloves beside it. She opened her new purse and took out a notebook and a shiny gold pencil. She may have written

Duster for desk
Kleenex
Glass jar for flowers
Air-Wick because he smokes
Paper for lining drawers

because the next day she brought each of these articles to work. She also brought a large black Bible, which she unwrapped lovingly and placed on the left-hand corner of her desk. The flower vase—empty—stood in the middle, and the Kleenex made a counterpoise for the Bible on the right.

When he saw the Bible he knew she had not been sent to spy on his work. The conspiracy was deeper. She might have been dispatched by ghosts. He knew everything about her, all in a moment: he saw the ambition, the terror, the dry pride. She was the true heir of the men from Scotland; she was at the start. She had been sent to tell him, 'You can begin, but not begin again.' She never opened the Bible, but she dusted it as she dusted her desk, her chair, and any surface the cleaning staff had overlooked. And Peter, the first days, watching her timid movements, her insignificant little face, felt, as you feel the approach of a storm, the charge of moral certainty round her, the belief in work, the faith in undertakings, the bread of the Black Sunday. He recognized and tasted all of it: ashes in the mouth.

After five days their working relations were settled. Of course, there was the Bible and all that went with it, but his tongue had never held the taste of ashes long. She was an inferior girl of poor quality. She had nothing in her favour except the degree on the wall. In the real world, he would not have invited her to his house except to mind the children. That was what he said to Sheilah. He said that Agnes was a mole, and a virgin, and that her tics and mannerisms were sending him round the bend. She had an infuriating habit of covering her mouth when she talked. Even at the telephone she put up her hand as if afraid of losing anything, even a word. Her voice was nasal and flat. She had two working costumes, both dull as the wall. One was the brown suit, the other a navy-blue dress with changeable collars. She dressed for no one; she dressed for her desk, her jar of flowers, her Bible, and her box of Kleenex. One day she crossed the space between the two desks and stood over Peter, who was reading a newspaper. She could have spoken to him from her desk, but she may have felt that being on her feet gave her authority. She had plenty of courage, but authority was something else.

'I thought—I mean, they told me you were the person . . .' She got on with it bravely: 'If you don't want to do the filing or any work, all right, Mr Frazier. I'm not saying anything about that. You might have poor health or your personal reasons. But it's got to be done, so if you'll kindly show me about the filing I'll do it. I've worked in Information before, but it was a different office, and every office is different.'

'My dear girl,' said Peter. He pushed back his chair and looked at her, astonished. 'You've been sitting there fretting, worrying. How insensitive of me. How trying for you. Usually I file on the last Wednesday of the month, so you see, you just haven't been around long enough to see a last Wednesday. Not another word, please. And let us not waste another minute.' He emptied the heaped baskets of photographs so swiftly, pushing 'Iran—Smallpox Control' into 'Irish Red Cross' (close enough), that the girl looked frightened, as if she had raised a whirlwind. She said slowly, 'If you'll only show me, Mr Frazier, instead of doing it so fast, I'll gladly look after it, because you might want to be doing other things, and I feel the filing should be done every day.' But Peter was too busy to answer, and so she sat down, holding the edge of her desk.

'There,' he said, beaming. 'All done,' His smile, his sunburst, was wasted, for the girl was staring round the room as if she feared she had not inspected everything the first day after all; some drawer, some cupboard, hid a monster. That evening Peter unlocked one of the drawers of his desk and took away the application form he had stolen from Personnel. The girl had not finished her search.

'How could you *not* know?' wailed Sheilah. 'You sit looking at her every day. You must talk about *something*. She must have told you.'

'She did tell me,' said Peter, 'and I've just told you.'

It was this: Agnes Brusen was on the Burleighs' guest list. How had the Burleighs met her? What did they see in her? Peter could not reply. He knew that Agnes lived in a bed-sitting room with a Swiss family and had her meals with them. She had been in Geneva three months, but no one had ever seen her outside the office. 'You *should* know,' said Sheilah. 'She must have something, more than you can see. Is she pretty? Is she brilliant? What is it?'

'We don't really talk,' Peter said. They talked in a way: Peter teased her and she took no notice. Agnes was not a sulker. She had taken her defeat like a sport. She did her work and a good deal of his. She sat behind her Bible, her flowers, and her Kleenex, and answered when Peter spoke. That was how he learned about the Burleighs—just by teasing and being bored. It was a January afternoon. He said, '*Miss* Brusen. Talk to me. Tell me everything. Pretend we have perfect rapport. Do you like Geneva?'

'It's a nice clean town,' she said. He can see to this day the red and blue anemones in the glass jar, and her bent head, and her small untended hands.

'Are you learning beautiful French with your Swiss family?'

'They speak English.'

'Why don't you take an apartment of your own?' he said. Peter was not usually impertinent. He was bored. 'You'd be independent then.'

'I am independent,' she said. 'I earn my living. I don't think it proves anything if you live by yourself. Mrs Burleigh wants me to live alone, too. She's looking for something for me. It mustn't be dear. I send money home.'

Here was the extraordinary thing about Agnes Brusen: she refused the use of Christian names and never spoke to Peter unless he spoke first, but she would tell anything, as if to say, 'Don't waste time fishing. Here it is.'

He learned all in one minute that she sent her salary home, and that she was a friend of the Burleighs. The first he had expected; the second knocked him flat.

'She's got to come to dinner,' Sheilah said. 'We should have had her right from the beginning. If only I'd known! But *you* were the one. You said she looked like—oh, I don't even remember. A Norwegian mole.'

She came to dinner one Saturday night in January, in her navy-blue dress, to which she had pinned an organdy gardenia. She sat upright on the edge of the sofa. Sheilah had ordered the meal from a restaurant. There was lobster, good wine, and a *pièce-montée* full of kirsch and cream. Agnes refused the lobster; she had never eaten anything from the sea unless it had been sterilized and tinned, and said so. She was afraid of skin poisoning. Someone in her family had skin poisoning after having eaten oysters. She touched her cheeks and neck to show where the poisoning had erupted. She sniffed her wine and put the glass down without tasting it. She could not eat the cake because of the alcohol it contained. She ate an egg, bread and butter, a sliced tomato, and drank a glass of ginger ale. She seemed unaware she was creating disaster and pain. She did not help clear away the dinner plates. She sat, adequately nourished, decently dressed, and waited to learn why she had been invited here—that was the feeling Peter had. He folded the card table on which they had dined, and opened the window to air the room.

'It's not the same cold as Canada, but you feel it more,' he said, for something to say.

'Your blood has gotten thin,' said Agnes.

Sheilah returned from the kitchen and let herself fall into an armchair. With her eyes closed she held out her hand for a cigarette. She was performing the haughty-lady act that was a family joke. She flung her head back and looked at Agnes through half-closed lids; then she suddenly brought her head forward, widening her eyes.

'Are you skiing madly?' she said.

'Well, in the first place there hasn't been any snow,' said Agnes. 'So nobody's doing any skiing so far as I know. All I hear is people complaining because there's no snow. Personally, I don't ski. There isn't much skiing in the part of Canada I come from. Besides, my family never had that kind of leisure.'

'Heavens,' said Sheilah, as if her family had every kind. I'll bet they had, thought Peter. On the dole.

Sheilah was wasting her act. He had a suspicion that Agnes knew it was an act but did not know it was also a joke. If so, it made Sheilah seem a fool, and he loved Sheilah too much to enjoy it.

'The Burleighs have been wonderful to me,' said Agnes. She seemed to have divined why she was here, and decided to give them all the information they wanted, so that she could put on her coat and go home to bed. 'They had me out to their place on the lake every weekend until the weather got cold and they moved back to town. They've rented a chalet for the winter, and they want me to come there, too. But I don't know if I will or not. I don't ski, and, oh, I don't know—I don't drink either, and I don't always see the point. Their friends are too rich and I'm too Canadian.'

She had delivered everything Sheilah wanted and more: Agnes was on the first guest list and didn't care. No, Peter corrected; doesn't know. Doesn't care and doesn't know.

'I thought with you Norwegians it was in the blood, skiing. And drinking,' Sheilah murmured.

'Drinking, maybe,' said Agnes. She covered her mouth and said behind her spread fingers, 'In our family we were religious. We didn't drink or smoke. My brother was in Norway in the war. He saw some cousins. Oh,' she said, unexpectedly loud, 'Harry said it was just terrible. They were so poor. They had flies in their kitchen. They gave him something to eat a fly had been on. They didn't have a real toilet, and they'd been in the same house about two hundred years. We've only recently built our own home, and we have a bathroom and two toilets. I'm from Saskatchewan,' she said. 'I'm not from any other place.'

Surely one winter here had been punishment enough? In the spring they would remember him and free him. He wrote Lucille, who said he was lucky to have a job at all. The Burleighs had sent the Fraziers a second-guest-list Christmas card. It showed a Moslem refugee child weeping outside a tent. They treasured the card and left it standing long after the others had been given to the children to cut up. Peter had discovered by now what had gone wrong in the friendship—Sheilah had charged a skirt at a dressmaker to Madge's account. Madge had told her she might, and then changed her mind.

Poor Sheilah! She was new to this part of it—to the changing humours of independent friends. Paris was already a year in the past. At Mardi Gras, the Burleighs gave their annual party. They invited everyone, the damned and the dropped, with the prodigality of a child at prayers. The invitation said 'in costume', but the Fraziers were too happy to wear a disguise. They might not be recognized. Like many of the guests they expected to meet at the party, they had been disgraced, forgotten, and rehabilitated. They would be anxious to see one another as they were.

On the night of the party, the Fraziers rented a car they had never seen before and drove through the first snowstorm of the year. Peter had not driven since last summer's blissful trips in the Fiat. He could not find the switch for the windshield wiper in this car. He leaned over the wheel. 'Can you see on your side?' he asked. 'Can I make a left turn here? Does it look like a one-way?'

'I can't imagine why you took a car with a right-hand drive,' said Sheilah.

He had trouble finding a place to park; they crawled up and down unknown streets whose curbs were packed with snow-covered cars. When they stood at last on the pavement, safe and sound, Peter said, 'This is the first snow.'

'I can see that,' said Sheilah. 'Hurry, darling. My hair.'

'It's the first snow.'

'You're repeating yourself,' she said. 'Please hurry, darling. Think of my poor shoes. My *hair*.'

She was born in an ugly city, and so was Peter, but they have this difference: she does not know the importance of the first snow—the first clean thing in a dirty year. He would have told her then that this storm, which was wetting her feet and destroying her hair, was like the first day of the English spring, but she made a frightened gesture, trying to shield her head. The gesture told him he did not understand her beauty.

'Let me,' she said. He was fumbling with the key, trying to lock the car. She took the key without impatience and locked the door on the driver's side; and then, to show Peter she treasured him and was not afraid of wasting her life or her beauty, she took his arm and they walked in the snow down a street and around a corner to the apartment house where the Burleighs lived. They were, and are, a united couple. They were afraid of the party, and each of them knew it. When they walk together, holding arms, they give each other whatever each can spare.

Only six people had arrived in costume. Madge Burleigh was disguised as Manet's 'LoLa de Valence', which everyone mistook for Carmen. Mike was an Impressionist painter, with a straw hat and a glued-on beard. 'I am all of them,' he said. He would rather have dressed as a dentist, he said, welcoming the Fraziers as if he had parted from them the day before, but Madge wanted him to look as if he had created her. 'You know?' he said.

'Perfectly,' said Sheilah. Her shoes were stained and the snow had softened her lacquered hair. She was not wasted; she was the most beautiful woman here.

About an hour after their arrival, Peter found himself with no one to talk to. He had told about the Trudeau wedding in Paris and the pot of azaleas, and after he mislaid his audience he began to look round for Sheilah. She was on a window seat, partly concealed by a green velvet curtain. Facing her, so that their profiles were neat and perfect against the night, was a man. Their conversation was private and enclosed, as if they had in minutes covered leagues of time and arrived at the place where everything was implied, understood. Peter began working his way across the room, toward his wife, when he saw Agnes. He was granted the sight of her drowning face. She had dressed with comic intention, obviously with care, and now she was a ragged hobo, half tramp, half clown.

Her hair was tucked up under a bowler hat. The six costumed guests who had made the same mistake—the ghost, the gypsy, the Athenian maiden, the geisha, the Martian, and the apache—were delighted to find a seventh; but Agnes was not amused; she was gasping for life. When a waiter passed with a crowded tray, she took a glass without seeing it; then a wave of the party took her away.

Sheilah's new friend was named Simpson. After Simpson said he thought perhaps he'd better circulate, Peter sat down where he had been. 'Now look, Sheilah,' he began. Their most intimate conversations have taken place at parties. Once at a party she told him she was leaving him; she didn't, of course. Smiling, blue-eyed, she gazed lovingly at Peter and said rapidly, 'Pete, shut up and listen. That man. The man you scared away. He's a big wheel in a company out in India or someplace like that. It's gorgeous out there. Pete, the *servants*. And it's warm. It never never snows. He says there's heaps of jobs. You pick them off the trees like . . . orchids. He says it's even easier now than when we owned all those places, because now the poor pets can't run anything and they'll pay *fortunes*. Pete, he says it's warm, it's heaven, and Pete, they pay.'

A few minutes later, Peter was alone again and Sheilah part of a closed, laughing group. Holding her elbow was the man from the place where jobs grew like orchids. Peter edged into the group and laughed at a story he hadn't heard. He heard only the last line, which was, 'Here comes another tunnel.' Looking out from the tight laughing ring, he saw Agnes again, and he thought, I'd be like Agnes if I didn't have Sheilah. Agnes put her glass down on a table and lurched toward the doorway, head forward. Madge Burleigh, who never stopped moving around the room and smiling, was still smiling when she paused and said in Peter's ear, 'Go with Agnes, Pete. See that she gets home. People will notice if Mike leaves.'

'She probably just wants to walk around the block,' said Peter. 'She'll be back.'

'Oh, stop thinking about yourself, for once, and see that that poor girl gets home,' said Madge. 'You've still got your Fiat, haven't you?'

He turned away as if he had been pushed. Any command is a release, in a way. He may not want to go in that particular direction, but at least he is going somewhere. And now Sheilah, who had moved inches nearer to hear what Madge and Peter were murmuring, said, 'Yes, go, darling,' as if he were leaving the gates of Troy.

Peter was to find Agnes and see that she reached home: this he repeated to himself as he stood on the landing, outside the Burleighs' flat, ringing for the elevator. Bored with waiting for it, he ran down the stairs, four flights, and saw that Agnes had stalled the lift by leaving the door open. She was crouched on the floor, propped on her fingertips. Her eyes were closed.

'Agnes,' said Peter. '*Miss* Brusen, I mean. That's no way to leave a party. Don't you know you're supposed to curtsey and say thanks? My God, Agnes, anybody going by here just now might have seen you! Come on, be a good girl. Time to go home.'

She got up without his help and, moving between invisible crevasses, shut the elevator door. Then she left the building and Peter followed, remembering he was to see that she got home. They walked along the snowy pavement, Peter a few steps behind her. When she turned right for no reason, he turned, too. He had no clear idea where they were going. Perhaps she lived close by. He had forgotten where the hired car was parked, or what it looked like; he could not remember its make or its colour. In any case, Sheilah had the key. Agnes walked on steadily, as if she knew their destination, and he thought, Agnes Brusen is drunk in the street in Geneva and dressed like a tramp. He wanted to say, 'This is the best thing that ever happened to you, Agnes; it will help you understand how things are for some of the rest of us.' But she stopped and turned and, leaning over a low hedge, retched on a frozen lawn. He held her clammy forehead and rested his hand on her arched back, on muscles as tight as a fist. She straightened up and drew a breath but the cold air made her cough. 'Don't breathe too deeply,' he said. 'It's the worst thing you can do. Have you got a handkerchief?' He passed his own handkerchief over her wet weeping face, upturned like the face of one of his little girls. 'I'm out without a coat,' he said, noticing it. 'We're a pair.'

'I never drink,' said Agnes. 'I'm just not used to it.' Her voice was sweet and quiet. He had never seen her so peaceful, so composed. He thought she must surely be all right, now, and perhaps he might leave her here. The trust in her tilted face had perplexed him. He wanted to get back to Sheilah and have her explain something. He had forgotten what it was, but Sheilah would know. 'Do you live around here?' he said. As he spoke, she let herself fall. He had wiped her face and now she trusted him to pick her up, set her on her feet, take her wherever she ought to be. He pulled her up and she stood, wordless, humble, as he brushed the snow from her tramp's clothes. Snow horizontally crossed the lamplight. The street was silent. Agnes had lost her hat. Snow, which he tasted, melted on her hands. His gesture of licking snow from her hands was as formal as a handshake. He tasted snow on her hands and then they walked on.

'I never drink,' she said. They stood on the edge of a broad avenue. The wrong turning now could lead them anywhere; it was the changeable avenue at the edge of towns that loses its houses and becomes a highway. She held his arm and spoke in a gentle voice. She said, 'In our house we didn't smoke or drink. My mother was ambitious for me, more than for Harry and the others.' She said, 'I've never been alone before. When I was a kid I would get up in the summer before the others, and I'd see the ice wagon going down the street. I'm alone now. Mrs Burleigh's found me an apartment. It's only one room. She likes it because it's in the old part of town. I don't like old houses. Old houses are dirty. You don't know who was there before.'

'I should have a car somewhere,' Peter said. 'I'm not sure where we are.'

He remembers that on this avenue they climbed into a taxi, but nothing about the drive. Perhaps he fell asleep. He does remember that when he paid the driver Agnes clutched his arm, trying to stop him. She pressed extra coins into the driver's palm. The driver was paid twice.

'I'll tell you one thing about us,' said Peter. 'We pay everything twice.' This was part of a much longer theory concerning North American behaviour, and it was not Peter's own. Mike Burleigh had held forth about it on summer afternoons.

Agnes pushed open a door between a stationer's shop and a grocery, and led the way up a narrow inside stair. They climbed one flight, frightening beetles. She had to search every pocket for the latchkey. She was shaking with cold. Her apartment seemed little warmer than the street. Without speaking to Peter she turned on all the lights. She looked inside the kitchen and the bathroom and then got down on her hands and knees and looked under the sofa. The room was neat and belonged to no one. She left him standing in this unclaimed room—she had forgotten him—and closed a door behind her. He looked for something to do—some useful action he could repeat to Madge. He turned on the electric radiator in the fireplace. Perhaps Agnes wouldn't thank him for it; perhaps she would rather undress in the cold. 'I'll be on my way,' he called to the bathroom door.

She had taken off the tramp's clothes and put on a dressing gown of orphanage wool. She came out of the bathroom and straight toward him. She pressed her face and rubbed her cheek on his shoulder as if hoping the contact would leave a scar. He saw her back and her profile and his own face in the mirror over the fireplace. He thought, This is how disasters happen. He saw floods of sea water moving with perfect punitive justice over reclaimed land; he saw lava covering vineyards and overtaking dogs and stragglers. A bridge over an abyss snapped in two and the long express train, suddenly V-shaped, floated like snow. He thought amiably of every kind of disaster and thought, This is how they occur.

Her eyes were closed. She said, 'I shouldn't be over here. In my family we didn't drink or smoke. My mother wanted a lot from me, more than from Harry and the others.' But he knew all that; he had known from the day of the Bible, and because once, at the beginning, she had made him afraid. He was not afraid of her now.

She said, 'It's no use staying here, is it?'

'If you mean what I think, no.'

'It wouldn't be better anywhere.'

She let him see full on her blotched face. He was not expected to do anything. He was not required to pick her up when she fell or wipe her tears. She was poor quality, really—he remembered having thought that once. She left him and went quietly into the bathroom and locked the door. He heard taps running and supposed it was a hot bath. He was pretty certain there would be no more tears. He looked at his watch: Sheilah must be home, now, wondering what had become of him. He descended the beetles' staircase and for forty minutes crossed the city under a windless fall of snow.

The neighbour's child who had stayed with Peter's children was asleep on the living-room sofa. Peter woke her and sent her, sleepwalking, to her own door. He sat down, wet to the bone, thinking, I'll call the Burleighs. In half an hour I'll call the police. He heard a car stop and the engine running and a confusion of two voices laughing and calling goodnight. Presently Sheilah let herself in, rosy-faced, smiling. She carried his trenchcoat over her arm. She said, 'How's Agnes?'

'Where were you?' he said. 'Whose car was that?'

Sheilah had gone into the children's room. He heard her shutting their window. She returned, undoing her dress, and said, 'Was Agnes all right?'

'Agnes is all right. Sheilah, this is about the worst . . .'

She stepped out of the Balenciaga and threw it over a chair. She stopped and looked at him and said, 'Poor old Pete, are you in love with Agnes?' And then, as if the answer were of so little importance she hadn't time for it, she locked her arms around him and said, 'My love, we're going to Ceylon.'

Two days later, when Peter strolled into his office, Agnes was at her desk. She wore the blue dress, with a spotless collar. White and yellow freesias were symmetrically arranged in the glass jar. The room was hot, and the spring snow, glued for a second when it touched the window, blurred the view of parked cars.

'Quite a party,' Peter said.

She did not look up. He sighed, sat down, and thought if the snow held he would be skiing at the Burleighs' very soon. Impressed by his kindness to Agnes, Madge had invited the family for the first possible weekend.

Presently Agnes said, 'I'll never drink again or go to a house where people are drinking. And I'll never bother anyone the way I bothered you.'

'You didn't bother me,' he said. 'I took you home. You were alone and it was late. It's normal.'

'Normal for you, maybe, but I'm used to getting home by myself. Please never tell what happened.'

He stared at her. He can still remember the freesias and the Bible and the heat in the room. She looked as if the elements had no power. She felt neither heat nor cold. 'Nothing happened,' he said.

'I behaved in a silly way. I had no right to. I led you to think I might do something wrong.'

'*I* might have tried something,' he said gallantly. 'But that would be my fault and not yours.'

She put her knuckle to her mouth and he could scarcely hear. 'It was because of you. I was afraid you might be blamed, or else you'd blame yourself.'

'There's no question of any blame,' he said. 'Nothing happened. We'd both had a lot to drink. Forget about it. Nothing *happened*. You'd remember if it had.'

She put down her hand. There was an expression on her face. Now she sees me, he thought. She had never looked at him after the first day. (He has since tried to put a name to the look on her face; but how can he, now, after so many voyages, after Ceylon, and Hong Kong, and Sheilah's nearly leaving him, and all their difficulties—the money owed, the rows with hotel managers, the lost and found steamer trunk, the children throwing up the foreign food?) She sees me now, he thought. What does she see?

She said, 'I'm from a big family. I'm not used to being alone. I'm not a suicidal person, but I could have done something after that party, just not to see any more, or think or listen or expect anything. What can I think when I see these people? All my life I heard, Educated people don't do this, educated people don't do that. And now I'm here, and you're all educated people, and you're nothing but pigs. You're educated and you drink and do everything wrong and you know what you're doing, and that makes you worse than pigs. My family worked to make me an educated person, but they didn't know you. But what if I didn't see and hear and expect anything more? It wouldn't change anything. You'd all be still the same. Only *you* might have thought it was your fault. You might have thought you were to blame. It could worry you all your life. It would have been wrong for me to worry you.'

He remembered that the rented car was still along a snowy curb somewhere in Geneva. He wondered if Sheilah had the key in her purse and if she remembered where they'd parked.

'I told you about the ice wagon,' Agnes said. 'I don't remember everything, so you're wrong about remembering. But I remember telling you that. That was the best. It's the best you can hope to have. In a big family, if you want to be alone, you have to get up before the rest of them. You get up early in the morning in the summer and it's you, you, once in your life alone in the universe. You think you know everything that can happen . . . Nothing is ever like that again.'

He looked at the smeared window and wondered if this day could end without disaster. In his mind he saw her falling in the snow wearing a tramp's costume, and he saw her coming to him in the orphanage dressing gown. He saw her drowning face at the party. He was afraid for himself. The story was still unfinished. It had to come to a climax, something threatening to him. But there was no climax. They talked that day, and afterward nothing else was said. They went on in the same office for a short time, until Peter left for Ceylon; until somebody read the right letter, passed it on for the right initials, and the Fraziers began the Oriental tour that should have made their fortune. Agnes and Peter were too tired to speak after that morning. They were like a married couple in danger, taking care.

But what were they talking about that day, so quietly, such old friends? They talked about dying, about being ambitious, about being religious, about different kinds of love. What did she see when she looked at him—taking her knuckle slowly away from her mouth, bringing her hand down to the desk, letting it rest there? They were both Canadians, so they had this much together—the knowledge of the little you dare admit. Death, near-death, the best thing, the wrong thing—God knows what they were telling each other. Anyway, nothing happened.

When, on Sunday mornings, Sheilah and Peter talk about those times, they take on the glamour of something still to come. It is then he remembers Agnes Brusen. He never says her name. Sheilah wouldn't remember Agnes. Agnes is the only secret Peter has from his wife, the only puzzle he pieces together without her help. He thinks about families in the West as they were fifteen, twenty years ago—the iron-cold ambition, and every member pushing the next one on. He thinks of his father's parties. When he thinks of his father he imagines him with Sheilah, in a crowd. Actually, Sheilah and Peter's father never met, but they might have liked each other. His father admired good-looking women. Peter wonders what they were doing over there in Geneva—not Sheilah and Peter, *Agnes* and Peter. It is almost as if they had once run away together, silly as children, irresponsible as lovers. Peter and Sheilah are back where they started. While they were out in world affairs picking up microbes and debts, always on the fringe of disaster, the fringe of a fortune, Agnes went on and did—what? They lost each other. He thinks of the ice wagon going down the street. He sees something he has never seen in his life—a Western town that belongs to Agnes. Here is Agnes—small, mole-faced, round-shouldered because she has always carried a younger child. She watches the ice wagon and the trail of ice water in a morning invented for her: hers. He sees the weak prairie trees and the shadows on the sidewalk. Nothing moves except the shadows and the ice wagon and the changing amber of the child's eyes. The child is Peter. He has seen the grain of the cement sidewalk and the grass in the cracks, and the dust, and the dandelions at the edge of the road. He is there. He has taken the morning that belongs to Agnes, he is up before the others, and he knows everything. There is nothing he doesn't know.

He could keep the morning, if he wanted to, but what can Peter do with the start of a summer day? Sheilah is here, it is a true Sunday morning, with its dimness and headache and remorse and regrets, and this is life. He says, 'We have the Balenciaga.' He touches Sheilah's hand. The children have their aunt now, and he and Sheilah have each other. Everything works out, somehow or other. Let Agnes have the start of the day. Let Agnes think it was invented for her. Who wants to be alone in the universe? No, begin at the beginning: Peter lost Agnes. Agnes says to herself somewhere, Peter is lost.

About Alice Munro

Munro is a Canadian writer, born in 1931 and raised in southwestern Ontario, which is often the setting for her stories. She began writing while at the University of Western Ontario and her first collection was published in 1968. Lauded as one of the greatest contemporary writers of fiction, Munro has received three Governor General's Awards for fiction, The Man Booker International Prize for her lifetime body of work, and in 2013 the Nobel Prize in Literature for her work as "master of the contemporary short story."

The Peace of Utrecht

I

I have been at home now for three weeks and it has not been a success. Maddy and I, though we speak cheerfully of our enjoyment of so long and intimate a visit, will be relieved when it is over. Silences disturb us. We laugh immoderately. I am afraid—very likely we are both afraid—that when the moment comes to say goodbye, unless we are very quick to kiss, and fervently mockingly squeeze each other's shoulders, we will have to look straight into the desert that is between us and acknowledge that we are not merely indifferent; at heart we reject each other, and as for that past we make so much of sharing we do not really share it at all, each of us keeping it jealously to herself, thinking privately that the other has turned alien, and forfeited her claim.

At night we often sit out on the steps of the verandah, and drink gin and smoke diligently to defeat the mosquitoes and postpone until very late the moment of going to bed. It is hot; the evening takes a long time to burn out. The high brick house, which stays fairly cool until midafternoon, holds the heat of the day trapped until long after dark. It was always like this, and Maddy and I recall how we used to drag our mattress downstairs onto the verandah, where we lay counting falling stars and trying to stay awake till dawn. We never did, falling asleep each night about the time a chill drift of air came up off the river, carrying a smell of reeds and the black ooze of the riverbed. At half-past ten a bus goes through the town, not slowing much; we see it go by at the end of our street. It is the same bus I used to take when I came home from college, and I remember coming into Jubilee on some warm night, seeing the earth bare around the massive roots of the trees, the drinking fountain surrounded by little puddles of water on the main street, the soft scrawls of blue and red and orange light that said BILLIARDS and CAFE; feeling as I recognized these signs a queer kind of oppression and release, as I exchanged the whole holiday world of school, of friends and, later on, of love, for the dim world of continuing disaster, of home. Maddy making the same journey four years earlier must have felt the same thing. I want to ask her: is it possible that children growing up as we did lose the ability to believe in—to be at home in—any ordinary and peaceful reality? But I don't ask her; we never talk about any of that. No exorcising here, says Maddy in her thin, bright voice with the slangy quality I had forgotten, we're not going to depress each other. So we haven't.

One night Maddy took me to a party at the Lake, which is about thirty miles west of here. The party was held in a cottage a couple of women from Jubilee had rented for the week. Most of the women there seemed to be widowed, single, separated or divorced; the men were mostly young and unmarried—those from Jubilee so young that I remember them only as little boys in the lower grades. There were two or three older men, not with their wives. But the women—they reminded me surprisingly of certain women familiar to me in my childhood, though of course I never saw their party-going personalities, only their activities in the stores and offices, and not infrequently in the Sunday schools, of Jubilee. They differed from the married women in being more aware of themselves in the world, a little brisker, sharper and coarser (though I can think of only one or two whose respectability was ever in question). They wore resolutely stylish though matronly clothes, which tended to swish and rustle over their hard rubber corsets, and they put perfume, quite a lot of it, on their artificial flowers. Maddy's friends were considerably modernized; they had copper rinses on their hair, and blue eyelids, and a robust capacity for drink.

Maddy I thought did not look one of them, with her slight figure and her still carelessly worn dark hair; her face has grown thin and strained without losing entirely its girlish look of impertinence and pride. But she speaks with the harsh twang of the local accent, which we used to make fun of, and her expression as she romped and drank was determinedly undismayed. It seemed to me that she was making every effort to belong with these people and that shortly she would succeed. It seemed to me too that she wanted me to see her succeeding, to see her repudiating that secret, exhilarating, really monstrous snobbery which we cultivated when we were children together, and promised ourselves, of course, much bigger things than Jubilee.

During the game in which all the women put an article of clothing—it begins decorously with a shoe—in a basket, and then all the men come in and have a race trying to fit things on to their proper owners, I went out and sat in the car, where I felt lonely for my husband and my friends and listened to the hilarity of the party and the waves falling on the beach and presently went to sleep. Maddy came much later and said, 'For heaven's sake!' Then she laughed and said airily like a lady in an English movie, 'You find these goings-on distasteful?' We both laughed; I felt apologetic, and rather sick from drinking and not getting drunk. 'They may not be much on intellectual conversation but their hearts are in the right place, as the saying goes.' I did not dispute this and we drove at eighty miles an hour from Inverhuron to Jubilee. Since then we have not been to any more parties.

But we are not always alone when we sit out on the steps. Often we are joined by a man named Fred Powell. He was at the party, peaceably in the background remembering whose liquor was whose and amiably holding someone's head over the rickety porch railing. He grew up in Jubilee as we did but I do not remember him, I suppose because he went through school some years ahead of us and then went away to the war. Maddy surprised me by bringing him home to supper the first night I was here and then we spent the evening, as we have spent many since, making this strange man a present of our childhood, or of that version of our childhood which is safely preserved in anecdote, as in a kind of mental cellophane. And what fantasies we build around the frail figures of our childselves, so that they emerge beyond recognition incorrigible and gay. We tell stories together well. 'You girls have got good memories,' Fred Powell says, and sits watching us with an air of admiration and something else—reserve, embarrassment, deprecation—which appears on the faces of these mild deliberate people as they watch the keyed-up antics of their entertainers.

Now thinking of Fred Powell I admit that my reaction to this—this *situation* as I call it—is far more conventional than I would have expected; it is even absurd. And I do not know what situation it really is. I know that he is married. Maddy told me so, on the first evening, in a merely informative voice. His wife is an invalid. He has her at the Lake for the summer, Maddy says, he's very good to her. I do not know if he is Maddy's lover and she will never tell me. Why should it matter to me? Maddy is well over thirty. But I keep thinking of the way he sits on our steps with his hands set flat on his spread knees, his mild full face turned almost indulgently toward Maddy as she talks; he has an affable masculine look of being diverted but unimpressed. And Maddy teases him, tells him he is too fat, will not smoke his cigarettes, involves him in private, nervous, tender arguments which have no meaning and no end. He allows it. (And this is what frightens me, I know it now: he allows it; *she needs it.*) When she is a little drunk she says in tones of half-pleading mockery that he is her only real friend. He speaks the same language, she says. Nobody else does. I have no answer to that.

Then again I begin to wonder: *is* he only her friend? I had forgotten certain restrictions of life in Jubilee—and this holds good whatever the pocket novels are saying about small towns—and also what strong, respectable, never overtly sexual friendships can flourish within these restrictions and be fed by them, so that in the end such relationships may consume half a life. This thought depresses me (unconsummated relationships depress outsiders perhaps more than anybody else) so much that I find myself wishing for them to be honest lovers.

The rhythm of life in Jubilee is primitively seasonal. Deaths occur in the winter; marriages are celebrated in the summer. There is good reason for this; the winters are long and full of hardship and the old and weak cannot always get through them. Last winter was a catastrophe, such as may be expected every ten or twelve years; you can see how the pavement in the streets is broken up, as if the town had survived a minor bombardment. A death is dealt with then in the middle of great difficulties; there comes time now in the summer to think about it, and talk. I find that people stop me in the street to talk about my mother. I have heard from them about her funeral, what flowers she had and what the weather was like on that day. And now that she is dead I no longer feel that when they say the words 'your mother' they deal a knowing, cunning blow at my pride. I used to feel that; at those words I felt my whole identity, that pretentious adolescent construction, come crumbling down.

Now I listen to them speak of her, so gently and ceremoniously, and I realize that she became one of the town's possessions and oddities, its brief legends. This she achieved in spite of us, for we tried, both crudely and artfully, to keep her at home, away from that sad notoriety; not for her sake, but for ours, who suffered such unnecessary humiliation at the sight of her eyes rolling back in her head in a temporary paralysis of the eye muscles, at the sound of her thickened voice, whose embarrassing pronouncements it was our job to interpret to outsiders. So bizarre was the disease she had in its effects that it made us feel like crying out in apology (though we stayed stiff and white) as if we were accompanying a particularly tasteless sideshow. All wasted, our pride; our purging its rage in wild caricatures we did for each other (no, not caricatures, for she was one herself; imitations). We should have let the town have her; it would have treated her better.

About Maddy and her ten-year's vigil they say very little; perhaps they want to spare my feelings, remembering that I was the one who went away and here are my two children to show for it, while Maddy is alone and has nothing but that discouraging house. But I don't think so; in Jubilee the feelings are not spared this way. And they ask me pointblank why I did not come home for the funeral; I am glad I have the excuse of the blizzard that halted air travel that week, for I do not know if I would have come anyway, after Maddy had written so vehemently urging me to stay away. I felt strongly that she had a right to be left alone with it, if she wanted to be, after all this time.

After all this time. Maddy was the one who stayed. First, she went away to college, then I went. You give me four years, I'll give you four years, she said. But I got married. She was not surprised; she was exasperated at me for my wretched useless feelings of guilt. She said that she had always meant to stay. She said that Mother no longer 'bothered' her. 'Our Gothic Mother,' she said, 'I play it out now, I let her be. I don't keep trying to make her *human* any more. You know.' It would simplify things so much to say that Maddy was religious, that she felt the joys of self-sacrifice, the strong, mystical appeal of total rejection. But about Maddy who could say that? When we were in our teens, and our old aunts, Aunt Annie and Auntie Lou, spoke to us of some dutiful son or daughter who had given up everything for an ailing parent, Maddy would quote impiously the opinions of modern psychiatry. Yet she stayed. All I can think about that, all I have ever been able to think, to comfort me, is that she may have been able and may even have chosen to live without time and in perfect imaginary freedom as children do, the future untampered with, all choices always possible.

To change the subject, people ask me what it is like to be back in Jubilee. But I don't know, I am still waiting for something to tell me, to make me understand that I am back. The day I drove up from Toronto with my children in the back seat of the car I was very tired, on the last lap of a twenty-five-hundred-mile trip. I had to follow a complicated system of highways and sideroads, for there is no easy way to get to Jubilee from anywhere on earth. Then about two o'clock in the afternoon I saw ahead of me, so familiar and unexpected, the gaudy, peeling cupola of the town hall, which is no relation to any of the rest of the town's squarely-built, dingy grey-and-red-brick architecture. (Underneath it hangs a great bell, to be rung in the event of some mythical disaster.) I drove up the main street—a new service station, new stucco front on the Queen's Hotel—and turned into the quiet, decaying side streets where old maids live, and have birdbaths and blue delphiniums in their gardens. The big brick houses that I knew, with their wooden verandahs and gaping, dark-screened windows, seemed to me plausible but unreal. (Anyone to whom I have mentioned the dreaming, sunken feeling of these streets wants to take me out to the north side of town where there is a new soft-drink bottling plant, some new ranch-style houses and a Tastee-Freez.) Then I parked my car in a little splash of shade in front of the house where I used to live. My little girl, whose name is Margaret, said neutrally yet with some disbelief, 'Mother, is that your house?'

And I felt that my daughter's voice expressed a complex disappointment—to which, characteristically, she seemed resigned, or even resigned *in advance*; it contained the whole flatness and strangeness of the moment in which is revealed the source of legends, the unsatisfactory, apologetic and persistent reality. The red brick of which the house is built looked harsh and hot in the sun and was marked in two or three places by long grimacing cracks; the verandah, which always had the air of an insubstantial decoration, was visibly falling away. There was—there *is*—a little blind window of coloured glass beside the front door. I sat staring at it with a puzzled lack of emotional recognition. I sat and looked at the house and the window shades did not move, the door did not fly open, no one came out on the verandah; there was no one at home. This was as I had expected, since Maddy works now in the office of the town clerk, yet I was surprised to see the house take on such a closed, bare, impoverished look, merely by being left empty. And it was brought home to me, as I walked across the front yard to the steps, that after all these summers on the Coast I had forgotten the immense inland heat, which makes you feel as if you have to carry the whole burning sky on your head.

A sign pinned to the front door announced, in Maddy's rather sloppy and flamboyant hand: VISITORS WELCOME, CHILDREN FREE, RATES TO BE ARRANGED LATER (YOU'LL BE SORRY) WALK IN. On the hall table was a bouquet of pink phlox whose velvety scent filled the hot air of a closed house on a summer afternoon. 'Upstairs!' I said to the children, and I took the hand of the little girl and her smaller brother, who had slept in the car and who rubbed against me, whimpering, as he walked. Then I paused, one foot on the bottom step, and turned to greet, matter-of-factly, the reflection of a thin, tanned, habitually watchful woman, recognizably a Young Mother, whose hair, pulled into a knot on top of her head, exposed a jawline no longer softly fleshed, a brown neck rising with a look of tension from the little sharp knobs of the collarbone—this in the hall mirror that had shown me, last time I looked, a commonplace pretty girl, with a face as smooth and insensitive as an apple, no matter what panic and disorder lay behind it.

But this was not what I had turned for; I realized that I must have been waiting for my mother to call, from her couch in the dining-room, where she lay with the blinds down in the summer heat, drinking cups of tea which she never finished, eating—she had dispensed altogether with mealtimes, like a sickly child—little bowls of preserved fruit and crumblings of cake. It seemed to me that I could not close the door behind me without hearing my mother's ruined voice call out to me, and feeling myself go heavy all over as I prepared to answer it. Calling, *Who's there?*

I led my children to the big bedroom at the back of the house, where Maddy and I used to sleep. It has thin, almost worn-out white curtains at the windows and a square of linoleum on the floor; there is a double bed, a washstand which Maddy and I used as a desk when we were in high school, and a cardboard wardrobe with little mirrors on the inside of the doors. As I talked to my children I was thinking—but carefully, not in a rush—of my mother's state of mind when she called out *Who's there?* I was allowing myself to hear—as if I had not dared before—the cry for help—undisguised, oh, shamefully undisguised and raw and supplicating—that sounded in her voice. A cry repeated so often, and, things being as they were, so uselessly, that Maddy and I recognized it only as one of those household sounds which must be dealt with, so that worse may not follow. *You go and deal with Mother,* we would say to each other, or *I'll be out in a minute, I have to deal with Mother.*

It might be that we had to perform some of the trivial and unpleasant services endlessly required, or that we had to supply five minutes' expediently cheerful conversation, so remorselessly casual that never for a moment was there a recognition of the real state of affairs, never a glint of pity to open the way for one of her long debilitating sieges of tears. But the pity denied, the tears might come anyway; so that we were defeated, we were forced—to stop that noise—into parodies of love. But we grew cunning, unfailing in cold solicitude; we took away from her our anger and impatience and disgust, took all emotion away from our dealings with her, as you might take away meat from a prisoner to weaken him, till he died.

We would tell her to read, to listen to music and enjoy the changes of season and be grateful that she did not have cancer. We added that she did not suffer any pain, and that is true—if imprisonment is not pain. While she demanded our love in every way she knew, without shame or sense, as a child will. And how could we have loved her, I say desperately to myself, the resources of love we had were not enough, the demand on us was too great. Nor would it have changed anything.

'Everything has been taken away from me,' she would say. To strangers, to friends of ours whom we tried always unsuccessfully to keep separate from her, to old friends of hers who came guiltily infrequently to see her, she would speak like this, in the very slow and mournful voice that was not intelligible or quite human; we would have to interpret. Such theatricality humiliated us almost to death; yet now I think that without that egotism feeding stubbornly even on disaster she might have sunk rapidly into some dim vegetable life. She kept herself as much in the world as she could, not troubling about her welcome; restlessly she wandered through the house and into the streets of Jubilee. Oh, she was not resigned; she must have wept and struggled in that house of stone (as I can, but will not, imagine) until the very end.

But I find the picture is still not complete. Our Gothic Mother, with the cold appalling mask of the Shaking Palsy laid across her features, shuffling, weeping, devouring attention wherever she can get it, eyes dead and burning, fixed inward on herself; this is not all. For the disease is erratic and leisurely in its progress; some mornings (gradually growing fewer and fewer and farther apart) she wakes up better; she goes out to the yard and straightens up a plant in such a simple housewifely way; she says something calm and lucid to us; she listens attentively to the news. She has wakened out of a bad dream; she tries to make up for lost time, tidying the house, forcing her stiff trembling hands to work a little while at the sewing machine. She makes us one of her specialties, a banana cake or a lemon meringue pie. Occasionally since she died I have dreams of her (I never dreamt of her when she was alive) in which she is doing something like this, and I think, why did I exaggerate so to myself, see, she is all right, only that her hands are trembling—

At the end of these periods of calm a kind of ravaging energy would come over her; she would make conversation insistently and with less and less coherence; she would demand that we rouge her cheeks and fix her hair; sometimes she might even hire a dressmaker to come in and make clothes for her, working in the dining room where she could watch—spending her time again more and more on the couch. This was extravagant, unnecessary from any practical point of view (for why did she need these clothes, where did she wear them?) and nerve-racking, because the dressmaker did not understand what she wanted and sometimes neither did we. I remember after I went away receiving from Maddy several amusing, distracted, quietly overwrought letters describing these sessions with the dressmaker. I read them with sympathy but without being able to enter into the once-familiar atmosphere of frenzy and frustration which my mother's demands could produce. In the ordinary world it was not possible to re-create her. The picture of her face which I carried in my mind seemed too terrible, unreal. Similarly the complex strain of living with her, the feelings of hysteria which Maddy and I once dissipated in a great deal of brutal laughter, now began to seem partly imaginary; I felt the beginnings of a secret, guilty estrangement.

I stayed in the room with my children for a little while because it was a strange place, for them it was only another strange place to go to sleep. Looking at them in this room I felt that they were particularly fortunate and that their life was safe and easy, which may be what most parents think at one time or another. I looked in the wardrobe but there was nothing there, only a hat trimmed with flowers from the five-and-ten, which one of us must have made for some flossy Easter. When I opened the drawer of the washstand I saw that it was crammed full of pages from a loose-leaf notebook. I read: 'The Peace of Utrecht, 1713, brought an end to the War of the Spanish Succession.' It struck me that the handwriting was my own. Strange to think of it lying here for ten years—more; it looked as if I might have written it that day.

For some reason reading these words had a strong effect on me; I felt as if my old life was lying around me, waiting to be picked up again. Only then for a few moments in our old room did I have this feeling. The brown halls of the old High School (a building since torn down) were re-opened for me, and I remembered the Saturday nights in spring, after the snow had melted and all the country people crowded into town. I thought of us walking up and down the main street, arm in arm with two or three other girls, until it got dark, then going in to Al's to dance, under a string of little coloured lights. The windows in the dance hall were open; they let in the raw spring air with its smell of earth and the river; the hands of farm boys crumpled and stained our white blouses when we danced. And now an experience which seemed not at all memorable at the time (in fact Al's was a dismal place and the ritual of walking up and down the street to show ourselves off we thought crude and ridiculous, though we could not resist it) had been transformed into something curiously meaningful for me, and complete; it took in more than the girls dancing and the single street, it spread over the whole town, its rudimentary pattern of streets and its bare trees and muddy yards just free of the snow, over the dirt roads where the lights of cars appeared, jolting towards the town, under an immense pale wash of sky.

Also: we wore ballerina shoes, and full black taffeta skirts, and short coats of such colours as robin's egg blue, cerise red, lime green. Maddy wore a great funereal bow at the neck of her blouse and a wreath of artificial daisies in her hair. These were the fashions, or so we believed, of one of the years after the war. Maddy; her bright skeptical look; my sister.

I ask Maddy, 'Do you ever remember what she was like before?'

'No,' says Maddy. 'No, I can't.'

'I sometimes think I can' I say hesitantly. 'Not very often.' Cowardly tender nostalgia, trying to get back to a gentler truth.

'I think you would have to have been away,' Maddy says, 'You would have to have been away these last—quite a few—years to get those kind of memories.'

It was then she said: No exorcising.

And the only other thing she said was, 'She spent a lot of time sorting things. All kinds of things. Greeting cards. Buttons and yarn. Sorting and putting them into little piles. It would keep her quiet by the hour.'

II

I have been to visit Aunt Annie and Auntie Lou. This is the third time I have been there since I came home and each time they have been spending the afternoon making rugs out of dyed rags. They are very old now. They sit in a hot little porch that is shaded by bamboo blinds; the rags and the half-finished rugs make an encouraging, domestic sort of disorder around them. They do not go out any more, but they get up early in the mornings, wash and powder themselves and put on their shapeless print dresses trimmed with rickrack and white braid. They make coffee and porridge and then they clean the house, Aunt Annie working upstairs and Auntie Lou down. Their house is very clean, dark and varnished, and it smells of vinegar and apples. In the afternoon they lie down for an hour and then put on their afternoon dresses, with brooches at the neck, and sit down to do hand work.

They are the sort of women whose flesh melts or mysteriously falls away as they get older. Auntie Lou's hair is still black, but it looks stiff and dry in its net as the dead end of hair on a ripe ear of corn. She sits straight and moves her bone-thin arms in very fine, slow movements; she looks like an Egyptian, with her long neck and small sharp face and greatly wrinkled, greatly darkened skin. Aunt Annie, perhaps because of her gentler, even coquettish manner, seems more humanly fragile and worn. Her hair is nearly all gone, and she keeps on her head one of those pretty caps designed for young wives who wear curlers to bed. She calls my attention to this and asks if I do not think it is becoming. They are both adept at these little ironies, and take a mild delight in pointing out whatever is grotesque about themselves. Their company manners are exceedingly lighthearted and their conversation with each other falls into an accomplished pattern of teasing and protest. I have a fascinated glimpse of Maddy and myself, grown old, caught back in the web of sisterhood after everything else has disappeared, making tea for some young, loved, and essentially unimportant relative—and exhibiting just such a polished relationship; what will anyone ever know of us? As I watch my entertaining old aunts I wonder if old people play such stylized and simplified roles with us because they are afraid that anything more honest might try our patience; or if they do it out of delicacy—to fill the social time—when in reality they feel so far away from us that there is no possibility of communicating with us at all.

At any rate I felt held at a distance by them, at least until this third afternoon when they showed in front of me some signs of disagreement with each other. I believe this is the first time that has happened. Certainly I never saw them argue in all the years when Maddy and I used to visit them, and we used to visit them often—not only out of duty but because we found the atmosphere of sense and bustle reassuring after the comparative anarchy, the threatened melodrama, of our house at home.

Aunt Annie wanted to take me upstairs to show me something. Auntie Lou objected, looking remote and offended, as if the whole subject embarrassed her.

And such is the feeling for discretion, the tradition of circumlocution in that house, that it was unthinkable for me to ask them what they were talking about.

'Oh, let her have her tea,' Auntie Lou said, and Aunt Annie said, 'Well. When she's *had* her tea.'

'Do as you like then. That upstairs is hot.'

'Will you come up, Lou?'

'Then who's going to watch the children?'

'Oh, the children. I forgot.'

So Aunt Annie and I withdrew into the darker parts of the house. It occurred to me, absurdly, that she was going to give me a five-dollar bill. I remembered that sometimes she used to draw me into the front hall in this mysterious way and open her purse. I do not think that Auntie Lou was included in that secret either. But we went on upstairs, and into Aunt Annie's own bedroom, which looked so neat and virginal, papered with timid flowery wallpaper, the dressers spread with white scarves. It was really very hot, as Auntie Lou had said.

'Now,' Aunt Annie said, a little breathless. 'Get me down that box on the top shelf of the closet.'

I did, and she opened it and said with her wistful conspirator's gaiety, 'Now I guess you wondered what became of all your mother's clothes?'

I had not thought of it. I sat down on the bed, forgetting that in this house the beds were not to be sat on; the bedrooms had one straight chair apiece, for that. Aunt Annie did not check me. She began to lift things out, saying, 'Maddy never mentioned them, did she?'

'I never asked her,' I said.

'No. Nor I wouldn't. I wouldn't say a word about it to Maddy. But I thought I might as well show you. Why not? Look,' she said. 'We washed and ironed what we could and what we couldn't we sent to the cleaners. I paid the cleaning myself. Then we mended anything needed mending. It's all in good condition, see?'

I watched helplessly while she held up for my inspection the underwear which was on top. She showed me where things had been expertly darned and mended and where the elastic had been renewed. She showed me a slip which had been worn, she said, only once. She took out nightgowns, a dressing gown, knitted bed-jackets. 'This was what she had on the last time I saw her,' she said. 'I think it was. Yes.' I recognized with alarm the peach-coloured bed-jacket I had sent for Christmas.

'You can see it's hardly used. Why, it's hardly used at all.'

'No,' I said.

'Underneath is her dresses.' Her hands rummaged down through those brocades and flowered silks, growing yearly more exotic, in which my mother had wished to costume herself. Thinking of her in these peacock colours, even Aunt Annie seemed to hesitate. She drew up a blouse. 'I washed this by hand, it looks like new. There's a coat hanging up in the closet. Perfectly good. She never wore a coat. She wore it when she went into the hospital, that was all. Wouldn't it fit you?'

'No,' I said. '*No.*' For Aunt Annie was already moving towards the closet. 'I just got a new coat. I have several coats. Aunt Annie!'

'But why should you go and buy,' Aunt Annie went on in her mild stubborn way, 'when there are things here as good as new.'

'I would rather buy,' I said, and was immediately sorry for the coldness in my voice. Nevertheless I continued, 'When I need something, I do go and buy it.' This suggestion that I was not poor any more brought a look of reproach and aloofness into my aunt's face. She said nothing. I went and looked at a picture of Aunt Annie and Auntie Lou and their older brothers and their mother and father which hung over the bureau. They stared back at me with grave accusing Protestant faces, for I had run up against the simple unprepossessing materialism which was the rock of their lives. Things must be used; everything must be used up, saved and mended and made into something else and used again; clothes were to be worn. I felt that I had hurt Aunt Annie's feelings and that furthermore I had probably borne out a prediction of Auntie Lou's, for she was sensitive to certain attitudes in the world that were too sophisticated for Aunt Annie to bother about, and she had very likely said that I would not want my mother's clothes.

'She was gone sooner than anybody would have expected,' Aunt Annie said. I turned around surprised and she said, 'Your mother.' Then I wondered if the clothes had been the main thing after all; perhaps they were only to serve as the introduction to a conversation about my mother's death, which Aunt Annie might feel to be a necessary part of our visit. Auntie Lou would feel differently; she had an almost superstitious dislike of certain rituals of emotionalism; such a conversation could never take place with her about.

'Two months after she went into the hospital,' Aunt Annie said. 'She was gone in two months.' I saw that she was crying distractedly, as old people do, with miserable scanty tears. She pulled a handkerchief out of her dress and rubbed at her face.

'Maddy told her it was nothing but a check-up,' she said. 'Maddy told her it would be about three weeks. Your mother went in there and she thought she was coming out in three weeks.' She was whispering as if she was afraid of us being overheard. 'Do you think she wanted to stay in there where nobody could make out what she was saying and they wouldn't let her out of her bed? She wanted to come home!'

'But she was too sick,' I said.

'No, she wasn't, she was just the way she'd always been, just getting a little worse and a little worse as time went on. But after she went in there she felt she would die, everything kind of closed in around her, and she went down so fast.'

'Maybe it would have happened anyway,' I said. 'Maybe it was just the time.'

Aunt Annie paid no attention to me. 'I went up to see her,' she said. 'She was so glad to see me because I could tell what she was saying. She said Aunt Annie, they won't keep me in here for good, will they? And I said to her, No. I said, No.

'And she said, Aunt Annie ask Maddy to take me home again or I'm going to die. She didn't want to die. Don't you ever think a person wants to die, just because it seems to everybody else they have got no reason to go on living. So I told Maddy. But she didn't say anything. She went to the hospital every day and saw your mother and she wouldn't take her home. Your mother told me Maddy said to her, I won't take you home.'

'Mother didn't always tell the truth,' I said. 'Aunt Annie, you know that.'

'*Did you know your mother got out of the hospital?*'

'No,' I said. But strangely I felt no surprise, only a vague physical sense of terror, a longing not to be told—and beyond this a feeling that what I would be told I already knew, I had always known.

'Maddy, didn't she tell you?'

'No.'

'Well she got *out.* She got out the side door where the ambulance comes in, it's the only door that isn't locked. It was at night when they haven't so many nurses to watch them. She got her dressing gown and her slippers on, the first time she ever got anything on herself in years, and she went out and there it was January, snowing, but she didn't go back in. She was away down the street when they caught her. After that they put the board across her bed.'

The snow, the dressing gown and slippers, the board across the bed. It was a picture I was much inclined to resist. Yet I had no doubt that this was true, all this was true and exactly as it happened. It was what she would do; all her life as long as I had known her led up to that flight.

'Where was she going?' I said, but I knew there was no answer.

'I don't know. Maybe I shouldn't have told you. Oh, Helen, when they came after her she tried to run. She tried to *run*.'

The flight that concerns everybody. Even behind my aunt's soft familiar face there is another, more primitive old woman, capable of panic in some place her faith has never touched.

She began folding the clothes up and putting them back in the box. 'They nailed a board across her bed. I saw it. You can't blame the nurses. They can't watch everybody. They haven't the time.

'I said to Maddy after the funeral, Maddy, may it never happen like that to you. I couldn't help it, that's what I said.' She sat down on the bed herself now, folding things and putting them back in the box, making an effort to bring her voice back to normal—and pretty soon succeeding, for having lived this long who would not be an old hand at grief and self-control?

'We thought it was hard,' she said finally. 'Lou and I thought it was hard.'

Is this the last function of old women, beyond making rag rugs and giving us five-dollar bills—making sure the haunts we have contracted for are with us, not one gone without? She was afraid of Maddy—through fear, had cast her out for good. I thought of what Maddy had said: nobody speaks the same language.

When I got home Maddy was out in the back kitchen making a salad. Rectangles of sunlight lay on the rough linoleum. She had taken off her high-heeled shoes and was standing there in her bare feet. The back kitchen is a large untidy pleasant room with a view, behind the stove and the drying dishtowels, of the sloping backyard, the CPR station and the golden, marshy river that almost encircles the town of Jubilee. My children who had felt a little repressed in the other house immediately began to play under the table.

'Where have you been?' Maddy said.

'Nowhere. Just to see the Aunts.'

'Oh, how are they?'

'They're fine. They're indestructible.'

'Are they? Yes I guess they are. I haven't been to see them for a while. I don't actually see that much of them any more.'

'Don't you?' I said, and she knew then what they had told me.

'They were beginning to get on my nerves a bit, after the funeral. And Fred got me this job and everything and I've been so busy—' She looked at me; waiting for what I would say, smiling a little derisively, patiently.

'Don't be guilty, Maddy,' I said softly. All this time the children were running in and out and shrieking at each other between our legs.

'I'm not guilty,' she said. 'Where did you get that? I'm not guilty.' She went to turn on the radio, talking to me over her shoulder. 'Fred's going to eat with us again since he's alone. I got some raspberries for dessert. Raspberries are almost over for this year. Do they look all right to you?'

'They look all right,' I said. 'Do you want me to finish this?'

'Fine,' she said. 'I'll go and get a bowl.'

She went into the dining room and came back carrying a pink cut-glass bowl, for the raspberries.

'I couldn't go on,' she said. 'I wanted my life.'

She was standing on the little step between the kitchen and the dining room and suddenly she lost her grip on the bowl, either because her hands had begun to shake or because she had not picked it up properly in the first place; it was quite a heavy and elaborate old bowl. It slipped out of her hands and she tried to catch it and it smashed on the floor.

Maddy began to laugh. 'Oh, hell,' she said. 'Oh, hell, oh *Hel*-en,' she said, using one of our old foolish ritual phrases of despair. 'Look what I've done now. In my bare feet yet. Get me a broom.'

'Take your life, Maddy. Take it.'

'Yes I will,' Maddy said. 'Yes I will.'

'Go away, don't stay here.'

'Yes I will.'

Then she bent down and began picking up the pieces of broken pink glass. My children stood back looking at her with awe and she was laughing and saying, 'It's no loss to me. I've got a whole shelf full of glass bowls. I've got enough glass bowls to do me the rest of my life. Oh, don't stand there looking at me, go and get me a broom!' I went around the kitchen looking for a broom because I seemed to have forgotten where it was kept and she said, 'But why can't I, Helen? *Why can't I?*'

Acknowledgments

Elizabeth Bowen, "Her Table Spread" from *Collected Stories of Elizabeth Bowen* by Elizabeth Bowen, copyright © 1981 by Curtis Brown Limited, Literary Executors of the Estate of Elizabeth Bowen. Used by permission of Alfred A Knopf, an imprint of the Knopf Doubleday Publishing Group, a division of Random House LLC. All rights reserved.

Morley Callaghan, "Last Spring They Came Over" appears in Morley Callaghan's *The Complete Stories, Volume Two* copyright © 2012, Exile Editions. Used by permission of Exile Editions o/b the Estate of Morley Callaghan. All rights reserved.

John Cheever, "The Country Husband" from *The Stories of John Cheever* copyright © 1978 by John Cheever. Used by permission of Alfred A Knopf, an imprint of the Knopf Doubleday Publishing Group, a division of Random House LLC. All rights reserved.

Mavis Gallant, "The Ice Wagon Going Down the Street" by Mavis Gallant, copyright © 1963, 1981 by Mavis Gallant. Originally appeared in *The New Yorker,* (December 14, 1963). Reprinted with permission of Georges Borchardt, Inc. on behalf of the Mavis Gallant Estate. All rights reserved.

Index of Stories

Index of Authors